Under Darkened Skies
A Novel
Sydney Gibson

Edited by A.E. Vikar and Associates.

Disclaimer: This is a work of fiction. Names, characters, businesses, places, events and incidents are either the product of the author's imagination or used in a fictitious manner. Any resemblance to actual persons, living or dead, or actual events is purely coincidental. Any content with cannot be used or distributed without the permission of the author.

Copyright 2020 Sydney Gibson

Cover art by
KM West Creative

To Khal and Megg,
The biggest purveyors of change in my life.
I don't think I would've finished this one without you two in my corner.

Chapter 1

I hated Chicago summers. Summer in the windy city always brought millions of humans, eager to descend upon the beaches, trying to squeak out every ounce of sunshine of the short summer. I stood at the large front window with a cup of coffee staring at the Sunday morning beach crowd. They would swarm the lake like lemmings on the weekend, crowding my front window with the unpleasant scenery of ill-fitting Speedos and large one-piece bathing suits better left covering tables, not pasty humans. It was the last few days of September, October would be here in the blink of an eye, with fall right on its heels. I'd begun counting down the days until the end of the summer heat, when I could have my lake back. If the weatherman was right, I had less than twenty days to go and it had been a long hot summer.

I grumbled to myself pulling the curtains closed, and walked into the kitchen, searching for those microwave waffles Aaron was obsessed with.

Closing the freezer, I stared at the numerous news clippings plastered all over the fridge door. Bold black headlines from the shooting at the convention in D.C., stared back at me. I frowned, in their eyes, the media genuinely thought the Latin Murders and ending Evan was *the one* true highlight of my police career. The local news outlets picked up the story and went hard on the reporting.

I was daily headline fodder for weeks on end. The picture of me holding the fancy commendation, the Superintendent grinning on my right, on behalf of the city for bringing down Evan and Rachel, was used by over three hundred news outlets. I was confident the Superintendent was going to use the image in his re-election campaign posters.

I frowned, turning away from the freezer, waffles in hand. The only upside to being paraded around like a prize winning horse? I'd been transferred to the training unit for an indefinite period of time. I no longer had to deal firsthand with the worst murders Chicago could throw my way. I'd just sit at a desk, sign off on reports, and approve overtime in a nice air conditioned office.

My new corner office sat one floor above the homicide unit with a window facing the opposite end of the lake, putting my old office view to shame. My name and rank, Captain Emma Tiernan, was painted in gold lettering on the simple glass door that offered little privacy from the office gawkers, curious if I was exactly as the media portrayed me. A serial killers last victim. A federal agency's bait trap for a serial killer.

It'd been almost eight months since the Latin Murders and the fallout from the FBI's undercover Operation Eclipse. I'd gone back to work a month after coming home from D.C., still working through everything. The lies, the pain, the numbness.

To be honest, I wasn't doing my best to work through anything. I was ignoring everything, hoping it would just go away like a bad case of food poisoning and I could flush it down the toilet.

I'd slip into long gaps of silence as I sat in my office staring at the stacks of case files sitting on the corner of my desk, thinking of everything and nothing at all. My brain was so cluttered and tangled, it was hard not to think, and harder to verbalize what I was thinking.

The only person I'd tolerate to be near me, was Aaron, and there were many days he'd simply exist with me in silence, eating whatever junk food he grabbed on the way in. I'd sit at my desk, brewing in stiff silence, staring at him or out the window, as the obnoxious sound of his aggressive chewing filled the room and cut through the odd tension I seemed to carry on my shoulders.

The worst of it hit when the national magazines picked up the story about Evan Carpenter and ran wild with the graphic details of his killings, along with the damage he inflicted on me, physically and mentally. Journalists pounded on my door to interview me, harass me. Desperate to get the exclusive scoop on my lesbian lover, turned double agent for the FBI. I was followed everywhere by the press, hounded for soundbites.

The most memorable incident was during a budget meeting with the Superintendent. A reporter snuck into the conference room, barraging me with questions and gory details of what happened on the hotel roof when I shot Rachel.

I sat with my head down, clenching my jaw until he was pulled away by a uniformed patrol officer. After that, the Superintendent realized the severity of the situation. He held a press conference where I released a formal statement, throwing a final bone to the rabid media. I sounded like a dying robot, reading from the written statement he provided, giving vague answers whenever Sasha was brought up. In time, the press grew bored and moved onto the next scandal.

Sasha.

Then there was Sasha.

I had not physically seen Sasha for months after Operation Eclipse ended and she was reassigned, sent away from me. Last I heard, she was with a new unit in the FBI, but I didn't know which unit and where. I knew I ruined things for her when I turned down the offer from my favorite Special Agent in Charge Dana Reagan to join a new task force. A united task force between the Chicago Police Department and the FBI. Another political move set up by my bosses to diffuse the fallout trailing behind a federal agency running an undercover operation on a Chicago

Police Department Homicide Detective and using her as serial killer bait, not as a resource. I was starting to believe the unit was another operation and swore I would never set foot in an FBI field office again.

As far as I knew, Sasha might be on the other side of the world.

We shared phone calls and texts here and there, but had not physically seen each other in close to six months. The FBI was keeping her on a tight leash. They weren't as excited about the media coverage like a police Superintendent looking to further his political career.

Luckily, in time, the Superintendent also moved on from my story since it no longer served his future political campaign, and I was left to sit in peaceful silence at a desk hidden away in the training unit.

Little in my life had changed. I went to work, went home, and let time pass as it saw fit. Eventually, I stopped thinking about the past every second of every minute of every hour of every day. Redundant, I know, but time was a lost construct in my life.

Even as the nightmares continued to rock me from sleep each night.

I reached up, wiping a dot of hot sauce off the laminated news clipping with a smile, and walked back into the living room. I groaned as I sat down, the coffee table was covered in the files and paperwork I brought home to catch up on before the weekend. I had four new recruit files to evaluate before they went to the review board to determine if the rookies could be cut loose on their own or held back for more training. I also spotted one of Aaron's homicide cases he'd left next to his half empty coffee cup.

I sat on my couch and picked up his file. I missed homicide cases and was curious what he was working on.

I flipped it open, recognizing the case number. It was

the Golden Mill Bakery murder. Aaron had been assigned as lead detective on the case. The baker and owner had discovered his wife was cheating on him and he lost his mind. He lured his wife and her boyfriend to the bakery where he then shot and killed them both. He then proceeded to dismember them, dumping their remains into his industrial bread mixer, making twelve loaves of very organic bread.

    I now understood why Aaron wouldn't touch any bread. I'd just assumed he was back on his low carb diet.

    I smiled with pride reading over his notes. Aaron ensured all officers and detectives involved, followed procedure the second he arrived on scene, creating an airtight case for a murder one charge. The defense attorney was already pushing for a plea of not guilty by reason of insanity, claiming his client was so upset about the end of his marriage, he went temporarily insane and blacked out.

    Meanwhile, Aaron and the prosecutor were pushing hard for premediated murder, and had the evidence to back it up. Including a strange confession made by the suspect. Aaron had written in the report that while interviewing the suspect he was very calm, and inadvertently confessed, claiming. *"My wife never liked my baking, until she became an ingredient."*

    As I sat reading through crime scene report, the doorbell rang. I figured it was Aaron with handfuls of doughnuts and beer, too lazy to use his own key. It was Sunday, and on Sundays Aaron and I would spend the day watching whatever Chicago team was playing or sit and watch the beach goers. Counting how many middle aged men wearing tiny speedos passed our front window.

    I set the file down on the table to run to the door, swinging it open and walking away, refusing to help Aaron. "It's okay to leave some stuff in the car so your hands are free to unlock the door." The guy had a bad habit of carrying everything at once.

"That would require multiple trips. You know I'm far too lazy to wash my gym clothes on the regular, let alone make two trips to the curb and back." Aaron kicked the door close as I took the box of doughnuts from him.

I shook my head, chuckling. "I'm going to shower. Keep tally of the speedos. I'm trying to get a summer total. I think this year was bigger than last year." I slid the doughnut box across the island, eager to dig in and have a late breakfast of doughnuts.

Aaron chuckled as he tucked away the beer in the fridge. "Aye, Aye, Captain."

I slugged him in the shoulder. "Shut up and find some more speedos. Try not to eat all the doughnuts?"

He shrugged. "I can't make a promise like that." He tapped the top of the box. "The girl at the Doughnut Spot gave us extra Boston cream."

"That's because she has a crush on you." I gave him a mild look of disgust. "And I hate Boston cream."

"Then more for me! Hurry up and take that shower. Lunch is your treat. Hot dogs and beer." He winked at me, half dancing to the living room double fisting doughnuts, groaning at a particularly large man donning a bright yellow speedo.

I walked away and went upstairs, laughing as he continued to groan and gag.

******

I stood in the mirror naked, looking at the visual history of my darkest moments. Most of my body was covered in scars, and every time I looked at one, it was a reminder of where I'd been and how lucky I was to be alive.

It was part of my ongoing therapy to look at myself, look past the scars, and reaffirm each day was a good day.

Regardless of what the past told me. What the scars told me.

I dried my hair as I sat in my small office, checking emails. I read over a short one from my father. He was still having difficulty digesting Rachel being Evan's sister, and the lies surrounding her. It hit him harder than any of us expected. She was someone he trusted, someone he saved, and in turn, she almost killed his only daughter.

My father had been pulled in by the FBI shortly after I was, to interview him about what he knew of Rachel. The FBI was so determined to tie up all loose ends regarding their rogue agent, they even brought in agents who might have shared an elevator, or cup of coffee with her. Rachel sneaking past their impenetrable walls without them knowing her biological ties to a serial killer, rocked the agency along with most of the world. Bringing up questions if the FBI could really be trusted to protect the public it served.

I tried talking to my father when I came home from the conference, but like me, he shut down when things hit too close to home. He'd only begun to answer my emails over the last week while on the Alaskan cruise my mother surprised him with. The fresh Alaskan air helped clear his mind and he began to talk and share more with me. He was closer to Rachel than I thought. He was her mentor, and never suspected her of being capable of such evil. Such pain.

In his latest email, he asked about my interview and the truth about the rooftop shooting. He'd never asked me about it, until now. It was like he wanted to hear the last pieces of the puzzle to put his mind at ease and bury the past. I started typing my reply when Aaron tapped on the doorframe.

"Hey, Emma. I forgot to ask, but would you mind helping me with that creepy bakery murder? I'm stuck on the final report for court and could use your ancient wisdom." He grinned, throwing me a wink. "I'll buy the pizza?"

"I thought we were doing hot dogs and beers?"

"After all the speedos I just saw, the last thing I want to look at is a hot dog." Aaron shivered, cringing. "Deep dish or thin crust? Before you ask, yes, I'm getting pineapple on my half."

"Thin crust and get pineapple on the entire thing. I'm feeling adventurous." I smiled when he playfully gasped.

Aaron left with a huge smile, doing his hungry hippo happy dance as he dialed the pizza place.

I closed my laptop and changed into an old Detroit Red Wings shirt. I'd email my father later, after a few more beers and I could trust the nightmares not to sink in too deeply. As I headed downstairs, I caught a glimpse of a picture of Sasha and I sitting on the far bookshelf. I picked it up and smiled.

We'd shared a quick phone call last week while she was waiting for a flight to North Dakota. She had plans to fly back to Chicago by the end of the month, finally tying up the last few loose ends for the new unit. I'd missed her terribly, but the distance between us was much needed. I needed to calm down and sort out the twisted thoughts in my head. I didn't want to take out my newfound short temper out on her while I untangled my mind. I also knew when she came back, everything would be completely new for the both of us. We'd have to start over as the Captain and the Federal Agent. Not the Detective and the Rookie.

I set the picture back on the shelf and ran downstairs when Aaron yelled asking if I wanted cheesy bread.

Chapter 2

The sun was bright when Aaron and I walked out of the courthouse. I agreed to go with him and sit in on the bakery murder pretrial hearing. I thought this would be a good test to see if I could still detach myself from cases like before. It'd been one of my greatest talents when I became a detective, separating myself from the gore and violence. I'd always succeeded in not getting too attached to the case, but that all changed when I became a part of the case and became a victim. I started to sympathize more, and see myself in the victims I was speaking for. It became incredibly difficult to look from the other side, be the investigator, not a victim.

Being a Captain on the administrative floor saved me from that. All I had to do was read reports, go to court occasionally, authenticate all chains of command with evidence, and serve as an expert witness when called. Regardless of the fact I was running a training unit, I was still one of the best profilers and homicide investigators in the city. But instead of testifying, I was now solidifying the facts and evidence other detectives found. I'd become detached and grown to like it that way. I'd grown to like the quiet whispers of shuffling paperwork.

The bakery murder pretrial hearing took longer than expected. At the last moment, the defense attorney revoked her clients insanity plea, switching it for a guilty and a deal for a reduced sentence in a mental facility. The prosecution discovered the bakery had hidden cameras throughout the building to monitor its pest problems. The defendant was caught clear as day dumping the remains of his wife and her boyfriend into the industrial bread mixer. The evidence was so concrete, they redirected into bargaining for a life at a mental health facility. Aaron and I still had to sit through the attorney's bickering, waiting in case any evidence outside of the footage was questioned.

We walked out of the courthouse close to two in the afternoon, I was starving and desperate for a drink. I stared up at the bright sun, Aaron stopping next to me. I sighed, soaking in the warmth of the sun, idly thinking about maybe taking a vacation to the absolute opposite end of the Earth to Australia. I could hang out with a few kangaroos and learn how to surf.

"I want a big greasy cheeseburger and an ice cold beer." He grumbled, tugging at his tie and breaking me from my daydream.

I nodded, turning to look at him. "As the senior ranking officer here, I call it a half day. We're off the clock." I smiled. I was tired and wanted nothing more than to escape the day and forget the gruesome details of the murder. Details that left my mind drifting to another murder case and Evan.

"Can't argue with a Captain." He grinned, pointing over my shoulder. "Oh, look! It's our favorite bar right across the street."

I held out my hand, motioning for him to lead the way.

Aaron and I took a booth in the back. I'd stripped off my uniform jacket, setting it on top of my briefcase with a frown. "The beer may have to wait. I always feel odd drinking in this clown suit."

"Sucks to be the higher paid." He shrugged, waving a waitress over. "But I'll have one in your honor, Emma." Aaron ordered a beer and an iced tea for me. He tossed the menu to the side, leaning back in the leather booth. "You hear from your Special Agent lately?"

I shook my head as I set the menu down. "She called

last week while waiting for her flight to North Dakota. She mentioned she might be back in Chicago next week."

Aaron nodded as his ice cold beer was set in front of him. I took my iced tea, dumping a bunch of sugar in it while he ordered for us. The thought of a greasy cheeseburger chased away the blues of not having a cold beer.

"Can I ask you a question?" I nodded at Aaron as the waitress walked away with our order. "Why didn't you two try to meet up? Have a secret rendezvous in a seedy motel on the outskirts of town? I thought you two really liked each other?"

I leaned back, fidgeting with the empty sugar packets. "It all became too much. Too much media pressure. Too much pressure from our bosses, too much pressure to fall into something happy after the nightmare. To be honest, my head was a mess and after the dust died down, I welcomed the break. I think Sasha needed it as well. We were thrown together in the middle of a huge rolling wildfire of shit." I sighed, looking out the window. "It doesn't mean I don't miss her or think about her every second."

Aaron grinned, pointing at me. "That's what I was looking for. And I get it Emma. I just want to see you happy, and that federal agent made you happy. She still makes you happy." He stood up. "I have to hit the head. Don't steal my fries before I come back."

I laughed as Aaron trotted off, stopping to flirt with the waitress. The man was always the charmer, always looking for the next great love of his life.

I leaned on an elbow, staring out the window, thinking about Sasha and how I was still very much in love with her. No matter how much I thought I should fight it.

I was mesmerized by the ebb and flow of the traffic

outside, not looking at Aaron as he sat back down. "Before you ask, I didn't drink your beer."

"You still feel weird about drinking in uniform out in public, don't you?"

Her voice was so soft, making me close my eyes at the sound. I took a deep breath as I turned to look at Sasha.

She grinned, picking up Aaron's beer, taking a large sip. She wore a plain black V-neck shirt with faded jeans. Her light brown hair was up in a loose ponytail, and she looked radiant in the simple makeup she always wore on lazy days.

I knew I was staring, but it'd been so long, far too long, since I'd seen her in person. It felt like I'd forgotten her. But my heart didn't as it skipped and pushed against my ribs.

I looked down at the iced tea, focusing on the lemon wedge as a wave of nerves smothered me. "When did you get in?"

Sasha glanced at her watch. "About an hour ago. I stopped at the station to surprise you. The desk sergeant mentioned you were at the courthouse with Aaron, told me his case had been pushed to a plea bargain and you two were stuck waiting on the lawyers." She reached for my hand, winding our fingers together. I swallowed hard at how perfect it still felt. "I was about to go back to the hotel. Then I looked across the street and saw this amazing looking woman staring out the window. I just had to come over here and ask her what her name was." Our eyes met as she grinned, and my heart skipped a few more beats.

Sasha stood, moving to sit in the chair next to mine. She grabbed my hand again, whispering. "I missed you, Emma."

I said nothing, only leaning closer to her. My hand fell to her cheek as I pulled in her for a kiss. I didn't care who saw us, I only cared Sasha was in front of me and I could finally kiss her after months of being apart. I felt her hand slide out of mine, falling to grip my upper thigh, making me gasp before breaking off the kiss.

The sound of Aaron dramatically clearing his throat ended the moment. "Would you two like a room? I know a place around the corner that charges by the half hour."

Sasha smiled against my mouth, laughing as I blushed. She turned to Aaron. "I don't even want to know why you'd know that." She hopped out of the chair, into his open arms.

Aaron picked her up in a massive bear hug. "Good lord, it's so good to see you, Sasha." He set her down as I took a nervous sip of tea, hoping to chase away the flush I knew covered my face. He motioned for the waitress to bring Sasha a beer as she sat back down. He smirked, staring right at me. "The Captain and I were just talking about you."

"Oh really? And what were you saying about me?" She ran a hand over my thigh, gently squeezing it.

Aaron drained his beer, eagerly grabbing the new one the waitress brought along with our food. Hopefully, I could stress eat away these nerves and the urge to kiss Sasha.

"Well, for one thing, you're the only person who can turn the Captain's frown upside down."

Even I laughed at his lame joke.

Sasha chuckled, stealing a fry from my plate. "Good thing I'm back in town for a while." She looked at me. "I hate to break up lunch with shop talk, but the unit is all set up. We'll be working out of the federal building downtown, in the basement." She shrugged when I gave her a look. "I know, but it's large enough for us to work in and I have access to anything we might need." She grabbed another fry. "And I've been indefinitely reassigned to Chicago."

She met my eyes when she said. She was just as nervous as I was about reconnecting.

I sighed as I fiddled with the ketchup bottle. "When do we start?" I was eager to get back into something other than evaluations, especially after helping Aaron with a few of his cases. I wanted to break up the monotony of paperwork and try to break apart the lingering fears I had with diving back into homicides cases. I also wanted a distraction from the massive elephant sitting between Sasha and I about our relationship and what our future would hold.

Sasha fidgeted with the pint glass. "Monday. I need to get settled back in the city. The first case is being sent over by courier from D.C. and won't be at my office until mid-morning Monday."

Aaron took a massive bite of his burger, mumbling through a full mouth. "Where are you staying?"

"I hope you never change, Aaron." She chuckled, handing him a napkin. "The bureau has me at an extended stay hotel. I'm moving into one of their federal apartment buildings later this week."

Aaron wasn't listening, distracted by the waitress flirting with him.

I took the small moment of privacy to lean over and whisper against her ear. "Stay with me, Sasha."

"Emma, I'll be fine at the hotel." She spun her glass around, she was nervous. I paused, leaning back. I'd been hesitant about everything, worrying every day about what I'd do when we were finally together. But as she sat next to me, within reach, I didn't want her anywhere else.

"We did live together once, and as I remember, it was far better than any hotel." I met her hazel eyes, and the hesitance in them. "I'll give you the spare key. Take your time to decide."

Sasha didn't answer, just squeezed my thigh again and looked away.

Aaron turned back to us, breaking the slow building tension with another one of his ridiculous jokes. The rest of the lunch was spent listening to Aaron talk about some of his strangest cases. I found myself staring at Sasha, half listening to Aaron. My heart kept telling me the things I already knew. I missed her, and I loved her with my entire being. Fear be damned.

At the end of lunch, Aaron glanced at his phone. "Shit, I have to meet the boys in a half hour for drinks before the game." He stood, throwing a few bills on the table before saluting me. "Thanks for the help and lunch, Captain. See you at home." He stepped to Sasha, grabbing her in another crushing hug. "As always, love to see your beautiful face, Agent."

I pulled on my uniform jacket, buttoning it up as Aaron ran out the door. I glanced at Sasha. "Can I give you a ride anywhere? I have a fancy company car today." I tried to lighten the air around us, ease the strange tension.

Sasha slipped sunglasses on as we stepped out onto the street. "If you're interested, Emma, I have the preliminary case notes from our first case with the unit at my hotel room. I know you officially don't start until Monday, but I know you like to look at evidence as soon as it comes in."

I stared at her, irritated the sunglasses were blocking her hazel eyes and whatever emotions were floating in them. I could always look in Sasha's eyes and know exactly what she was thinking.

"Can you grab them and then go back to my house? I really want to get out of this uniform." I dug around in my pocket for the car keys. "Please tell me the dress code for this new unit is a little less formal?"

Sasha grinned. "It's more relaxed. You'll have to go back to those terrible, yet perfectly tailored, detective pantsuits you used to wear." She cocked an eyebrow, looking me over. "But this uniform is still very, very impressive on you."

I picked up on the gentle attempt at flirting. Mildly amazed at how tentative we were both acting. Where we once were so quick to fall into each other's arms, it now felt slow and painfully cautious.

I frowned, plucking at a loose thread on my sleeve. "I'll take the pantsuit over this any day." I motioned towards the alley behind us. "I'm parked back there."

I took a few steps and let Sasha catch up to me. There was a strange silence hanging between us. It was as if we both were struggling with what to say, versus just attacking each other and ripping our clothes off in the middle of the street. Making up for the lost time.

I swallowed hard, unlocking the car. Throwing my briefcase into the trunk, I slid into the driver's seat, fighting the urge to attack Sasha and rip her clothes off.

Our conversation during the drive was minimal, just Sasha giving directions to her hotel. I waited for her as she ran up to her room, running back out a moment later with a large suitcase and briefcase, tossing them into the back as I pulled away.

Back at my house, I pushed the door open, smiling at the memories of her and I living together. I set my briefcase down next to the side table as I pulled off my jacket. "You know the house, Sasha. I'm going to run up and change, then we can start."

Sasha smiled as she set her bags and briefcase down. "Thanks. Hey, does Aaron still keep his good beer in the back of the fridge?"

I nodded with a grin. "He certainly does."

I watched as she walked into the kitchen like she'd never left this house, like we hadn't been separated for the last six months. It reminded me of when we lived together, when she was just Sasha, the pain in the ass partner I fell in love with. I smiled, sighed and headed to my bedroom.

As I hurried downstairs, I paused in the middle of the staircase, watching Sasha on the couch. Her brow furrowed as she sifted through yellowed pages.

She was still the same woman I'd fallen in love with. I'd realized it the moment she sat next to me at the bar. She might be a federal agent, but everything I felt for her was still the same. It was just the lingering distance and emotions built off lies that made things gently awkward and fearful. We'd been through the tunnels of hell and survived, yet we both still had open wounds and healing scars from what we went through. I sighed, hoping my love for her could overcome the damage.

I sat on the couch, brushing against her arm. She smiled, leaning into me, nodding at the beer next to hers. "I'll buy him more, but you look like you could use a drink, Emma."

I laughed. "Aaron won't care, considering he eats more food than he pays for."

Sasha laughed before setting a file in my lap. "This is what I've been given so far, more should be coming on Monday as it's dug out of the archives."

The file itself was aged and yellowed, obvious it'd sat at the bottom of a filing cabinet, untouched for a decade or two. I opened it and saw the case date was dated from the summer of 1983, well over thirty years ago. I smiled, shaking my head at the handwritten reports and pages typed with a broken typewriter. I missed that aspect of police work. The attention to detail necessary when you had to hand write the whole report, then type it up on a typewriter with missing keys.

The first page chased that smile away. This cold case was a sexual assault and murder of a seventeen year old girl while on a school field trip to the nation's capital.

Angela Heaten was on her senior class trip to Washington D.C., traveling from a small town on the edge of Cedar Rapids, Iowa. She'd gotten separated from her class while walking down the National Mall and was reported missing later that day by one of the class chaperones.

The police searched the area and interviewed her classmates, but nothing came from it. They continued to search for two days until a park ranger checking the grounds around the Lincoln memorial, found Angela's body early in the morning, tucked up and behind Lincoln.

The coroner's report revealed she'd been sexually assaulted and violently beaten. Trace evidence had been collected, but unfortunately, back then DNA was still a pipe dream forensic tool in its early stages. They had swabs, skin samples, fingernail clippings and fibers pulled from her body. But nothing ever came of the evidence, and some it was lost due to the poor handling of it while in storage. The police had no witnesses, no suspects. There was nothing but a dead body and unreliable trace evidence.

The crime was quickly labeled a random act of violence and shelved after a few more months of investigating dead end leads.

I finished reading the file and was confused. I wasn't sure why the first case for a behavioral science unit cold case division, would be a decades old murder with no clues, no substantial evidence, no suspects, and no witnesses. I closed the file and tossed it on the coffee table.

"Okay. I'm lost. Why this case? It seems pretty clear it was a random homicide buried by poor police work. You should hand this over to Internal Affairs and let them sort through it." I looked at Sasha sifting through the stacks in front of her.

"Read it again, Emma. You should know nothing is ever random."

I raised an eyebrow. "I read it. Cover to cover, there's little to nothing there." I waved a hand at the file. "Aside from shoddy police work and poor evidence handling, it's literally a dead end. I'm not sure where we'd start. Dead ends are hard to revive."

Sasha gave me a hard look. "Dead end? Then tell me why in the Sergeants notes, did he write it was a pretty clear case of random brutality and stopped all further testing of the trace evidence his team collected. Even when the FBI expressed interest in using the collected DNA samples as a possible test for the new DNA identification process they'd been developing? If it was just a random act with nothing to go on, why not let the FBI use it as an experiment? Why keep it from a federal agency eager to further a forensic technique and possibly find a murderer?"

It took me a moment to answer her barrage of questions.

This Sasha sitting next to me was Special Agent Natasha Clarke. She no longer needed to keep her true talents as an investigator hidden. I smiled as her clear and concise words reminded me of the times I lectured her as my rookie. *Look between the lines for the little things that don't make sense in the overall picture. That's where you'll find the answers*

I flipped pages, scanning over them once more. "I can see his point. DNA testing back then was like introducing electric lightbulbs to the candle burners of the world. It didn't make sense and seemed like a hokey form of police work. I don't see anything wrong with his decision. It would've just dragged the family through endless amounts of pain waiting for the results, if ever there were any. Then there's the work of trying to pinpoint a suspect without the aid of a massive DNA database like we have now. It would've been a waste of manpower and time."

Sasha stared at me with a slight smile as I ranted. The same admiration from her days as my rookie, radiated in her eyes, even as I was obviously shooting down her astute observation. When I finished rambling, she sat for a moment in silence before speaking. "Are you done, Emma?"

I shrugged as she picked up another file, handing it over. "Good. Because you need to look deeper, read between the lines. The Sergeant is hiding something. This case landed back on the top of the pile after thirty years at the request of Angela's parents. They heard the FBI opened a new unit for cold cases like this, and asked for the file to be pulled from storage and reopened. Word has it they were talked out of cooperating with the FBI in the first few days of the case. Told it would be a waste of time and manpower. My gut feeling the Sergeant swept this particular case under the rug on purpose." She reached over, tossing another file onto my lap. "The whole thing stinks of a cover up."

I opened the file. It was the personnel file of the sergeant in question. Sergeant Anthony Bellico of the D.C. Metro police Department, was the first responding officer on scene that day. I read over his personnel file. Bellico was a heavily decorated police officer, which lead him to becoming a Sergeant early in his career. He was highly successful with very few blemishes on his record. The only large black mark was a single unsolved homicide on his record, Angela Heaten. The Heaten case was the question mark hanging over Bellico until he retired from the department five years ago.

I closed the file, setting it on top of the rest. "I have to admit, it's suspicious. He has an almost perfect record, a ton of commendations, loved by his bosses and the public he served. I find it unusual for a man who saved old ladies and rescued kittens out of trees, would walk away from this particular case without putting forth the heroic effort that fills his file."

Sasha leaned back on the couch, tucking a leg under her. "Exactly. The psychology behind why he didn't put in the effort is going to lead us to answers." She gave me a light smile.

I let it sink in for a moment before closing the files. "Where should we begin with this one then?" I leaned back into the couch. Even though it was breadcrumbs, I was intrigued to see where Sasha was taking this. Intrigued to see this side of her.

She set the files in her hand down, letting out a slow breath. "This is where I look to you, Emma. I'm not, nor ever was, an experienced street detective. I'm lost as to where we start looking. I'm used to fresh cases with clear suspects to chase. Not a cold case with long dead leads." She grinned. "Even though I had a really great FTO in the homicide unit, I'm still a bit of a rookie."

I smirked, motioning to the coffee table. "We need to go back and look at the physical evidence, which I'm hoping still exists within the D.C. Metro archives." I looked at her with questioning eyes. My rank and pull would only get me what I wanted in Chicago. Outside of the city, I was just another jerk in a fancy uniform. "But I don't have that kind of juice to barge in and ask for what I need."

Sasha nodded, reaching into her bag for her phone. "Let me make a call." She stood and walked into the kitchen. I didn't bother to try and eavesdrop, instead turning my attention to the pile of old files.

There was something strange with this case. Far too many few holes were covered up with half assed reasons. It intrigued me, if anything, and I wanted to know why Bellico just gave up and walked away, leaving this case unsolved. I knew a million retired cops who had that one case they dreamed about solving. The one that got away. Maybe the Heaten case was Bellico's one that got away.

I heard Sasha end the call. I quickly turned to her as she sat down, leaning into my side. "D.C. Metro still has all evidence collected from the Heaten case. It's in their storage warehouse on the Maryland side of the Potomac. I just have to get the go ahead to move it into our custody and we're good to go." Her tone was very authoritative, something I'd never really heard from Sasha. It made me curious about this side of her. The federal agent side.

I crossed my arms, leaning my head back as I looked at the ceiling. "Alright, how long will that take?" I was concerned the small details weren't already taken care of. Especially if this case was handed to Sasha as a starter case, the remaining evidence should've been pulled and sent with the case files sitting on my coffee table. Experienced cop or not, anyone who's watched enough CSI would know that's where you start. Organizing the evidence into one place and plotting your next move.

Sasha dropped her phone on the couch. "A day or two at most. I guess they have to physically dig out the boxes, why?"

I sighed, rubbing the bridge of my nose. "I hate waiting for information." I smiled at her. "You know, rule number fifteen." I shook my head at the list of random rules of investigation I kept and how they were never in any order, they just came out when I needed them. I also vaguely remembered irritating the hell out of the woman next to me when I threw them in her face as we drove to crime scenes.

    Sasha smiled, looking down at her hands. "Rule thirty one. Wait for no one, especially when it comes to critical information." Sasha met my eyes, her smile turning serious for a moment. "Emma, what happens next?"

    I let out a heavy breath. "We review the evidence and whatever tests that were done, then go from there. I'll want to re-interview officers and witnesses." I was staring at the ceiling, my mind trying to lay out all the puzzle pieces I had, and the ones I still needed.

    I felt her hand slip into mine as it laid on the cushion next to my thigh. "I meant with us."

    I rolled my head to the side, looking into her soft hazel eyes.

    I squeezed her hand, pulling it into my lap. "I don't know, Sasha. Do we have to plan it out? Or can we take it one day at a time? I think we're both on a blank slate with each other. The only thing I know for sure is what I still feel for you." I sucked in a slow breath, setting our hands back down. "The relationship we did have, I don't want again. It was built on lies and fear." I looked in her eyes, keeping a soft tone. "I want to start over with you, Natasha Clarke. Like I said months ago, I know it's going to take time and I'm still working through things." I paused, temporarily lost at what to say next.

    Sasha tugged me closer. "I know, Emma. I want to start over. I know it'll take time. This is so new for me. It didn't help the FBI kept me away from you for so long. It's made things feel awkward, new, different." She reached up, brushing a few pieces of hair away from my face. "From this moment on, you'll get Natasha and only Natasha." She held her hand against my cheek. The warmth of her palm soaked into my skin. I nodded in agreement. The time forced between us had created a very tentative situation.

Sasha leaned forward, removing the small space between us. I gasped as my mouth opened slightly, my eyes falling to her lips. Just as we were about to connect, Aaron barged through the front door, barely sober.

He grinned at the sight of Sasha and I sitting on the couch and threw his hands up in the air. "Ladies! I'm home!" He stumbled over, flopping down the couch like a whale, shoving himself in-between us. He huffed, barely holding his head up. "I'm so excited to have the team back together." He rolled his head to look at Sasha. "You know Emma here buys better groceries when you're around? The real fancy stuff."

"No, I didn't know." She leaned forward to look at me with a smile. I rolled my eyes and sighed.

Aaron sighed, rubbing his eyes. "True story. She buys the better meat, the better cheese and those expensive potato chips." He suddenly leaned over, laying a sloppy kiss on her cheek. "I thank you for your return. I've missed the fancy kettle cooked potato chips." He then rolled his head in my direction. "Captain, I'm going to take a quick nap. When I wake up, the three of us are going to the grocery store for more fancy food." Aaron wiggled himself free and wobbled, holding his hands out to steady himself. He then stumbled towards the basement door, half walking, half falling down the steps before slamming the door shut.

Sasha laughed, standing up. "It's not even five in the afternoon."

"He does that sometimes. Day drinks and talks too much." I glanced at the clock over her shoulder. "I should probably go grocery shopping without him. When he tags along it's like having an eight year old with me. He just wants doughnuts, chips, and peanut butter chocolate cereal."

Sasha collected her files, stuffing them into her briefcase. I grabbed a few, handing them to her. "I can give you a ride to the hotel, or you can come with me. Help pick out some *fancy* potato chips."

Sasha shook her head with a smile. "I have to make a few calls. See if I can expedite the rest of these files and get them before the end of the week." She finished stuffing her briefcase. "I'll grab a cab."

I nodded, following her to the front door. As she opened it, I placed a hand on her elbow. "Hang on a second." I ran to the kitchen, digging in the junk drawer for the extra set of keys Aaron had given Sasha months ago. I jogged back, handing them to her. "You're more than welcome to stay here if you feel like it. This was your old set." I smiled at the small Chicago Bear keychain Aaron had linked around the keys.

Sasha palmed the keys. "Thanks." The air suddenly turned thick with tension, I scrambled to speak.

"Will you come back tonight for dinner? Please?"

She met my eyes, still smiling. "I'll do my best." She tucked the keys into her pocket.

"Dinner is usually around eight and it's Aaron's night to cook. So, it'll probably be his nine alarm chili and cornbread."

Sasha paused, and as if no time had passed between us, she leaned forward, kissing me gently on the cheek. "I'll definitely try to hurry things up." She kept her smile, turned and walked out the door.

I let out a heavy sigh the second the door closed. This was going to be harder than any case I ever had to solve.

Chapter 3

I spent the rest of the day grocery shopping. Aaron made dinner when he woke up from his three hour nap, epic hangover in tow. We spent the rest of the day sitting in the kitchen talking about the end of summer and the recent department gossip.

I kept fidgeting, glancing at the clock, waiting for Sasha. I didn't expect her to show up on the doorstep and join me for a casual dinner. I'd felt how strained things were, regardless of how desperate we were to climb over the small walls built up between us.

I left Aaron to clean up his mess and went upstairs to my bedroom to finish the email to my father. When it was sent, I changed into pajamas and busied myself with organizing my clothes. I'd stuffed my old patrol blues in the back, followed by the bland detective pantsuits. I pushed the Captain's uniform to the middle and moved the suits up. I was thrilled to be getting out of the stiff uniform. But as I pushed through the untouched suits, the painful memories of my time as a homicide detective flooded through. I cringed at the memories of Evan, and eventually gave up organizing and closed the closet door. Opting to read a book and wait for the impending heartburn from Aaron's chili to strike. I glanced at the bedside clock, it was a quarter to midnight. I had tomorrow off before I started working with Sasha and returned to the world of the FBI. I hoped a day would be enough time to prepare and get my head back in the game.

I crawled into bed with my book. A silly fluff fiction I'd picked up a few days ago while waiting for my coffee at the bookstore.

I leaned back into the pillows, reading the first page, when the front door opened and closed. I paid little attention to it, figuring Aaron was heading out for Tums or more beer. I flipped to chapter one as a soft knock tapped on my door.

"Aaron, you don't always have to knock. It's not like I'm up here with a girl or anything." I straightened my glasses, rereading the sentence the knock interrupted.

The door creaked open. "I'm grateful to hear there are no girls in here with you. I might get a little jealous if there were." I turned to Sasha, grinning in the doorway. "I'm sorry I missed dinner. I got caught up in a conference call and chasing paper."

"Be glad you missed the chili. It was pretty intense." I set the book in my lap, tipping my head down to hide the silly grin covering my face. "I'm sure there's some leftovers, if you're interested."

Sasha shook her head, walking into the room and sat on the edge of the bed, looking over her shoulder. "I can't sleep at the hotel. The suite feels like a dorm room."

I reached out, laying a hand on her upper arm. She immediately covered it with hers. The silly grin on my face grew just from her touch. "You're more than welcome to stay here. I can sleep on the couch, or bunk with Aaron." I pushed the book off to the side and went to drop my hand from her arm to get up.

She held onto my hand. "Or we could share the bed." Sasha held onto my hand tighter when she felt me flinch. "It's just sleep, Emma. Nothing more."

I cleared my throat. It was apparent in the way she was looking at me, the expression on my face betrayed my cool exterior, revealing the nervous panic washing over me.

"I know." The words rasped out as I gently pulled my hand from hers, rolling over to sit next to her. "It's not like we haven't shared a bed before, for sleeping purposes." I stood up from the bed.

Good lord, this was painful. I was painful to listen to. I

shook my head, moving to the closet for extra pillows, talking to Sasha over my shoulder. "Did you need something to sleep in? I have shirts and sweatpants you can borrow."

Sasha shook her head, picking up the bag she dropped at the door. "I got it covered." She stood, looking at me as I turned around, arms filled with pillows. "Bathroom still over there?" She smirked, pointing behind me, and the dimple that often infiltrated my dreams, appeared.

I nodded, biting my bottom lip, holding back a grin. "Still there."

Sasha moved to the bathroom while I fidgeted with placing pillows on the bed. I pulled down the blankets, slipping under them. I sighed, focusing on anything else to settle my racing heart. I heard Aaron rummaging around in the kitchen, then climb the stairs like he did every night before he went to bed. He tapped on the doorframe before poking his head in. "Hey Emma, you good?"

I smiled and nodded. Aaron's routine would include locking up the house, grabbing a snack, and check on me. He started it from the moment I came home from the conference, broken and exhausted. The nights following the conference, he'd find me crying in bed. Other nights he'd find me blankly staring at the walls. On those nights he'd pull me out of bed, hug me, then make me watch a crappy movie with him until I passed out. In time, I got better, and the nightmares lessened, but he continued to check on me nightly. "I'm good, Aaron. Thanks."

"Copy that. I'll grab the doughnuts in the morning."

Aaron turned to leave when he heard the bathroom door open, shooting me a cautious look. I held up my hand as Sasha walked out, grinning. "Hey you! Sorry I missed the chili. I heard it was one of your best?"

Aaron couldn't contain his massive grin. "No worries, Sasha. There's plenty left. You can have some for breakfast. It goes great with coffee."

"I think I'll stick to just coffee." Sasha dropped her clothes next to her bag. She wore an old FBI academy shirt with thin cotton sleep pants. Aaron chuckled when he caught me blatantly staring at her, and winked at me, throwing us a salute. "I'll see you both in the morning." He tapped on the door frame once more before closing the door.

Sasha crawled into bed, rolling over without a thought to her side. I sighed, lying on my back, riddled with nerves. I reached to turn off the light, settling into the pillows, about to say something to Sasha, when I felt her slide closer. Her arms moved across my stomach and pulled me against her body, like she always did when we slept together. I let out a soft sigh, laying a hand on top of hers.

I knew what she was doing. Trying to reinstate our old routine to chase away the nerves. It was working as I felt her sigh, then her breathing slow down into a gentle up and down. She was asleep within three breaths. No sign of hesitancy or fear of being this close to me.

*****

It was the first night in months where I slept through the entire night without a nightmare. There were a few times I had to shut my libido down when I felt Sasha's body press against mine in certain places.

I looked at the clock with a yawn. It was only a little after eight in the morning. I sighed, rubbing my eyes before looking at the warm body next to me. Sasha had her back to me, tangled up in blankets and lightly snoring.

I shifted, moving to spoon her when her cell phone

began to vibrate on the side table. Sasha's hand shot out, grabbing the phone. She answered it with a mumble. I heard someone on the other end as she rolled over on to her back, her arm covering her face.

"Send it to the office. No, I know I'm not at the hotel. I'll be at the office in a half hour, leave it at the front desk and I'll sign for it when I get there." Sasha groaned. "Yes, Agent Natasha Clarke, BSU Cold Case Division. That's me. I swear to God, some of you people need to work on your listening skills." Sasha hung up, tossing the phone on the bed with a groan. She rolled her head, catching me blatantly staring at her. "Morning."

I smiled. "Morning, how did you sleep?"

Sasha moved to sit up, running hands over her wild bed head. "Better than I have in a very long time. I hope I didn't hog too much of the bed. It's been a minute since I've shared one."

I raised my eyebrows, smirking. "Just the usual amount of hogging."

Sasha playfully slapped my arm. "You're probably going to tell me I still snore, aren't you?"

I shrugged. "Actually."

Sasha shook her head, pushing back the blankets. "Well, you were mumbling about speedos in your sleep." She cocked an eyebrow. "Is there something I need to know?" She smirked as she grabbed her bag, pointing towards the bathroom. "You mind?"

"Go ahead. The towels and soap are in the same place." I yawned again, enjoying the ease between us.

Sasha paused at the bathroom door. "How do you feel about joining me?" I swallowed hard as she blushed at her words. "Um, I mean at the office. The D.C. field office sent over the final files. That's, uh, what the early phone call was about." She fiddled with her bag. "I know you don't start until Monday, but I have to go in now to sign off on the chain of evidence. I'll be there for most of the morning. I can show you around and we can start reviewing the files."

I nodded slowly, still stuck on her asking me to join her in the shower. I cleared my throat, looking away. "Sure, yeah, I'll stop by. I have the day off and it'd be good to get a jump start." I picked at a loose thread on the blanket as Sasha walked into the bathroom, speaking over her shoulder.

"Perfect! I'll give you the address to the Federal Building and get you on the visitor's list."

When the water turned on, I had to occupy myself from indulging in memories of sharing a shower with Sasha. I rolled out of bed absently tidying up the almost spotless room. Eventually, I had to leave the room and head to my office.

I paused at the small desk to grab a few recruit files, when Aaron yelled from the bottom of the stairs asking what I wanted for breakfast. I sighed as he rattled off the different cereals he had. All of them sugary and meant for kids.

I quickly turn to yell back at him and ran smack into a fresh out of the shower, only wearing a towel, Sasha.

We collided with a collective oomph, her hands falling to my upper arms as she had tried to steady herself. Her wet hair soaked through my shirt, and the smell of my shampoo hit my nose. I swallowed my heart back down into my chest, and looked down, mumbling "Sorry, Aaron's being annoying about breakfast."

Sasha looked up, meeting my eyes, a soft sensuality washing over hers. She leaned back, biting her bottom lip. It only took a moment before she moved, closing the small distance between us as her lips captured mine. Her arms slid around my waist, her hands pressing flat against my back as she kissed me hard. She gently bit my bottom lip, forcing me to moan against her mouth.

My hands fell to her bare shoulders, my fingers pressing into her wet skin. She was warm from the shower and as I drew slow, light fingers across her, Sasha pushed harder against me. She broke the kiss to lean back, reaching for the top of the towel.

I didn't stop her. I wasn't going to stop her.

I wanted her as much as she wanted me, it was just a matter of who was going to make the first move.

She tugged the towel free, letting it drift slowly down her chest to fall to the floor. I took a slight, unsteady breath.

Just as the towel slid down to reveal the top of her breasts, Aaron burst into the room, holding up a box with a cheery cartoon Koala bear on it. Aaron had his eyes glued to the back of the box, not aware of the situation he just walked in on. "I found this multigrain organic crap cereal in the back of the cabinet."

I grabbed the towel, wrapping Sasha up, pulling her close before Aaron turned and got an eyeful.

Aaron finally looked up. His eyes grew wide as he blushed. He cleared his throat, turned on his heels and walked out as fast as he came in, mumbling. "I forgot Sasha was here."

I brushed past Sasha closing the door, leaning my forehead against it with a sigh. "He's been doing that for six months. Barging in like a nosy mother. I need to retrain him." I turned to Sasha, her back facing me.

"I understand. I forgot he lived here." She dropped the towel, allowing me a view of her bare back. I squeezed my eyes closed. The moment had been ruined and left me anxious. I took a second to calm down and opened my eyes to catch Sasha slipping into her bra and shirt. "But I couldn't resist. It's been a minute, Emma." She pulled on her jeans, tuning to face me. She gave me a weak smile, stuffing clothes in her bag.

She moved past me to the door. I grabbed her elbow, stopping her. "For whatever reason, I'm nervous. But it has nothing to do with you. I'm nervous because it really has been a minute." I met her eyes, silently translating what I meant.

She nodded. "I know. I'm nervous too." She shifted her bag, looking away. "But I can wait, Emma." She leaned forward, placing a slow, soft kiss against my cheek. "I'll leave the directions to the office on the fridge." Sasha left the room and went downstairs, where I heard Aaron fumbling around his awkward apology.

CHAPTER 4

After taking a long hot shower followed by a quick ice cold one, I stood in front of my closet staring at my clothes. I had no burning desire to put on any of my old detective suits or the stiff Captain's uniform. I decided on a decent pair of jeans and a nicer button down, dressing quickly before moving to make the bed. I lingered for a moment on Sasha's pillow, running my hand over it, wishing I could figure out what why I was so anxious.

Was it because I didn't know this Sasha?

She was still the strong, forward woman I met a year and a half ago. Granted, she was far more aggressive and authoritative as a federal agent. But I was used to that working in law enforcement. Federal agents were always a little more aggressive and authoritative. It came with the fancy gold badge and title of Agent.

Yet, there was something that left me tentative to make the first move with her.

I grabbed the blankets and extra pillows tossed to the floor, when I saw her FBI Academy shirt laying on the floor. I picked it up and sighed. Maybe I was scared because I fell in love with a woman who was now a complete stranger to me.

I folded the shirt, neatly setting it on the pillow. Regardless of what it was, I knew I was still in love with her, but afraid to close the gap time shoved between us. I sighed, smoothing down my shirt before walking downstairs to find Aaron drinking coffee, looking over reports.

He looked up with an uneasy frown. "Sorry, about earlier. You haven't had an overnight guest in a long time." He cringed. "I interrupted a possible reunion, didn't I?"

I shrugged, pouring a cup of coffee. "You did, but you're forgiven." I leaned against the counter, reading the address Sasha had stuck on the white board under Aaron's request for more ice cream.

Aaron squinted at my outfit. "Are you going to work? You never get this dressed up on your days off. You just sit around in those nasty sweatpants and whatever t-shirt you slept in the night before."

I shot him a dirty look. "When did you become my fashion police?"

"When those sweatpants became more disgusting than my gym shorts, Emma."

I frowned. "They're my favorite pair of sweatpants. But yes, I'm going downtown to the federal building. Sasha got the rest of the files sent to her. She wants to show me the new office we'll be working in."

Aaron nodded. "Well, let me be the first to say it. Welcome back, Detective."

*****

Standing outside the mundane dirty beige federal building, I frowned. I'd walked past this building a million times in my life, only thinking it was a silly bank owned building, when in reality, it was the Midwest hub for the FBI. I shook my head, questioning again why I was doing this, took a deep breath and walked in.

After going through more security than the airport, I asked the girl at the front desk to point me in the direction of Agent Natasha Clarke's office. She politely smiled and asked for my identification. I handed her my badge wallet, leaning on the desk as she made a handful of phone calls, glancing at my badge and face every two seconds.

Five minutes later, she hung up, sliding my wallet back. "Captain Tiernan? Agent Armstrong will be up to escort you to Agent Clarke's office." She then slid a plastic

ID card towards me. The word visitor stared back at me in bold blue letters. "You weren't expected until Monday, so I can only provide you with visitor access. But I can give you your employee badge now. You'll have full access to the building Monday morning when you've been added into the system. It won't work until then." She gave me a knowing smirk when she saw my disappointment.

"Thank you." I took the small plastic white card with my picture from the Chicago Police Department, my name and title in black letters along the bottom. I tucked it into my pocket as I clipped on the visitor badge. The young girl issued a hearty welcome to the FBI and sat back down to answer the phone. I smiled and walked to the small set of chairs to wait for my escort.

Ten minutes later a baby faced male agent walked over. He had blonde hair with a gentle red tint to it, bright brown eyes and an eager smile. He held out his hand as he approached. "Captain Tiernan? I'm Agent Peter Armstrong. I apologize for making you wait, I was held up in records." His handshake was firm and pleasant. "I'll escort you to the basement where Agent Clarke is working."

I nodded as we stepped into the elevator. The kid started talking a million miles a minute about the FBI, leaving me no room to interject. I let him drone on about the history of the building as he hit the B button for the basement.

When the elevator started to move, he turned to face me. "It's a pleasure to meet you, Captain. I've heard so much about you, and I should admit, I'm a bit of a fan."

I kept my eyes on the floor indicator, watching how far deep into the bowels of the building we were going. "Hopefully it's all good things." I tried to give him a genuine smile, but knew it came out more bitchy than genuine.

"Of course, it is! I've admired your case work in the Chicago Police Department." Armstrong's idle chatter suddenly grabbed my attention.

I turned to face him. "My case work?" I was suddenly on edge. I knew the FBI were professional snoops, but I didn't want it thrust in my face.

"Well you know, the Latin Murders and Evan Carpenter. I did my final case study at the academy on Operation Eclipse and the events that followed. It was very interesting how everything tied together at the end. It blew my mind when I read Evan and Agent Fisher were siblings and how she set you up as bait to draw Evan out. I admire your strength to keep investigating after what you went through. The fight in the parking garage where you almost perished? What an incredible night." Armstrong's eyes met mine. "Is it true Evan walked Agent Fisher right out of the hospital minutes before you arrived?"

I felt an intense hot wave of anger wash over me.

I'd not talked about Evan or Rachel to anyone aside from my therapist. Hearing the most terrifying moments of my life casually recapped, brought up a hidden rage I'd spent the last six months of my Captain's salary on trying to forget. I stared at the young agent with fierce intensity, fighting to stay calm. He continued rambling as he fidgeted with his cufflinks.

"It's truly an unbelievable case and series of events! We were the first class of agents allowed to look at the files. Especially since it involved the BSU. Can I ask? How did you deal with it? Finding out Agent Fisher was betraying you? Never mind the fact Operation Eclipse was a masterpiece of undercover work."

His last words sent me over the edge, and I snapped. "When did you graduate from the academy, Agent Armstrong?

His eagerness faded as he met my steely gaze. "Almost two months ago, ma'am."

I nodded and laughed, irritated. "Do me a favor and shut up. I don't want to hear another goddamn word about Evan Carpenter or Rachel Fisher. You'll *never* understand exactly what happened reading a few case notes put together by uninformed assholes like you. She did not betray me. We had nothing more than a professional working relationship, so there was nothing to betray. She was manipulated to the point she had no control over her actions, or thoughts. But I'm glad I served as a lab rat for you to study. What I really want right now, is for you to fill this elevator with silence." I took another deep breath to steady my anger. "If you utter another word about *my work*, I'll make sure you're assigned to the worst corner of the bureau spending the first twenty years of your career hand sorting fingerprint files. Understand?"

I didn't realize I was almost yelling at the kid until I finished and watch Armstrong's face turn beet red.

He swallowed hard, uttering. "I'm… I'm sorry… I just thought… I didn't know."

I felt no guilt for tearing into a fresh out the academy rookie. He pushed my buttons. Hard. I glared at his red face. "Think before you speak. Useful advice for any cop."

The young agent nodded, turning to stare at the elevator doors. I turned back to the floor indicator, closed my eyes, and leaned my head back against the elevator wall.

Armstrong took my advice and let the elevator fall into awkward silence.

*****

Armstrong led me through the basement hallways to

a large concrete encased office. If you want to call an old basement storage room with a few desks, an office. Sasha was elbow deep in old evidence boxes running the length of a large folding table. Armstrong walked over to her while I admired how well her dark blue pantsuit fit.

    The young agent interrupted her to let her know I was here. Sasha glanced my way, thanking him. He smiled briefly, before tipping his head down and avoiding all eye contact as he left the room.

    I walked over to an ancient metal desk that looked like Hoover himself used it, poking at a box filled with files.

    "Emma, come look at these." Sasha held up a thick file yellowed with age.

    I sat down at the desk, taking the file. It was the initial crime scene report for the Heaten case. I couldn't help but smile at the hand drawn crime scene diagrams. A technique that was standard in police work in the eighties, but became obsolete over the last twenty years. Old school cops couldn't generate animated graphs, they couldn't electronically map body position, or use lasers to bounce off walls for exact measurements. Everything was hand drawn and the margins filled with handwritten notes and thoughts.

    The file also held stacks of photographs with negatives attached to them. I set the photographs to the side. I didn't want to look at them right away, I wanted to read the report then compare the photos to the notes. It was how I found inconsistencies.

    Heaten's body had been found behind the Lincoln memorial, twisted in an unnatural way that suggest she was possibly dumped postmortem. The medical examiner found evidence of sexual assault and listed cause of death to be a combination of strangulation with blunt force impact to the sides of her skull. The girl suffered a violent, gruesome death.

    The medical examiner also noted if strangulation hadn't killed her, the large blood clots on her brain would've slowly killed her.

    I continued reading the crime scene report. A rape kit had been completed at autopsy. Some fibers were lifted off her clothing, but it came back inconclusive. The technology wasn't advanced enough to tear down a fiber. Then track that fiber to the date it was made, what it was made into, where it was sold and who bought it. The same went with the rape kit. DNA was collected, but no way to test it or compare it to a suspect. I shook my head and wondered how many cases would've been closed if people had believed in the power of DNA thirty years ago.

    I finished the report and moved to the hand drawn map and the body positioning. I then turned to the photographs. I tried to look at them with a clinical, detached eye. I was looking at a brutally murdered seventeen year old girl. I had to look past the violence and look at the puzzle and read the evidence.

    The pictures were old and hazy, but the graphic images still told a story. The body was bruised with no blood pooling under her. It was evident she was murdered then taken to this spot and dumped. That at least correlated with the report.

    I looked at the photographs of her hands. There were no defense wounds which struck me as odd, but meant she may have known her attacker. I moved to the photos of her face, and for the first time in my career, I had to look away. It wasn't because of the violence of the crime. I'd seen crime scenes ten times worse, ten time more brutal.

    What forced me to look away was the girl looked like a young Sasha.

A flashback of the night in the warehouse where Sasha bled out on the table in front of me, struck, and struck hard. The memory hit so fast, I had to set the photo face down and lean against the desk. My hands shaking as I gripped the edge to steady them.

I took a deep breath. Maybe I did jump back in too soon.

I rubbed at my temples to chase the memories away. The room was silent aside from the gentle whisper of Sasha turning pages, mixing with the hum of the overhead fluorescent lights. I focused on the hum, breathing in and out to lower my heart rate. I needed to calm down before I dug further into the evidence, or I wouldn't find anything but more bad memories.

I took a few more steadying breaths, trying not to draw attention to my mild panic attack. I didn't want Sasha to know I was struggling. She'd feel guilty about bringing me in and hold me back a little longer. As much as it drudged up hidden fears, I would have to push through the small walls that built up in the time between the Latin Murders and now. I had to.

I stood up, moving to the evidence box next to Sasha and started pulling out evidence bags one by one. Everything was there. Angela's clothing, the fibers collected from the scene, and small random pieces of trace evidence found on, and around, her body.

I suddenly paused, remembering my status as a guest in this building, and looked at Sasha. "Do you mind?"

She gave a small smile. "Go ahead. You've been listed as part of the chain of evidence and I honestly have no idea where to start with the clothing. I was trying to find the initial, unedited evidence collection reports."

I nodded my thanks and walked to one of the many long tables in the room. I found a roll of clean white paper, tore off a large piece and laid it on the empty table in front of Sasha. I covered the tabletop, glancing at Sasha as I taped the edges down. "This basement is fairly large for an office."

"It is. Agent Reagan suggested we move down here. Apparently if this first case is success, she'll be adding more agents and team members. But for now, it's just you and me." She chuckled. "I know, the trouble making agents sent to the dark basement. It's very cliché.

I let out a breath. It was cliché, but I found another angle to it. "I see it as back at the beginning. Partners again." Sasha's cheeks turned a soft pink as she tipped her head down.

I turned back to the evidence box, pulling out a paper bag containing Angela's clothing. After slipping on a pair of gloves I started removing the contents. Angela had been wearing a plain light pink t-shirt with a long forgotten band logo on it, and a pair of faded stone washed jeans. I carefully laid out the clothing, examining each piece as I went. It took less than a minute before something caught my eye.

I picked up on the blatant fact her clothing was clean and completely free of any stains. No blood or body fluid stains. That didn't make any sense with the injuries she suffered.

I leaned over the table. "What does it say in the initial crime scene report about her clothing? Did the crime scene tech make any notes about it? Bloodstains?"

"Let me look." I heard pages flipping behind me. "There's no documentation about any stains on the clothing. Just a footnote the clothing was removed before autopsy to preserve evidence collection of fibers. But nothing about stains, why?"

I turned to face Sasha. "Tell me what you think.

Looking at those photos, the girl was severely beaten. She had lacerations and contusions all over her body, yet there's no blood on her clothes. Don't you think that's unusual?"

She stood, moving to stand next to me with the file in her hand. "Are you suggesting the body was dressed after she was murdered?"

"Maybe. Can I see the photographs again?"

Sasha handed them over. I swallowed hard as I flipped through them, fighting to pay attention to details and not scare myself like I did earlier. I frowned, pissed at myself for not noticing it at first glance. The clothing was clean, spotless. I handed the photos back. "My question is, why wasn't it noted the victim could've been dressed postmortem? There's nothing, no notes, and I find *that* incredibly unusual even for almost thirty years ago. It's a big thing to overlook even if you have to hand write everything. Something doesn't feel right about it, about this." I waved a hand over the evidence sitting on the table.

Sasha looked at the photos, at the clothing, then back at the file. "You're right. It's strange. The crime scene investigator noted the cleanliness of the area of where the body was dumped and went into great detail about the rest of his findings. But that's all insignificant compared to not mentioning the possibility of the body being dressed after death."

I glanced at Sasha, her brow furrowed in intense thought. I now saw why it was hard for her to keep up the image of a fumbling rookie. Her intensity towards the job was admirable and hard to hide. I reached over, pointing at the name of the investigator. "Tom Latham. We need to talk to him. Can you make that happen?"

"I can do my best." Sasha pulled out her phone, walking out of the basement office as she dialed.

I flipped through the file she left on the table, reading through Latham's report again. With every word read, I started to feel the slow creep of suspicion up my spine.

Officer Tom Latham was very thorough in his reports. Noting almost everything including the position of the sun at the time of discovery, but he left out a key point of no bloodstains on the clothing. In my mind, a rookie investigator would find that a telltale sign the body had been redressed before it was dumped behind the memorial.

I flipped the file closed when Sasha silently appeared next to me. She held up a thick file bound with tired rubber bands. "This is Latham's personnel file. I'm waiting for Armstrong to get back to me with his current address and phone number."

"How did you get this so fast?" I looked at her with slight admiration of her ability to make things appear out of nowhere. A skill that would've been valuable back in the homicide division.

"I requested the personnel files of everyone who worked on the case. I wanted to get a larger scope of who was involved and get to know them. I'd planned on reading all of them to eliminate suspects one by one. The rest of the personnel files are around the corner in the brown banker's boxes stacked up by the coffee machine." She smirked, tilting her head. "I believe it was rule number twenty nine of Lieutenant Emma Tiernan's rules of investigation? Cast a wide net of suspects. The larger the better?"

I grinned, weighing the heavy file in my hand. "It's actually rule number five." I motioned to another metal desk that looked like Sasha had claimed as hers. "Let's take a look at Tom Latham."

I rolled my chair up next to Sasha's desk and split up

the file, handing her a large chunk.

The pages I had were the end of career highlights for Latham. He had an impeccable record even in the last few years of his job as Lead Crime Scene Investigator for D.C. Metro police. There were no blemishes in his record for mishaps in evidence collection, or with cases that fell apart in trial because of a lack of attention to detail. If cases were lost, it wasn't because of Tom Latham's work.

Latham's file was filled with commendations for cracking large cases, and he retired out of the department at twenty five years served on the dot. I chewed my lip, hoping his memory was still fresh about this case. I knew retirement opened a door for people to easily forget the job. I'd been mildly guilty of that in my short retirement when Aaron had to remind me daily the radio codes I forgot as we drove to scenes.

Sasha interrupted my thoughts, reading aloud from Latham's file. "He graduated from Georgetown in 1976 with degrees in physics and biology, then went to the police academy, class of '77. He worked foot patrol for five years then transferred to the crime scene unit. The department was desperate for college graduates and his biology degree fit the bill. He looks almost spotless on paper. A good officer, a good investigator. I don't really see a connection here, or why we need to look at him, Emma." Sasha sighed as she sifted through more pages.

"He's pretty clean, but for someone who obviously is well known for his attention to detail and not missing a step, something is wrong. I don't understand why he'd miss such an important fact as unstained clothes but remember to detail the exact position of the sun at discovery of the body. You get my point?" Her eyes focused on mine as she listened. "Bloodstains or lack of, take precedence over the sun hanging at high noon. I've got a gut feeling he did it on purpose, or was told to leave it out of his report."

"True, but it could've slipped through the cracks. All these reports are handwritten. It could've been easily overlooked."

I had to smile at her devil's advocate way of thinking. This Sasha, this Federal Agent Natasha, was my equal intellectually and she would openly challenge my ideas. I found it to be intriguing and invigorating.

"No, I don't think it was an oversight. But again, that's my gut feeling. I want to talk to this guy. I want to look in his eyes to know if it was just a bad day for him and he missed it, or if he was told to miss it."

Sasha sat with a furrowed brow, thinking. She wasn't accustomed to the street way of thought. She'd spent very little time as a street detective. Sasha was looking at the case through a paper pushers' eyes. If it wasn't on paper, it wasn't going to be looked at too closely. She never had the experience of the streets like I did where you physically picked apart the layers until you found the root of the mystery.

Sasha tossed her half of the file back at me as her phone rang. She sighed before answering. "Armstrong, did you get it for me? Okay, good. Thank you." She quickly grabbed a piece of paper and started jotting down notes. "Got it. Thank you, Agent Armstrong." She hung up, setting the phone on the desk with another heavy sigh.

I looked at her, curious. "Sasha, can I ask a question? Was this a promotion or a demotion? I get the feeling this assignment to the basement was you being gently pushed out of sight after my media storm splashed onto you and the bureau." Sasha was hit just as hard by the media. She was followed, dragged through the gutter, and cast doubts on the FBI for allowing their agents to have far too much leeway. It was one of the reasons why the FBI kept her busy and away from me for months. I was the thorn in the rose bush of a successful operation.

Sasha glanced at the ceiling. "Neither. It was an amicable sideways shift. Agent Reagan gave me the temporary title of SAC for this new unit, but until it gets off the ground and is proven to be successful, it's just a title." Sasha took a breath. "Fisher slipping through our fingers, more so mine, was not looked upon as favorable by the upper brass." She met my eyes. "And us. They had a hard time accepting our relationship and how I let it compromise Operation Eclipse."

I flinched, ignoring the bit about our relationship. "An amicable sideways shift? I've never heard that one. Nor have I heard of anyone being punished by promotion to agent in charge of a new unit."

Sasha laughed. "Let's just say everyone's has their secrets, including my bosses."

I shook my head with a smirk. "Ah, I see. Mutual blackmail."

Sasha just shrugged to say *I don't know what you mean*. I left it at that. I knew Sasha would tell me anything I asked of her, and at the same time, I wasn't ready for more secrets to be revealed. I had my fair share of that over the last year.

"Let's go talk to Latham. I'm curious what he has to say." I stood up, wiping my hands on my jeans. Trying to wipe away the nervous sweating.

Sasha leaned back in the chair. "We'll go first thing Monday. I still have to procure a company car for us and set up your expense account."

I blinked at her. "An expense account?"

"Yup. You're technically a federal employee and everything you do on their time has to be accounted for." She gathered the files, stood and walked over to the box, dropping them in. "By the way, Morgan is back in town for a couple of days. She's between cases and we're going to meet up for dinner." Sasha turned to me. "You're more than welcome to join us. She asks about you every time she calls."

I picked up my notes, sliding them into my back pocket and smiled. I did kind of miss Morgan. She'd become a friend when we were study buddies, learning medical terms together. "I think I'll join you. I'm intrigued to hear what new stories Morgan has. It's still hard to believe she's an agent."

Sasha laughed. "You're telling me. I've known her for years and she still manages to surprise me." She finished packing up the boxes, grabbing her briefcase. "I can give you a ride home if you'd like."

"Sasha, will you stay over tonight?" The words shot out like a broken firecracker. "I mean, you left your academy shirt at my house.

She grinned, stepping closer. "I could be persuaded to spend the night, Captain Tiernan." Her hand fell to my arm, squeezing. "But we'll have to tell Aaron I'm staying over."

I suddenly wanted to kiss her, but we were in the middle of a damp basement in a federal building. I swallowed hard. "I'll text him as soon as we leave."

Sasha laughed, dropping her hand. "I'll tell Armstrong we're heading out for the day. He can come and lock up."

"Can you also apologize to Armstrong for me? I might have lost my temper on him." I stepped into the elevator, leaning against the wall. A wave of exhaustion washed over me, giving a warning of the nightmares to come later.

Sasha leaned over, pushing the lobby button. "Let

me guess, he asked about the Latin Murders and Fisher?" I gave her a confused look. She smiled, leaning into my side. "I went off on him the first day he was assigned as my administrative assistant. He hit me with a barrage of questions and wanted to know about my relationship with you, and if you really were an Ice Queen like your reputation once suggested."

I let out a slow breath as her arm slid across my back, pulling me closer. "And what did you tell him?"

Her eyes locked on mine. "I told him never refer to the woman I love as the Ice Queen, or I'd make sure he would be placed on motor pool duty cleaning out the cars for the first fifteen years of his career."

"You didn't?"

"I did." She hesitated before speaking. "And I'm still in love with you, Emma." Her voice dropped at the end.

Before I could reply, the elevator doors opened and Sasha stepped away, letting her arm fall away. She smiled at the woman at the front desk. "Will you please tell Agent Armstrong I'm leaving for the day? I'll be back on Monday with Captain Tiernan." She then turned to me, holding up car keys. "Would you like to drive?" She smirked as the keys jingled from her fingers.

I laughed, shaking my head. It'd always been a point of contention between us when it came to who was going to drive when we were partners. I'd never let her, and it drove her nuts. But things needed to change, it was time for change. "I think it's finally time you start driving us around, partner."

Chapter 5

Sasha drove us to a restaurant over in Wrigleyville. The Saturday night crowd was thick, but I spotted Morgan from blocks away in her Cubs shirt and black jeans. I smiled as she turned, grinning at the sight of Sasha and I walking together. She trotted towards us, almost knocking Sasha down with an aggressive bear hug. When she released Sasha, she folded her arms, giving me a once over, eyebrow cocked. "Tiernan. It's nice to see you started eating again. Fill out those pantsuits Sasha loves so much." I caught Sasha blushing as Morgan held out her arms. "Give me a hug, you old copper!"

I laughed, hugging the smaller woman. "How are you, Morgan?"

She let go of me with a dramatic sigh. "I miss my partner here. I've been stuck over in New Jersey working on wire taps, listening for hours on end about some Mafia goombah's hair routine. The mafia boys do love their hair products." She rolled her eyes. "And my new partner is beyond boring. He doesn't let me eat pizza in the safehouse or in the surveillance vans." She huffed. "Anyways, enough cop talk, let's eat!" She pushed herself in between Sasha and I, linking her arms in ours, yanking us into the restaurant.

As I picked at a piece of chocolate cake, I began telling Morgan what it was like to have Aaron as a roommate. I knew she had a tiny crush on Aaron, but I wasn't going to call her out on it. "Aaron's like a little brother, big brother rolled into one. I'm glad he's in the house."

Sasha interrupted me. "Except for when he has bad timing." She winked, grabbing my hand under the table, squeezing it as Morgan raised her eyebrows. Sasha pushed my phone over, silently reminding me to tell Aaron she was staying over, when a rowdy group flooded into the bar.

A large group of sweaty, dirty men all wearing matching softball shirts burst into the doors, laughing and yelling at each other. It was obvious they'd just come from a late summer softball game. I just smiled at Sasha and Morgan, signifying there was no point in trying to talk until the group settled into their drinks and quieted down. Both smiled back in silent agreement.

Just as I motioned to the waitress to bring us another round, I glanced up as one of the larger sweaty men, looked over, squinting at Sasha. His face suddenly broke out in a wide grin as he stood and rushed towards our table. As he was two steps away, he hollered. "SASHA! HOW THE HELL ARE YOU?!"

Sasha turned around, smiling back at the man stomping his over. She stood up with her arms open, hugging the rather large man. Sasha was so caught up in an embrace, she didn't notice the flicker of jealousy in my eyes. "Danny! It's so great to see you!"

I felt awkward and stared at the last inch of beer in my glass. Morgan stood and high fived Danny, still in Sasha's embrace "What's shakin', Dan the Man?"

Sasha stepped out of the hug and grabbed a chair from another table, pulling it up to ours. She swatted the seat. "Sit! I had no idea you were in Chicago!"

Danny sat down roughly in the chair, still grinning. "Jesus, Sasha, I haven't seen you since the academy. Where the hell have you been?" He was completely focused on her and didn't notice me, adding to the increasing awkwardness. Sasha was very comfortable with Danny, and I watched as her demeanor changed and her body relaxed. Making that small ping of jealousy grow and surge through my veins.

"I've been shuffled to the basement. I'm taking lead on a new unit Reagan is trying to get off the ground." Sasha caught me watching the strange reunion with a frown. "Oh, I'm sorry! Danny this is Emma. Emma Tiernan. She's my new partner on this new project."

Danny turned to me with a salesman grin. He was attractive in that rugged cop way, and as he shook my hand, I could tell he was checking me out. I smiled innocently to myself. It always made me chuckle on the inside when men looked at women the way they do. Always undressing us with creepy silence and lecherous stares.

"Danny Edmonds. It's great to meet you, Emma. I attended the academy with these two fine ladies, and man, did they give me a run for my money." He wrapped an arm around Morgan, squeezing her into the slab of meat that was his shoulder. "This one here, beat my top score at the firing range." Morgan shrugged, blushing as she sipped her beer. He then pointed at Sasha with the beer bottle in his hand. "And this one? I asked her to dinner at least three hundred times, and three hundred times she turned me down." He winked at her, earning a blush and sheepish smile in return.

I nodded with a tight smile on my face as the jealousy ramped up.

Danny took a sloppy sip of beer. "So, you've been assigned to work the cold cases with my girl here? What field office are you with? I don't think I've ever seen you around the office." He had a cheeky, but charming, way about him. And I hate it.

I clenched my jaw, my teeth creaking under the pressure. "I'm not FBI. I'm a Captain with the Chicago Police Department."

Danny looked at me, then at Sasha. "Chicago PD? How did you wrangle that one, Sasha? You know how hard it is to mix agencies, let alone local with federal." He paused as it finally sunk in. "Wait. You're Emma Tiernan? Not *the* Emma Tiernan from Operation Eclipse?" I watched as Sasha and Morgan tensed up from the words falling out of his mouth.

"Emma is an incredible detective and Reagan asked for her assistance with the new unit." Sasha scooted her chair closer to me, adopting a soft tone. Trying to ease the building tension she undoubtedly saw on my face.

Danny patted Morgan on the back. "Well here's to her being good enough to get you out of the basement and back upstairs where you belong. I still think its bullshit they shuffled you down there after that business with Fisher on the rooftop. That was some fucking crazy gung ho shit." Danny took a large drink as Morgan met my eyes, silently asking if I was okay. "What actually happened up there? They haven't released that part of the report. I heard crazy Fisher tried to stab you with that nutjob Carpenters knife. How did you get out of that one, Sasha?"

I had enough of Danny's overwhelming bravado and his crass disregard for what Sasha and I had gone through. The rooftop incident was not a war story to be tossed around over drinks. I stood, glaring at the sweaty mass of jerk wad. "I shot and killed Fisher as she was about to shoot Agent Clarke. There was no stabbing, or attempted stabbing. So, I'd suggest you don't run your ignorant mouth about a case you have no clue about." I held my hand up when Morgan stood up, reaching for me. "I need to leave before I punch him in the face." My temper was at a tipping point. I was tired of people trying to tell me what I'd been through while mauling the truth. Danny gaped at me as I walked out, hearing him ask Sasha if I was *that Captain* from the rooftop.

I pushed through the half full restaurant and out into

the city streets, taking deep breaths of the cool air. I might show on the exterior I was completely fine, but inside, I was still dealing with the aftermath of Evan, shooting Fisher, and the mess in between. It was always just under the surface ready to spill out if I didn't fight to keep my emotions in check.

I looked around the street, deciding to walk to the corner, grab a cab, and call Aaron to meet me in his man cave with all the beer he had and one of his action movies. I made it to the corner when a small hand grabbed my elbow.

"Whoa, Captain! Slow it down. Sasha's right behind me, we're going to walk you home."

I sighed hard, looking down at the sidewalk. "Sorry about the outburst."

"Look, you don't have to tell me, I get it. I saw more than I wanted when we took down Evan in the lab." She slipped her arm into mine, pulling me into her side. "Danny's a giant dumb frat boy. He always tried to get in Sasha's pants at the academy, it's probably why he was in the bottom half of our class. Too dumb and too focused on chasing tail. He's in the white collar unit. Holed up in a windowless office, sifting through bank accounts all day long. He's jealous Sasha and I became sweet field agents and caught amazing assignments."

I leaned into her, letting out a slow breath. "I lived the nightmare. I lived through it. I don't need to be reminded of it by random assholes."

Morgan sighed, laying her head on my shoulder. "I know. But I'm glad you and Sasha are back in each other's lives. You need each other." She met my eyes with a smile.

Sasha walked up, slightly flustered. "I'm so sorry about Danny, Emma. He runs his mouth without thinking."

"It's fine, Morgan already gave me his backstory." I

grabbed her hand, looking down the street. "I know it's early, but I think I'm going to head home."

Morgan let go of my arm. "You know what, I think I'm going to call it an early night too." I caught the slight wink she threw Sasha. "Call me in the morning and we'll get breakfast. Invite that handsome Aaron along, if you don't mind."

Sasha hugged Morgan, whispering something I couldn't hear. Morgan gave me a quick hug before flagging down a cab.

I walked back to the car with Sasha in awkward silence. Danny's words still grating on already frayed nerves.

Back at the house, Aaron was in the basement with the door closed, an aggressive action movie shaking the walls. I felt my phone vibrate the moment Sasha closed the front door. It was from Aaron telling me he'd locked himself in the basement for the rest of the night. The added winky face made me laugh.

I looked back at Sasha locking the door. "It's only nine o'clock. I know I'm being a bit of a party pooper. If you want to go back and spend the evening with your friends, it's fine."

Sasha laid her hands on my biceps. "I think there was something we were talking about this morning that Aaron interrupted. Do you want to go upstairs and finish talking?" Sasha grinned, her dimple in full effect. I felt my heart begin to race. I swallowed hard, letting her hand fall into mine as she led us upstairs.

She leaned against the door, closing it with her weight. I heard the soft click of the lock as I stood against my bed. Sasha pushed off from the door and walked towards me, stopping inches away from me. Her eyes locked on mine as she whispered. "Do you remember the first day we met?"

"You were wearing your patrol blues. Excited and filled with the rookie jitters." I reached up to brush some hair from her face.

Sasha closed her eyes with a soft sigh. "You made me jittery, not the brand new gold detective badge in my sweaty hand. It was you, Emma. You made me nervous with how beautiful you were, still are." She leaned forward, brushing soft lips against my cheek. "How strong you are. How you make my heart skip every time you look at me." Sasha moved her kisses to the edge of my mouth. I couldn't hold back, and gently pulled her chin up so I could fully kiss her. Softly at first, until I felt her push against me. I moved my hands to her shirt, unbuttoning it to glide my hands across the bare skin I dreamt about for months.

My hands fell to her bare sides. I smiled when I heard her gasp at my warm touch as the cool air drifted into her open shirt. I dragged fingers over her stomach, when I felt the gentle ridge of her scar.

I paused. A twinge of raw emotion surged through my palm as I pressed it against her. I pulled away from her lips, stepping back to look it. It was pink, still healing and larger than I remembered. I ran my fingers over it, swallowing down tears. "This is my fault. I did this." I glanced at her wrists, wincing at the thin white lines of scar tissue there.

Sasha looked down, grabbing my hand to press it against her stomach. "No, Emma. You didn't do this. You didn't do any of it."

I gently pulled away, tears rising as memories of that night rushed forward. I moved away from Sasha to sit on the edge of the bed, cradling my head in my hands. "Every night, when I close my eyes, I see them. Rachel and Evan. I can't chase away the memories of what happened, what happened to you." I looked up at Sasha, tears streaming down my face. "I keep going over everything, asking what if? What if I'd done one thing different, you wouldn't have those scars. If I'd just pulled the trigger the first time, everything would've been different. Inside and out." I stared at the fraying edges of the rug on the floor. "That's what makes me nervous. I'm afraid I'll lose you again."

    Sasha sat down, wrapping me in her arms. "You'll never lose me, Emma. I promise." She kissed my temple, murmuring in my hair. "I can wait until you're ready. I love you so much, Emma. Never forget that." She kissed me again. I raised my head, looking at her. Even through the soft smile, I saw the immense amount of guilt she carried. I sighed and leaned into her, crying.

    Sasha held me until I cried myself out and fell asleep in her arms.

*****

    The next day, Sasha's office called with Latham's address and we left the second she'd scribbled it down. The flight to Virginia was short, filled with reviewing the case notes Latham took that day. As we walked out of the terminal, I laughed at the government sedan waiting for us in the first spot. Sasha grinned and opened the passenger side door, motioning for me to take a seat. "I'm driving."

    I read over Latham's personnel file as we drove to his home in Springfield, Virginia, a large suburb outside of the nation's capital. I looked out the window, admiring the quiet neighborhood Latham lived in. It reminded me of the suburbs outside of Chicago. Quiet, green, and full of people working on their lawns. For a moment, I forgot I was in the south and suddenly missed my parents.

Latham lived in a ranch style home that was very middle American. As we pulled up to the address scribbled on the piece of paper Sasha handed me, I spotted a woman kneeling by the flower beds lining the front of the house. I tucked the personnel file under my seat and stepped out.

I waited for Sasha as the woman looked our way, smiling as she stood to investigate who her strange visitors were. Sasha fell to my side, and I glanced at her with a wink. "If you don't mind, I'll take this one. Latham is a street cop, and no offense, but you might throw him off with your federal pantsuit."

Sasha nodded. "I was going to suggest you take lead. But let me handle the introductions, I've a little more tact than you do with first impressions." She threw up a small smirk. I chuckled, this Sasha was quite the match for me. She didn't back off where she once did as my rookie.

"How can I help you?" The woman held her smile, brushing dirt off her jeans. Her voice was gentle with a hint of deep south in the way she pronounced you.

"We're looking for Mr. Tom Latham. I'm Special Agent Sasha Clark and this is my partner, Captain Emma Tiernan." Sasha held out her hand in a warm, professional greeting.

The smile tightened as she shook Sasha's hand. "You're looking for Tom? May I ask what you want with my husband?" She looked between Sasha and I, thoroughly scrutinizing us.

"Mrs. Latham, there's nothing to worry about. We'd like talk to him about some of his old cases. We need his expertise on a cold case that fell into our lap. Do you know where he might be?"

"Can I see your badges?"

I grinned reaching for mine. She had the same tone my mother did whenever someone came knocking on our door looking for my father. Hard, protective, and skeptical.

Sasha nodded, pulling hers out of her pocket, handing it to Mrs. Latham. I dug out my Chicago badge, handing it over. As Mrs. Latham looked at mine, she chuckled. "You're a long way from home, Captain."

I shrugged. "Just a little. But I heard your husband is one of the best in his field." I figured the flattering comment would ease her demeanor and build some trust.

Mrs. Latham returned the badges with a smile. "Wait here. I'll get him for you."

I stood in the yard looking at the attention to detail in every corner. The flowers were perfectly spaced apart. Not a single weed was forcing their way through the cracks in the pavement, and the grass looked like it was cut every other day. Even the house was well kept, clean and polished. Everything was perfect. All this meticulous attention to detail, and yet Latham left out a key point in his investigation.

I frowned at the sudden thought of how I wished I'd stuck to my early retirement plans and settled into the normal life I planned with Sasha. I wanted a perfect house in a quiet neighborhood where my only concern was to weed the flower beds. I dreamt of a quiet life when we moved down here, and in this moment, I wanted it again. I wanted it more now than when I actually had it.

I glanced at Sasha. "I want a house like this when I grow up."

"You do have a house like this, with a lake view." She gave me a confused look.

"I know, but I want this. I want a quiet life, gardening in the middle of the week. I envy those who have normalcy." I met her eyes as I said it.

She held the gaze for a second before looking down. "It'll be yours one day. Ours, one day. You have the strong will to make anything happen, Emma."

Mrs. Latham appeared, chasing away the daydream. "Tom is on the patio. He said to head on back and meet him. Go up the drive, he's off to the right, reading the paper. If you ladies need anything, please holler."

Sasha spoke for both of us. "Thank you, Mrs. Latham. I promise this won't take too much time and we'll be out of your hair before lunch."

She waved us off. "Oh, it's no bother. You're not interrupting anything but some overdue weeding." She gave us one last smile before walking back to the flowers.

I followed Sasha to the back yard where we found Latham sitting at a patio table reading the Washington Herald. Sasha spoke first. "Mr. Latham? Hi, I'm Agent Sasha Clarke and this is Captain Emma Tiernan. We'd like a few minutes of your time."

Latham set his paper down. "Yes, my wife told me there were two lady cops in our front yard. Nice to meet the both of you." He motioned to the empty chairs. "Please, take a seat and fill me in on why you're visiting an old retiree on this fine afternoon."

"Well, we're here to talk to you about a cold case that landed on our desk. We're part of a newly formed cold case unit for the FBI, and we need your help." Sasha was putting on the full professional tone. I cringed a little with Latham at the mention of FBI.

Latham nodded. "I'll help you any way I can. I've been off the job for some time now, so I'm not sure how much I can help. Retirement has allowed me to forget a few things here and there."

Sasha glanced my way, giving me a small nod to take over.

I leaned forward. "Mr. Latham do you remember the Angela Heaten case? It was back in the summer of 1983?"

Latham tensed at the name and stared at me, mulling something over. "Vaguely. It's been a long time since I worked that one. I can't promise I remember everything. Is it being reopened?"

I leaned back in the chair, taking a more casual approach. "Yes, by the request of Angela's parents. They've never found closure and hoped with today's technology, we might be able to find a new lead. I went through some of the files, and a few things grabbed my attention. You were the lead crime scene investigator, correct?"

Latham studied me. "Yes, I was. I assume that was one of facts was in the files you read?" I knew by his tone I wouldn't be able to play the dumb cop with him. He was as sharp as his crime scene reports portrayed him, but he'd easily fall back into the old forgetful retiree if I pushed too hard.

"I read over your whole report, which is full of outstanding work. I have to give you credit for being so thorough and detailed back then. It must've taken you at least three hours to fill out the reports. I confess, I had a hard time sticking to filling out the traffic incident reports back when I was on patrol, and that was click and select on the in car computer." I shook my head with a smirk.

"How long were you a patrol officer? Where was it again, Chicago?" He squinted.

"I was patrol for five years. Mainly on Chicago's south side then up on the east side when I was promoted to homicide detective. I'm still at the five seven nine, but riding a desk with butter bars these days. No more traffic tickets and hot summers, but don't get me wrong, I sometimes miss pounding the pavement."

Latham grinned, my tactic working. "I bet you don't miss being called meter maid or getting cornered by the little old ladies who lost their car in the Piggly Wiggly parking lot." He chuckled, shaking his head as he remembered the old days.

I'd finally made a connection through our shared connection as patrol officers. You could only understand a patrol officers' pain if you yourself had been one, walking the streets in polyester pants and twenty pounds of extra gear.

Latham leaned forward. "What do you want to know about the Heaten case? I remember everything. It was the only case I couldn't close."

"You have an incredible attention to detail. I see it in the way you take care of your house. But the Heaten file, something caught my eye and it's bothering me. I think you might know what it is."

Latham looked out in the backyard, his face darkening as he went back to that day in 1983, standing at the crime scene. He didn't speak, so I continued. "I just want your help. Why didn't you document the victim's clothes had no bloodstains on them, or there were signs the victim was possibly redressed postmortem?"

Latham turned and met my eyes. I'd hit a nerve with my question. "Pardon me, Agent Clarke, but would you mind finding my wife and asking her to bring us some lemonade? I'm getting a little thirsty."

Sasha glanced at me. I nodded, silently communicating she should go get that lemonade. Latham wasn't going to say anything more in front of her. No street cop, retired or active, ever felt comfortable around a federal agent. Most federal agents never pounded the pavement or understood the unspoken rules of being a street cop.

"Of course, I'll be right back." Sasha stood up with a smile, walking back down the driveway.

Latham waited until she disappeared. "I did initially

document it. It was the first thing I noticed. Her clothing was absolutely spotless. Not a spot of blood or speck of dust on it. Something inconceivable for the violence she endured. I also noted I suspected her body was dressed after the attack and her subsequent death. I even went to the coroner and had him note it in his report. I bet that detail is missing from his report?"

"It is. There appears to be a lot missing from all of the reports. The only reason I caught it, was because you documented the position of the sun. Something so minor in the overall scene, yet you missed her clothing being clean. It stuck out and didn't make sense for a man who had the career you did. That's why I'm here. Something isn't right about this case and I can feel it." I took a slight breath. "What really happened?"

Latham took a deep breath, letting it out slowly. "I don't really care anymore. This damn case has bothered me for years. I'm retired, so what's the point in trying to hide it anymore?" He closed his eyes, working up the nerve to tell me the truth. "When I filed my full report, it was kicked back to me. I was told it needed to be edited. I went over the whole thing again, making sure I included everything I felt was crucial to the crime scene. Adding in the position of the sun and wind, then submitted it again. This time it was hand delivered to my desk by the lead homicide detective working the case. He ordered me to edit it down even more. I was confused, telling him everything pertinent to the investigation was there. He threw the file down on my desk and told me to call the Captain."

Latham paused, clenching his jaw as more memories were coming to life. "I was told to remove the notes on the victims clothing. The Captain thought it was insignificant to the case since there was no stains or body fluids on them. I tried to debate it was crucial to the entire case. The lack of blood showed there was a second crime scene we needed to find. I was told since we lacked the manpower or equipment to investigate the clothing properly, it was an open and close case of random violence and I was to move on. I fought with the Captain, telling him if we ignored it, we'd lose the first crime scene and any chance of finding a suspect. He told me I had no argument and to follow his direct order. Take it out of my report, resubmit, and move on. I tired going to Internal Affairs but got nowhere with them aside from threats of demotion to meter maid or termination. I needed the job at the time, so I went with it. I had a new family and knew I'd never find another department with such a heavy black mark on my file."

He frowned, the sadness and shame of choosing the job over justice haunted him. Latham looked me dead in the eyes. "I've regretted not fighting harder. I know if we found that first crime scene, we would've found who killed that girl."

"It's not your fault. You did your job, better than anyone else. I understand how hard it is to fight the upper management. Now you have the opportunity to do what should've been done." I hesitated, then took a chance. "Do you happen to have the original reports? The unedited one?"

Latham grinned "I do. I kept it locked up with my old comic books. Something deep down told me to hold onto it."

"Do you mind if I take it? And can you give me the names of the lead homicide detective and the Captain in charge? I need to have a chat with them."

"I can. It's not like they can hurt me if the feds are on the case" Latham picked up a pen and tore off a corner of his newspaper, scribbling names. "You'll want to talk to Captain John Walker and Steve Exeter. Exeter is retired, but you can find him in the security shack at the country club up in Fairfax. Be warned, he's a fat angry bastard." I sensed the immense amount of distaste Latham had for Exeter. I knew right away talking to him would require more effort than I'd been used to pushing papers around my Captains desk for the last few months.

Sasha appeared around the corner with a tray of glasses full of lemonade, looking like an overpaid waitress in her pantsuit. Latham stood the second she slid the tray onto the patio table. "Let me go get that file for you, Emma. I'll be right back." He disappeared into the house as Sasha sat next to me.

"Which file is he getting for you?"

"The original unedited case report for the Heaten crime scene. He also gave me two names we need to investigate when we get back to the office and then probably interview them. Latham confirmed my suspicions. Someone is hiding something, and it isn't him. He was just pushed into falling into line and hiding facts."

Before Sasha could question further, Latham came out of the house. He handed me an envelope, a little thicker than I expected. "Here. This is the original. Everything's in there. I've had it in my safe for almost three decades. My wife got on me about throwing it out last spring. I'm glad I ignored her." Latham smiled with a wink as I took the envelope.

"Thank you, Mr. Latham. This will help." I slid the envelope into Sasha's briefcase.

"Don't thank me, just close this case. Call me if you need anything more. I'd like to put this one to bed and spend the rest of my days with a clear conscience." He gave me a hard look full of determination.

I stood, shaking his hand. "I promise, Tom. I'll do my best to bring Angela and you justice. Thank you again."

Sasha stood with me. "We appreciate your time, Mr. Latham. I apologize if we've interrupted your day."

He waved her off. "Don't worry about it. I should apologize for asking you to get the lemonade, but I don't trust feds. Never have, never will."

She grinned. "I don't blame you. I don't trust them either." She turned, walking back down the driveway towards the car. I thanked Latham again and gave him my card in case he thought of anything else.

Sasha was already in the car by the time I made the end of the driveway. I climbed in. "What are you thinking?"

"Why does everyone hate federal agents?" She squinted at the maple tree in the yard. "I was a police officer. I worked the road for a few years. I chased jerks in the heat of summer, took my licks like everyone else."

I laid a hand on her thigh, squeezing lightly. "Think about when you were a street cop and IA came barging in, or when the feds showed up taking over your case. They'd always tear it apart and take credit for all the work you did. Street cops hate the feds because they have no real understanding of what's it like to be shot at, spit on, beaten up and called every name in the book for writing a parking ticket. Federal Agents see the cleaner side of crime and deal with it from a distance. They also don't spend long hot summers in the city wearing dark polyester pants, pounding the pavement, sweating your ass off."

Sasha sighed. "I've done that, Emma. I went into the FBI to have a career. When I was in the department I was shuffled around and ignored by the boy's club."

I leaned over, kissing her on the cheek. "I know, but all street cops see is the gold badge and the three letters. They don't see the amazing woman behind it."

She blushed, starting the car. "I did learn from the best." She took my hand, lacing our fingers together.

*****

As we drove to the hotel, I secured the original file in the secret pouch in my briefcase. I'd look at it later, but first wanted to track down Steve Exeter and get an idea of who I'd be dealing with.

I looked over at Sasha as she navigated the late afternoon traffic. "Can you do me a favor and locate a Steve Exeter? He was in the department with Latham. I need to locate his personnel file and current address." I paused. "When you were working Metro, did you ever hear of a Sgt. Anthony Bellico?"

Sasha furrowed her brow, taking a breath. "Emma, I never worked at Metro." She looked away. "That was another lie, a cover story. I was on the books at Metro as a part of the narcotics team, even had a fake badge issued to me, but every day I went to work, I went to the FBI headquarters. I spent my days sifting through intelligence with Morgan."

It didn't surprise me her time at Metro was a lie. One of many thrown into my lap.

I nodded, turning to look out the window at the lines of cars all stuck in heavy traffic. The silence thickened and almost grew too unbearable when I asked. "Can you at least try and get me Exeter's file?" I held out the scrap of newspaper with Latham's handwriting. "We also need Captain John Walkers file and Bellico's. I want to look into those three before we expand our list of suspects."

She took the scrap of newspaper. "Emma, I…"

I shook my head, not wanting to talk about it. "We should start on Exeter as soon as possible. He could be the weakest link." I leaned against the window. "Latham told me he's a bit disgruntled, he may not hesitate to throw

others under the bus if pressured."
	"I'll make a few calls as soon as we get to the hotel." Sasha's voice was soft, guilt tinged around the edges of her tone. I said nothing as I continued to watch the traffic. I knew with every small step her and I took, there was a possibility of more lies being revealed.
	It wasn't her fault, but it didn't sting any less.

Chapter 6

I waited in the lobby of the hotel while Sasha checked us in. I fought flashbacks of the last time we were in a hotel and sighed, wishing my lingering thoughts of hurt would disappear. It was smothering and filled more of my being then I wanted.

I stared at the ugly mural hanging over an even uglier couch facing the concierge desk, losing myself in the painting, desperate to numb my thoughts.

"We're all set, Emma. Up on the fourth floor." Sasha gave me a room key with a smile. The car ride had been awkward, leaving a tension between us. "If you'd like, you can head up to the room and settle in. I asked for two beds." She paused. "I didn't want to assume anything."

"Thank you." I slid the room key in my pocket, bent down and grabbed Sasha's bags.

"While you get settled, I'm going to run over to headquarters. I had Exeter's file pulled while waiting for the clerk to run my credit card. It's ready for us."

"I can go with you." I shifted her suitcase in my hand.

She looked past me, at the mural. "I have to meet with Reagan in an hour. Update her on our progress." Sasha knew how much I disliked Reagan. How much I hated her.

My jaw clenched as I forced a smile. "I can avoid her, it's a big building. I want to go through Exeter's file and maybe work on finding Walker's. I know you feds have the databases, and you did give me federal clearance."

Sasha walked towards the elevators. "Okay, let's drop our things and go together. When we're done, we can go to dinner and form a game plan."

I followed her, we were only in D.C. for a few days. I suggested we tackle Exeter first, since he was retired and least likely to bend to politics or a massive retirement payout like a Captain might.

Another stiff silence fell in the elevator as we rode up. I wanted to get to work, but knowing I was walking back into the building of lies, it left me unsettled. I stared at the fake wood grain of the elevator, when Sasha laid a hand on my arm. "Emma, whatever you don't want to do or wherever you don't want to go, tell me. You're more important to me than any case and career ever will be."

I swallowed hard, looking into her eyes. "Doesn't it bother you? Does any of it bother you? You don't seem to show it if it does." I paused, trying hard to keep an even tone as I asked the question that had been eating at me for months. Sasha never showed much emotion regarding in the days and months following the end of Operation Eclipse. Granted, her focus was always on me and how I was doing, but it was hard to let her in at times. She felt closed off, keeping me at a distance.

Sasha took a slow breath, looking down at her hand. "It does bother me, all of it. I dream about the rooftop, the warehouse, and the night I almost lost you forever. I rarely sleep a full night where I don't dream of how I could've done it all differently." She turned to face me. "What bothers me the most, is how much I hurt you, Emma. The dreams, I can overcome. I can take sleeping pills, do hypnosis, even start heavily drinking before bedtime." She gave me a sad smile. "But I'm scared I can never show you, tell you enough, how sorry I am for the lies and the hurt I caused. I wish things were very different." Sasha stopped, moving her hand from my arm, tucking it behind her back. "I feel your hesitation with me, and it scares me more than staring down a psychopath with a gun pressed to my head."

The elevator door opened slowly. "But I'll fight for us just as hard as I did in the beginning." Sasha picked up her briefcase. "Until you tell me to stop." She exited the elevator, the sad smile still on her face.

I watched her walk as I followed a few steps behind. She'd answered my nagging question, tenfold. The only thought I was left with was, would I be able to overcome the fear, the damage in my heart and mind, to be the woman she once loved?

*****

Sasha drove us to the FBI building, and I was grateful to give up the need to always drive. D.C. traffic was far worse than Chicago traffic could ever hope to be, and I was already on edge. More when the beige building of nightmares and lies fell into my line of vision.

I entered the building with Sasha, clenching my jaw as I walked across the inlaid seal on the floor. The last time I walked into the lobby, I was limping, and my world had been ripped to shreds.

But after a few steps, I couldn't help but smile as I noticed many an Agent, man and woman, smile at Sasha as she strode down the hallway to the intelligence division, she once worked in. The woman was beautiful and her confidence as a federal agent was quite a turn on. I found myself staring at her, she had the same impact on others as she did me. It also didn't hurt her dark blue pantsuit was a perfect fit, highlighting her curves.

Sasha stopped quickly, forcing me to bump into her because my eyes were locked on her pantsuit, not where I was walking. I blushed as I heard her laugh. "Eyes on the road, Tiernan." She pointed at the door in front of us. "This is where Exeter's file is kept." She opened the door, and we were greeted by the soft hum of multiple computers. Sasha kept talking as she held the door open. "The hard copy I'll pick up after I meet with Reagan, but you can read over the digital copy while I'm in the meeting." Sasha moved to a terminal along the far wall, pulling a chair over. As I sat down, she leaned over, clicking into the system.

"I set you up with a user ID and a password. When you're logged in, change it like you would at the station." Sasha leaned closer as she maneuvered the mouse, her light perfume mixed in the stale air. I sighed as I felt her press against me, hearing the smile in her voice as she whispered. "Username is CPTTiernan and the password is…" Sasha bent forward, brushing her lips along the shell of my ear. "Onthecounter."

I couldn't hold back the shiver that rocked my body. I knew I was blushing like an idiot. The password was in reference to our almost first time together, on my kitchen counter. I was lost in the sound of my heart pounding, quickly interrupted by Sasha bringing up the database on the monitor.

I fidgeted as Sasha moved away, ending all physical contact.

She smoothed out her shirt. "I shouldn't be more than an hour. You have access to everything you need, Emma. If you want hard copies, make notes and I'll have one of the interns pull the files." I nodded as I slowly turned to look at her, still feeling flush from the small, intentional movements and words. She was smirking when I caught her eyes and had to force out a thank you. Sasha nodded, still smirking as she walked out. "If you need me, text me."

As soon as the door clicked closed behind her, I let out the breath I was holding and leaned forward on my hands. Sasha still had an effect on me like no other and was highly aware of it. No matter how guarded I felt I had to be, it was trumped by the simplest touch from her. With one touch and one well-placed soft breath, she had me unraveling in a hard plastic chair. I shook my head and took a deep breath, trying to refocus.

The database was exactly like the one I used daily back in Chicago, but with fewer restrictions. In a few clicks I was looking at the full unedited personnel file of Steven Phillip Exeter.

Exeter, aged fifty four, had been a police officer in Metro for thirty years when he retired less than two years ago from riding the front desk as the midnight sergeant, taking walk in reports and complaints. I scrolled through his police academy records, hoping to find something to use against him in the interview.

Exeter was nothing to write home about. He ranked barely above passing in academics and physical agility. His police record was very boring and bland. He never really moved forward until the last five years of his career when he made sergeant, but he also never had any missteps that could point to him being a crooked cop. He floated under the radar and above it just enough to stay out of trouble. I clicked through some of his scene reports. Exeter was nowhere near as thorough as Latham, but his reports were clear and concise. It showed he cared a little about the job he was tasked with.

I clicked and read over some of his evaluations. That's where I noticed an anomaly. The last fifteen years of his career, his department evaluations had a higher score than any of his previous ones, and the supervisor who signed off was Sergeant Anthony Bellico. I clicked through the forms and saw he was evaluated higher than ever in his career and Bellico wanted to pull him into the narcotics unit he supervised. Stating Exeter had a solid set of street smarts and his presence could benefit the unit.

I scribbled a few notes, excited I'd uncovered a possible lead. Exeter's other evals stated he wasn't a team player and had been reprimanded for neglect of duty. The guy had been caught sleeping in his squad car more than twice and was terrible when it came to be dealing with simple citizen complaints. But when Bellico took over his evaluations, Exeter became a gold star officer. Leading me to believe Exeter had some dirt on Bellico and was using it as leverage.

    I wanted to look at the hard copy of Exeter's file. Having a hard copy in my hand gave me better insight, as if I could read the emotion and thought process in the handwriting of others. I searched through the database and found Bellico's file. I wrote down the case file number for an intern to pull. I'd barely glossed over Bellico's before I saw it was a massive file with multiple lateral transfers from other departments before he landed in Metro.

    I sat back, excited with the find when my mind drifted to another file that could be tucked in this database. I sighed and began typing as I glanced at the clock. My hour alone was almost up.

    I paused as I slid the mouse over the execute search button and clicked go.

    Within three seconds, Special Agent Natasha Clarke's file was laid out in front of me. I took a shaky breath as I looked at her complete record, professional and personal. It was like the one Aaron managed to snag when I was starting to grow suspicious of her.

    But this was the hard truth, unedited and laid out in front of me in black and white. Sasha hadn't lied when she told me her homelife growing up was less than spectacular. Her younger years were spent moving in and out of temporary foster homes throughout Chicago. Her mother was a negligent alcoholic, and eventually gave up full custody of Sasha to her grandparents when she was barely a teenager.

Her grandparents made finishing high school and taking on college a little easier, and Sasha thrived in a loving home. She graduated with a bachelor's degree in criminal justice from the University of Illinois and walked right into the police academy. Graduating at the top of her class, Sasha hit the streets of Chicago and became an up and coming officer. For two years she was on the fast track to detective, closing out the small cases she was lead officer on, along with taking night classes for forensic science.

I smiled, one way or another, I'd have met this incredible woman.

I clicked a few more times, diving into her federal file. When Sasha applied, her application was pushed to the front of the line. She was three weeks out from graduation, when she was selected and pulled into Operation Eclipse.

The operation had been in the planning stages for close to five years, at the height of Evan's killing spree, after attacking his biological sister, Rachel Fisher. Sasha was a brand new FBI agent when she was placed with me, watching as I became the new target of a serial killer.

This is where the blemishes in Sasha's perfect career began to appear.

She'd fought hard numerous times to leave the operation. There were disciplinary actions filed by Reagan and other supervisors, advising Sasha to stick to the task at hand and not allow her emotions to cloud her actions.

I sifted through statements and reports of my daily activity. They started out incredibly detailed and thorough, mainly about my background and routines. But as time wore on, Sasha's reports became shorter and less descriptive. Two page detailed reports became two paragraph quick entries. She wasn't lying when she told me she'd fought to leave it all behind for me.

I clicked through more notes from her supervisors

about her losing focus, when I found her resignation letter, glossing over it.

It was a standard professional resignation letter until I got near the bottom.

It is in my heart of hearts I can no longer successfully continue this investigation and the personal surveillance of Detective Lieutenant Emma Tiernan of the Chicago Police Department. I can no longer lie, nor continue to lie to someone I've fallen in love with. I will choose her over any future I may have with the Federal Bureau of Investigation. Police work has always been my passion and my focus, but I can no longer, with deep conviction, say that I will be able to forgo my feelings for Lieutenant Tiernan to continue the mission I was tasked with. Effective immediately, I'm submitting my full resignation from Operation Eclipse as well as from the Federal Bureau of Investigation. My voluntary termination forms are attached to this letter.

I swallowed hard as I looked at the date of the letter. Sasha filed her resignation the day I was attacked in the basement lab of the medical school. The day my life was ripped apart and all of the lies were laid bare.

The door creaked open. I clicked out of Sasha's file and pulled up Bellico's file. "I found Bellico's personnel file. How long until we can we get the hard copy?" I cleared my throat, putting on a serious face, hoping I hadn't been caught nosing around in places I didn't belong.

Sasha gave me a tight smile as Reagan walked in two steps behind her. I stood up, my blood racing at the sight of the other Agent.

Reagan gave me one of her shitty professional smiles. "Hello Emma, it's great to see you."

"I can't say the same." I stared past her at Sasha, her

eyes boring holes in the floor.

Reagan laughed. "Still a little upset with me, I see." She crossed her arms over her chest. "Agent Clarke has filled me on your progress and I'm quite impressed at how fast you two work." Reagan looked around the large room. "She has the file you requested, and I'll gladly get you the others." Reagan matched my steely glare. "This case is important to us. It's left a mark on the agency and the Metropolitan Police Department. I came down with Agent Clarke to say hello and to inform you, whatever you need in this case, I can and will provide. I want this case closed with Angela's murderers facing long overdue justice."

Reagan's gazed turned intense. "I also want to issue an off the record apology, Emma." She softened her glare, her smile turning genuine.

I knew instantly what she meant.

I nodded, glancing at Sasha. "I'd accept it, but on and off the record, it's going to take some time."

Reagan gave me a curt nod. "Understandable." She then turned to Sasha. "Everything is set up. There are expense accounts and full federal access to whatever you may need." Reagan dug into her pocket, pulling out a thin black wallet, handing it to me. "You may need this. It holds a little more weight than your gold star."

I took the wallet from her, opening to reveal an FBI badge with a temporary agent ID card.

"I'm deputizing you, Emma. You'll be a probationary agent until the case is closed, or you could make the right decision and come to our side."

"Are you offering me a job?" I truly hated this infuriating woman.

"I have been for the last year, Emma." She smirked. "I'll leave you two to it."

Reagan left the room as I slapped the wallet shut,

jamming it in my back pocket. "I don't understand you federal people."

Sasha shrugged with a smile. "I don't either." She paused. "The job offer is real. We discussed it at the end of the briefing. You're brilliant and her bosses are pushing hard to recruit you." Sasha walked closer, laying a hand on my shoulder. "I wouldn't be against it. I love working with you." She looked over at the monitor with Bellico's files. "Did you find what you needed?"

"I did." I held out the scrap of paper with the names and file numbers I wanted. "We need the hard copies for these two. I want to surprise Exeter tomorrow morning. He works at the country club in Fairfax, still there by his tax records from last year."

Sasha chuckled, squeezing my shoulder. "Good work, Detective." She dropped her hand. "You ready for dinner?"

I caught her hazel eyes and swallowed the lump forming. I felt different after reading her file and the resignation letter. I made a note to talk to Sasha, push through the pain and hurt I carried. She had a story and if I loved her, I had to ask her to share it with me. I had to learn who Sasha Clarke truly was and then let her in.

Sasha neatly folded my notes, slipping them into her pocket. "Let's go then. We can hit the hotel, change out of these clothes. I want to take you to the best little diner on the edge of the suburbs. Close to where we used to live." I felt her tense up as it slipped out. I grabbed her hand, winding my fingers in hers. "Sasha, we have a past, and most of it is good memories." I smiled to put her at ease.

"I know. It's a past I miss." She turned away, holding the door to let me walk out into a bustling hallway full of suited agents trying to save the world one shiny badge at a time.

Chapter 7

At the hotel I took a shower to wash away the feeling of being in that building. Being in anything FBI related left me feeling smothered and sweaty.

I stepped out of the steamy shower, wiping the mirror to stare at myself. The dark circles under my eyes were slowly fading away as sleep came easier these days. I was still tired and a little too thin for my liking but returning to a healthy inside and outside was going to take time. At least that's what my therapist told me.

I toweled my hair dry as I heard Sasha outside rustling through her suitcases.

I pulled on a pair of jeans and a bra, avoiding the mirror as the steam dissipated. My upper body was covered in scars and if I caught glimpses, I'd stare at them for far too long, allowing the memories of how I got them sink in and swallow me in darkness.

I looked around the bathroom for my shirt. Grumbling when I realized I'd forgotten to grab it when I rushed into the bathroom. "Shit." I grabbed a towel, holding it over my chest as I opened the door. Sasha stood on the other side of the room, holding up a shirt from her suitcase. I stepped out and tried to run to my suitcase before she turned, catching me half naked.

The shirt was in my hands, and as I dropped the towel on a chair, Sasha turned. "Oh hey, I didn't know you were all done." She smiled when she saw me, then I watched as her eyes scanned my barely covered body. Her smile faltered as she lingered on the scars.

I tried to turn my body away from her stare. "I forgot a shirt." I closed my eyes, fighting the short burst of panic. Sasha had never fully seen my body in the light like this. I always hid it from her as best as I could.

I sighed as I pulled on the shirt, not noticing Sasha

had closed the distance between us until I felt her hand on my arm. "Emma." Her voice barely above a whisper as I turned to her. Her eyes were glassy as she pulled her gaze away from the scars littering my body.

I shook my head, tugging my arm free. "Sasha, no."

"Yes. Let me look at them."

I hesitated, trying to ignore her soft request. I wanted nothing more than to disappear into myself and hide. I'd become more self-conscious over the last few months as some scars deepened. Physically and emotionally.

Sasha stepped in front of me, her hand still on my arm, a gentle reminder I was safe with her. I sucked in a slow breath and faced her, hearing her gasp as I lowered the shirt. I flinched when warm fingers grazed over the smattering of scars on my shoulder, then to the thin one hiding under the edge of my bra. I held my breath as her hand fell to the oldest scar trailing the length of my abdomen, clenching my jaw as she pressed her open palm against it.

I'd never let her touch them or look at my bare skin when we were together. I made sure I was covered, or the lights were conveniently off.

She lifted my right arm holding it in both hands, holding it up to the light. The deepest, messiest scar laid there, running the length of my forearm. It was the scar that reminded me how precious and fleeting life was. "Why do you hide these?"

I closed my eyes, desperately fighting the urge to run. "They remind me of all the times I failed." I clenched my jaw, hating how delicate her touch was.

She ran a thumb over my wrist before pulling it up to her lips, kissing the ragged skin. I shivered as she whispered. "Surviving is not failure."

Sasha pulled me closer as she leaned forward, kissing the scar on my bicep from when Fisher shot me. She ran her hand down my arm, settling it on my hip as she stepped back to look right in my eyes. "If I could take them all way, I would."

I was caught in the emotion drowning me and struggled to find the words. I slowly leaned forward and kissed her, letting her slide her arms around my shirtless back. Goosebumps covered my skin from the warmth her hands funneled into my body.

I held her face with both my hands as I kissed her softly, slowly. It felt like a first kiss. A first kiss that reminded me of the silly romance movies I watched. Slow and purposeful. I missed this woman in my arms and wanted to take it slow, savoring her as I fought the mix of emotions rolling through me. Sasha *could* take all my scars away.

I parted from her lips, leaving Sasha breathless and flushed. I wanted to go further, forgo dinner and lay her on the bed, but something held me back. It could be the nerves I felt from Sasha seeing the pure physical violence on my body, the road map of my life.

I pulled on my shirt, making Sasha frown. I smirked as I ran a hand down her cheek. "That's for the login and the password." Sasha groaned as I walked past her to grab my jacket and came up behind me. She wrapped her arms around my waist, holding me against her front. "Emma, I mean it. I wish I could take it all away."

I turned into her arms, tilting her chin up, forcing her to look at me. "You are. Little by little. Just stick with me. I know I'm excruciatingly slow." I swallowed, licking my lips before I confessed I'd read her personnel file in the archives. "I read your file."

Sasha glanced away with a nod. "I knew you would."

Her hands slid down my back. "I requested them to declassify my resignation letter knowing you'd read it at some point." She grabbed the hand holding her chin. "It's still all true. I still love you as much as I did from the first time I saw you, Emma. I wanted you to go in my file and read everything. I'm not hiding anything from you anymore. I'm done keeping secrets."

I wound my fingers in hers. "Over dinner I want to hear all about your grandparents and how they raised you to be this incredible woman." Sasha grinned, blushing as she went to walk towards the bathroom, I squeezed her hand before letting go. "Sasha, for what it's worth, I do love you. Just as much as I did when you had me pinned against that old squad car, kissing me senseless."

Sasha turned a darker shade of red. "I know. We're just taking it slow this time." I nodded, trying to smile for her benefit. "Don't worry Emma, it'll happen. Even if I have to wait thirty years for you, I will." She let go of my hand, walking to the bathroom as she picked up her clothes.

I let out a sigh as the door clicked close. I needed to get over whatever was holding me back with Sasha, and fast.

*****

The diner Sasha took me to screamed old southern country. It was a mom and pop run diner, half full as the early dinner hour fell upon the city. We were on the edge of the capital, near the suburb where we once lived. I even vaguely remembered driving past this diner on my way to classes.

I smiled as Virginia had two sides to it, hidden behind a curtain. One side was the bustling back and forth of the heartbeat of the nation's capital. The other was the rolling hills and quiet manners of the south.

I looked out the window as we sat in a booth, staring out at the hills pushing up around the diner and the houses in the small suburb across the street. Sasha set the menu back in its spot as the waitress left with our order. "Morgan and I came here every weekend during the academy. We'd spend most of the day cramming for whatever test we had that week." She smiled. "This booth to be exact. I felt like I wore a hole in the seat from nerves." She pointed past me at a small bulletin board that held Polaroids of customers. "Morgan is up there on the wall of fame. She won the Cherry Blossom Festival pie eating contest. Took down fifteen pies in one sitting. No one has yet to match her record or beat it."

I laughed as I turned, easily spotting Morgan's picture hanging near the top. "That girl has a gastronomical gift." I turned back to Sasha as a cup of coffee was set in front of me. "I want to hit the country club first thing tomorrow. Catch Exeter by surprise." I was suddenly consumed by my work brain. Slipping into my old detective habits, forgoing normal life for work. Something was nagging at the back of my mind about Exeter and I wanted to talk about it.

Sasha nodded, stacking creamers. "Who exactly is Exeter? I didn't get a chance to look at his file."

"Exeter was listed as the lead detective on the Heaten case. He kicked back Latham's report at the request of his bosses. Latham suggested we talk to him and a Captain John Walker. He said both are shady and could use the pressure after all these years. I'll need to find Walker's file, but I want to wait on that. Digging in a Captains personnel file will start raising red flags. I'd much rather sit and poke at a bitter retired police officer, over starting a whirlwind of suspicion." I sipped the coffee. "It's already suspicious Latham told me Exeter was the lead detective on the case, and yet there's nothing in his file stating he'd ever officially transferred to the homicide unit. I just have him working the road under Bellico until he was close to retirement."

Sasha raised an eyebrow. "What else did Latham tell you while I was getting lemonade?"

"I told you most of it on the way back. This case reeks of a cover up. Latham is still bitter about how the case was handled, and I'm beginning to have a sinking feeling of what we're getting ourselves into. Nothing is thicker than blue blood, or more dangerous." I set the coffee down, running my finger around the edge of the cup. I knew the further we dug, things could get risky if this was a major cover up. Street cops would get vicious if they felt someone was digging too deep in things better left with the dead bodies they buried.

Sasha sighed hard and sat back against the red vinyl booth. "Blue blood. The thin blue line, the brotherhood mentality of street cops. Once a cop, always a cop and you never betray each other. They always say blood is thicker than water, well blue blood is the thickest and treading into a sea of it is asking for trouble. I've run into the wall a few times in Chicago as rookie officer. I had to prove my worth to the old boys club over and over." She shook her head. "Should we just ignore this case? I mean if you have a gut feeling we're digging up something buried a long time ago, something many want to stay buried. Should we bother? Is the risk worth it?"

"We can't ignore it. We have to find the truth. We owe it to Angela and her parents to find out who did this. I hate breaking through the blue line and pointing fingers at cops, but more than that, I hate crooked cops who defy the justice system they've sworn to serve." I smiled at the waitress as she set a plate of scrambled eggs and pancakes down. "I feel that's where we failed with Evan. No one wanted to own up to the truth about him when we were kids. Because of that, he slipped through the cracks in the system and scared cops." I spoke harder than I wanted, shaking my head as I pushed a fork into a soft steamy pile of pancakes. "Sorry, I know I'm still bitter." I reached for the syrup. "I want to talk to Exeter. There's something about him and his connection to Bellico that has my gut spinning. There's no reason why he would keep kicking back an impeccable crime scene report."

"I had Bellico's file pulled from the archives. It should be at the hotel when we get back." She picked at her club sandwich before taking a bite.

"I'd like to interview him before we go home." I cut into syrup soaked pancakes, trying to reel in my building anger.

"I can make it happen. I already called Metro. They're tracking down his current whereabouts. He retired last month and disappeared off the map."

I made a mental note about his retirement. Bellico was slowly becoming my number one suspect.

I glanced at Sasha as she cut her sandwich in half. When she wore regular clothes, jeans and a tight shirt with the old beat up leather jacket she adored, she looked so vulnerable. Not the tough, un-bendable federal agent who'd saved my life a few times.

I tried to smile, wanting to shift the conversation away from murder. "Tell me how you met Morgan, and how on earth did she become an FBI agent?"

Sasha grinned with a chuckle. "I kept running across her as a road patrol officer. She was always in some trouble with her small petty crimes, and always managed to talk her way out of being arrested, trading information for freedom.

She's a smart girl, just needed stability. I took her under my wing and forced her from the streets by always sneaking up on her right when she was about to rip someone off. In time, I got her to listen to me. She straightened up her act and, in a few months, she forced her way into being my new roommate. She just showed up on my doorstep with all her stuff and pushed past me, claiming my office was now her bedroom. When I applied to the FBI, she applied as a joke, never expecting a recruiter to come knock on our door. He was extremely interested in her Russian language skills and offered to ignore her minor indiscretions. Morgan has the IQ of a genius, but never had the right resources to cultivate it. We were accepted together and went to the academy, graduating number one and two in the class. She became my best friend, my sister, and the only family I could count on."

  Sasha smiled as her face softened. "She saved my life once. A story I've never told anyone." Sasha paused as she pushed her plate away. "I was on patrol in the worst parts of Chicago on the midnight shift and had a traffic stop go south." She paused again. I saw the memory flickering across her eyes. "The driver was a street thug six times my size and affiliated with one of the toughest south side gangs. He hated cops and charged me even before I reached the driver's side door. I was knocked on my ass before I knew what hit me and he started using my face as a punching bag. I had no chance to call for backup or reach for my gun. Morgan was in the alley next to us, trying to sell some stolen cell phones when she heard me yelling." Sasha gave me a tight smile. "The girl is like a spider monkey and jumped on his back. She sprayed at least three cans of pepper spray into his face until he fell off me. She kept him down with a knee to his balls, using my radio to call for help. The thug is seventy percent blind in prison, and I'm alive."

I reached across the table, grabbing her hand. My jaw clenched as a new wave of anger slowly slid into my body. I vaguely remembered hearing Aaron talk about helping the traffic unit investigate a traffic stop that turned ugly. A female officer caught by surprise and beaten.

That female officer was sitting across from me, holding my hand.

Sasha shrugged. "When backup finally arrived, Morgan told them I'd brought the guy down and she was just an innocent witness. That was when I decided to leave the streets to become a federal agent. I was tired of the raw violence. The hurt, the pain, and the familiarity of the households I pulled kids out of." She sighed. "I was accepted to the academy two weeks before my detective test results came back, and I was approved transfer to the homicide unit. Your unit." She sighed, letting go of my hand, picking at cold fries. I kept my hand on the table where her hand once was. "I wonder what would've happened if those test results came back two weeks sooner."

"You would've hated me two weeks sooner." I nodded at her plate. "Finish your sandwich, you don't eat much anymore. You're thinner."

Sasha smirked. "Yes, Doctor." She pulled the plate closer. "I hope I'm not pushing, but do you think you'll ever go back to medical school?"

"I don't know. There's a lot of *will I ever* left to answer." I went to expand, and tell her chances were I'd just ride out my time and retire. Then spend my golden years watching speedos, eating doughnuts in old sweatpants. I smiled at the silly thought, about to ask Sasha her thoughts on joining me in glorious doughnut filled retirement, when my phone vibrated with a message from

Aaron.

Hey, Emma. A weird package showed up at the front door this afternoon. No return address. I took it to the lab to have it checked it out, just in case. You want them to open it after it's been cleared? p.s. how's the hot agent and you doing?

I sent him a reply to go ahead and fill me with the details as he got them. I then answered his question about Sasha with one word

Slow.

I set the phone down, pushing my plate away with a huff.

Sasha reached over, scooping a forkful of my eggs. "Who was that?"

"Aaron. A suspicious package landed on my door step this afternoon. He took it to the lab and wanted to give me a heads up." I was more irritated than concerned. I'd gotten random fan mail from creeps and true crime junkies in the days following the Latin Murders and Operation Eclipse, so a box on the front step wasn't out of the ordinary. Most of the time I'd bring the letters to the lab, then let the human resource department do what they did to scare off the weird pen pals I was accruing daily.

I shrugged with a smile. "Aaron will take care of it. I trust him." I motioned to the waitress to bring the bill. "Let's go back to the hotel and go over those files."

Sasha nodded in agreement as she took the bill before I could grab it. "The FBI is paying for this one."

I sighed. "When will you let me pay for one of our dates?"

Sasha cocked an eyebrow. "I didn't know this was a date. If I'd known it was a date, I would've taken you somewhere nicer and made you pay."

I chuckled. "This was perfect. It's a part of the real you. Thank you for sharing it with me, giving me a deeper look at the life of Natasha."

"Can I take you on a real date when we get home?" Her cheeky grin echoed one of a girl asking her high school crush out on a first date.

I smiled and stood up, holding my hand out. "How about I just make you dinner at my house."

She grinned wider as she took my hand, letting me pull her gently up until we were inches away. I had to take a slow breath. Anytime this woman was inside my orbit, I would lose more of my resolve to take it slow.

Her eyes fell to my lips. "As long as Aaron stays far, far away from the house the entire night."

"I promise." I wound my fingers in hers, smiling like an idiot as we walked out of the diner together.

CHAPTER 8

Back at the hotel, my bed was covered with the Exeter and Bellico files. I'd pulled them apart into different sections for Sasha and I to look at individually. Two sets of eyes working to find any patterns or key points I could use in the interview. Sasha was sifting through the thinner file of Bellico, which had us both concerned. Exeter's file was thick, filling at least three or four file folders. Bellico's only filled one.

"Emma, the intern said this was all he could find in our database and Metro's. I had him check three times. This is it." Sasha handed me the thin file. I opened it up, looking at the cover sheet for Anthony Louis Bellico. Fifty three years old and retired from the Metropolitan Police Department as of last summer.

I flipped through his school records, and academy records before hitting a large gap of nothing. Nothing but the last ten years of his service in Metro. He was a lateral transfer from a small police department in Oklahoma that no longer existed after it was absorbed by the county. No records from that department made it over to fill his file and give a better insight on who Bellico was. In Metro he was quickly promoted to Sergeant on a whim and a hope he knew what he was doing. There were some case reports that stood out as going above and beyond the call of duty, but the rest was vague. Vague and suspiciously empty. "Your guy said Bellico just retired?" I asked, skimming over standard performance records.

Sasha gave me a curt nod. "Over the summer. He put his twenty five in, filed his papers and walked out on a Friday afternoon a civilian. A week after his retirement party, Bellico just faded into the wind and disappeared. None of his friends in the department knew where he was headed to, nor do they remember him talking about some grand retirement plan of buying a fishing boat down in Key West." Sasha flopped back onto the bed, rubbing her eyes. "I read over his file at least six times. Nothing stands out, Emma."

"Everything about this file stands out, Sasha." I sighed hard as I set it on my lap. "I think Bellico is the key here. He's obviously hiding something. Hopefully I can pressure Exeter to talk about him." I tossed the file onto the floor with my briefcase, leaning forward. "Nothing is ever easy." The words came out in a raspy whisper. I was tired. Tired of the bullshit circles we kept running in.

Sasha propped herself up. "Are you already frustrated? I never expected that from you at the start of a case." Her tone had a hint of sarcasm and it hit a raw nerve.

I gave her a hard look. I *was* frustrated. I'd lost my patience over the last few months as I pushed paper from one corner of my desk to the other. "I'm not used to digging through the files of old lazy cops and coming up with nothing and sorting through piss poor attempts to hide secrets." I waved my hand at the files strewn around the room. "This is why I hate law enforcement at times. It's a game of secrets and lies to some while so many others suffer." I stood up quickly, my temper coming to a tipping point. I'd dug through Exeter's file for the last few hours and found he was a lazy cop, and more than likely a dirty lazy cop.

Bellico was starting to shape up to be the same thing. I knew it'd be only a matter of time before I'd be pulling apart the ugly cover up of a teenage girls' murder. I stepped over the files and walked to the window, staring out onto the city as the sun set. I leaned against the cool glass of the window, trying to calm frayed nerves. "Maybe I should've waited longer before jumping back into all of this."

"You can quit anytime, Emma." Sasha's voice was soft as she spoke, but it still caught an edge. I clenched my jaw, pressing my hands harder against the glass. "I won't quit. I can't." I tried to control my tone, failing miserably.

I couldn't quit. This case reminded me too much of my own life. Unanswered and messy. I felt like I had to solve it for Angela and prove to myself I could still do this job. Do this job and fight for all the other Angela's out there waiting for someone to be their voice for justice.

"You don't have to work this case. Maybe I pulled you in too soon." Sasha's voice was close, her hand pressed against the small of my back. The simple touch overwhelmed me, and I had to move away from it. I pushed away from the glass, keeping my eyes on the capital building lit in the distance. "What else was I supposed to do? Continue to sit at a desk, stapling and collating papers? Collecting a paycheck before I was forced into retirement? That's not who I am."

"Maybe, but I don't want you to jump back into the minds of evil if you aren't ready."

I turned quickly, staring at Sasha. "I never was ready. I wasn't ready for someone like Evan to set up shop in my mind and torture me." I looked in her eyes. I was furious, and the anger was about to rush out of me like a busted dam. "I was never ready for him, Rachel, you. All of it." I paused as I saw her flinch. She nodded, taking a step back. I went to reach for her. "Sasha, I didn't mean that like it sounds."

She held up a hand. "I understand. I do. I understand I'm the one who has to pick up the pieces I broke out of you. I understand when you look at me, you don't see the same woman you met. I'm basically still a stranger to you." She furrowed her brow, her infamous temper rising. "This case is going to be dirty, tough. I can already tell we're digging into the dark corners of the shadows all monsters hide in, to find the truth. You don't have to stay on just because you feel like you need to or because I asked it of you." She looked away as her jaw clenched. "You make this very hard, Emma." She turned away from me.

Her words dug at that nerve, pushing my temper to the brink of failing. "It's only hard because I don't know where my trust is. With you and within myself. You honestly expect me to run back to the way it was day one? Back to Sasha Garnier the bumbling rookie? To a Goddamned lie?" My tone was harder than I wanted, the words flooding out before I could stop them.

Sasha spun around, her face flushed as I'd hit a button. "What do you want from me, Emma? One minute you're so distant, playing the professional co-worker and the next moment you kiss me like I've never been kissed before, making my knees buckle. This back and forth, it's just like it was in the beginning." She stepped closer, poking me in the chest right above my heart. "Because you've tucked this away again, hiding it from me and any chance you might want to give me to fix this. Fix us." Her gaze turned hard. "I told you I'd fight for you for as long as it takes, but I *will not* continue to endure cameo appearances of the ice queen when I've left the door wide open for you to know who *I am*. Natasha Clarke, the dedicated agent and the woman who is still so stupidly in love with you it's slowly destroying me." She dropped her hand from my chest, still flush. "Figure out what you want, Emma."

I watched her for a minute as she angrily picked up files and started throwing them into her briefcase.

One thing was clear, Sasha would fight me kicking and screaming all the way. Second, I knew exactly what I wanted in that moment. I took quick strides over to her, grabbing her elbow as she was tossing a stack of files onto the floor. I pulled her to face me, and she looked up at me with sad, frustrated eyes. "Emma, I'm tired."

    I said nothing as I moved both of my hands to the sides her face, pulling her into a deep kiss.

    In that moment, I knew exactly what I wanted. Her.

    I felt her try to pull away, but held her gently as my lips moved across hers. Sasha moaned as she gave in, pressing her body closer against my chest.

    I knew I was slowly destroying myself and her. She was right, I shoved my heart away, once again, out of self-preservation. But this woman, who's lips were the softest I'd ever kissed, would fight day after day with me, next to me. I felt her hands slide up, lying flat on my back, fingers digging into the fabric of my shirt. I pressed my forehead against hers, whispering against her lips. "You're the only thing I know I want, the rest..." I shrugged. "Fuck if I'll ever figure it out."

    A lone tear slid down her cheek. "Then stop fighting me. I'm not holding anything back from you." I brushed away the tear with a shaky hand. Sasha caught my hand before it fell completely away. Kissing my fingers, looking in my eyes, she searched for any signs of me pulling away or stopping things right as they started, like I had the last few times we were this close. I smiled lightly, giving her the cue, she was waiting for. Sasha closed the distance between us, kissing me hard as her hands moved up to hold my face. She kissed me with determination and longing, and it made my head swim.

    She pressed her body against mine, walking us to the edge of the bed, forcing me to fall back onto the files covering the bed. Sasha looked over my shoulder and frowned. She stood, grabbing my arms, and pulled me up. She then leaned over the bed, sweeping an arm across the neat piles I'd made, throwing the files to the floor with a thud. Single pages fluttering in the air to scatter across the room like confetti.

Sasha smirked, pressing a soft kiss to my cheek, her hands moving to the edge of my shirt. She kissed the edge of my jaw as she pushed her hands up and under my shirt, making me gasp at the sudden warmth. I felt her smile against my ear as she whispered. "I feel you every time my heart beats."

I squeezed my eyes shut as her warm breath fluttered across my ear, mixing with those warm hands touching very sensitive skin. I didn't want to wait anymore. I moved back from her enough to tear off my shirt, no longer caring if she saw every scar. I just wanted to feel her again.

Sasha ran her hand down the middle of my chest, making me shiver. She bent forward and kissed me softly, before moving down my neck, to my shoulder and the scar there. She pushed me gently back onto the bed, sliding up next to my body as she looked over me in the full light the hotel room offered. She pressed soft kisses down the middle of my chest, stopping at the scar underneath my bra. The gunshot wound that almost took me from her forever. She traced the edges before her hands moved across my stomach as she bent to kiss the thin scar running along my abdomen.

It was intensely intimate, her soft lips pressing against the faded ridges of skin. I closed my eyes again, trying to hold back the tears I knew were threatening to spill. I'd never let anyone that close to that part of me, until her.

Sasha moved up my body, kissing me on the lips as she hovered above me. Stopping only long enough for me to reach up and tug at the edge of her shirt. I sat up, yanking the shirt over her head, allowing her fast access to remove my bra. I sighed hard at the first touch of her palm covering my breast. It'd been far too long since I saw her, touched her, felt her skin mold to mine. Sasha straddled me, pulling my face up to hers again as she kissed me harder, her tongue finding mine in a familiar dance. I moaned as both hands covered my breasts, forcing me to push harder into them. I moved quickly, rolling her underneath me as I propped myself up on my elbows. When I looked into haze eyes, I saw nothing but pure love, asking for forgiveness in a silent gaze amplified by the flush covering her body.

I pushed a few strands hair away from her face, my fingers dragging slowly down her cheek. "I love you. My heart is still yours, even when the ice grows too thick and I lose myself."

Sasha smiled, pressing her fingers against my lips. "We can talk later. Right now, no talking, only touching and kissing."

I smirked, leaning forward to brush my lips against hers, pulling a moan from her as I pressed my hips against her. Sasha pushed up, wanting to increase the contact between us. I kissed her as I ran my hands down the soft skin I missed and dreamt about in between nightmares. I found the top of her jeans and before I unbuttoned them, Sasha arched up, grabbing my hands with her, helping me to pull off her jeans. I leaned against her as my hand ran up her thigh, to the one spot that made me groan as I felt how ready she was for my touch. I slid two fingers in easily, pausing as I heard Sasha lightly whimper, the sound alone almost taking me over the edge. I moved slowly as she matched my rhythm, our eyes locking as I pulled more moans from her, quickening my pace with every movement of her hips. When I felt she was on the edge, I pulled my hand back, making her shudder and shiver at the sudden loss of contact.

I kissed her stomach as I moved myself down to settle between her legs. I kissed her thighs softly before I gave her what she wanted and needed. The first soft touch of my tongue, Sasha pushed up and off the bed, pushing her hips down, tangling her fingers in my hair. I held her hips as she moved with me. I slid my fingers back in her, feeling her clench around my fingers as she moaned my name in a desperate way that made the ache between my legs unbearable. When she finally came down from the waves that rolled through her body, Sasha was breathless, biting her bottom lip as she gasped for air. I ran my hand over goose bumped skin as I laid on top of her, pushing my thigh between her legs, pressing against her. I wanted more.

Sasha grabbed my face, holding me still, looking in my eyes. "Do you know how hard it was to wait eight months and not attack you that day Aaron interrupted us?" She licked her lips through short pants.

I nodded as I smiled, teasing her as I brushed my lips across her, gently biting her bottom lip. "We should probably make an earnest attempt to make up for lost time." Sasha smirked as I teased her again, raising her hips up and pressing down against my thigh. The move distracted me enough to let her push her hand into my jeans, taking her turn at taking my breath away.

"We certainly do."

******

Two hours later, we both collapsed into a dreamless exhausted sleep. The morning traffic rolling outside the window, woke me. I looked around the room, smiling at the mess we made. The bed looked like it had been through world war three, only leaving a top sheet to cover both of us. The files that were once in neat orderly piles, were thrown all of the room, making me grin. I rolled over, snuggling into Sasha's side, laying my head on her chest as I listened to her heartbeat and the slow breaths she took as she slept. I ran my hand across her stomach absently, never quite getting enough of the way her skin felt against the palm of my hand.

I felt her sigh as my roaming hands woke her up. "This room is a disaster." Her voice was raspy and tired. I sat up, looking over the mess with her. She kissed the corner of my mouth. "I guess we could've used my empty bed instead of throwing papers around like a mad woman."

I laughed, shaking my head. "Why do we always fight right before we sleep together?"

Sasha pushed some hair from my face. "Because we're really, really, and I mean really good at makeup sex."

I sighed, leaning against her hand as she cupped my cheek. "I'm sorry."

Sasha shook her head. "Never be sorry for what you feel." Her hand fell to my chest, pressing over my heart. "As long as you let me in here, you will never have to apologize for anything." I felt the tears rise as I looked into the eyes of the woman who could tear down all my walls with one look, one simple touch. I just had to keep letting her tear down those walls. I leaned forward to kiss her, when the hotel phone rang. Sasha glanced at it. "Do you think we were too loud last night?"

I shrugged as I reached across her, gently pressing my body against hers as I answered it. "Hello?"

"This is the concierge desk. We have a courier package at the front desk for a N. Clarke? It can be collected at your earliest convenience." I thanked the cheery voice and hung up, looking down at Sasha still focused on my naked chest pressed against hers. "Eyes up here agent. You have a package at the front desk" I smirked as Sasha blushed. "We should go check that out and get ready for Exeter."

Sasha frowned. "Sometimes, particularly the times when you're naked with me, I really hate my job."

I laughed as I kissed her forehead, moving away so I could get up. "We finish this interview and we can go home. Go on that dinner date you promised me." I carefully stepped over the files on the floor, walking to the bathroom, feeling Sasha stare as I walked to the bathroom naked.

After a quick shower, I found Sasha picking up the mess we made, wearing an old Chicago Police Department shirt that barely covered the tiny underwear she wore. I smiled at the sight, suddenly hating my job. "Go take a shower. I'll clean this mess up."

Sasha set a small stack of paper on the bed, sighing hard. "Good thing you're so anal about organization. Most of this mess is still in its original piles." She turned and walked over, sliding her hands around my waist. "I called the country club. Exeter is on duty in an hour. We can grab breakfast, then head over." She quickly kissed me before moving to the bathroom. I found myself staring as she bent over to grab a fresh set of clothes. I was about to throw the towel on the bed and follow her, when Aaron's ringtone broke my trance.

I frowned deeply as I answered it, watching Sasha close the bathroom door. "You have really bad timing."

"Sorry, not sorry. That package I called about yesterday?" His voice was firm, serious. I only heard him like this a handful of times, usually when the shit hit the fan.

"What is it, Aaron?"

"Yeah, I'm fine, but the lab boys looked over the package and opened it this morning. This shit is fucked up, Emma. I sent you a picture. I think you need to get home as soon as possible."

I pulled the phone away, clicking on the text he just sent. "Hang on." The picture showed a plain brown shipping box with the top open. Inside was a Polaroid of a mouth making the *shhh* shape. On top of the picture sat a dismembered hand. The index finger positioned up against the lips of the mouth, making a perfect morbid picture of someone shushing whoever opened the box. I closed the text, clicking back over to Aaron. "What the hell is that?"

"The lab is running the fingerprints now. I'm on the way to meet them at the house so they can process the front step. The box was addressed to you, Emma. Captain Emma Tiernan." He paused, let out a slow breath. "I've got a couple guys working on tracking the package, where it came from, but it's hard with no return address and a generic shipping label." Aaron paused again. "There was a note tucked behind the picture." I heard the soft crinkle of a plastic evidence bag. *"Stop asking questions you don't want to know the answer too. Shhhhhh!"* He huffed in frustration. "What the fuck is going on, Emma?"

I ran a hand through my damp hair, eyes darting around the room. "I don't honestly know, but I have a feeling someone is pissed about us poking in the past. Call as soon as you get a hit on the fingerprints and if anything else comes up. Sasha and I are doing one quick interview and then we'll be on our way back to Chicago. This package, do it like we always used to."

"Roger that, Captain. Full chain of evidence, no one but you, me, and the agent get to look at the lab results. I'm on it." Aaron took a breath. "Be careful, Emma."

I bit the inside of my cheek as he hung up and took another look at the text.

It was now crystal clear Sasha and I were treading into treacherous territory.

I set the phone down on the side table next to my briefcase. I let my stare drift to the files on bed, listening to the shower. I would have to tell Sasha about the package sitting in the lab back in Chicago, but wanted to hold off until after we interviewed Exeter. I needed positive identification on the hand before I started sharing ideas and speculating who our suspects were. I turned to the bathroom as I heard Sasha drop something, cursing softly. I sighed, I really, really hated my job right now.

I moved the rest of the files, missing the times I'd leave everything to rush into the shower with Sasha when we lived a few blocks over.

I closed my eyes, I knew I was in love with her but convincing the lingering darkness she was worth more than anything, was daunting. Mix that with the overwhelming need to protect her, this was going to be harder than I ever thought. I knew I was different, and she'd see through my thin veils and saw how much I changed over the last few months.

I finished sorting the files as Sasha walked out of the bathroom, drying her hair. "I'll be ready in ten, then I'll get the car. We can stop at the front desk to grab the package on the way out."

I nodded, shoving more files into my briefcase. "Let's play Exeter by ear. Whoever he takes to better, will take the lead."

"Sounds like a plan." Sasha smiled as she slipped her gun and holster onto her hip. She looked up, catching the look on my face, immediately reading the minute fear in my furrowed brow. "Are you okay, Emma?"

I nodded lightly, looking away from her, knowing there was more to her simple question. "I'm a bit tired. I didn't get much sleep last night." I smiled at the memory of her and I. The way her skin felt under my lips.

Sasha stepped closer, placing a gentle hand on my arm. "If I'm pushing too hard, or going too fast, tell me. Last night…" She looked at me.

I cut her off, laying my hand on hers. "Don't. The only way out for me is to push through." Those hazel eyes could read right through my soul if I let her.

Sasha gave me a soft smile "I know. And I'm with you every step of the way." She moved back, picking up my jacket, handing it to me. "Let's get this interview done and go home."

*****

In the elevator down, I couldn't stop staring at Sasha's reflection as she read emails on her phone. I wanted to heal, physically and emotionally for her. She was my whole world and so much more. She was the light in the dark that continued to consume me, pushing me out through the other side. When I slept next to her, the nightmares never came. It was as if they were afraid of ruining the foundation of hope she provided me. For a moment before the elevator dinged, I saw a glimpse of having a future with her. All of her.

Sasha glanced back as the doors opened. "I can feel you staring." She winked before stepping out and walking towards the Concierge desk. I playfully frowned, trying to cover up my thoughts and the obvious staring. I went to make a sly comment, when the girl behind the desk set a medium sized box on the counter. A cold shiver of recognition filed down my spine.

As Sasha signed for the package, I pulled out my phone and opened the picture Aaron sent less than an hour ago. The box on the counter eerily matched the one sitting a foot away. "Sasha, wait, don't open that." My tone caught her by surprised, and she quickly turned.

"What's wrong, Emma?"

I motioned to the girl at the desk, smiling politely at Sasha and me. "Who dropped this off? What did they look like?"

The girl gave me a wide eyed look. "I don't know, ma'am. I just started my shift ten minutes ago. This was already here, and I was only told to make sure someone signed for it."

I clenched my jaw, gripping my phone as I glanced at Sasha. "There are gloves in my front pocket, grab them and move the box to the conference room over there." I paused, lowering my voice. "Do not open it."

Sasha nodded, reaching into my jacket pocket to grab the gloves I always kept in there. It was an old habit I feared I'd carry all the way to the retirement home. You never know when a crime scene would spontaneously fall in your lap. I dialed the non-emergency number for the Metropolitan Police Department. Sasha slid the gloves on, a look of concern and confusion on her face. The phone rang twice before a gruff voice answered. "Metropolitan Police, how may I direct your call."

"This is Captain Emma Tiernan of the Chicago Police Department. I need to request an evidence technician to meet me at the Grand Court Hotel, conference room three on the first floor."

The gruff voice huffed. "This better not be a joke."

The gruff voice gave me an idea. I couldn't ram my way into getting a tech over here without causing some jurisdictional issues and a flood of officers descending on the hotel. I knew I was talking to an older officer who was minutes away from retirement and very thin on patience, like most desk sergeants. "It's not. I'm here for a conference and I need to win a bet. I'm arguing with an FBI agent about fingerprint powder. She thinks white powder is best on glass, I say silver. We've been arguing for hours." I rambled on, hearing the gruff voice sigh with exasperated irritation.

"Please hold while I connect you to a supervisor." I could literally hear his eyes roll.

"Thank you." I let out a slow breath, nodding to Sasha to grab the box.

I followed Sasha as she carried the package to the nearest empty conference room. I closed the door behind us as she sat the box down. A few seconds later, the hold music was interrupted by a firm voice. "This is Lieutenant Harvey."

"Lieutenant Harvey. Captain Emma Tiernan, Chicago Police Department. I'm currently working with the FBI on a joint task force. The agent I'm partnered with received a piece of evidence that needs on the spot processing. Can I borrow one of your techs? Have them come out, take a few pictures, dust for prints?" I was staying calm and kind, knowing if I made a bigger deal out of the package than was necessary, it would bring unwanted attention. "The FBI is taking the jurisdictional responsibility on this one. Your tech won't be held responsible for anything other than assisting. I can have the agent speak to you if you'd like?"

There was a slight pause, followed by a heaving sigh. "Is it a bomb? I have to ask per policy before I send someone out on an assist. Doesn't the FBI have their own teams?"

I smiled, hoping it would echo in my tone. "Not a bomb, Sergeant. Like I said, it's just a small piece of evidence and the local FBI teams are tied up for hours. I just need fingerprints pulled, and I hate waiting for the feds to decide if I'm important enough or not. I want to grab as much fresh leads I can before I take it to the big boys and ruin everything. All I need is a camera and some fingerprinting equipment." I laid down my softest, calmest tone. The tone I'd often reserve for victims' families. "I promise I'll take the heat, call this number. It's my Chicago office, they'll confirm who I am and the agent standing next to me. And again, the FBI will be taking this one." I smiled, my bullshit game was on point today.

 After a few more minutes of gentle back and forth, the Lieutenant promised if I checked out, he'd have a team out in fifteen minutes. Mumbling how much he also hated federal agents and their gung ho hurry up and wait ways. When I hung up, Sasha had an even more concerned look. "Can you please fill me in?"

 I took a breath while reaching into the top of my boot for the knife I kept there. "I have a hunch."

 I caught her eyes as I pulled out the knife. I gave her a weak smile "New habit. I don't trust to carry just a gun anymore." I opened the knife, handing it over. "You remember rules twenty and four of evidence preservation?"

 Sasha shook her head as she ran the knife slowly along the edge of the box top, holding the box top closed, exactly as I'd shown her in her first few days as my rookie. Use surgical precision to cleanly open the box while looking for possible traps. She set the knife down, stepping to the side as she lifted the lid, opening the box. Sasha peered in, jumping back. "What the hell?"

 I let out a slow breath, moving to the box, lifting the lid open with the tip of the knife. My jaw clenched when I saw the contents. Sasha moved closer to me, as if I was her shield from the box. "Emma, is that what I think it is?"

I nodded slowly, taking a few pictures with my phone, sending them all to Aaron.

Inside the box was a pair of human ears, looking as if they'd been recently removed from the owner by the blood pooled underneath them. The ears were placed on the edges of a black silhouette of a head, right where the ears sat on a human. In big white letters, scrolling around the ears, read.

You don't want to hear the truth.

I let the box lid drop closed as I stepped back from the table, gently pulling Sasha with me. I opened the picture of the package in Chicago, handing the phone to her. "Aaron sent this earlier. Came to my front door, addressed to me. He has the lab running prints while they search for trace evidence." I folded my arms as I looked at Sasha focusing on the gruesome image. "I'm willing to bet my second retirement, these two boxes are connected. Someone knows we're digging and doesn't like it."

Sasha handed the phone back, folding her arms as she glared at the box. "We started this case less than a week ago. How would anyone know?"

"That's the million dollar question, and the answer will take us to the main suspect." A light knock on the conference door startled the both of us. I walked over to the door, hand on my gun, opening it slowly to reveal a young evidence tech, grinning with his hands full of equipment.

"Captain Tiernan? Lieutenant Harvey sent me over to assist you and the FBI."

I nodded, reaching for the cases in his hands. "I'll take these, please wait outside until we're finished."

The young tech blankly let me take the equipment. I smiled again as I pushed the door closed on him. "Sorry, must maintain scene integrity." The tech stammered a few indiscernible words as the door shut on his face.

I set the equipment at the other end of the table and began sorting through what I'd need. Sasha picked up the camera. "Why call them if you're not going to use them?" She motioned towards the door and the tech fidgeting behind it. "I could've called in a call for an FBI team."

"I'm not ready to get the word out about these little gifts yet. In time yes, I'll make it known we have received the message loud in clear, but I want the upper hand. I also want to document this before we see Exeter, in case he in some strange way is connected. Plus, your teams don't know the meaning of discretion. Most of the gossip I hear in Chicago come from loose lip tech teams, FBI tech teams." I set a few brushes and vials of fingerprint powder down. "The box is going to your secret office at the FBI. Only the lab techs you trust can be allowed to look at this, process it. And everyone has to keep their mouth shut."

Sasha raised an eyebrow as I pulled on gloves, I shrugged. "Or you can carry it on your lap for the flight home? Up to you. I'd rather drop it off and start the identifying process while we're in the air."

Sasha gave me a look. "There's no way I'm carrying dismembered ears anywhere on my lap." She moved to stand next to me. "Remind me to start the report when we're done, start covering our asses, and justify your rogue decisions."

I laughed. "We're already in the basement, how much more trouble can we get into?"

Sasha and I worked silently and smoothly. I held silent pride watching her work. It was apparent all the small things I'd taught her in Chicago, became second nature to her. She documented everything with photographs as I lifted a few partial prints here and there. The interior of the box was almost spotless regarding latent trace evidence. I was more determined now to get it to the lab where it could be examined with a fine tooth comb.

After we finished, I secured the entire thing in a large plastic tub I'd requested from the front desk. Ten minutes later I opened the conference room door, startling the tech who had taken a seat on a side chair. I handed his cases of equipment back. "Please tell Lieutenant Harvey thank you."

The tech nodded, but obviously confused as Sasha walked past him with the plastic tub in her arms, talking to the FBI lab on her phone.

"Uh, yeah, sure thing, Captain."

"My partner over there will send your boss a letter of thanks for your assistance today." I looked at his name tag. "Thanks again, P. Shaya. Your work here will not go unappreciated." I patted the kid on the back and hustled after Sasha.

She gave me another dirty look. "You give me more paperwork, and I might ask for a new partner."

We drove quickly to the federal labs where Sasha pulled strings to start the full evidence processing procedures and to ensure all reports were sent directly to me or her. She also coordinated for the Chicago field office to meet with Aaron and do the same with my package. I couldn't help but chuckle as Sasha's ever present charms worked on shy nerdy lab techs. Lab techs who had clearly never seen a woman like Sasha walk anywhere near their orbit. After multiple promises of Sasha's eyes only, we left.

Silence filled the car as we drove to the country club to tackle Exeter.

I was tired and concerned Aaron hadn't called or messaged, and found myself staring out the window. Lost in thought as I tried to navigate the tiny paths of this maze we found ourselves on.

"Emma, do you think your father could help us out with this new evidence?" Her voice cut through the contained silence of the stuffy federal sedan. I shifted in my seat. "My father?"

Sasha nodded as she kept her eyes on the road. "He worked extensively with the Russian and Italian mafias in his career, right? It might be a hunch, but these gift boxes of ours, reek of mafia retribution." Sasha looked at me as she stopped at a light. "Morgan once told me a story of how her uncle was running drugs for a family out of Moscow. Whenever someone spilled secrets, they'd lose a body part. The body part would be sent to their families or whomever was responsible for that person as a warning."

I frowned. "That's fairly brutal." I turned to look out the front windshield. "I can ask my Dad. He did spend most of his career working with the mafia in Chicago, worked on a couple task forces. He might know who or what we're dealing with." I sighed. "It'll be a few days before I ask. I haven't heard from him since my last email about Rachel. It's still a sore spot with him, he trusted her." I faded off, letting my eyes latch onto a couple of runners struggling up the hills of the quiet suburb we entered.

"It was an idea. I also asked Morgan to stop by when we get back to Chicago. If it's okay with you, I want her to look at the boxes, see what she can come up with." Sasha sucked in a slow breath as she turned into the entrance to the country club. Leaning forward in the driver's seat, she looked at the massive white building. "I will never understand the draw of these places. Even if I was a millionaire, I'd never join one."

I chuckled as she pulled into a parking space clearly reserved for the member of the month. "They have nice

Sunday brunches." I reached for my briefcase in the back seat.

"Don't tell me you're a member?"

I nodded slowly as I removed my gun from the briefcase. "The yacht club on Lakeshore drive near the pier. Elle was given a free membership from one of her clients. We'd go every Sunday for brunch and bloody Mary's, trying to escape the city for a few hours." I paused, tucking the gun onto my hip. I glanced over at Sasha, softly staring at me. I smiled and slid out of the car before anything more was said.

I rarely, almost never, spoke of Elle, but when I did, the same soft look came over Sasha's face. Making me want to walk away before she asked the questions I knew she was dying to ask.

I stretched, taking a deep breath of the spring air, and soaked up the sun. I pushed my sunglasses on as I scanned the area. There were masses of rich couples dressed in whites and pastels as they walked to tennis courts or to pro golf lessons. All prim and precise, these people walked with a sense of self entitlement that irked me.

I felt Sasha stand next to me as I spotted the security guard shack off to the right. I watched a large man lean against the door, ogling every passing short skit. It was apparent he didn't fit with the country club esthetic. His uniform was disheveled, the baseball cap with security in bold white letters, was pulled down as he squinted at the sun with bleary eyes, suffering a massive hangover. His face was half shaven and the mustache instantly gave him away as a former cop. I motioned towards him. "That's Exeter."

Sasha laughed. "The mustache gave him away."

I gave her a half shrug as I started walking towards the shack. The large man was too occupied to even notice

Sasha and I walking up. I cleared my throat, trying to pull his attention away from the young girl in the tennis skirt, bending over to pick up her tennis racket. He dismissed me with a meaty wave. "The main entrance is back to the left."

"I'm looking for Steven Exeter." My tone was firm, loud, working perfectly in its desired effect as the large man tore his bloodshot eyes away from the girl and moved them to me, sizing me up.

"Who are you?"

I put on a professional smile, taking off my sunglasses. "My name is Emma, what's yours?" I was trying to keep it cool. If I threw out a badge, he'd clam up and I'd get nowhere but to the bar for bottomless mimosas.

He tugged on his wrinkled shirt, looking at Sasha, then back to me. "You two have the cop stench all over you." He tipped his dirty baseball cap. "Steve Exeter at your service, you found me." He motioned for us to come inside the shack. "I figured someone would be coming for me when I heard the Heaten case was back on the table." Exeter motioned to a couple of folding chairs near the main desk of the shack. "Coffee?"

I shook my head no, Sasha taking my lead with a politely whispered no. Exeter shrugged. "So, who do you work for?"

Sasha spoke for the both of us. "I'm Agent Clarke of the FBI and this is Captain Tiernan of the Chicago Police Department. We're with an FBI cold case unit. The Heaten case came across our desk last week."

Exeter laughed as he filled a dirty cup, flopping himself down in the old leather chair behind the desk. "Only a matter of time before that one rose to the top like rotten milk." I watched as he took a sip, dribbling most of his coffee down the grey security shirt. "I'm assuming you already spoke to Latham?"

I gave him a hard glare. "Let's just cut to the chase. What can you tell us about the Heaten case, Anthony Bellico and John Walker?"

Exeter leaned back in his chair, smirking in a way that made me feel dirty. "You two are far too pretty to be cops." He ran a hand over his mustache. "Bellico. I can't tell you zip about him, the fucker disappeared like a bad magic act two days after his retirement party. I have no idea where he is or what he's doing. He just upped and bailed on everyone. We had plans to go fishing in Florida at the end of this month, but after calling his phone and getting no answer, other than a sorry this number is no longer in use, I gave up. Bellico was always a bit of a loner asshole."

I found myself looking away from Exeter to stare at the bulletin board full of memos. "What about John Walker, he was a Captain and worked with Bellico at the department, where can we find him?"

Exeter reached into a desk drawer and pulled out a raggedy planner, stuffed to the gills with bits and pieces of paper. He flipped through it one handed until he plucked a stained business card out, tossing it across the desk. "You'll find him down at the capital. Walker is trying to link in with a private security firm taking on government contracts. I'll say this though, good luck getting anything out of him. He's equally tight lipped as he is tight assed." Exeter chuckled at his own joke. I sighed. I wanted to yell at this fat slob as I continued to feel his greasy eyes on me.

Sasha reached over and took the card, flashing the grin that could open doors and classified files without a second thought. "Thank you. Now can you fill us in on what you know about the Heaten case?"

Exeter took another large, sloppy sip from his coffee. "That case was a pile of what the fuck, the moment I showed up." Exeter shifted his greasy stares to Sasha "I was first officer on scene, and from the word go, the whole thing stank of something and it wasn't just death."

Sasha nodded. "Can you tell us what you saw? How did you work the scene?"

Exeter grinned, licking the bottom of his mustache in a way that had bile rising up in my throat. "Are you single, Agent? I'd love to take you out for crabs one night."

Sasha kept her composure. "That's a lovely offer, but sadly, I'm very much taken." She shot a quick glance at me before pushing forward. "Can you tell us anything? Any little thing you remember could be a huge help."

Exeter licked his lips as he stared at Sasha in a way that made me want to pound his face in. "Um, yeah. I'd seen my fair share of murders and sexual assaults, but this one stood out. It was really weird. I called in Latham to help process the scene. I knew he had more of a brain in his head then the rest of the jack holes out there. I stood with him as he worked the scene. Even he mentioned a few times he felt there was something off about the scene."

Exeter swung in his chair. "I might've been a lazy bastard in my time, but I never dicked around when it came to cases like this one. After a few hours of Latham and I working the scene, Bellico popped up like a bad rash. He'd just been promoted to Sergeant, so he was all gung ho, always taking charge and showing off his best power stance at scenes. But this time he was quieter than usual. He pulled me to the side and told me to forget everything I'd seen, and if I was questioned, to keep my mouth shut. Bellico cornered Latham and told him the same. I felt bad for Latham after his reports kept getting kicked back in his face. Mine was only kicked back once before I picked up what was being thrown down. They wanted to cover this mess up and I honestly could give two shits why. Not my fucking business or place to start digging in holes better left covered."

My anger rose at a rapid rate. This fat sloppy ex-cop before me was an uncaring asshole. Sasha sensed I was growing furious. She bumped my leg with hers to silently tell me to keep my cool. Sasha scribbled some notes before asking. "Is there anything else that seemed unusual to you?"

Exeter shrugged. "Not really, Latham documented everything. If I know the old fart, he probably kept triplicate copies of his handwritten reports." He shifted forward, leaning on the desk. "Listen, I'm not the only one who knows you're fishing. Walker called me two days ago, letting me know the case had been reactivated by the feds. I honestly don't care anymore, it's been close to thirty years and I collect a piss ant of a paycheck from this country club to stare at nice asses, on top of my retirement." Exeter now looked at both Sasha and I with clear intensity. "Whatever, whoever killed this poor girl, wants to leave it buried. Walker called me to warn me to keep my mouth shut and give you the run around, but I always hated him. He's the one you want to grill, and Bellico. They were the assholes who forced the black marker in our hands to hide the parts they didn't want us to share with the world and the family. That girl didn't deserve that. I wish I could give you more, but I don't have any more to give. All I can say is, watch out for Bellico, he's a stubborn shitty bastard." The phone ringing off to the side ended Exeter's mini diatribe, he snatched it up. "Security. Yeah, alright, I'll be down in a minute." He dropped the phone back onto its cradle. "Well ladies, I have to take a report on a ripped Louis Vuitton purse an old bitty got caught on a door."

He stood up, smoothing out his shirt. "Hard to believe I once was a real police officer." Exeter tugged on his baseball cap and walked towards the door, holding it open for us. He took a lingering look at us, lingering a little too long on Sasha. "You two know where to find me if you have more questions." He winked at Sasha. "And if you ever break up with that boyfriend of yours, my dinner invite still stands."

I felt Sasha's hand on the small of my back, pushing me gently as she could sense I was two steps away from punching his lights out. She issued a professional thank you to Exeter before walking us out to the car.

I leaned against the trunk, folding my arms, clenching my fists. "Fat greasy fuck."

Sasha held out the business card for Walker. "He is, but he isn't the first, or the last greasy fuck I'll have to deal with. At least he didn't stonewall us." She cocked an eyebrow. "But that invite for free crab may be too hard to pass up."

"You're kidding, right?" I was shocked, my fists were clenched so tight, I was sure I could've made diamonds out of coal.

Sasha laughed. "Maybe, it's almost crab season around here, and it's been a minute since I had a nice crab dinner." She squinted. "But I could be persuaded to turn him down if you have a better offer."

I leaned forward my voice low as I whispered against her ear. "My better offer is, me kissing that one spot right above your left hip that makes you shiver and moan." I held my smile as Sasha blushed, biting her lips as she swallowed hard. She stumbled over her words when she finally spoked. "I think you win. Um. Should we tackle Walker or find Bellico first?"

I was enjoying watching Sasha blush and fidget. "Bellico first. If we can crack a Sergeant under the Captain, it'll give us more leverage to work Walker."

Sasha nodded, still flushed as she looked around the

country club. "Are the Sunday brunches really that good to waste the money to come here?"

I reached out, gently grabbing her forearm. "I'll take you when we're home. Start a new tradition with you." Sasha met my eyes, a slow grin forming. She was about to say something when my phone rang. I held up my hand to Sasha as I stepped away from her, showing her it was Aaron.

"You're killing me with the radio silence." I turned, squinting at the tennis courts in the distance.

"Sorry, Emma, shit's been crazy around here. I picked up two more homicides on top of your creepy box." I could hear Aaron was walking as he was talking, "I got an ID back from the lab. They ran the fingerprints and got an immediate hit. They're still working on the rest, but I wanted to call you as soon as I got it in my hands."

I looked at Sasha watching a group of women guzzle mimosas. "Shoot."

"Your set of hands belong to Anthony Louis Bellico. He was a sergeant over in Metro. Freshly retired as of last summer." Aaron's tone was even as it always was when he read off evidence reports to me. He had no clue Bellico was on my suspect list. Was, now being the key word.

My stomach dropped as I listened to Aaron go over the other details of Bellico I already knew. I thanked him when he told me he'd have the file waiting for me when we got home, hopefully with the rest of the evidence reports. I hung up the phone, closing my eyes, the frustration building, I barely heard Sasha.

"Where do you think we should start with Bellico? Family? Friends? Family might know where he is."

I looked up, letting out a breath. "I know where he is, at least pieces of him."

Sasha stared at me, her eyes filled with confusion

and a glint of fear of what I'd just said.

"Can you pull some strings? Get the last known address for Bellico?" I had no idea where to go next with the piece of information Aaron just casually laid on me. I only knew we had to look at Bellico's house for clues of why I now owned his dismembered hands.

Sasha nodded slowly, pulling out her phone. "What do you mean, pieces of him, Emma?"

As I went to tell her, her phone rang. She glanced down at the caller ID before answering it. "Agent Clarke." Sasha turned slightly away from me, folding her arms as her brow furrowed. "Are you sure? You ran preliminary DNA and blood type?" Sasha took a steady breath. "That's fine, just send the final report back to the Chicago office. I'll be there within the next few days. I also want you to classify this report as high priority, only I or Captain Tiernan will have direct access. After that I only want SAC Reagan to have access and no one else." Sasha turned, locking onto my eyes. "I also need you to pull his last known address and get it to me ASAP." She issued a few more quick instructions before hanging up. Sasha held onto her phone tightly. "The lab identified the ears."

I sighed. "Bellico?"

Sasha nodded once. I pushed off the car. "Aaron called to tell me our lab came back with identification for the hands. Fingerprints got an immediate hit the second they ran them." I stared up at the trees, pausing my thoughts as I gently marveled at how the leaves were slowly turning color as the signs of late fall were taking hold. It was almost November, but it felt like late spring at the country club. The days were still warm, and people walked around in summer clothes. It took a small edge off the fact I was now in the middle of a gruesome case. One that was slipping closer to a fresh homicide.

"Emma, what is going on?"

I looked down at her, pulling off my sunglasses. "I don't know, Sasha. All I know is we need to get to Bellico's house and find out who did this to him and why they're sending the pieces to us."

She looked at me, and I was suddenly taken back to a day when there was a madman chasing us. I heard her phone beep. She cocked an eyebrow, reading the message. "Records found Bellico's most recent address. It's over in the next county, should only take us a half hour to get over there if we leave now."

I tossed the car keys to her. "Then we better get going."

Chapter 9

The car ride over to Bellico's last known address was tense. I read Aaron's email to Sasha, filling her in as she drove. Bellico's hands had been removed with a blunt cutting tool, leaving ragged edges on the wrist bones, before being posed and locked in place when rigor set in. The rest of the evidence was still being processed, but so far it appeared the box was clean of any fibers, or dust, that could be used in identifying who packaged the hands. There wasn't a damn fingerprint worth saving on the entire thing, just half partials and smudges.

Aaron also wrote the medical examiner would be taking a closer look at the areas where the hands were removed, in hopes of figuring out the exact tool used and run it through the massive database the FBI had. Better than driving to the local hardware store with autopsy photos.

I clicked my phone off, tossing it in the console. I pressed my temple against the car window, rubbing at my forehead. "I don't think I'll ever get used to this feeling."

Sasha glanced over as she raced through the streets towards the highway. She'd been on edge the moment I told her who the ears belonged to. "Thinking about retiring again?"

I kept my eyes on the gentle rolling hills of Virginia encasing the houses built around them. I sighed at the question. "I don't think I'll ever get used to the feeling of hunting suspects, or the feeling of being hunted." I purposely ignored Sasha's light comment about an impending second retirement. "This case is turning into a fractured pane of glass. The next lead could shatter it, leaving us in pieces."

Sasha reached over, laying a warm hand on my arm, squeezing. "I'm here with you. We're in this together."

I knew what she was doing, trying to keep me from constantly slipping into my fortress of solitude. It was a temptation every day as I struggled with what this case had thrown at us, on top of everything I'd left untouched with the Latin Murder case. I looked over at Sasha, her hand still firmly on my arm as she focused on driving, and said nothing. I placed my hand on top of hers, running my thumb over her knuckles. She smiled lightly at my touch, squeezing once more as I turned my attention back to the window and tangled thoughts.

I held onto the scrap of paper Sasha wrote the address on, leaning over in my seat looking at mailboxes on my side trying to locate Bellico's house. We were over in Loudon County now, close to Leesburg. Bellico's address listed him living in a quiet suburb full of families. Obvious government, military, and law enforcement families.

The houses oozed American pride in their ever present flags and clean, neatly manicured lawns. There were smatterings of Christmas decorations going up, mixed with the odd Thanksgiving decoration. My heart had an unconscious ache when I saw the mix of decorations. I'd not celebrated a proper holiday in years. Not with my family. Not with Aaron, aside from drinking and watching the Thanksgiving Day parade when a snowstorm canceled his flight out to Seattle to spend the holidays with his family. I didn't give a damn about the holidays since Elle. There was no point.

I closed my eyes as a quick memory of our last Christmas together hit me harder than I wanted.

"Oh, here we go." Sasha quickly hit the brakes, jolting me forward in my seat, jolting me out of the memory. I leaned over, looking at the house she stopped in front of. It was a simple, plain white ranch style house that looked exactly like the others around it. Nondescript, plain aside from the small American flag swaying in the slight breeze at the top of the garage. The lawn was overgrown a bit, looking as if it had missed almost two weeks' worth of maintenance. I double checked the address in my hand. "It's a match." I looked out the front windshield, scanning the neighborhood. "Park in front of the next door neighbor's house. We'll walk up." I turned quickly in the seat, still leaning over Sasha's side, very close to her face as she looked at me, slightly biting her bottom lip. Her heartbeat visibly racing in her neck.

    I looked at her lips, and back in the hazel eyes that made my heart skip a few beats and my skin prickle. The energy between us was always present and thick. It didn't matter we both had boxes of body parts waiting in labs for us, our hearts were always begging for us to touch and move closer.

    I cleared my throat, leaning back in the seat, unbuckling my seat belt and making a smooth exit out of the car. I walked to the trunk to pull off my blazer, the day had grown warmer since this morning. I tucked it into my duffle bag as Sasha met me at the trunk.

    "Your gun is visible." She swallowed hard, collecting herself.

    I cocked my head as I dug in the bag. "I know. I'm starting to roast in this southern sun and polyester, Second, this neighborhood is oozing law enforcement and military. If we make it clear we're cops, the neighbors might cooperate with answering questions about Bellico, and offer their insight on what kind of neighbor he was."

    Sasha smiled with a nod, and as she pulled off her blazer, I had to look away as the dark grey shirt she wore underneath stretched tighter, hugging her curves.

    Sasha sighed, laying her blazer next to mine. "It's a shame I wasn't your rookie longer. I could've learned a lot from you, and how to pick up the small details around me." I knew she was hinting at much more. I shook my head as I straightened up, adjusting the bulky holster on my hip making room for my badge as I clipped it next to the holster. I stretched, looking at the house for any of those small details. Sasha was digging around in the trunk, settling her holster on her hip when I felt her hand press against the badge on my hip, making me gasp lightly. "You know, you could use that fancy FBI badge Reagan gave you."

I glanced at her hand covering the badge. Her fingertips were warm on my stomach even through the light dress shirt, it added to the warmth I felt from the sun beating on me. I swallowed hard. "I know, but I prefer sticking to my Chicago badge. I don't want Reagan getting the *slightest idea* I'm considering her job offer."

Sasha smiled as she dropped her hand, her fingers grazing my stomach. "Fair enough, but it would be nice to think of you as my partner for real, Agent Tiernan."

I took a step away from the trunk, closing it. "I already am your partner, Sasha." I said it softly as I pushed the trunk closed.

With a deep breath, I moved to the front door of the house, speaking over my shoulder as Sasha caught up. "Look for anything in the windows, or on the door. We only need the smallest amount of probable cause to gain entry. Piles of mail, signs of forced entry, anything. If we can't find it, I'm going to need you to call in a favor and get a warrant." I silently kicked myself for not asking for a warrant the moment I got a positive ID on Bellico's hands.

"I have a warrant ready and waiting for us. I just need to send a text to Armstrong, and it'll be my possession within fifteen minutes." Sasha grinned. "I had one drafted up as soon as the ears were identified."

I grinned, shaking my head. "Maybe Armstrong is worth something, get us that warrant. In the meantime, we still need to get in the house. So whatever bit of probable cause we find, run with it. I want in that house."

I walked to the garage door as Sasha set to work getting the warrant in our hands. I tugged on the door, finding it locked. I walked around to the front door, same thing. The whole house was locked up tight. Sasha and I peered in the front windows and saw nothing. The blinds and curtains were drawn closed like Bellico had taken off on vacation and sealed up the house.

We both walked to the back of the house. The backyard was large with an immense patio obviously designed for entertaining. A large barbeque sat next to a jacuzzi, both covered up for the season. The next door neighbor was out in his backyard, watering his flowers and eyeballing us. He took a moment before finally walking towards us, calling over the fence. "Hello there! Is there anything I can help you with?" His tone was a gentle but firm. I spotted the boxy shape of a pistol hiding under his oversized polo.

Sasha thankfully took the lead, she was always better at casual conversation than I was. I was too tired and too jaded to care enough to play the polite back and forth with concerned citizens. While Sasha made nice, I kept looking around the house.

She explained to the neighbor what we were doing at the house, skirting the truth, when he revealed he was a county deputy. Sasha glossed over our intentions, telling the neighbor we were on a welfare check favor for Metro. Bellico had missed some inane conference the FBI was holding for retired law enforcement. I had to hold the smile back as I listened to the pile of dribble falling out of her mouth, eagerly devoured by the friendly deputy.

I moved to the farthest window on the back of the house as the deputy began telling Sasha he'd not seen Bellico in a few weeks, but he remembered seeing the old Chevy Tahoe Bellico drove, leave the house early one morning. The deputy assumed Bellico was taking another one of his long fishing trips. Sasha continued to question the deputy, who carried a shy grin as he did his best not to look at Sasha's other assets. I shook my head at him when I caught him staring. He flushed red for a second before returning to direct eye contact with my partner.

I laid my hands on my hips as I squinted at the house, trying to find any scratch, ding, or crack that would lead me to believe foul play was at work. I sighed, focusing on a large willow tree darkening the backyard with its shade, when I heard the soft buzzing. I craned my head towards the sound, closing my eyes to focus on the buzzing and tune out the other noise around me. The buzzing synced up with the click of the air conditioning unit incessantly going on and off in the time Sasha and I had been in the backyard. The unit struggled to keep up with the demand on it. I moved further away from the groans of the air conditioning unit, focusing harder on the buzzing.

After a few seconds, I pinpointed the buzzing. It was coming from inside the house.

I walked to the far window at the back of house, the one closest to the willow tree. The buzzing was loud, and I had to stand up on my toes to see the ledge of the high set window. What I saw made me clench my jaw and whisper. "Shit." I took a deep breath and tapped on the window, scattering a handful of flies mashing themselves against the window in a desperate attempt to escape.

I turned to Sasha still talking to the deputy. "Excuse me, Agent Clarke?" The sound of her full title made her stop mid laugh and turn immediately in my direction, her eyebrows raised in silent question. "I found our probable cause." I waved at the window.

Sasha politely excused herself from the deputy, walking over. "And that is?"

I pointed to the window. "Hear that buzzing?" I tapped on the window to show her the flies scattering. "You know what all those flies mean, don't you?"

Sasha clenched her jaw. "Carl, my old road partner taught me to look for this on my very first dead body call. The more flies the longer it's been."

"The patio door, I'm sure we can pry it open." I grabbed her elbow lightly, pulling her towards the back patio door.

"I can pick the side door into the garage quicker." I looked at her confused as pulled her elbow free, digging her in back pocket. "Agent Adams taught me how to pick locks the three weeks into our friendship."

I huffed, following Sasha. I was thankful we were out of view of the deputy. There was no need to get more people involved, more jurisdictions involved. Sasha knelt and went to work on the door, using a lock pick set she'd pulled from her back pocket. I watched, marveling at how quickly she worked on the lock. It only took her a handful of seconds before she stood up, turning the handle and opening the door. She turned to me with a smile, waving her hand. "Ladies first."

I rolled my eyes unlatching the holster on my hip, pulling my gun out to rest at my side. "Thanks." Standing at the edge of the door, I peeked in and saw the Chevy Tahoe was missing. I took a slow step inside the garage, scanning the dimly lit room. Sasha was close behind me as I walked towards the door leading into the house.

I put my hand on the doorknob, testing it and finding it unlocked. I glanced back at Sasha. She nodded and stood off to the opposite side. Counting off to three, I pushed the door open and immediately gagged as the smell hit of us like a brick wall. I quickly grabbed the door, slamming it closed as I rushed out of the garage, gulping fresh air, desperate to clear the smell out before I threw up in the driveway.

Sasha looked pale, just as pale as the first time we went to the morgue in Chicago. She looked up at me, cringing. "That smell. There's a body in there. A very dead body."

I nodded quickly. "Yes, and it makes perfect sense why the air conditioner is running until it explodes." I wiped at the sweat beading on my forehead. My heart racing with my mind. "We have to go back in and find out who it is." I let out a slow breath. I didn't want to go back in there. It would be my first dead body in months, and my fear was pushing memories up. I gripped my gun tighter, trying to funnel some of the fear out, and steady the shiver running down my spine.

"Can't we call a crime scene unit in?" She glanced over her shoulder. "Maybe let a tac team go in there and secure it." She grimaced, looking at the back window where the flies continued to buzz.

"We could, but it'll take too much time and it'll bring the locals down here in force. I want to look at whoever is in there before a hundred pair of boots trampled the evidence." I stared at her for moment, until it clicked in my head. "Wait here." I jogged back to the car, digging in my duffle bag. It was my old go bag from my days as a road officer in Chicago. As a second thought I'd brought it with me on this trip and dumped it in the trunk, purely out of gut instinct and habit. I dug around until my fingers wrapped around the black nylon bag that held the old respirator issued to every officer on day one. I pulled it out and smiled, I'd only used it once during tear gas training. I slammed the trunk down and ran back to Sasha.

    I pulled the mask out of the bag, handing it over. "Wear this. It should cut the smell down." I walked back into the garage grabbing a handle full of clean rags. "I need your set of eyes as much as mine." Sasha shook her head trying to hand it back to me, I held her hands. "Wear it, Sasha. I'm adjusted to the smell of death more than I'd like to admit. Years of homicides in the heat of Chicago summers has ruined my sense of smell and made me hate barbeques." I smiled tightly as I took the mask, helping her put it on. I then handed her a pair of gloves. "I'll call it in and take the blame for not waiting for backup. It should give us at least ten minutes to grab a first look." Sasha adjusted the mask as I made a quick call to the local Sheriff's department, informing them of the situation and to send out an evidence team as soon as possible. I dropped my phone into a pocket, taking a large breath. "Are you ready?"

    She gave a short nod, gripping her gun tighter. I took a deep breath of clean air before clamping the thick rags over my nose and mouth and pushed the door open. I had to clench my jaw as the strong odor of death pushed through rags. Holding my gun up, I walked into the house, shivering. The house was frigid as I navigated through the tidy kitchen, the air conditioning had done its job. I scanned quickly, making my way to the far end of the house where the window of flies was. We walked past a bathroom, a bedroom, a master bedroom. All of them were tidy, bland, signs a bachelor lived here. The house was empty, clean, and void of life. It gave an added eerie feeling to the entire house. I glanced back at Sasha to check on her. She gave me a quick thumbs up and nodded to keep moving.

    The last room was tucked in the back of the house,

the door was closed. I paused, taking a minute to prepare myself.

    I felt Sasha's hand on my shoulder, gently reassuring me. I swallowed hard, fighting through the smell as it grew thicker, burying itself in the rags and my clothes. I held my breath as I dropped my hand from my face to open the door. Turning the knob, I kicked the door open, covering my mouth again. The room was pitch black, and the buzzing sound burned in my ears. Feeling around for a light switch, I flicked the lights on, illuminating the pure horror before us.

    In the middle of the room laid a badly decomposed body. It was hard to tell ethnicity or gender by the swelling and bloating consuming the body. I coughed at the sight, dropping my eyes to the floor to calm down as I walked further into the room. I glanced up, and knew it was Bellico. The hands and ears were missing from the body.

    Bellico was splayed out on the floor. A plastic sheet laid underneath his body in an attempt to keep the body fluids from seeping into the floor. The room was a mess. There was a desk tipped over, bookcases on their sides and files strewn all over as if someone was searching for something. Looking around the room, my eyes fell to a large mason jar with two eyes floating in a clear liquid sitting next to a large shipping box. A shipping box similar to the ones sent to Sasha and I. That's when I drifted my gaze back down to Bellico and noticed his eyes had been removed. The dark empty sockets bore into my eyes, so deeply I had to turn away as I mumbled multiple curse words. I met Sasha's eyes, shaking my head as I left the room in a hurry.

    I ran out of the garage and into the backyard, leaning on my knees under the willow tree as I gasped for air. The gruesome scene in that room hit me harder than I expected. It shook me to the core, and I had to get out of there as soon as possible. My hands shook as I holstered my gun and leaned against the tree, fighting the tears welling up in my eyes. I stared at the tree as sirens filled the air.

    I composed myself just as the first deputy came into the backyard. He looked over me, his hand on his gun. I pointed at the house. "Inside. The Agent is still inside with the body." He nodded and went rushing into the house. I heard his gags and coughs as he came running back out with Sasha two steps behind him. She looked at me as she ripped off the mask. The look in her eyes silently asking a million questions. I just stared back at her as another wave of deputies flooded into the yard.

    Sasha switched into Agent mode, taking over the scene, directing the deputies to set up a perimeter as she moved to meet the evidence techs and prepare them. I walked past the sea of uniforms cluttering the driveway, encouraging the neighbors to come out of their houses and start gawking. I walked to the car with my head down, digging out a fresh pair of clothes out of the trunk. The smell of death was stuck on my clothes and no matter how much I washed them, it would never leave. I walked over to the ambulance on standby, smiling at the young EMT. She let me change my clothes in the back and dump my ruined suit into a biohazard bag. I double bagged it and tossed it in the trunk. I'd have to take the bag to the local dump and burn my clothes. I sat on the hood of the car, trying to shake out the feeling still rattling in my bones. I'd been on a million crime scenes, a million different violent crimes, I'd survived Evan, and yet one simple glimpse of Bellico rotting into that floor, I was the verge of a total collapse.

    I turned away from the house, looking at the mountains cresting behind the house across the street. I was trying to distract my mind and photographic memory that had just forever captured the crime scene.

I didn't hear Sasha call my name until I felt her hand on my knee. I looked at her, smiling for her benefit to prevent her from asking if I was okay for the hundredth time.

She picked up on my forced smile. "They're about to remove the body. The medical examiner is going to rush the autopsy for me. The techs are combing through the room where we found him and the rest of the house." Sasha let out a shaky breath. "The next door neighbor was only able to tell me Bellico was a quiet neighbor. He kept to himself but would help out when it was asked of him. He also said he hasn't noticed any strange cars at the house or strange people knocking on the door. The last time he saw Bellico was almost three weeks ago when he, and what appeared to be an old cop friend, sat on the patio drinking the day away." Sasha folded her arms, trying not to stare at me. "I showed him the pictures of Exeter, Latham, and Walker. He didn't recognize any of them. Just said it sounded like the two were old buddies from the force."

I kept my gaze on my hands in my lap. "Try to get a description from him. Maybe we can have a forensic artist draw something up. The lack of any sign of forced entry lead me to believe Bellico knew his killer and let them in."

"He already volunteered and is sitting down with his departments sketch artist right as we speak." I heard her take a deep breath. "It's going to take hours to process the scene. How about you go back to the hotel and try to rest." Her tone was gentle. She motioned to the masses of uniforms around us. "I'm pretty sure the entire county is here to help, plus some. I'll stay here until it's all done. The FBI is sharing jurisdiction with the county. It's their homicide, but we'll be allowed access to the evidence since it's connected to our case."

I slid off the hood, opening the driver's side door for

the extra clothes I grabbed for her. I handed Sasha the clean set of clothes. "These might not fit you, but you need to throw those clothes out. You smell really bad."

Sasha couldn't help the small smile that crept across her face. "Thanks. You do owe me a new suit after this." Her hands covered mine as she reached for the clothes. "What else do you have in that bag?"

I shrugged. "Everything I think I might need on the road. It's a leftover habit from when I was a patrol officer and still had the stomach for the job." The last part slipped out. I smiled, trying to hide my fear. "I'll meet you back at the hotel. I've seen all I need to, and I want to call Aaron, fill him in on this new development." I took the car keys Sasha held out. "Call me if you need a ride." I felt bad for leaving her, but knew in my shaken state, I'd be useless.

"We can go home tomorrow. It'll take a while for the evidence to be processed." Sasha's voice was still gentle as she reached for my hand. "In the meantime, we can take a few days off."

I nodded and said nothing as I looked in her eyes. I grabbed her hand, winding my fingers in hers. "Be careful Sasha, call me if you need me."

Sasha sighed. "If you *need me,* Emma, call."

I smiled as I moved away from her and sat in the driver's seat. I watched her in the sideview mirror as she walked back to the circle of techs suiting up, asking if she could change somewhere. I sighed hard as I started the car.

I only got a few blocks away from the subdivision until I pulled off onto the side of the road and broke down. I cried with my forehead pressed against the steering wheel, fighting my panic with every tear. I was slowly crumbling inside and didn't know how much longer I could hold strong in this job and for Sasha.

*****

It took longer than I'd wanted to get back to the hotel. Virginia traffic was thick, and having barely paid any attention to where we were going as Sasha drove, I had to rely on the crappy GPS on my phone. It was almost an hour before I got back to the hotel and into a hot shower, scrubbing away the lingering stench of death.

As I sat on the bed Sasha and I shared, now back into a pristine state thanks to housekeeping, I called Aaron. Rubbing my wet hair with a towel, staring out the window as I listen to the phone ring three times before Aaron answered. "Hey! How's my favorite part time federal agent and the full time agent she loves."

I tossed the towel off to the side onto a chair. "We found Bellico. Sasha is still at his house processing the scene with the county sheriff."

"Processing the scene? Let me guess you found Bellico in a non-responsive forever state?"

I smiled at his morbid sense of humor. "Exactly. We're coming home in the morning. This case is getting messy and spreading across too many jurisdictions for my liking. Sasha and I are going to pull everything into one pile, hopefully back in Chicago. I'm getting tired of the bad memories Virginia holds." I rubbed my eyes as I drifted quickly to the other times I'd endured in this state. Lies, betrayal, the death of a serial killer, and the death of the normal life I thought I was living. "I'm thinking we need to take the reins and make the FBI lead on this. Control the flow of information of evidence and statements." I sighed hard.

"You okay, Emma?"

I chuckled. "I think that's the one question I'll never be able to truthfully answer." I paused, looking up at the hotel ceiling. "I don't know, Aaron. Something about what was in the room got to me, it broke through my walls and shook me like I was rookie again staring at my first dead body. I think I'm getting too old for this shit. I'm losing my edge." Before he could answer with is usual big brother advice, I kept on. "I need you to light a fire under Dr. Willows. Tell her it's a favor for me and she'll rush the rest of the reports. The rest of it, I'll work with you when we're back home."

"Not a problem, Captain. I'll call Willows as soon as I hang up." I heard him scribble notes in the background. "Oh, and Emma? You're not getting too old for this shit, you're just getting too stubborn to talk to someone, anyone, about everything you still have bottled up. Talk to Sasha. She loves you and will be there at the end of the day, no matter what you tell her."

I clenched my jaw at his words. He was right, but I sure as shit wasn't going to openly admit I was my own worst enemy. "I'll think about it. Clean the house before I come home, or I'll double your rent."

Aaron laughed. "I don't pay any rent, but ten four. The house shall be spotless upon your arrival. Be careful Emma, get you and Sasha home safely."

I smiled and hung up the phone, setting it on the table next to the bed. I leaned on my knees and stared out at the window for what seemed like hours until my brain finally begged me to lay down and close my eyes.

I fell into a deep sleep, curled up in the middle of the bed in old sweatpants and t-shirt.

I dreamt of Elle that night. I hadn't dreamt about her in years since her death or dreamt at all in the last few years. It was always nightmares that plagued me. The dream was of Elle and I, standing on the edge of the lake. It was quiet and calm around us. The gentle sounds of the lake was the only sound I could hear. I stared at Elle as she turned to me, smiling, warming my heart and easing the strange sense of imbalance chasing me since I flipped the light switch on in Bellico's room.

Nothing was said between the two of us as she walked closer and closer. My eyes welled up as I looked at her. My heart ached for her in a way that wasn't like before, it was an ache that felt like I was betraying Sasha. Elle moved closer to me, reaching out to place her hand over my heart, forcing me to look down at it and clutch her hand in mine. She whispered against my ear. "Your heart is no longer mine. She deserves more from you."

I closed my eyes tight as I whispered to her. "I know."

I woke up with a start when I heard the door open, the room was now dark. I had slept through the afternoon and night took its place. I waited as my eyes adjusted to the minimal light in the room. I wasn't as tense as before. I was calmer now, even as the bed dipped next to me. A warm body pressed against my back as I felt her arms slide around my waist, the smell of her shampoo filling the air.

Sasha's hair was still damp as she snuggled into me, whispering. "Are you okay? I've never seen you like that. I was." She paused, hesitating to finish the sentence.

I found her hand and pulled her closer. Wanting more contact with her as my heartbeat only for her. "I shouldn't have left you."

"Don't worry, I just got back. I saw you sleeping and didn't want to wake you. But then I couldn't resist." I felt her sigh against me. "Everything is handled, we can go home in the morning. The Sheriff's office is working with the FBI labs, so we don't have to worry about information getting lost in transit. I have promises all across the board we will get final reports by the end of this week. I have the county canvassing the neighborhood and running interviews wherever they can. Hopefully it'll turn up a lead." I heard her yawn and stretch against my back. "I'll tell you the details over breakfast, but right now, I'm tired and all I want to do is get some sleep."

I felt in the way she squeezed my hand she was worried about my reaction at the scene, and wanted to talk about it, but was holding it back for my sake. I rolled over in her arms, looking at her face in the soft light streaming through the window. She smiled and leaned into my hand as I pressed it against her cheek. I ran my thumb across the soft skin, pulling a grin from her. She did deserve more from me.

I said nothing as I laid my head over her heart, sliding my arm across her waist. I caught her by surprise, and it took a moment for her to settle her hand on my back, running it up and down as she held me. I whispered against her chest as a few tears slid free. "You deserve more from me, Sasha. I promise." I closed my eyes to hold back the tears, when I heard her whisper. "I love you, Emma."

I fell asleep in her arms and for a moment, and forgot the things trapped in my mind.

CHAPTER 10

Standing in the long line, staring at the endless list holiday flavors of coffee and wondering why anyone would pay six dollars for an over sugared cup of coffee, I smiled at the sudden thought of Sasha. I'd let her sleep in and snuck out of the hotel to enjoy the odd warmth early November in Virginia had to offer, making me wonder where the hell time went to? We started this case near the end of summer, and now I was staring at jolly turkeys and Santa's, telling me the blonde roast was the best. I felt better after sleeping in Sasha's arms and letting myself go, giving her a little more of me. But I still needed the largest coffee in the world to feel human the morning after finding Bellico.

Reading the calorie count of a gingerbread muffin, I'd oddly noticed how holiday driven the world around me had become, also noticing I'd missed Thanksgiving by three days. I'd lost myself in work and taken Sasha with me. But not once did she mention the holiday or a family who needed her at the bountiful harvest table. As I waited for the woman in front of me order a cup of coffee with more components than a genetic structure, I felt my phone vibrate in my pocket.

I sighed and answered. "Hi, Mom."

"Emma! My long lost daughter!" My mother's cheery voice forced a grin across my face. "Where in the world are you? Your father and I stopped by your house on the way home from the airport and Aaron told me you were on a case in Virginia?"

"Hang on a sec, Mom." I held the phone down as I ordered two large orange juices, two large black coffees, and as a last thought, two pumpkin muffins. "Sorry, Yes. I'm on a case in Virginia with Sasha. It's a cold case, and as much as I'd love to tell you about it, I really can't." I paused as I walked to the other counter to wait for my order. "This case is a tough one, a weird one." I rubbed at my eyes, bits of the crime scene sneaking its way back in. "How was the trip?"

My mother paused before she answered. She picked up on the small undertones in my voice. She of all people, knew me better than I knew myself. "The cruise was much needed. Your father and I had fun. Saw some bears, went ice fishing and he took a million pictures. It was good for him. I think he's finally letting go." She took a breath. "When are you coming home?"

I smiled at the young man behind the counter sneaking googly eyes at me as he made the coffee. "Sasha and I leave in a few hours after she wakes up."

I could hear her smile on the phone. "And how is the lovely Sasha?"

I bit my bottom lip. "She's good. We're working together again. I think I told you that before you left on the cruise. It's interesting to see her as a federal agent. She has an immense amount of talent and is stronger than I ever imagined."

"Emma, you know I'm not asking about her criminal investigatory talents. *How are you two?*"

I sighed as I took the drink tray pushed towards me. "We are." I paused trying to find the words. "Getting there." I didn't say anything else as I walked out of the bustling coffee shop, and back out onto the quiet street.

"Hmm. Not much of an answer, Emma. But I know how hard it was for you for the last eight months and not having the time to reconnect and sort through everything." I heard my father in the background shout out a hello. "Your father says hello."

I smiled. "Tell him hello back. How's he doing?"

"Better. He misses you. I miss you. So, here's the deal." I laughed as my mother cut to the chase like always.

"We all obviously missed Thanksgiving. Your father and I want to do a post-Thanksgiving pre-Christmas family dinner. We haven't done it in years, and I think it'd be good for all of us to start some new holiday traditions." I wanted to object, but she didn't give me the chance. "This weekend drag your ass to the house. Bring Sasha, bring that Aaron and we'll have a Tiernan family holiday dinner. And don't you dare make up a work excuse, you haven't done a holiday in three years."

Her tone meant business, I wouldn't win with her. My mom the fierce prosecutor would find a way to negotiate me into showing up against my will. "Okay. I know Aaron will be there. Wherever there are piles of free food, that's where you'll find him. I'll have to ask Sasha. She might have family obligations or work."

"Well, tell her she's more than welcome to come. Your father and I haven't seen her in ages, and I want to spend some time with the woman who makes my daughter smile."

I rolled my eyes. "I'll ask as soon as I get back to the hotel. Then call you when we get home and RSVP." I walked into the hotel lobby. "I have to go, I'm about to walk into an elevator and I'll lose you."

"Call as soon as your back in the windy. I love you Emma, we miss you."

I grinned at the simple motherly words that meant so much in the moment, chasing the edge of darkness away. "I love you both so much." I was still smiling as I hung up and tucked the phone in my front pocket. I even hummed a little to the elevator music version of build me up buttercup.

Slipping into the room, Sasha had moved to the middle of the bed. She was clutching to the pillow I'd used, lightly snoring. She was in a deep sleep by the heavy rise and fall of her chest as she slept. I set the drink tray on the small table across from the bed, next to the window. The curtain was open a crack, allowing the morning light to sneak across the bed as if it was trying to take my place next to Sasha.

I opened my coffee to add cream and sugar, smiling as the aroma of fresh coffee reached the sleeping woman. She shifted in her sleep, opening sleepy hazel eyes, and in the raspy morning voice I loved, she asked. "Please tell me you got me one of those?"

I nodded slowly, setting her coffee and juice on the table. "I even got you one of those silly pumpkin muffins."

Sasha perked up immediately and rolled out of the bed, almost pouncing on the muffin I set out. She grabbed the muffin, bending down to kiss me on the lips, smiling against my mouth as she mumbled. "What did I do to deserve you buying me junk food?"

I watched her as she curled up in the chair, she wore an old Chicago Police Department flag football t-shirt that hung off her, making her look like a little kid. The little sleep shorts she had on, ones that left little to the imagination, pulled all my attention to her long legs. "My mom called while I was getting breakfast." I had to focus on my coffee to refrain from touching her.

Sasha raised an eyebrow. "Uh oh. Are you in trouble for not calling or visiting?"

I threw a crumb at her. "No. Well, not really. My dad and her want to do a holiday dinner since Thanksgiving was missed and Christmas is fast approaching. With this case, I don't know if I, we, will have time to celebrate." I took a sip of coffee. "She invited you and Aaron." I set the cup down, picking at the lid as my nerves rose. "But if you have other plans with your family, she'll understand."

Sasha held her half demolished muffin. "What day and time?"

"This Saturday. I have to call her and confirm as soon as we get home." I felt my heart ache. I'd not done a holiday since Elle was alive. I was nervous at the thought of bringing Sasha to a family gathering. Even though she'd spent time with my parents and Aaron, it was another part of my life I was opening up to her and it frightened me. "But if you have family stuff you need to do, I understand. We missed Thanksgiving because of this case. I didn't even realize it."

Sasha set the muffin wrapper down, leaned across the table and grabbed my hand. Looking at our hands together, she shrugged. "Aside from Morgan, you're my only family Emma. My grandparents now live in California with the rest of my family, and that part of the family I don't really know because of my mother." She looked up meeting my eyes. "I want to start new traditions with you." We held each other's gaze until her phone started beeping from across the room. She turned, looking at it with a hard sigh. "I think that's the email from I'm expecting from the lab." She looked back with a smile. "Are you going to eat that?" Sasha pointed at my pumpkin muffin, still in the paper bag.

I pushed it towards her. "They're both for you. I didn't know how far I'd have to bribe you to come to my parents' house."

Sasha hopped up, snatching the muffin as she jogged across the room to her phone. I felt my heart skip at the slight sight of her rear end poking out from the sleep shorts. From over her shoulder, she smirked. "Bribery and muffins will get you everywhere, my dear." Sasha's smirked remained on her face as she sifted through emails, tucking pieces of hair behind her ear. The small movements, the smiles, the way her eyes lit up when she woke up and looked right at me, Everything. It was proof she deserved everything I could give her and more, I just needed to continue to convince my heart and mind I could give it to her.

    Sasha flopped down on the bed on her stomach, holding the phone out. "The lab has some results, but it looks like the entire scene is a swamp of evidence. It's going to take them a few days, maybe a week or two to sort through everything and get me a final report. But they've confirmed the ears we were sent are Bellico's. The medical examiner matched it to his head as well as the DNA matched his." As I took the phone from her hands, scanning the emails, she clutched my pillow again, tucking it under her chin. "It looks like we get a small vacation from this case. Bellico was a link to a lot of possible leads. Until we get a better idea of who sent us those gift boxes and killed him, we might be stalled for a while." She sighed as she snuggled deeper in the pillow, concerned. "I think you need a break too. We both do." I nodded slowly as I glossed over forensic reports, my scientist mind working overtime. I leaned forward in the chair, thinking and reading. Sasha's voice softened. "Emma, yesterday. What happened? I've never seen you like that."

    My jaw clenched as I closed the emails, setting her phone down next to the untouched orange juice. I kept my eyes on the floor as I struggled with the emotions of yesterday begging to flood my being. "The scene got to me. I don't know exactly what it was." My eyes drifted up to her. "Somewhere I lost my stomach for all of this. My heart, my stomach, my ability to look past the violence and at the puzzle pieces of evidence." I ran a hand through my hair. "I'm sorry for falling apart and leaving you, but I couldn't..." I let out a shaky breath, I had to stop talking before I fell apart again.

Sasha reached for my hand, sliding to the edge of the bed. I took it without a thought, allowing her to pull me to the bed. She wrapped me up in her arms as I sat on the edge of the bed and she sat behind me. Sasha set her chin on my shoulder. "You don't need to ever apologize for anything, Emma. It was a rough scene. This case is rough." Her heartbeat was steady as she pressed her front against my back. "You're more important than this case. I know I've said that a million times." She paused, taking a deep breath. "I don't want to lose you again. To this case, to the monsters we're chasing or anything else. I couldn't bear it." Sasha squeezed me tighter.

I ran my hands over her arms as she held me, letting my gaze drift to the window. "Let's go home."

*****

Aaron picked us up from the airport, bear hugging us the second we walked out of the terminal. For the drive back to the house, I sat in the backseat of his car while he and Sasha discussed work. I was shivering, not excited Chicago had embraced winter faster than I wanted. Leaving the lovely heat of the south and running face first into a Midwest winter, left me grumpy. I was also grumpy about the case halting for the moment mixed with the impending Tiernan family dinner.

I'd not spent much time with my family, or anyone outside of Aaron, since the weekend of the conference in D.C. Only having one thing to think about at a time, allowed me far too much time inside my head, diving deep into the things I'd tried so hard to ignore.

Leaning my head back, I watched the city float by, listening to Aaron tell Sasha about his latest case. A bungled heist at a liquor store that left two bodies, the store owner shot in the ass, and a shitload of questions. I half listened as I watched a few stray snowflakes swat against the car window.

Aaron was asking Sasha if she could look at the case file when we got back to the house. I sighed, rolling my head to catch his eyes in the rearview mirror. "Go back and re-interview the store owner. I bet you can get him to bend and admit he shot himself in the ass to make it look like armed robbery. It's a simple insurance scam gone wrong. That liquor store has been failing since I was on patrol in that district. The owner has tried to sell it, burn it down and condemn it. Each time, the insurance company denied his claims. The two dead bodies you have, I bet my salary they're his cousins. That whole family is a bunch of dumbasses with records longer than my left leg."

Aaron grinned, pointing at me in the mirror. "That's why you're still the best, Captain." I couldn't help but smile with the dramatic eye roll I gave him.

My smile grew as Aaron parked in front of the house, happy to be finally home. As I pulled our bags out of the trunk, Aaron came to help, nudging me lightly in the shoulder. "Mom called, family dinner this Saturday?"

I nodded as I sighed, grabbing Sasha's bag. "You can't fight a former county prosecutor. So, yes. Family dinner this saturday. Our version of Thanksgiving Christmas." I hefted the bag up, glancing at Sasha as she opened the front door. Aaron took the bag from me, looking at me with a concerned look. "You haven't done a holiday since…" He drifted off with a half-smile.

"I know, Aaron." I pulled out the remaining bags, closing the trunk. "Sometimes, things have to change." My eyes were still focused on the door, watching Sasha reappear to help with the bags.

Aaron smiled, following my gaze. "Yeah they do, and she's more than worth it." He winked at me, tossing Sasha one of the lighter bags as she laughed. I took a deep breath, following the two into the house.

I had a difficult time sleeping that night and the next few nights, always sneaking out of bed after Sasha passed out to the world, my mind too full to settle. I'd sit in my office reading over emails and the small pieces of reports the labs and the Loudon County Sheriff sent us. I was losing myself in work, instead of figuring out why I'd been so bothered by the Bellico scene, or why I wasn't sleeping when there was a beautiful woman in my bed every night.

I couldn't sleep the night before the family dinner, and it was starting to catch up. I was grumpy when Aaron woke me up, making noise in the kitchen trying to make coffee. I'd poured over Bellico's record and autopsy report into the early hours, finding nothing that could give me an edge in moving the case forward. There were fiber samples the lab was working on tracing, and Aaron had managed to track down where the packages had been sent from. He was currently awaiting the CCTV footage from the shipping store to review, hoping that would give us something.

I walked downstairs to a bedraggled Aaron, eating microwave waffles. He winked at me and nodded towards the kitchen window. "Look, it's the first big snow of the season." I looked out the window and saw huge fat white flakes falling from the sky, covering everything in a thick blanket of snow. For a split second, I had a glimmer of hope the spontaneous blizzard would force my mother to cancel. Aaron picked up my thoughts, chuckling. "The weather channel said the worst will be over by lunchtime. Dinner is still a go. Your mom already texted me." He grinned, waggling a floppy waffle at me. "I'll meet you guys at mom's house. I have to go pick up a surprise for Sasha before dinner."

I folded my arms and stared out the window, barely hearing anything he said. I barely noticed when he left the kitchen. I was tired and found the falling snow entrancing. I stood there for a while, watching, until warm hands slid over my shoulders, pulling me back into a warmer body. "It's a much better view upstairs in bed, than standing in front of this window." I felt her shiver lightly. I turned to look at Sasha, sleepy faced and beautiful. I ran my hands up her arms, warming her up. "I know. I just like watching the snow as it first falls. Did you sleep well?"

"I'd sleep better if I could wake up and have you next to me." The tone in her voice had a hint of sadness in it.

I changed the subject. "Mom messaged Aaron. Dinner is still on. Seems she *will not* let the first blizzard of the season stop her."

Sasha smiled, her hands falling to my hips. "Why am I not surprised she's equally as stubborn as you?" She kissed the corner of my mouth. "Go upstairs, get into bed and sleep for a few more hours. I have a few things to do before dinner, but I promise to wake you in time to get ready." She grabbed my hand with hers, pulling me with her. "I'm about to lock you out of the emails if you don't at least take a night off." I shot her a look as she smiled over her shoulder. "You're not the only brilliant detective in the house." Sasha pulled harder as I groaned slightly, letting her drag me back upstairs.

I fell into bed, falling asleep in a matter of seconds. I dreamt of the Bellico scene and woke up startled, covered in sweat as the image of his eyes in the jar wouldn't leave me. I pushed up in the bed, my heart racing and my eyes trying to adjust to the darkness in the room. I ran a hand over the spot next to me, hoping to find Sasha. I frowned when I found her side of the bed cold. I heard her talking downstairs on the phone. I slid out of bed, more exhausted than before. I opened the bedroom door, moving to meet her downstairs, when I caught her tone. Sasha was agitated as she spoke to whoever it was on the other end of the phone. It was obviously not a work related call. I leaned against the doorframe, eavesdropping.

"You can't keep calling every time you're in trouble. Just because I'm an FBI agent and you're in a federal prison, doesn't mean I can help you out. You put yourself there years ago. No, don't. Stop it, before I hang up." Sasha paused for a moment. When she spoke again, her tone was more frustrated. "No, I'm not coming to visit this year. Why? Because the last two years all we've done is fight. I have to go. I'll call next month, and the money should be in your account by morning."

I stepped back into the room as Sasha issued a hasty goodbye, throwing her phone on the counter, groaning, and whispering curse words under her breath. I walked to the bathroom, starting the shower as I tried to decipher the unusual conversation I'd just overheard. I instantly thought it was Morgan she was talking to, but then I remembered Morgan was running wiretap surveillance in New Jersey, not a federal prison.

My mind raced as I pulled off my pajamas and stepped into the hot water. I leaned against the shower walls, my heart sinking at the thought Sasha was hiding something from me. Again.

After a lengthy shower, I walked into the bedroom to find Sasha already dressed. She looked gorgeous in a simple grey dress with her hair up in an elegant ponytail. She was putting the final touches on her makeup when she caught me staring at her in the mirror. "Hey, you." She grinned, smoothing out the nonexistent wrinkles in her dress. "I hope this is okay?"

I smiled, biting my bottom lip. "More than okay. You're absolutely stunning." I walked past her to the closet, rooting around to find something decent to wear. "You do know it's just my parents and Aaron? Pretty casual." I stared at her for a moment, fighting the itch to ask who she was talking to downstairs.

"I know, but I wanted to look good for you and be presentable for your parents." The nerves were heavy in her voice. I grabbed a pair of dress pants and one of my nicer sweaters, tossing them on the bed, smiling at Sasha.

"There's nothing to be nervous about, they already know you. You've already impressed them when you saved my life a few times." I sat on the edge of the bed. "I'm the one who's ridiculously nervous. It's the first holiday I've spent with my family since… Elle." Her name fell out of my mouth in a whisper. I glanced up at Sasha, smiling at me with soft eyes. She opened her mouth when her phone rang, grabbing it with a heavy sigh. "Dammit, it's Reagan. I have to take this." Sasha left the room, closing the door behind her. I heard her clipped tone, giving Reagan a quick update on the case.

I finished dressing before Sasha returned. She leaned against the doorframe with a grin. "You look amazing." She stepped closer, sliding her arms around my waist. "Are you ready? We need to get going. The snow has slowed down, but the roads will be messy."

I helped Sasha with her coat and the large bag of gifts she pulled out of the closet. I gave her a look. She just shrugged. "If you're a good girl, there might be something in there for you." I raised my eyebrows and opened the door. The cold air was thick, cutting right through my coat. It was still snowing, and the roads were sloppy. I pulled my collar up, tucking my chin in. "I'll drive."

I held the door for Sasha and watched her walk to the car, suddenly feeling very normal, nothing like a homicide detective investigating a series of brutal homicide cases. I almost felt like I did three years ago.

In love and happy.

******

Traffic was at a dead stop, amplifying my slow burning frustration. The snow had picked up to a gentle, almost movie like, fat snow. I turned on the police radio at the top of the console. The radio chatter told us there was a massive car accident up ahead of us on Lakeshore drive. We'd be stuck for almost an hour while crews tried to clear the scene. I looked over at Sasha, shaking my head as I turned off the radio. She smiled, patting my arm. "We should only be a little late to your parents."

I groaned and fished my phone out, texting my mom to let her know we were stuck. I could've called her but being on the phone was the last thing I wanted to do as I looked out at the sea of red taillights cutting through the white snow. I tossed the phone onto the dashboard, leaning my head against the cold glass. Reaching over, I tried turning on the regular radio, only to find every single one of my presets had switched over to all christmas music, all the time. I groaned again. "Why? It's not even two weeks into December."

Sasha's hand fell to my shoulder, squeezing it. "Emma, it's that time of the year. Everyone is in the holiday spirit." She poked me. "Don't be such a grinch."

I closed my eyes, clenching my jaw. "I don't like the holidays, haven't in a few years. They stopped having meaning for me. It's just another day off, unless I pick up the overtime."

The last holiday I enjoyed was a few months before Elle died. It was perfect picture of what Christmas should be. Our house was perfectly decorated. A Christmas tree sat in the front room with presents spilling out from underneath. Stockings were neatly hung by the fire, with joy coursing through our veins. We'd gone to her parents for dinner, then spent a quiet Christmas night together. It was perfect, and I never knew how to recreate it on my own, or ever really wanted to. Until now. But now, I had no idea where to start. I'd rather avoid it than stumble through trying to start new traditions with Sasha. My mind was too distracted by the case to want to stop and bake cookies.

The soft Christmas music in the car mixed with the whisper of the heat blowing around us. Sasha's voice almost startled me when she spoke, breaking the trance I was in. "Tell me about her."

I opened my eyes, turning to look at her. "Who?" I knew who she was asking about, I just didn't want to talk about her.

"Elle. Tell me about her. You've never told me about her. The woman who captured your entire being. The woman I don't want to replace, because I know I never can, or will." There was a touch of sadness in her voice, making my heart hurt. The dream I had a few nights ago was my sign to let Sasha in. Let her be the woman to take Elle's place.

I took a deep breath. "Sasha, please. I don't want to talk about it." I turned my gaze out the windshield, clenching my jaw. The red brake lights taunting me as they refused to move. I was trapped.

"No, Emma. Don't brush this off. I want to know about her, who she was, how she snagged your heart. All of it. You carry her with you every day and I want to know who I'm trying to make room for as I struggle to rebuild something with you. The other night, you told me I deserved more. I think I deserve to know about Elle. I want to know her. I want to know anyone who had you completely like she did. Maybe I could learn something from her." Her voice was soft. Heartbreakingly soft.

    I chewed on my bottom lip, trying to fight the usual response of grumpy anger and being a jerk and ask about her phone call. I sighed, rubbing the bridge of my nose. I did promise Sasha more. I took a deep breath, my eyes latching on the SUV's brake lights directly in front of us. It took a few moments of silence between the two of us, highlighted by Nat King Cole singing *The Christmas Song*.

    The words fell out slowly, as if they were hesitant to fill the air as much as I was to speak them. "Elle. Elle was an Architect. A brilliant architect. She was beautiful, intelligent, feisty and didn't put up with my crap." I looked at Sasha, her big hazel eyes saw through me just like Elle's blue eyes once did, but Sasha saw all of me. Every fractured piece. She nodded for me to continue. I tipped my head down, staring at my hands. "I met her at a charity benefit when I was a rookie."

    I told Sasha everything about that first date. Then the second and third date. Our trip to New York City and our first fight because I'd picked the wrong subway train and it took us all the way to Brooklyn, instead of Times Square. I told her how we picked the house and bickered about renovations, and how I still hated the coffee table in the living room. I then told Sasha about the accident, losing Elle, all of it. I fought back tears as I told Sasha what it was like to see Elle in that bed, leaving me slowly. The tears that slipped out, were ones of finally letting go of Elle liked she asked me to in the dream.

    I felt Sasha's hand on my cheek as she wiped away my tears. "Emma." I leaned into her hand, opening my eyes and looking at the woman I knew would replace Elle and more. She was shivering as she ran her thumb across my cheek.

"Sasha, you're cold." I moved from her touch, reaching into the backseat. "I have a blanket back here." I stretched into the backseat, my fingers grazing the soft blanket I kept there for emergencies. I almost had it in my grasp when I felt her hands fall to the sides of my face, stilling me, pulling me back to look at her.

We were inches apart. Sasha's eyes were glassy, and I saw I'd finally let her in, and she knew it. I went to say something, Sasha shook her head and closed the space between us, kissing me tenderly but full of passion. When we broke apart, we were both breathless. Only the sounds of our breaths and Nat King Cole's voice, filled the car. I ran the back of my hand across her cheek, whispering. "I love you, Natasha. With everything I have left to give."

She smiled, kissing me again. This kiss was less tender, more passionate. It grew warmer in the car as we continued to kiss, fogging up the windows. The need in me rose quickly, I wanted Sasha.

Before I could say anything, I felt Sasha's hand on my thigh, pushing down. I realized she was using me to balance as she reached between my legs for the seat adjuster underneath me. She lifted up, pushing the seat as far back as it could go. I clutched her thigh as she climbed over the console and into my lap. She pulled off her coat as she straddled me, letting the edge of her skirt ride up her legs, making my breath catch at the sight of her strong, smooth thighs. My hands immediately moved on their own, my fingers running up to meet where the edge of her skirt had stopped. The simple touch of my fingers on her skin pulled a moan from her as she leaned forward in the seat. She held my face as she found my mouth with hers. The need in both of us was at a high, we both wanted the same thing. To give ourselves over to each other wholly, completely, even if it was in a car trapped on the highway during a Chicago snowstorm.

As her tongue found mine, my hands moved further up her skirt. Sliding to the inside of her thighs, I felt the heat radiating from her, making me moan and push my mouth harder against hers. My hand grazed the edge of her panties. Sasha backed away from the kiss, leaning into my shoulder. Her mouth brushing against my ear as she whispered. "Emma, please."

My heart stopped at the deep, simple sensuality of her plea. My hand acted on its own, pushing the simple cloth barrier out of the way, finding Sasha more than ready for me. As my fingers found their way easily into her, Sasha wrapped her arm around my neck, burying her face into my shoulder as she kissed my neck, biting it lightly as my fingers found a slow rhythm that pulled painfully soft moans from her. Her hips moved with my hands, and Sasha sat back, her eyes locking on mine. So much was being said between us as she matched my movements. She leaned back against my hand, her own hands searching out the top of my dress pants. I scooted up to give her better access, and before I could blink, she unbuttoned them and her hand pushed past the waist of my pants, her fingers filling me. The sensation forced a large moan out of me as I pushed hard against the seat. It took me a minute to catch up to her rhythm, but when I did, I leaned forward, wrapping my free arm around the woman I loved. Holding her close to me as our hands synced up, pulling moans, groans and whispers of curse words from each other. I kissed the bare skin of her chest, wanting so badly to have more room to strip our clothes off so I could feel every inch of the incredible woman I was beyond in love with.

Sasha shifted her hand and hit the right spot. I came hard and loud, moaning her name against the kisses I laid on her chest. The noise I made, sent Sasha over the edge. I felt her shudder and contract against my fingers, letting out a deep, delicious moan. I held on to her tightly as she rode out the wave of ecstasy.

Both of us were disheveled and breathless in the foggy car. I pulled her close, holding her tightly as I let my heart rate return to normal. I kissed a flushed cheek, whispering against her ear. "Do you still need that blanket?"

Sasha giggled, running a hand down my neck. "Actually, can you crack the windows? I'm burning up." She leaned back in my arms. "I love you."

I squeezed her hips, feeling the need to have her again rush over me. I leaned forward to kiss her again when the car behind us angrily honked its horn. Sasha and I both turned to look out the front windshield to see traffic starting to move.

Sasha sighed, pushing herself off my lap, trying to fix her skirt as she returned to the passenger seat. I fixed my pants and pulled the seat back up, just in time before the next round of honking hit. I put the car in gear as Sasha looked in the mirror, trying to smooth out her hair. "Does it look like I just made love to my girlfriend in the car?" Sasha glanced over, a huge grin on her face.

"It kind of does, but my mom won't notice. Aaron will, but I'll kick him in the shin if says anything inappropriate at the house." I reached over, pushing a few strands of hair out of her face before kissing her cheek. Sasha turned up the music in the car before she grabbed my hand, our fingers falling into a perfect pattern together.

Our hands never parted until I pulled into my parents' driveway an hour later.

Chapter 11

My parents lived in the Chicago suburb of Clarendon Hills, in a house that looked a lot like Ferris Bueller's. Perfectly midwestern and perfectly Chicago. I laughed at the same old Christmas decorations from my youth littering the lawn and hanging off the roof. My parents loved Christmas and did their best to get the decorations up as soon as possible.

I stood at the front of the car staring at the house, taking a deep breath. The snow continued to fall in fat snowflakes, adding to the atmosphere of the decorations. It wasn't Christmas, but in that moment as I stood in front of the house, Sasha's arm sneaking into mine, it certainly felt festive. I looked down at her, bundled back in her coat, her free hand holding the gift bag she bought, she looked beautiful. I pulled her tighter into my side. "Aaron's already here, and I'm sure he's pressuring mom to start dinner without us."

"We're only fifteen minutes late. I'm sure she held him off."

We walked to the front door and before my finger grazed the doorbell, the front door swung open. I was immediately scooped up into a crushing hug from my mother. "My daughter has returned!"

I rolled my eyes as she kept a death grip on me. I glanced at Sasha as she was helped inside by my father before she was also swept up into a hug. I had to break the hug off so I could get my mother into the house before we froze to death. The second she let go, I was caught in another bear hug from my father. When I was free from him, I saw Aaron coming my way. His goofy grin on his face as he held a half-eaten dinner roll in his hand. I went to call him out, when I heard Sasha yelp, mixed with another female's voice. I looked at Aaron as he gave me a quick hug.

"You'll see, Captain."

He walked with me into the front living room where Morgan and Sasha were hugging, talking over each other. Morgan looked my way, winking. "Surprise! Aaron picked me up from the airport this morning and your awesome parents have kept me hidden all day." She held out her hand for a high five, never breaking from the best friend hug she was ensconced in. I smiled, shaking my head as returned her high five.

I stood there with Aaron, watching the two women strike up a conversation with my mother. My mind was thankfully empty and quiet. No crime scenes, no misery, no desire to read lab reports or emails. I was actually in the here and now for once in my life.

I felt my father come up next to me, throwing an arm around my shoulder. "Looks like the family is all here, wouldn't you agree, Emma?"

I glanced up into his blue eyes. There was a hint of sadness mixing with the joy of having this family dinner. I slid my arm around his waist. "I couldn't agree more."

He kissed the top of my head like he did when I was younger. "Let's go eat. I'm starving and your mom has been fighting Aaron off for the last hour. He wanted to start without you the second he walked in the door." I laughed as he told Sasha and Morgan to break it up and head to the dinner table. He leaned closer as we walked to the dining room. "Can I get you to join me in a cigar and scotch after dinner?"

I nodded, knowing it was his code for wanting to speak to me in private. "I would love that, Dad."

He smiled, again kissing the top of my head. "Go sit by your lady, and enjoy this dinner your mother made us."

I hugged him one more time before taking my seat next to Sasha. Her hand fell to my thigh, squeezing in a way that said so much without saying anything at all.

I would enjoy this night as much as possible. Burn it into my memory so I could fall back on it when the darkness threatened to swallow me whole.

Dinner went better than I could've imagine. I laughed more than I had in a long time, all because of the strange dynamic between Morgan and Aaron. They'd tell extravagant stories and bounce off each other like a perfect comedy duo. Sasha's hand never left me for long. She'd lay a hand on my thigh, my shoulder, my arm. It was as if she wanted to maintain some sort of physical connection with me at all times.

After dinner and a group decision to wait on dessert, Morgan, Aaron, and Sasha sat at the table with my mother, listening to her intently as she shared stories about first cases as a rookie prosecutor, then slid into what it was like raising me as a dirty, mute teenager brought home from Detroit by my father.

My father nodded at me as he stood from the table. I took his cue, following him to the study he used as an office. It was large, cozy and felt like a library in England. There were bookshelves, a leather couch, fireplace and an antique desk that looked like it belonged in an old private eye's office from the forties. It was one of my favorite places in the house. A room I often exhausted in college when I needed a place to sprawl out and study in peace.

I sat down on the couch as my father knelt in front of the liquor cabinet. "Scotch or your usual whiskey?" He looked over his shoulder at me.

"Scotch, please."

My father handed me a glass of scotch as he sat in the large chair by his desk, digging in his cigar box. He offered one to me. I took it just to hold it, and maybe smoke it later. I'd not smoked a cigar in years and although I loved the smell, I wasn't a smoker and found myself gagging after two puffs. But the cigar brought a sense of familiarity, calm, as I held it.

My dad leaned in his chair looking out a large window. It was still snowing, making the night appear almost eerie as the moon reflected off the white snow.

"Your mother is going to heavily suggest you stay tonight, since the snow is going to be hell to drive in." He looked at me as he lit his cigar. "It's good to have you home, Emma."

I nodded, sipping the scotch, letting it sit in my mouth before swallowing it. "It is. I'm glad Sasha dragged me home." I winked with a chuckle.

He took a large drag on the cigar and let it out, filling the study with the wonderful aroma of cigar smoke. "How's your case going? It's a cold case, right?"

"It stalled out. Sasha and I hit a crime scene a few days ago. It spiraled out into a giant mess with so much evidence it may take weeks until we can start pursuing leads again." I shifted in my seat. "Maybe you can help me out. You've worked in the mafia world, gang task forces, for years. There's something about this last crime scene and the pieces of evidence Sasha and I received. I need some advice. I don't know what to look at first." I looked up to see him cringe. I knew where his head was at. Sitting in this study was more than indulging in some quality father daughter time.

"Dad, Rachel. She wasn't your fault. She was long gone well after you met her, and no one had any idea she'd turn out to be who she was." I took a shaky breath. "Even Sasha. Sasha never had any idea who Rachel was. She was kept in the dark during the whole operation."

My father chewed on the cigar, his eyes drifting back

to the window. "It doesn't take away the fact I handed you right over to a psychopath. A psychopath who almost killed you." He rubbed his forehead. "It still bothers me, Emma. You're my daughter. My only daughter and if I lost you, especially because of something I did." He paused, smirking. "Do you remember when you tried to hold me up in the alley all those years ago? You looked like a dirty little boy. I almost threw you a right hook until I looked in your eyes and saw so much." His face fell.

I blinked back a few tears, focusing on the amber liquid in the bottom of the glass. "Dad, you saved my life that day. I wouldn't have the life I do if it wasn't for you taking pity on a dirty kid trying to rob you with a cracked lighter." I sighed, looking at him. "Rachel and Evan would've eventually found me. They were consumed, driven. Don't carry the burden of that. Because of you bringing Rachel into my life, it also saved my life. The FBI was able to discover who she was sooner and got to her faster." I bit the inside of my cheek. "Dad, you have to let it go."

My father pulled his gaze from the window, looking right at me. "So do you, Emma. We both do." He pointed with his glass towards the door, where laughter filled the kitchen. "You have to for that woman out there. Sasha. She's so much like your mother." He paused. "Your mother is the reason why I'll let this all go and moved on. All for her. Why? Because your mom will fight me every day until there's no darkness left. She's the reason why the job never got to me. For every horrible crime scene I was called to, for every horrible act I witnessed humans commit against each other, I had her to come home to. Then I had you to come home to. My little family kept me whole." My father stood up and sat next to me on the couch, throwing an arm around me. "Sasha loves you more than any of us can put into words. She'll be the one person who holds the darkness, and the demons, at bay as they try to sneak in through the cracks." He took a deep breath. "Mom fought me tooth and nail after you came home from the conference and we all learned the truth about Rachel." I looked up at him, he grinned and kissed my forehead. "You also have me, Emma. Anytime you want to sit and talk, call me. We can share war stories."

I nodded as I leaned into his side and took a deep breath. "I think I'll take you up on that. There's so much in my head and heart. It's hard to talk to anyone who doesn't understand. They haven't seen it, experienced what I have." I blinked back tears.

He whispered. "I know, Emma."

We sat in silence. I thought about how different my life would be if I hadn't chosen this man as my first mugging victim. My father took a deep breath, letting me go. "So, kiddo. Tell me about this new case. How can I help you?"

I leaned back in the couch, my eyes drifting over to the window to watch large snowflakes float down. "Sasha and I received boxes. Mine had a severed hand in it, hers had severed ears. The crime scene we stumbled upon had a jar of the victims' eyes on a table, ready to be shipped." I paused, swallowing hard as the crime scene came back to life. "The victim was brutalized. His body parts were harvested and sent off like simple telegrams."

My father stubbed out the rest of his cigar and leaned against the edge of his desk, furrowing his brow in thought. "Hmm. Do you think I could look at the scene pictures?"

"If you come over to the house in a few days, I'll have the files. I think Sasha would be okay with you taking a look. We're trying to keep a tight lid on this. Anytime we go talk to someone, they end up dead."

My father smiled. "Not a problem. I know how to keep my mouth shut." He walked around the study. "What you've described, it kind of reminds me of the drug gangs out of Columbia. They were always big on sending out messages to their rivals, or whomever they felt they needed to keep quiet and in line." He drank most of his scotch in a single gulp. "There was one gang who would send body parts in the manner of see no evil, hear no evil, speak no evil. I believe it was either the Alvarez Cartel or the Demongo Brothers Cartel. Many of the federal agencies would receive unsavory daily packages back in the eighties when the cocaine wars were at their peak. I remember being called more than once to the FBI field office to assist with processing the packages." He let out a breath. "If you give me a couple days, I can hit a few friends up and see if I can get my hands on more information. I think my old patrol partner ended up in the DEA."

"Sounds good. Anything at this point will help. I'll give you a couple of names and see if you can wipe the dust off the files of these old retired cops I'm hunting." I paused. "Only if you want to, Dad. I don't want to drag you into this mess."

He grinned. "You're not dragging me into anything. Once a cop, always a cop. I could never rest when the puzzle of a mystery was handed my way."

I smiled back and walked over to him, hugging him, catching him slightly off guard, until I felt his strong arm wrap around me. I rasped out. "Dad, I owe you so much. The life you gave me. All of it."

My father patted me on the back and leaned back, tears in his eyes. "Emma, your mother and I owe you more. You gave us a life we never dreamt of."

A small knock on the door broke the moment. Sasha pushed the door open, smiling as she poked her head in.

"Hey, I hope I'm not interrupting, but Morgan and Mrs. Tiernan are ready to serve dessert."

    My father chuckled. "The pumpkin pie is best when its fresh out of the oven." He patted me on the back, kissing me on the cheek. "I love you, my favorite daughter." He winked at Sasha as he left the room.

    "He's right. My mom's pumpkin pie is the best when its fresh." I grabbed her hand, pulling Sasha after me and towards the sounds of Morgan and Aaron fighting over the biggest slice.

    After dessert and a few more drinks, it was determined, more so demanded by mother, that no one leave the house. The storm had shifted into a blizzard and the cars were all buried in the driveway. Morgan and Aaron were excited to stay over after being told there'd be breakfast in the morning, and my dad pointing out the basement had an extensive movie collection with a couch and extra bedroom. The two ran downstairs like little kids and disappeared. I helped clean up the kitchen as my mother sat with Sasha and went through albums of photos of me as an awkward teen. I left the two alone, setting about putting away the leftovers.

    When I was finished, I found Sasha in the living room with my mother. They were laughing, holding one of my catholic school photos. My father snuck around and grabbed my mother, kissing her on the cheek. "Time for bed. It's late and well past everyone's bedtime."

    My mother sighed, leaning into his side. "It is late." She glanced at the clock on the wall, it was almost midnight. I was also desperate to get to bed and sleep. My mother held onto my father's hand as she walked towards us. "Your old room is set up and ready to go, pajamas are out on the bed. Anything you need, find it yourself. You used to live here." My mother winked at me, patting me on the cheek. She then hugged Sasha. Stepping back, she looked at the both of us as she reached for my dad's hand. "It's good to have you home, both of you." She smiled as she was tugged gently away. "Good night girls! See you in the morning!" My dad half scooped her up, carrying her down the hall.

I turned to Sasha, looking at the photographs lining the walls. I saw her looking at the few my mom still had up of Elle and I. I moved to stand next to her, staring at the photos of family holidays past, and a couple of Elle and I as we moved into the house by the lake. I looked at Sasha, she was smiling as her eyes roamed over my life. My very private life that only Elle and Aaron had been a part of. I ran my hand down her arm. "Are you ready to share a twin bed?"

Sasha turned, shocked. "A twin bed?"

I nodded. "Yes, a twin bed." I bit my lip to hold back the smile when Sasha asked again about the twin bed. I opened the door to my old room, and sighed at the time capsule. Science and police memorabilia dotted the walls. Books from my youth filled shelves and a few of my old sweatshirts hung in the closet. Sasha slugged me when she saw the queen sized bed. "You know, I was kind of looking forward to sleeping on top of you in a twin bed, Emma."

I blushed as I picked up the pajamas on the bed, holding out the extra pair to Sasha. "I hope you don't mind staying here. My mom is a tough one to fight when it comes to hazardous weather and driving. Ever since." I drifted off. Losing Elle had changed the entire family.

Sasha went to grab the clothes from my hand. "Oh wait, let me grab my things from downstairs." Sasha whisked out of the room.

I walked around my old room, pulling down the

blankets. I truly missed being home. The quiet safety and warmth it always offered almost made me forget the life I'd lived and was living. I sat on the edge of the bed as I pulled off my clothes, slipping into the oversized pajamas my mother kept for guests.

Sasha pushed into the room as I started to pull on the bottoms. She leaned against the door with a smirk. "Are you sure you need the bottoms? It's pretty warm up here."

I looked in her eyes and what I saw in them, echoed what I saw in the car, sending a shiver through my body. I stood up, pulling the pants over my hips. "We're at my parent's house, Sasha." It was an excuse as I broke away from the deep stare of those hazel eyes.

Sasha frowned, pushing off the door. "I know. But can't blame a girl for trying." She set her bag down. "There's something in there for you." She picked up the pajamas, reaching down as she walked to the bathroom, removing a small gift wrapped box and handing it to me.

"Sasha, you don't have to. Christmas is weeks away."

She shrugged, walking into the bathroom. "I know."

I held the small gift on my lap, looking at the small imperfections in the wrapping at the corners. I slid my finger under the edge and tore off the paper to reveal a small shadow box with two gleaming police badges inside. I stared at the two silver Chicago badges, set perfectly in the black background. It took me a minute to recognize my old patrol badge. The other, I drew a blank on.

Sasha walked back into the room, I glanced up at her. "What is this?" She sat down on the edge of the bed, swimming in her own oversized pajamas. She leaned against me, tapping the glass.

"That's your old badge and this one." She tapped over the second badge. "Is mine."

I furrowed my brow, confused. She smiled, running her fingers along the edge of the shadow box. "Do you remember when I told you a long time ago, I'd kind of always knew about you?" I said nothing, only nodding. "I met you a long time ago. Four months out of my last FTO phase, you came into my life. I was working perimeter for a double homicide and there you were, working the scene. That day was the first day you crawled into my heart and I couldn't shake the effect you had on me. It was just a few minutes here and there, you smiled and were polite. More polite than most of the detectives I had to deal with." Sasha looked at me with glassy eyes. "I remember you with Elle. I saw you with her once when she came to visit you at the station. I saw how happy you were." Sasha moved away from me. I reached for her arm, sliding my hand into hers. "The last time I saw you before I became your partner was two weeks after she passed away."

Sasha looked at our hands together. "The only thing I could think of was how much I wanted to bring that light back into your life. To see the radiant, beautiful lady detective who captured my heart with a smile. I had no idea I would ever fall so far into love with you like I did." She took a shaky breath, letting it out as she focused on the badges. "Aaron helped me find your old badge in the closet in the basement. I wanted to give you mine to tell you, and show you, because of you, I'm who I am now." Sasha sniffled as tears slid down her cheeks. I reached up, wiping them away as Sasha leaned into my hand. "Emma, I love you. I want you to have this because it's a part of who I am. The real me, the eager patrol officer who wanted nothing more than to do the right thing and just happened to fall in love at first sight."

I swallowed hard, fighting back tears and pulled Sasha into my arms, holding her tightly as she whispered against my chest. "I know I can't replace her, I don't want to."

"Sasha you are a part of my heart and my family." I took a breath. "You know, I remember you. That day in the station as I handed off a prisoner to you for transport to the county lockup. There was something about you."

I closed my eyes at the memory of the beautiful patrol officer who sent tingles through my hand when we touched. The memory surged to the front of my mind the moment Sasha began telling her story. But Sasha looked different then, her face was hidden by the obnoxious patrol hat we all had to wear. Then everything in my mind became cloudy as I lost Elle and began my spiral into darkness and obsession with work. Sasha leaned back in my arms, smiling weakly as I wiped her tears away. "All it means, is that no matter how hard I try, I can't get rid of you." I leaned forward and kissing her. I stood up and set the badges on the table next to the bed. I then crawled into the bed, holding out my hand, silently asking her to join me. There was nothing left to be said in the moment, I just wanted her in my arms. Sasha slipped under the blankets, snuggling into my side as she laughed against my chest. "Too bad I had to ruin the moment. I was going to try to get you to fool around in your parent's house."

"Of course, you did."

We fell asleep in each other's arms, wearing oversized pajamas in my parent's house.

*****

The next morning, I woke up late, later than I had in a long time. I stretched and found Sasha missing. I frowned, suddenly understanding how she felt when I wasn't there in the mornings when she woke up. Cold and lonely. I rolled out of bed and dug around in my old closet, finding some of my old police academy sweats, yanking them on as I looked out the window. The entire world outside was a blank white canvas. Completely untouched by humans and beautiful. I was secretly glad my mother forced us to stay over. I would've gotten the car stuck, and no matter how much of our own heat we created, Sasha and I would've had a rough night.

    I walked downstairs, finding my mother in the kitchen making coffee and setting out plates for breakfast. She cocked an eyebrow. "Have a good night, did we?"

    I blushed, rolling my eyes. "Mom, we wouldn't do that in your house. Well, not as long as you were home." I chuckled with my mother, reaching for a muffin. "Where's Sasha?"

    My mother waved towards the study. "In there, talking shop with your father. They got up at the same time, and you know how cops are. Can't leave anything alone for more than a day."

    I glanced at the study. For some reason I didn't want to delve back into the case just yet and ruin the peaceful feeling I woke up with. My mother pushed a cup of coffee my way. "Go see if the children are awake. They were up late watching every action movie in your father's collection."

    "Yes, ma'am." I held back the smile when I found Morgan and Aaron on the fold out couch, both passed out and cuddled up into each other. I suddenly wished I had my phone so I could take a picture.

    It didn't take more than a moment before Morgan let out a yawn. She opened one eye, dramatically sniffing the air. "Is that fresh coffee?" I nodded, holding out the cup. She shifted out of Aaron's arms, taking the cup as she leaned against the back of the couch. I expected some sort of sassy comment from her about waking up in the arms of my best friend.

"How much did you two drink last night? He's dead to the world." I swore I saw a line of drool in the corner of Aaron's mouth.

"We finished a bottle of rum I found in the liquor cabinet. Don't tell your mom, it looked old." She nodded at Aaron. "You know he's adorable? I don't know how you didn't snatch him up after all these years."

I sighed. "I think its self-explanatory, since I find your best friend equally adorable, and she's a girl."

Morgan laughed. "You got me there, Captain." She took another sip of coffee, sighing in pleasure. "I think I might ask him out on a date. If you're okay with that?"

I grinned. "I'm okay with that, but be warned, he's high maintenance." Just then Aaron woke up and saw me standing over him. He sat up quickly, looking for his gun. "Emma! What's up? You okay?"

I shook my head, still grinning. "Everything's fine. Mom wanted me to shake you two out of bed and go help with breakfast."

Aaron ran a hand through his messy hair, yawning. "No problem." He squinted at me, taking in my outfit. "Shit, are those your academy sweats? I think you're the only person in the world who kept their PT sweats and have them fit better. Last time I saw you in those, they were baggy and looked like you stole them from your dad." Aaron glanced at Morgan. She smiled, handing him the coffee. Aaron blushed, tipping his head down to hide it.

I reached over, patting his shoulder. "Don't worry, she kept your honor intact." Morgan and I laughed as Aaron turned a brighter shade of red.

I headed back upstairs leaving the two alone and ran into my Father as he refilled two cups of coffee, smiling and motioned towards the hallway. "Come to the study, Sasha and I have a few things to go over with you."

Inside the study Sasha was working at the computer. She had all the FBI files pulled up as well as the crime scene photographs from the Bellico scene.

She smiled when I walked in. "Hey, you, your Dad and I were talking this morning. He's got a few good ideas of where to start looking." She stood up from the desk, taking the cup of coffee from my father as he sat in her place. "He thinks the crime scene photographs show tactics that look like a gang he dealt with out of Columbia and hit the Midwest, and East Coast pretty hard in the eighties. He also put a call into his old DEA contacts. It might not get us far with the Heaten case, but at least if we can start moving on Bellico, it's something."

I sat on the couch watching my father do what he did best, analyze evidence and piece together clues. Sasha sat next to me, leaning into my side, taking in my clothes. "You kept your academy sweats?"

I rolled my eyes. "They're warm and oddly comfortable." I looked at Sasha, her eyes were softer, more relaxed than last night. I reached up, brushing some hair from her face. "I have an extra set if you want to borrow them."

Sasha leaned into my hand, laughing. "No thank you. I set mine on fire as soon as I was done and graduated. So many horrible PT memories." She shivered, snuggling deeper into my side.

I laid a hand on her thigh. "You're cold. I'll go grab that extra set." I stood when Sasha jumped up, grabbing my wrist.

"Oh no, I'm totally fine. But I'll happily dig around in your closet and see what other things you have hiding in there." Her hand fell into mine as she told my father we'd be right back. He waved us off, mumbling something, deeply engrossed in his thoughts and the files.

*****

I laid on the bed as Sasha dug through my closet. My mother had kept everything I abandoned from my teen years and the occasional laundry days from college. Sasha stepped out wearing one of my old Detroit Red Wings sweatshirt. It was so big it hung down to her knees. She grinned, holding out her arms as the sleeves covered her hands. "Were you a giant kid? This thing is huge. And the Red Wings? You were raised in Chicago, shame on you."

I groaned. "I was born in Detroit. The Red Wings were spoon fed to me from the moment I was born. And I was in a weird phase when I bought that. I was trying to hide my gangly, skinny, awkward body and rebel against being the adopted kid."

Sasha crawled onto to the bed, straddling me. She leaned forward, kissing me. "Why would you ever want to hide this?" Her hands slid under my sweatshirt, drawing goose bumps as her hands ran over my skin. "Oh, and I'm keeping this sweatshirt." I felt her push her hips down, making me moan as my hands went to her thighs, holding her still.

"The whole house is awake, Sasha."

She smirked as she wiggled against my stomach. "I know, but the shower looks soundproof." I smiled at this bold version of Sasha. It was apparent our talk in the car and last night had broken down some of the walls between us. The desire and need radiating between Sasha and I was at an all-time high. My resolve would falter in a matter of minutes if she kept moving her hips like that.

Sasha rolled off me and stood up. She peeled off my

giant sweatshirt, quickly followed by the old t-shirt she'd worn to bed. She paused before walking into the bathroom turning on the water to let it get hot. I went to roll out of bed and follow her, when her phone rang from her inside bag. Sasha hollered over the running water. "Can you please ignore that, especially if it's the office?"

I found her phone in the bottom of her bag, about to hit ignore when the number flashing across the screen caught me by surprise. It was the number for the federal penitentiary down in West Virginia. My stupid photographic memory had memorized all the useless phone numbers I used on the job. County jails, state prisons, federal prisons, they were all stuck in my brain from the occasions I had to interview prisoners or drop off a new inmate. Never mind the fact Sasha had a heated conversation with an inmate at a federal prison yesterday.

I stared at it, debating.

I hit accept and said hello.

My fears and concern from the last time Sasha was on the phone before we left the house was too much to forget. The operator on the phone spoke in a bored tone. "Agent Natasha Clarke, will you accept a call from Alison Porter?" I whispered yes as the operator sighed. "Agent Clarke, I know this is the third time your mother has requested a phone call with you. She's been saving her phone time for an extended call this month. Let me put you on hold while I connect you." It was evident the operator was familiar with Sasha.

I gripped the phone in my hand, a wave of guilt washing over me, and I walked into the bathroom. I handed the phone to a half-naked Sasha. She smiled, until she saw the number. I swallowed hard. "You should probably answer this, it's your mother."

Sasha's face went pale as she took the phone.

She slowly closed the bathroom door as I turned and walked back to the bed. I heard her talking in hushed tones. I picked up the Red Wings sweatshirt Sasha discarded on the floor, holding it in my hands, realizing I'd crossed a line with Sasha by answering her phone.

Maybe I wasn't completely free of my misgivings and lingering mistrust of what happened in the past.

Sasha's voice raised as she snapped at her mother. I glanced at the bathroom door, dropping the sweatshirt on the bed and decided it was better to leave the room.

CHAPTER 12

The smells emanating from the kitchen pulled me like a fish on a hook. I was starving and needed to eat something, eat away the building guilt. On the way, my father poked his head out of the study and stopped me, a notepad in his hand. "Emma, come here a second. I think I have something for you."

I folded my arms and sat on the couch as he sat down at the computer. "I dug through some of my old case files and notes from my days chasing cartels. I think there's a possible drug connection here. What you and Sasha described to me, and what I saw in the pictures, it points to a drug cartel revenge kill."

He handed me an old spiral notebook, tapping the cover. "In there, you'll find case numbers the federal agent can pull out of her national databases. The photos aren't as high quality as you have now, but it'll give you something."

I nodded as I sifted through the scribbles of an eager young detective. Smiling at how he and I were far more similar than I thought. "I sent word to one of my old federal buddies. He was a DEA agent who worked with me when the Chicago Police Department and the DEA developed a task force. His name is Angus Duncan. Gus for short." I raised an eyebrow at my father, who smiled. "I know. But he's from a Scottish Irish family out of Boston. He's exactly what you imagine him to be with a name like that, but he owes me a favor or three. He's still with the DEA and moving up into the world of politics as the right hand man to the soon to be new Drug Czar." My father leaned back in his chair. "I'll call you when he gets in touch with me."

"Thanks Dad, this will help. Having access to similar evidence will be huge. I just have a weird feeling about this whole case. The cold case that turning into fresh homicides." I closed my eyes, leaning my head against the back of the couch and letting out a heavy sigh.

"What's wrong kiddo?"

I stared at the ceiling. "I did something stupid upstairs, Dad."

Did you get her pregnant?" My father chuckled, reaching for his coffee.

I shook my head, hiding a small smile. "One, no. Two, do you really think I'd do that in your house with you and mom home?"

He laughed harder, shrugging. "The way you and Sasha look at each other, we expected it. Anyways, what did you do? And for the record, it'd be nice to have grandkids to spoil one day."

I let out a deep breath. The thought of kids was the furthest from my mind. I didn't even fully trust the woman I loved more than life, let alone think of having children with her. "I answered Sasha's phone." I looked at my dad. "It was a call from the federal penitentiary down in West Virginia. A collect call from an inmate there." I ran a hand through my hair, tugging on the ends. "The inmate is her mother."

His eyes widened a little as he set the notepad off to the side. "Interesting. I'm going to assume Sasha has yet to tell you about her mother?"

"She has yet to tell me a lot about her family. Just that she was raised by her grandparents and Morgan is the only person she calls family." I looked up. "And you, mom, me." I glanced down at the large rug on the floor, wringing my hands. I felt even worse about the simple act of answering her phone and what it meant in the long run. Sasha had become a part of this family a long time ago when she spent nights by my side at the hospital, watching over me when my parents couldn't.

"Emma, you're going to have to trust her. You

already trust her with your heart, give the rest to her. We all know what happened last year. It was out of her control." My father leaned closer. "She saved your life a few times, if you can trust her with your life, well, you know what I'm getting at. We all have secrets, kiddo, you included." I felt his strong hand on my shoulder, squeezing to emphasize his point. "Apologize to her and talk. I think she'll forgive you."

I covered his hand with mine, lightly smiling. "I never thought this would be this hard, going back to case work while navigating loving and trusting someone."

My father stood up, kissing me on the forehead. "It's because you kept your heart locked up for far too long. As for the case work, sometimes even the best falter when it gets to be too gruesome for the strongest stomach." He walked back to his desk, collecting his notes. "Maybe it's a sign you should retire again."

I smiled. "I think you and mom want me to retire again. Go back to a quiet life without death, criminals, and badges stuck on my hip."

He nodded with his back turned to me. "I want you to live the best life possible and it might not be in this career anymore, Emma." He looked over his shoulder. "Take it from an old grizzled law man. Sometimes when you see the light at the end of the tunnel, its best to walk towards it and walk right on out."

I went to ask him to explain what he meant, when I heard Sasha walk past the office, calling after Morgan. I stood up, tugging on my sweatshirt. "Looks like mom has breakfast ready. Let's take a break, dad." I walked out of the office with hands full of his notes and notebooks. When I walked into the kitchen, I saw Sasha wearing her dress from last night, her bags sat by the counter. Sasha walked in from the dining room with Morgan close on her heels.

"Can you give me like two more minutes to finish breakfast?" Morgan was slightly pouting as she held a very full plate in her hand.

Sasha glanced up, her eyes dark with anger. She was pissed, pissed at me. "I need to get back to my apartment, Morgan. Work called. I have to meet Reagan in an hour."

I reached for her arm. "Sasha, I can drive you home."

She stepped away from my reach, pushing a few more things into her bag. "You should stay, spend some time with your family." The edge in her tone could cut paper to shreds.

Aaron popped out of the dining room as my father moved past him, waving for my mother to stay back. It was obvious Sasha and I needed to talk, but Aaron was oblivious.

"Hey ladies! Sasha, I hope you're not bolting before breakfast. Mom's French toast is the best you'll ever have."

"Sorry, Aaron. Duty calls." She forced a smile, reaching for her bag.

Aaron looked at me, silently asking what the hell was going on, I shook my head at him, then gently grabbed Sasha's arm. "Sasha, I'm sorry. Can we talk upstairs?" I kept my voice low, trying not to bring more attention to us and the tension hovering in the air.

Sasha gave me a hard look. "I need to go, Emma." Her voice was still edged, there was no way I would win this battle. Her infamous temper was at the brink of spilling out and Sasha was doing her best to keep it in since we were at my parent's house.

"Let me take you home." She tensed up under my hand.

Aaron broke in, handing his car keys to Morgan. "Here Morgan, take my car. Drop Sasha off at her apartment and come back. And if you're interested, I'll take you to lunch." I knew he was trying to diffuse the situation as fast as possible before both of our tempers turned the heavy silence into an all-out screaming match.

Sasha grabbed the keys, smiling at Aaron. "You're the best, Aaron." She turned to her best friend. "I'm leaving *now*, Morgan."

Morgan pouted and ran to get her coat, mumbling to Aaron. "I'll be back as soon as I can."

Aaron gave me one last look, I shook my head again. Our silent signal that I'd tell him as soon as I could. Aaron nodded slowly and walked back into the dining room.

Sasha lifted her bags up, turning towards me. I spoke before she had the chance. "I'll meet you at home in a few hours and we can talk."

Sasha swallowed hard. "I think it's better if I go back to my apartment for a few days. I haven't been there since before we left for Virginia the first time." Her words bit deep. Sasha had been staying at my house since Latham's interview and was showing signs of eventually moving in.

"Sasha, I'm sorry. I don't know why I answered the phone."

Sasha offered a weak smile. "I do. You still don't completely trust me." She shifted the bags on her shoulder. "And I don't know if you ever will, Emma." The tone in her voice broke my heart deeper than any thoughts of mistrust ever could. I went to reach for her, but she moved away, shaking her head. "I would've told you if you just asked me."

Before I could say anything more, Morgan shot out from the dining room, half eaten piece of French toast in her hand, wearing Aaron's winter coat. "I'm ready if you are, Sasha." She then walked over, hugging me, whispering against my ear. "I'll be back in a few. I can't ever talk Sasha out of working when the great Reagan calls upon her, but

I'll give it the old college try. Aaron and I are taking you and the parents out for lunch, so get dressed in something other than these sweats." She poked me in the side before moving towards the front door.

Sasha went to leave, when I grabbed her elbow again, her cheeks flushing a bright angry pink. "Wait, at least take these with you. It's my dad's old notebooks and a few contacts who can help us with the Bellico case." I picked up the notebooks, gently shoving them into the bag on her shoulder. "He agrees it could be drug related. Please read over them. I'll contact the DEA agent he knows."

She nodded. "I'll look at them and call you when I get the results back from the lab. Take a few more days with your family, Emma. We'll meet back in the office on Monday and see what comes next."

The tone in her voice was nothing but business, no hint of emotion at all. The flush of anger on her cheeks was the only sign she was upset. I held onto her elbow. "You can go to the house if you want. It's your home too, Sasha. I want you there. I made a stupid mistake, please, let's talk about it."

Sasha sighed. "I'll call you when I have the lab results."

I knew there was no bargaining with her in this moment. I let go of her elbow, whispering. "I love you."

I watched as she squeezed her eyes shut and walked away from me. "Tell your parents thank you for me."

Morgan hollered through the house at my parents she would return and to save her some food. I stood in the kitchen until I heard the front door click shut.

I walked back upstairs as my heart sank. I didn't want to see my parents or Aaron right now. I sat on the bed, staring at the small frame with our badges in it. Why was this so hard for me? Trusting her completely. I wanted to, I had to. She had my heart and yet I was clinging to the past, being too stubborn to think clearly. Every time I told her I loved her, I meant it. I just had to get my lingering fears on board. Sasha was all I would ever want in my life, and if I lost her, I would lose myself. I held my head in my hands and groaned. This was harder than anything I'd ever done in my life. Loving someone and letting them love the mess I was.

*****

I showered and changed into an old pair of jeans and flannel button up. I packed up my academy sweats and Red Wings sweatshirt, laying the shadow box on top. I ran downstairs just as Morgan walked back into the house. She pointed at me. "You. We need to talk."

I nodded and motioned for her to follow me into the study. I closed the double doors behind us as Morgan flopped down onto the couch. "You know one day you'll have to let go of all your hang-ups about Sasha before she's had enough and runs like I would've a long time ago." Morgan gave me a hard look.

I moved to where my father kept the good scotch, pouring a glass for each of us. "I know, trust me, I know."

Morgan eagerly took the glass, downing most of the scotch in a sip. "I got an earful on the ride back to her lame apartment. An apartment that's bare and cold compared to your house. I know she's pissed at you if she's opting to go back to that boring shit box the FBI pays for." Morgan crossed her legs under her. "Look, Emma. I'm not going to tell you the deal with her mother. I think that's something you two need to talk about, but it's not what you think it is."

"I don't have any thoughts about it."

Morgan laughed, pointing at me with her glass. "Bullshit. If you didn't, you would've left the phone alone and defiled that shower like you should have." Morgan paused. "Ask her when she's cooled down. She'll tell you everything you've ever wanted to know. Sasha has been waiting for you to ask, but she's more afraid you'll leave if you find out some of the shitty details of her life, because she can see every day you still don't trust her."

I swallowed the scotch, wincing at its delicious burn. "Morgan, I'm afraid to lose her too. But there's something in me that won't let me stop being stupid at times. I can't ignore the past and all of the things in my head." I tapped my temple. "It's a bit of a mess in here."

She raised an eyebrow. "Maybe you need therapy?"

I raised my eyebrows back at her. "I've been in therapy for almost a year. It's helped with the nightmares." I let out a sigh, staring at the little bit of scotch left in my glass. "This case is getting to me, testing me more than I thought it would. I can't detach, I can't separate my fears or myself from the violence." I sat on the edge of the desk. "I often think I search out the small things to keep Sasha away, so she won't have to see my eventual implosion and collapse when this all gets to be too much." I took a deep breath, looking out the window. "Did she tell you how I lost it at the last crime scene?"

Morgan moved from the couch to sit next to me. "She did, and it scared her. She had no clue how to help you as she watched the fear and panic run across your eyes." Morgan patted me on the back. "She knows you're walking a thin line between falling apart and keeping it together, but it also means you can't keep using her as the punching bag. She's also riding a thin line, the last year was a pile of shit for her too, add in an absentee criminal mother, and well." Morgan moved to stand in front of me, eye to eye and held onto my shoulders. "Look Captain, she's with you for the long haul. But I don't know if you being an asshole and doing stupid things that push her way is going to keep her around much longer. She loves you, loves you more than anything else in this world. So, I say this, she's my best friend and I *will not* let you take her down with you as you implode." Morgan squeezed me. "You love her, I also know that. Give her a couple of days, then ask her. She'll tell you everything about her mom and her life. After that, get through this case and for the love of God, figure out if you want to be a cop anymore. But love that girl like I know you do." Morgan grabbed me in an awkward hug. "Don't fuck it up any more than you have." She let go, winking. "Give her a day. And this is the last time I give you a secret friends pep talk. Two is my limit. Oh, Sasha has no idea about this one, I'd like to keep it that way. Get. Your. Shit. Together."

Morgan drained her scotch, handing the glass back to me before she rushed out of the room. I heard her and Aaron laughing with my parents. I poured another glass and stared out the window, Morgan's words sitting heavy on my shoulders.

*****

I skipped lunch, choosing to go home and work. I hated the way the house felt empty without Sasha and Aaron filling the silence with laughter and silly bickering. I sat in my office reading over the notes my father had given me, aching for Sasha to walk into the room like she always did when I was working too long. It'd only been a couple of weeks since she had sort of moved in, but it felt like forever and it didn't feel right not having her here.

Leaning back in my chair I reached for the phone to call her. I missed her and wanted to hear her voice even if she yelled at me for being an idiot. I went to text her when the phone lit up with an unknown number. I recognized the area code as a number out of D.C., I took a breath and answered. "Captain Tiernan."

"Captain Emma Tiernan? I'm an old friend of your pops. The name is Angus Duncan, but you can call me Gus." The hard edges of Boston sat in every syllable the man spoke.

"He just emailed you this morning." I leaned against my desk. It was late afternoon and I'd left my parents' house less than two hours ago.

"He did and I owe that man a multitude of favors. So, when he reaches out, I do my best to answer as fast as possible."

I closed my eyes as I remembered the last person who repaid a favor to my father, Rachel. I cleared my throat. "Well, I appreciate your quick response, Gus. I'm sure he filled you in about the current case I'm working on?"

"Yeah, and it also appears the DEA and you are on a similar trail. This Bellico case fell across my desk two days ago. Looks like Bellico's garage was full of drug manufacturing equipment. Large amounts of chemicals and laboratory grade gear. The FBI lab is still testing the chemicals and other pieces of evidence your team collected. But at first glance, I can tell you, your man was definitely dabbling in something he shouldn't have."

I paused. I didn't remember seeing any photos of drug paraphernalia and chemicals, but then again, I was more focused on how Bellico and his body parts fell into my lap. "Do you think you could assist Agent Clarke and I with the Bellico case?"

I heard the creak of a chair in the background. "Definitely. I think our cases are tied together. It's giving me wicked flashbacks of the eighties when I was chasing a real evil Columbian drug lord." Gus cleared his throat, his accent somehow getting thicker. "Can you and Agent Clarke meet me at the DEA field office in Chicago next week? I'll be on your side of town for a meeting with the boys. I'll bring whatever notes I have."

"That's perfect. Is there anything you need from us?"

"Won't be necessary, Captain, I have everything I need. I'll forward you a few more case files to peruse through that I think could help you connect some of the dots. I also have a file on Bellico from his short stint working undercover for us." Gus paused for a moment. "One last thing, this is going to be some heady stuff we're digging into, kid. The drug cartels don't take too kindly to cops digging in their business, especially us federal cops. Are you sure you want to push deeper into this? The DEA will gladly take it over and share the information."

His voice was dripping with extreme caution. My father had hinted at the same thing as he showed me old crime scene photos. I took a breath, steadying my gut. "I have a job to do. I have two murders to solve and the only way I can do that is if I continue to push for answers. It's not like I haven't dealt with monsters head on."

"I heard, kid. You're a tough one, Captain Tiernan, you have the admiration of a lot of us." I knew he was hinting at the Latin Murders and Evan. I was pretty certain the entire law enforcement world knew about some of the worst days of my life. I said nothing in return, allowing Gus to change the subject to details of the meeting.

I hung up with Gus and smiled as his emails flooded my inbox. The man was definitely on top of his game. I went to call Sasha when an email from her fell into my inbox above Gus. They were the finalized lab reports with a few more scene photos attached.

She was keeping her distance.

I shut off the computer, went downstairs and grabbed the last few bottles of beer Aaron left in the fridge. I went into the basement, grinning at how clean Aaron kept it, a far cry from his office at the station. I flopped down on the leather couch and drank, losing myself in a favorite TV show. I passed out in a beer buzz as the laugh track filled the eerie silence of my house.

I woke up a few hours later, the house still empty. I groaned as a hangover was settling in.

Shuffling up the stairs I saw it was close to midnight, making me wonder why Aaron wasn't home. Grabbing a glass of water, I leaned against the kitchen counter holding my head. I wasn't tired after the almost six hour nap in the basement and decided to go read over the lab reports. I also wanted to check my phone, see if Sasha had called.

Walking through the kitchen I noticed the deadbolt on the front door was locked. I stared at it, swallowing hard. I never locked the deadbolt until Aaron came home. He'd broken his key off in the deadbolt weeks ago and was still being lazy about replacing it. It wouldn't lock from the outside since his key was still lodge inside the tumbler. I stared at the door for a few more seconds, trying to think if I'd locked it on accident when I came home.

Clutching the glass of water, I walked to the side table, opening the drawer and grabbed the Glock 22 I kept there as a backup. I slipped the gun into my waistband and climbed the stairs.

At the top of the stairs, the light to my bedroom was on, the door cracked open. My heart began to beat a little faster as memories of Evan and how he was able to sneak into anywhere unnoticed, raced through my mind.

I crept up the stairs, removing the gun and gripping it tightly as my hand pushed the door open, and took a deep breath.

"Emma, it's me."

Sasha sat on the edge of my bed, her head down as she fidgeted with her hands in her lap. I walked into the room, setting the gun down on top of my dresser. I wanted to scoop her up in my arms, but paused as her soft voice filled the room.

"My mother was arrested for the last time when I was at Quantico. Federal drug trafficking charges that will have her behind bars until my grandchildren have grandchildren of their own." Sasha looked at me. Her eyes red and puffy. She was tired, and looked as if she'd been crying for hours. She held her gaze as she continued. "She left me when I was seventeen, dropping me off at my grandparents' house and never really showed up again. I changed my last name to Clarke, same as my grandparents when I turned eighteen. They were more parents than she ever was. I've only seen her twice in my life since then. Once at my police academy graduation where she snuck into the back of the hall, and then last year at Christmas. I made the trip down to see her after she begged me. Turns out she only wanted to see me because she found out I was an FBI agent and hoped I could get her charges reduced."

She sniffled and turned away, directing her eyes back to a random spot on the floor. "She was a drug mule for a Mexican drug cartel out on the West Coast. I looked into her case to help with her appeals, but I also wanted to know more about the woman. After I read everything she did, her charges, I never ever want to help her. She's where she belongs." Sasha folded her arms across her chest as I moved to sit next to her, careful not to touch her. Even though she was in my room, on my bed, she was pissed at me. And I didn't blame her.

"Sasha, I should've asked you."

She angrily nodded. "Yes, you should have, Emma. I

would've told you. I *have* wanted to tell you. She's been calling more and more, playing the regretful neglectful mother, now more than ever, thinking I can pull a deal out of my ass for her and get her multiple life sentences reduced." She turned, giving me a hard look. "You have to trust me Emma, or we're never going to make it."

Her hard, direct tone pierced my heart. I whispered, biting my bottom lip as my eyes welled up. "I know."

Sasha sighed as she looked at the ceiling, anywhere else, but me. "I went back to the apartment. I didn't want to come here. I walked around that cold box of an apartment I wanted to call home, but you weren't there in any way. Just blank walls and cold hardwood floors. I didn't want to come here so soon, giving you the idea you'd broken me and won." Sasha closed her eyes. "But you have broken me. You have won, Emma. All of me. And I can't imagine a life without you, even when I'm so angry at you for not trusting me. Thinking at any moment I'm going to pull the rug out from under you and confess I'm someone I'm not again."

I moved closer to Sasha, our legs brushing against each other. I wanted to say something, but the air crackled with a thick tension, telling me she was far from done talking. Her face was flushed, and her tone was filled with the struggle not to lose it on me or break down into tears.

Sasha laid a hand on my thigh. "I know you struggle with demons every day. I know every day could be the day you break apart and lose yourself in the darkness that lingers from Evan. I know every day you carry a fear of something I know you cannot describe to me, and I will never ask you to." She turned suddenly, facing me. "I'm here, Emma. I'll fight with you for as long as I can. All I'm asking is for you to trust me. I know I already have your heart, as you have mine, but I need you to trust me. Trust that I will be here until the end. Trust me to tell you the things you want to know about my past." She let out a soft sigh. "I thought about all of this for the last few hours. I'm still upset with you, but I wanted to come home. To you. I found you on the couch in the basement passed out and came up here to leave the hard copy files on your desk along with the file on my mother. I want you to know everything I have left to show you." She paused. "Then I found it hard to leave." She then nodded at her bag by the door. "I also forgot the sweatshirt."

    I couldn't help but smile at the sight of the red material of my old sweatshirt half hanging out of her bag. "I brought it back with me, hoping I could give it to you." I turned to Sasha, her eyes glassy with unshed tears. I reached up, pressing my hand against her cheek. "I do trust you, Sasha. You're the only one who keeps coming back when I push you away. You fight me tooth and nail, you chase the demons away as they fight so hard to stay in my mind." I watched as she shut her eyes, her hand coming up to cover mine. "I made a stupid mistake answering that phone and assuming something I should've just asked you about." I felt her sigh. "Sasha, I'm not sure about much anymore. I don't know if I can continue being a cop after this case is closed. But I do know I love you and need you. You make me whole for the first time in a very long time and I will fight for you as hard as you fight for me."

    I suddenly stopped talking, and pulled her into my arms. I smiled when I felt her arms slip around my waist, her hands lying flat against my back. "Tomorrow, I want you to tell me everything there is to know about Natasha Clarke. But for right now, I just want you here, in our home, in my arms." I paused, swallowing down the lump in my throat. "I promise." I spoke carefully, keeping my voice even. "I never break my promises."

We sat for a few moments in silence.

Sasha moved first, letting go of her grip on me and moved to her bag, pulling out a thick stack of files. She set them on the bed, and spoke. "These are the hard copies of what I emailed you. I also pulled the files Gus Duncan forwarded to me." I picked them up as she gave me a curious, confused look. "Who is this Agent Duncan from the DEA? His name pushed through my work email with a high security clearance, higher than I've ever come across, outside of Reagan.

I grabbed the files, setting them on my lap. Work was the last thing I wanted to deal with right now. "He's an old friend of my dad's. A DEA contact from the eighties who has information that could help. It appears the Bellico case landed on the DEA's desk. He was possibly cooking up drugs in his garage. Th evidence we collected peaked the DEA's interest."

Sasha folded her arms across her chest. "I read that in the lab reports. The chemicals and equipment point to him trying to manufacture cocaine and meth."

I sighed, shaking my head. "How did this cold case lead to a fresh homicide case with drug cartel involvement? We're investigating the murder of a sixteen year old girl. Not a cop turned to drug dealer."

Sasha shrugged. "I have no idea, Emma. All we can do is follow the leads and if it gets too hot, I've been instructed by Reagan to turn it over to the narcotics division and return to the Heaten case. But only if it turns out Bellico's case and ours have nothing to do with each other."

I stared at her as my sinking feeling grew. Something was off. Not only did Duncan warn us to be cautious, but now Reagan was sticking her nose deeper into our business when she promised to leave us alone. "I don't know if I like where this case is going. I have a bad feeling." Sasha nodded in agreement. I stood up, collecting the files and dumping them in my desk drawer. "We're off until Monday. Let's make the most of it."

I walked to the far corner of my room, kneeling at the bottom of a bookshelf, removing a thick stack of yearbooks and photo albums. I sat next to Sasha, setting the stack in her lap. She scrunched up her brow. "What is this, Emma?"

I tapped the side of the photo albums. "Those are the albums my mom doesn't have. I stole the albums with the most embarrassing pictures years ago and stashed them here." I tapped the top album. "These are my yearbooks from high school along with every awkward moment of my teen years. Going back to the day my parents adopted me, all the way up until I graduated from the academy. This is everything I am. This is who I am."

Sasha half smiled, flipping through the one album. She laughed, stopping on a page filled with me wearing that horrid Red Wings sweatshirt. "You weren't kidding about the sweatshirt being your only wardrobe choice. Did you wear it every day?" She held up a page where in every picture, I was enrobed bright red material.

I nodded, smiling sheepishly. "I told you. I was gangly and skinny."

Sasha giggled as she flipped through more pictures before she stopped, holding out her hand. "Will you sit with me and tell me the stories behind every one of these."

I grinned, nodding. "Let me get more beer first. A lot of these stories can't be told without liquid courage."

Sasha grinned. "I love you, Emma Tiernan. Every gangly, skinny, awkward amazing inch of you. I always will."

My face suddenly grew warm as I blushed. I walked over to her, grabbing her face gently with both hands, kissing her deeply as she held onto my wrists. I pulled away just enough to look in her eyes, and whispered. "I love you, Sasha. From this moment on, you have my complete trust." I smiled as I waved at the photo albums. "No one has ever seen these pictures or heard the story of how I was suspended in tenth grade for a month. I stole all of the biology lab frogs and set them free, only to have them get squished in the parking lot."

Sasha blinked as a tear rolled down her cheek. I brushed it away as she laughed. "Am I in love with a juvenile delinquent?"

I kissed the corner of her mouth. "It appears so." I kissed her once more before running down to the kitchen to grab the beer. When I ran back up to the bedroom, I found Sasha wearing the sweatshirt, laying on the bed, flipping through the endless albums. I sighed as I looked at her, and out of nowhere it fell out of my mouth. "What do you think about kids? Having them?" In that moment staring at Sasha wearing my clothes, I knew I wanted a future with this stubborn woman. The whole future of a house, kids, a dog and a home. I felt myself letting go of the trust issues with this remarkable woman before me.

Sasha looked up, her eyes bright as she smiled, answering so much more than my random question. She grinned as she pointed at a picture of me dressed in traditional German lederhosen standing next to my mother. "First, explain why in the world do you look like the German girl on the beer bottles I stole from my grandfather?" I rolled my eyes and opened the first beer, dropping myself down next to Sasha as I told her the story of being forced to participate in the German festival when I was seventeen.

In this simple moment, I forgot all about the cases and the heavy warnings hanging over us like storm clouds. I hoped I could keep them in the back of my mind for now.

193 Under Darkened Skies – Sydney Gibson

I'd deal with them later when we went back to work.

CHAPTER 13

Sasha left the house, going on a late night food run. We'd spent most of the day, and night, discussing my awkward teen years that became semi awkward college years. For the first time in a long time, I told someone how I became a Tiernan. I told her about the failed attempt at mugging my dad in a dirty alley, and instead of being arrested, I was taken away to a better life. When I finished, all Sasha had to say was. "Remind me to thank your dad every time I see him." I saw exactly why in her eyes, and in the way she kissed me.

I broke up the storytelling announcing I had an overwhelming craving for tacos from the late night taco joint by the station where we first met on a prisoner transfer. Sasha hopped up from the bed, pulled on a pair of jeans, still wearing the baggy sweatshirt, and offered to grab the tacos. I smiled as she quickly kissed me, grabbing her gun and slipping in it the waistband of her jeans, promising to be back in an hour.

I sat on the bed staring at my entire life in photographs as the front door clicked shut. I sighed, collecting the albums and shoving them back on the shelf. I felt lighter having shared so much of my life with Sasha. Maybe I was getting closer to healing through and through. I yawned, picking up the file Sasha set on top of her briefcase. It was her mother's file.

I walked to my office, bringing the shadow box with me. I sat down at the desk, setting it right next to my monitor where I'd always see it, I laid my hands over the file, taking a deep breath before opening it.

Alison Porter had a long rap sheet filled with drug crimes starting when she was a young teenager and took her well into her adult life. Simple possession charges became intent to distribute charges. Those charges morphed into intent to manufacture, sell and traffic large amounts of narcotics. She'd been imprisoned throughout the country in numerous county jails, before finally ending up at a federal penitentiary with a multitude of felony charges, keeping her behind bars for the rest of her life.

    I skimmed over the county jail records. Alison spent time at couple in Illinois, a handful in California, one in Detroit and a few down in Florida. I paused at her time in Detroit, shaking my head at the fact she'd been there around the same time I was dumped into the foster care system as an infant. I moved on to the rest of her criminal record before I dwindled on my biological parents and their death.

    Sasha's mother was a junkie who'd been swallowed up into the drug culture and pushed her way into the profiting side of it. Her record was dotted with assault charges, fighting drug dealers or other junkies who tried to rob her. Never mind the litany of assault charges against law enforcement officers. Alison was not a shining example of how to be an upstanding citizen. She'd always chosen herself and her addiction over anything, anyone, else. Including her own daughter.

    I flipped through the rest of her file, staring at the most recent booking photograph of the woman taken on the day she was processed as an inmate at the federal prison in West Virginia. Sasha looked a lot like her, but happier, healthier, and just so different on so many levels, I couldn't describe it with words. Sasha was simply everything her mother wasn't.

    The last page in the file was the custody trial verdict between Sasha's grandparents and her mother. The custody battle started while Alison was serving a six month sentence in California, the same year Sasha was a junior in high school. Her grandparents had been raising Sasha for most of her life and decided it was time to gain full custody, give her some stability. The judge's comments at the bottom of the document, caught my attention.

The mother in this case has no hesitation to rid herself of what she claims to be a burden in her life. Her only daughter. I hereby award the grandparents full custody and from this date on, Alison Porter will only be allowed supervised, prearranged visits with her daughter until her eighteenth birthday. It will also be noted, Ms. Porter shows no remorse for the loss of her daughter, nor shows a desire to accept any rehabilitation programs offered by the court and her counsel.

Sasha's mother had given her away like it was nothing, like she was nothing. It broke my heart to pieces. I shoved the file away, ignoring the endless reports from child services, documenting the poor living conditions and signs of neglect Sasha endured.

Reading the file, I fully understood why Sasha wanted to keep that part of her life in the dark. It wasn't something a child would be proud of, having a junkie criminal for a parent. I stood up, tucking the file back into Sasha's bag. I wanted to burn it, there was no reason for me, or Sasha to ever see it again. I also understood why Sasha was so tenacious, fierce. She'd lived one hell of a life and survived.

I contemplated crawling into bed, hiding under warm blankets, when my phone rang downstairs. Jogging down the stairs I scooped it off the counter, smiling as I answered. "Aaron, let me guess you're not coming home tonight? Staying with the parents an extra night? I know how much my mom loves you."

Aaron chuckled. "She does love me. I wonder if she

has a crush on me. But, no, I left the Tiernan homestead a few hours after you. I wanted to let you know I'm going to be taking a certain federal agent to dinner and we both decided it would be best if you and your federal agent had some alone time." I heard the smirk in his tone. "Just calling to let you know the house is yours tonight. Get at it all over the place. Just don't stain the furniture."

I rolled my eyes as I leaned against the kitchen island. "Aaron, don't be disgusting." I blushed at the sudden memory of Sasha and I on the kitchen counter.

He laughed. "I know. I'll be home later tomorrow. Oh, Emma, before I forget. The Sheriff down in Virginia called, I took the call when I stopped into the station earlier. They have some evidence they'd like to share with you. It looks like the neighbor across the street may have seen someone leaving Bellico's house the night he was murdered. The deputies are sending you the interview notes and the composite sketch." Before I could open my mouth, Aaron cut me off. "I told them to send it ASAP. I know you better than you know yourself, Captain Detective Tiernan. The files will be in your office at the station first thing in the morning."

I smiled as I pushed around my never used spice rack, wiping dust off the top. "You're the best, Aaron. I'll see you in the morning, also tell Morgan I said hi. I think you two make a cute couple." I hung up as he began to stammer, laughing. I loved when I caught Aaron off-guard.

I let out a slow breath, tapping the edge of my phone on the counter, staring at a jar of cinnamon. Finally, some forward movement in the case. I felt renewed about digging deeper into things. Maybe we could pass off the Bellico murder to the deputies and focus on the Heaten case. I was hopeful Bellico's murder wasn't connected to the Heaten case, but deep down in my gut, I knew I was skating on a thin sheet of hopeful ice.

    Lost in thoughts about the bizarre bits and pieces we had on both cases, I didn't hear Sasha come through the front door. Only catching the delicious smell of tacos as soon as they entered the house. I moved to help Sasha struggling with two giant bags of food as she walked in the kitchen, setting them down on the island. "I don't know if my eyes were bigger than my stomach, but there's twenty tacos, a large nacho, and some of those cinnamon churros you love." Sasha laid her hands on her hips, surveying the massive amount of food. "This might be too much." She cringed, giving me a shy look.

    I laughed, digging through the bags of food, enjoying the delicious smells coming out of grease spotted brown bags. I pulled out a handful of tacos, offering one to Sasha. "Good thing they're just as delicious cold as they are fresh." I unwrapped the wax paper and took a healthy bite, enjoying every greasy dripping inch of the taco, smiling as Sasha moaned over her own first bite, taco sauce dripping down her chin. I reached over with a napkin, wiping it off, when Sasha grabbed my hand, slightly embarrassed at the mess she was making. I leaned over, kissing the same spot on her chin. "Don't be embarrassed. I have watched you inhale a pumpkin muffin in a matter of seconds."

    Sasha grinned, kissing me back and blushing as she changed the subject. "Is Aaron coming home soon?"

    I shook my head, taking another bite. "Nope. He took the night off to take Morgan on a dinner date. The house is ours." I smirked. "He called while you were out to let me know the Sheriff's office in Virginia pulled together a composite sketch of the suspected last visitor to Bellico's house. He's having it sent to my office. We can look at it on Monday along with the interview notes from the neighbors."

Sasha cocked an eyebrow, smirking as she slid her phone across the island. "Or you can look at it now. It popped up in my email a little while ago. One of the on scene deputies took a liking to me and went out of his way to be oh so very helpful. He called while I was standing in line listening to a couple of drunks bitch about the Bears lack of defense." She grabbed another taco while I picked up her phone, opening the email.

I narrowed my eyes, holding the phone closer to scroll through the attached images. "Is there anyone in the law enforcement world who doesn't take a liking to you? Exeter asks you out for a crab dinner. Bellico's next door neighbor tells you his life story while flexing his muscles. The FBI lab boys all swoon at your simplest movements, and now you're roping in polite southern deputies." I tried to play up the jealous tone in my voice, but doing a poor job hiding the truth. I was jealous. Painfully jealous.

Sasha laughed. "Can you blame them?" She held her arms out to cheekily say, *come on look at me.*

I opened my mouth in mock shock. "No, but maybe I'll sleep in the basement tonight. Wouldn't want any of your prospective suitors to think you're taken. I hear crab dinners can be lovely with the right company."

Sasha's smile faded. "The basement?

I nodded slowly with a slight smirk, returning to the composite sketch. I suddenly tuned out Sasha desperately trying to backtrack. I scrolled through the picture a few times until I pointed at the sketch. "Is it me, or does this look exactly like Magnum P.I.? I think either the neighbor was seeing things, or our mystery guest was wearing a disguise."

Sasha leaned over my shoulder for a better look. "Emma, I hope you know I was kidding about what I said." Her gaze dropped to the phone. "Oh, wow. You're right. This looks exactly like Tom Selleck. Big bushy eighties mustache, curly dark hair. Even down to the dark blue Detroit Tigers hat." She walked over to her briefcase, removing her
laptop and started an image search. When she was done, she swung the laptop around to face me. There was an exact image of the composite sketch in a promotional picture for the show. The sketch and promo picture looked eerily alike, the only difference was one was a police sketch. That, and I highly doubted Tom Selleck was our murderer.

I leaned against the counter, staring at the laptop and composite sketch on Sasha's phone. "Someone has a twisted sense of humor." Sasha grabbed another taco as I sifted through more images. "Do you still want to interview the neighbor?"

I sighed. "I do, but it might not be worth a trip down there. Call your deputy *boyfriend* and see if we can arrange a video conference with the neighbor." I inadvertently emphasized the word boyfriend as I clicked on a few more pictures. "Also, find out if the neighbor has a sketchy record. Sometimes attention seekers come out of the woodwork when they see flashing blue lights and crime scene tape." I went quiet as I got lost in old video clips of Magnum P.I. "Man, I forgot how good this show was."

I was so distracted by the television show, I didn't notice Sasha walk away from the counter and tacos. I was also too busy adding the show to my Netflix queue, I didn't feel her move behind me until two hands came around my waist, pulling me into her front and away from the laptop.

A warm hand slid under my shirt, covering my breast, squeezing in a possessive way as the other one dipped below the waistband of my jeans. Her fingers teased my skin as I gasped at the sudden sensation of her touch. Sasha kissed my neck, before taking my ear lobe between her teeth, sending shivers through my entire body as she bit gently.

I gasped, leaning forward to grab the edge of the counter to steady myself. She let go of my earlobe, whispering against my ear. "What were you saying about that deputy? The one you called my boyfriend?" Her hand pushed past my underwear, her fingers tracing slow circles around sensitive skin, making me ache. I gasped and tried to push back into her, wanting more from her as my heart pounded and my body instantly responded to her touch. When Sasha felt me push into her, she pulled her hand free, spinning me around to face her. I reached out for her, desperate to kiss her and continue what she started.

She intercepted my hands, guiding one down to waistband of her jeans as her other hand kept a firm grip on my hip. The top button of her jeans was already unbuttoned as she slowly pushed my hand past them and her underwear, pressing my hand against her hot wet skin. I bit my lip to hold back the moan at how wet she was. Sasha tilted my chin up, forcing me to look in her eyes. "No one does this to me. No one ever will. Only you, Emma. It will only ever be *you*."

I swallowed hard at the sight of her almost black eyes, knowing she was telling the truth. I licked my lips. "Sasha, I was being stupid. Jealous." It came out as a desperate whisper, fueled by the desire I constantly felt for this woman.

Sasha grabbed my face, kissing me hard. I kissed her back, forcing her mouth open wider as my hand moved on its own, fingers covering the short distance to where she needed me. When she felt me slip easily inside, Sasha moaned against my mouth, shoving me back against the counter as she pushed herself down on my fingers. Her thigh came up hard between my legs, pressing against where I ached for her. It drove me crazy with need for her to touch me. I pulled my hand free from her, a soft protest falling from her lips. I wanted, needed, her naked now. I reached for her shirt, ready to rip it to shreds, when she caught the look in my eyes.

She nodded, pushing my hands away. We communicated silently as she ripped off her shirt, my mouth covering every inch of skin revealed to me, licking and biting. Her jeans were the next to come off as I knelt in front of her, my hands sliding up her bare thighs, asking her to open wider for me.

I took a moment to soak in the sight of a naked and flushed Sasha. Her hands ran through my hair, gently tugging me forward.

I honored her request. Suddenly very glad Aaron was nowhere near the house. "You're so beautiful, you make me jealous. So fucking jealous." I whispered, looking up at Sasha. Her eyes glistened as she smirked. I moved closer, kissing the inside of her thigh, eager for a taste.

The front window shattered like a bomb hitting it, followed by the bright orange and yellow burst of flames as a bottle exploded on impact, engulfing the wooden coffee table in fire. Sasha screamed as I reacted on instinct, pushing her to the floor, covering her with my body to shield her from flying glass and the rapidly spreading flames in the living room. I stood up as soon as I realized it was a firebomb, running for the fire extinguisher I kept next to the stove. I yelled for Sasha to get out of the house and call 911, she yelled back, but I ignored her, screaming. "Get out of the goddamn house now!" I was fighting my panic, focused on getting her out of the house.

The fire extinguisher had enough juice to put out the medium-sized fire covering the table and some of the couch. I then moved to the window to deal the small flames riding the edge of the front window curtains.

I looked out the shattered window, down at the sidewalk.

A figure, dressed in dark clothing, stood in front of my house, glaring right at me through the massive hole in the window.

I reached for my hip, forgetting I'd left my gun upstairs. I clutched onto the fire extinguisher as I yelled at the figure. "Hey! Stop!" The figure didn't move an inch until Sasha came running up behind me, her gun drawn as she yelled for me to get out of the house. Her attention was quickly drawn to where I was looking.

The figure yelled through the broken window, a hint of laughter in his voice. "You keep chasing fire and you're gonna get burned, Agents!" He was a young man with the beginning of an old smoker's raspy voice with a slight accent to it. I instantly recorded it into my mind.

Sasha bolted towards the front door, ripping it open and running down the front steps after the figure. I watched as he ran off down the street the second she hit the top step, yelling over his shoulder. "This was the first of many messages if you don't back off!" I yelled at Sasha to stop as she was swallowed up into the night.

Sirens sliced through air, the street filled with cop cars and fire trucks. I ran outside to meet the first responder, looking over my shoulder for Sasha, swallowing down a hard lump of fear. She'd just ran after a maniac, a maniac who tried to kill us. My heart was pounding, more for her safety than the fact my house was almost burned to the ground.

I spoke to patrol officers, giving them details and directions, ordering them to find the kid and get Sasha back to the scene. I knew it was a feeble attempt, trying to find a kid wearing all black in the middle of the night, but I had to try.

I stood with my hands on my hips staring at the busted front window and wisps of smoke filtering out into the cold night. The damage wasn't as bad as it sounded when the window broke. There was charred furniture, and the carpet was covered in broken glass. One officer found glass fragments from the bottle, hopeful for fingerprints or chemical evidence. I quickly assessed the scene, there was snow on the ground, but my sidewalk was a busy one. There was no way to track footprints, especially with the boatloads of firefighters and cops trudging through my yard and house. I grabbed a firefighter. "Call the arson squad and tell your guys to be careful not to smash any more evidence."

He nodded and yelled for the Lieutenant on scene, rushing towards him with my instructions. I turned to the sound of someone running through the snow. Sasha grabbed my arm as she stopped in front of me, looking around the scene with wide eyes. "You okay?"

"Where the hell did you go?" I was furious with her, opening my mouth to reprimand her, when I glanced at the blood running down her right arm just above the wrist. "Shit, Sasha, you're bleeding." I grabbed her by the shoulder, dragging her to the ambulance.

"I'm fine. Some glass hit my arm when the window shattered. It's just a small cut." I heard the slight tremor in her voice as I waved down a paramedic.

"She has a deep laceration on her right arm, might be some glass in the wound." I helped Sasha into the back of the ambulance, sitting next to her as the paramedic went to work. I looked at the gash on her arm, pieces of glass embedded in the wound caught the light, reflecting fear back at me. The wound was deep and would need more than a few stitches. "Sasha, it's more than a cut. You'll need to go to the hospital for debridement and stitches." My mind started to drift to the last time I saw blood on her arms. I swallowed few times to keep that night in the warehouse far away.

I took a slow breath as the paramedic agreed with my diagnosis. I sat back, sucking in deep breaths through my nose. I'd seen Sasha hurt a few times, and every time it happened, it got harder and harder to digest. My heart felt like it was going to explode out of my chest. Sasha tried to refuse the paramedics help, claiming she wanted, needed, to stay and assist with processing the scene.

I turned, giving her a hard glare. "Sasha, you're going to the hospital. I can't have you bleeding out when there's more than half of the city's finest and bravest at my house." I tried to smile to ease her, but she caught the fear in my eyes. "Please, just go for me." I sat on my hands so she couldn't see how badly they trembled.

Sasha hung her head down, slowly nodding. "Fine, but I expect you to be right behind me." She grabbed my hand, looking out the back of the ambulance at the red blue lights. "What the hell just happened?"

I sighed, trying to hold back in the shakes. My adrenaline was dumping out fast, fear replacing it just as quick, along with vivid, unforgotten memories. "I don't know."

"Where the hell is Captain Tiernan and Agent Clarke?!" Aaron's voice boomed through the side of the ambulance.

I went to open the back door to flag him over, when it was yanked open. Aaron jumped in, dropping to his knees in front of us. "I got here as fast as I could. Morgan's here too. We heard dispatch put out the call on the way back from dinner." He paused, letting out a breath. "What the fuck happened?" He laid a hand on my forearm, squeezing. He was hyped up, full of adrenaline and anger. I'd seen him like this once before and knew he wouldn't stop until he found every single person involved in the firebombing of my home, his home.

Sasha spoke first. "I think we're getting ourselves into something that's going to take us for the ride of our lives." She quickly broke down what happened, telling Aaron how she chased the man a few blocks before the night just sucked him up and he disappeared. I looked at the ceiling of the ambulance, whispering to myself. "It may even cost us our lives."

I leaned back against the supply cabinets, clearing my throat when Sasha was done. "Aaron, we're going to monitor the scene until the arson squad gets here. Sasha has to go to the hospital to get her arm cleaned and stitched. You and I need to work on saving whatever evidence we can."

Aaron shook his head. "No, you're going to the hospital with Sasha. Morgan and I will stay here and monitor the scene. She's already out there yelling at the firefighters for stomping all over the living room." He swallowed, trying to refrain from slipping into his big brother protector mode. "You're not staying here tonight. Go back to Sasha's FBI apartment. You'll be safe in an FBI owned building. Stay there until I figure out if this was random or not. You've got a lot of enemies, Emma. It could be pissed off gangs, or it could be related to the cold case you're working." Aaron smiled tightly at me. "And before you ask, this case is mine. I'm the first detective on scene, so relax." I went to open my mouth to refuse, when Aaron stood up, holding me by the shoulders. "Not a word Emma. Sasha needs you."

He looked at Sasha. "I'll come pick you up at the hospital when we're done here." Aaron hopped out of the back, slamming the door. I then heard him yelling instructions as he walked away and back into the chaos on my front lawn.

I glanced at Sasha. The only reason I wanted to stay at the scene was because I couldn't handle seeing her hurt. I had far too many times before, and it invoked such a rage and fear deep inside of me, I didn't know how to control it. I never wanted to go back to the time when I thought I'd lost her. It was too dark of a thought.

All I could do in the moment was reach for her, wrap an arm around her, and hold close as the paramedic climbed in to let us know we we're leaving for the hospital. He smiled as he told the hospital was expecting us. Apparently, an Agent McAdams had placed a priority call along with strict instructions no one was to know we were coming. I gave the kid a weak smile, before turning to look out the square back window. Sasha and I fell into a thick

thick silence as the ambulance navigated the bumpy streets of Chicago.

At the hospital we were escorted to a room at the far end of the emergency room. The nurse mention it was generally reserved for difficult prisoners and high profile patients. I remained silent, watching as the on call doctor made the same assessment I did of Sasha's injury, telling her how lucky she was an artery hadn't been nicked. I guess knocking her to the floor when I did, saved her life.

I furiously paced around the room, half listening to the doctor, trying not to look at Sasha. Every time I did, I would focus on the blood and residual fear that came with it.

I sat across from Sasha as a cheery nurse cleaned her arm. The silence between was still thick and heavy when the nurse left the room, explaining the doctor would be back in a moment to close the wound.

"The guy ditched his sweatshirt. I grabbed it and gave it to the evidence techs before I found you. Hopefully, trace can find something." Sasha broke the silence, her legs nervously swinging off the edge of the gurney she sat on. She wouldn't look directly at me.

I leaned forward in the hard plastic chair I sat in, nodding slowly. After a moment I looked up. "Don't *ever* do that again." My voice came out harder than I wanted, startling Sasha.

Sasha furrowed her brow. "Do what?"

"Run off like that, chasing some creepy asshole who just firebombed our house, trying to kill us." I was trying to keep the anger out of my voice, but was failing miserably.

Sasha let out a breath. "It was instinct, Emma. It's what I'm trained to do."

"You're not a Goddamned street cop

anymore! You're smarter than that." I leaned back in the chair, folding my arms, clenching my jaw. "You should've gotten out of the house when I told you to." I pointed my chin at her arm. "That could've been worse, you could've been burned." I paused as my mind ran the gauntlet of what if's? All of them far worse than the last, all of them making my heart tighten.

Sasha shook her head. "Jesus, Emma. I'm a cop. We chase the bad guys."

"He could have shot you! You don't know what he had hidden in his sweatshirt. He could've easily led you into an alley and shot you before you knew what happened." I was bouncing in my seat, my anger on the verge of exploding. I leaned forward on my elbows, covering my face. I was drowning in the fear of losing Sasha again because of someone wanting us to back off this case. I'd lost her once because of a case, hell if I'd let it happen again.

"I'm okay, it's not a big deal. It's a few stitches." Her tone was slightly aloof, and it hit my raw edges.

I stood up quickly, stepping to stand right in front of her. "No Sasha! It is a big deal. I will not risk your life again! I will not allow you to go blindly into the dark chasing after a shadowy figure. I don't care if you're a federal agent, or the best damn cop this world has ever seen. I will not lose you! I cannot lose you again!" The words came out slow, shaky. "If you die again, I die with you." I quickly grabbed her hand, pushing it against my racing heart. "You are the only reason this still beats."

Every syllable was riddled with heartbreaking truth. If I lost her, I would lose myself in the dark hole I was crawling out of. She was the only reason I continued to fight my demons when they threatened to take over and devour what little light I had left inside my heart.

I watched as she swallowed hard, her eyes locking onto mine as they turned glassy. "Emma." She pressed her hand flat against my chest. "I..."

The doctors cheery hello broke the tension as he walked into the room, chattering away, flipping through Sasha's chart. He paused with a soft smile, looking between us. "Are you ready, Ms. Clarke? I think about ten stitches will close this up nicely."

I nodded at the doctor. "She is, yes. But please double check for any missed shards of glass."

Sasha's eyes never left mine as I stepped back, letting her hand fall away. Her fingers caught the ends of mine, squeezing them before I took another step back to allow the doctor to slide over on a rolling stool. I blinked back tears. "I mean it, Sasha." She nodded once, holding back her own tears.

I sat back down in the cold plastic chair, keeping my eyes on the floor, when my phone vibrated in my pocket. I pulled it out, Morgan's number flashing across the screen. I pointed at the phone as I stepped out of the room. Sasha sighed. "Please, tell her I'm okay."

"Morgan, what do you have for me?" I leaned against the wall just outside of Sasha's room, rubbing at the bridge of my nose. A hell of a headache was building. I needed a handful of Tylenol and a shot of whiskey.

Morgan blew right into it. "We got a unique shit salad on our hands, Captain. Aaron's still at your house with the techs, but we found your creepy firebomber, four blocks from the house. He had your address scribbled on a piece of paper with traces of accelerant on his hands." Morgan paused, sighing. "How's Sasha? Aaron told me her arm caught some glass." Morgan was doing her best to keep her nerves in check.

I leaned my head against the wall, staring at the

flickering fluorescent lights that gave everything a strange green aura. "Sasha's alright. We'll be going home in the next hour. She'll have a few new stitches and some antibiotics, but she's okay." I cleared my throat, changing the subject back to the arson suspect before I broke down. I was running on fumes, barely holding it together as the last few threads of adrenaline filed out of my veins.

    I swallowed down the thought of locking myself in a closet, crying until I ran out of air. "Are You taking the fire bug to the station for questioning?"

    "Oh, we aren't taking him anywhere but the morgue. We found your guy with two clean bullet holes to the forehead." Morgan lowered her voice. "This isn't good Emma. This has cartel all over it."

    I sighed hard and looked back in the room at Sasha. She was smiling as she chatted with the doctor. "We'll be at the FBI office as soon as Sasha is cleared. We need to debrief, and I need to look at whatever evidence you guys collected. Can you get an ID on the fire bug?"

    "Already on it, should take less than a half hour. fingerprints are still intact."

    "You're the best Morgan. I'll fill Sasha in on the way to her office. Have Aaron meet us when he's all done." I rubbed at my eyes. Exhaustion was creeping its way in with the pounding headache. I hung up with Morgan and walked to the window, folding my arms as I watched Sasha with the doctor.

    I wasn't lying when I told her she was the only reason my heart still beat. I made a silent promise right then, that no matter what happened in this case, I would keep her safe. Regardless if it cost me my own life.

Chapter 14

I waited until the doctor finished bandaging Sasha's arm before walking back into the room. I thought about how much hated hospitals as I stood in a corner, waiting for the nurse to leave the room. She'd slipped in like a ghost, white pharmacy bag filled with antibiotics in her hand. Chipper smile and pure efficiency.

I sighed, frowning, wishing she'd hurry up and leave. I hated the draining fluorescent lighting hospitals used, washing everything and everyone out. I hated the smell of hospitals. They always smelled like a bouquet of emotions in every strange odor that passed by. Death, rebirth, never-ending sickness.

Lastly, I hated the sensory memories standing in a hospital always thrust into my mind. Over the last year, I had spent my fair share of days in this sterile environment, and I wanted to leave as soon as possible.

I held the door open for the nurse as she pushed the small cart out, smiling as she went to the next room, on to the next broken person to repair. I glanced at Sasha as the door closed behind me, and saw how tired and sore she was in the way she held her bandaged arm, slumping ever so slightly in the middle of the bed. She straightened up when she heard the door close, and gave me a weak smile. "Hey, the doc says I'll be fine by the time the stitches need to come out. No lingering damage, just a nasty cut." She poked the bag next to her. "Antibiotics for the next two weeks and a follow up appointment with my doctor in three."

I nodded slowly, holding my hand out. She smiled and took it, pushing her weight on me as she slid off the paper covered gurney. Sasha looked up in my eyes for a second before letting go, reaching for her wallet and phone. "Did Morgan have anything to say?"

Leaning against the edge next to her, I watched her. She was tired, more tired than she wanted to show me. Her movements were slow, sluggish as she rubbed her eyes.

"They have the firebug, found him a few blocks from the house. Dead, and it looks like a professional kill. All of it looks a little too perfect for a random act of violence. Morgan and Aaron are collecting what evidence they can, then they'll meet us at your office for a debrief." I paused as Sasha turned to look at me, her brow furrowed as she processed what I just said.

"Dead?" She tucked her phone in her pocket, and tried to cross her arms, flinching when she hit a sore spot. "I chased him for at least two blocks before he took a hard left into an alley, where I lost him." Sasha rubbed her eyes again, letting the information sink in. She huffed, shaking her head. "Well, let's go to my office. I'll call Morgan on the way, see if she ran him."

"She's already on it. We should have his name by the time we get to the office." I pushed away from the edge and stood in front of Sasha, laying my hands on her upper arms. "Maybe we should take you home instead. You're still coming down from shock. I'd rather have you safe and warm, instead of chasing paper."

Sasha covered my hand, lightly patting it. "I'm fine. We need to chase the fresh leads. This case is getting shitty, and the faster we work, the less chance we have of falling in deeper." She swallowed hard.

When she looked in my eyes, her normally bright hazel eyes were dim, sad. I went to say something, anything to persuade her to go home with me and rest, when she gave me a tight smile. "I promise, I'm fine. We have work to do." Sasha pulled my hand from her arm, slipping her fingers in mine. "Rule twenty nine, never let a hot trail go cold."

I shook my head. "Unfair using my own rules against me."

Sasha winked. "All's fair in love and war." Her hand moved from mine to rest on my elbow. "Come, we have work to do, Captain."

She pulled me out of the room. I watched as she took a deep breath and put on the ever-present professional smile. It made me ache to take her home, take her away from this case and whatever we were spiraling into. I snaked an arm around her waist, pulling her closer to my side as we walked past the nurse's station. I looked up, grumbling at the sight of Agent Armstrong leaning over the desk, flirting with a pretty nurse.

Agent Armstrong straightened up when he heard Sasha call out his name in her stern agent voice. He barely made eye contact with me. I chuckled, it was clear he was still afraid of me.

He stuttered over his words. "Agent Clarke, Captain Tiernan. Agent Adams instructed me to pick you up and drive you to wherever you'd like."

I smiled, letting her walk in front of me to the desk. As she signed her release forms, she barely looked at the young agent. "We need to go back to my office. Take us there and then you're free for the evening." She set the pen down on the clipboard, looking at Armstrong. "Are Agent Adams and Detective Liang still working the scene?"

Armstrong nodded quickly as his eyes darted to bandage on her arm. I silently begged him to ask, act like the rude jerk I knew him to be. I needed to punch something, preferably him. "Agent Adams was finishing up when she called me, and Detective Liang is still working the first scene. I was told nothing else other than to come here immediately."

Sasha turned to me, her mouth curling into a small

smirk. "Ready?" I stepped towards her, placing my hand on the small of her back, feeling her instinctively press back into my hand.

"Let's go find out who our fire bug is."

*****

Thankfully, Armstrong kept his mouth shut during the ride to the office. He'd only glance at me in the rear view mirror, then look away just as quickly.

I finally let a smile creep across my face as we walked into the elevator at the FBI field office. "That kid is deathly afraid of us. I feel bad, maybe I should apologize for tearing him a new asshole."

Sasha laughed. "Don't. I like him fearful. He was burning holes in my arm, fidgeting and trying to hold back the millions questions I knew he wanted to ask." She closed her eyes with a sigh, slumping against the elevator walls.

I moved closer, laying a hand on her shoulder. "We can do this later."

Sasha kept her eyes closed as her hand covered mine. She said nothing until the elevator stopped. Her hand dropping away as she right herself, smoothed out her shirt, and walked out of the elevator. I followed her, running a hand through my sooty hair, determined to pick her up and take her home, when I heard Morgan's voice.

"Sasha! You better be okay, and you better not lie to me." Her voice was firm with worry.

I walked around the corner to see Sasha locked in a tight embrace, Morgan's small arms squeezing the life out of her. "I'm okay, and that's the truth. Emma witnessed the doctor stitch me up. You can ask her for verification of my semi clean bill of health."

Morgan glared at me as she let go of her death grip. "Is she okay?"

I nodded. "She's fine, but we need to get her to bed as soon as possible, she needs her rest."

Morgan winked at me. "Look at you, always grabbing at any opportunity to get my Sasha into bed."

I laughed at the joke, welcoming the break in tension. Morgan trotted past us as Sasha went to sit one of the vintage metal chairs. She was trying hard to not let on how tired she was, but I saw through it, and it worried me. Sasha never let anyone see any of her moments of weakness.

I walked towards Sasha, sitting on the desk behind her as Morgan fired up her computer. Three clicks and an image of the FBI seal was projected on the large white wall we faced. Morgan clicked again, and the seal was replaced with a mug shot of young Hispanic male, with short dark hair and tattoos on his neck and chest.

Morgan turned, angling herself between us and the mug shot. "Alejandro Arturro Alatano, also known as Triple A. Twenty three years old with a rap sheet longer than his age in length. It wasn't too hard to get an identification. As soon as his fingerprints hit the system, it lit up like Vegas at night and set off four different local and federal alerts. He has, had, ten different warrants out for his arrest." Morgan clicked again. Triple A was a well-known low level soldier for whatever gang or cartel would pay him. He's not tied to a major cartel at this time, just a freelance operator. He worked mainly on the south side, but would float through the entire city of Chicago. His talents were firebombs, arson, simple battery and carjacking. It was only recently did he start trying his hand at dealing at the street level. Dishing out dime bags, nickel bags of weed and meth."

A couple more clicks, and the crime scene photos darkened the wall. I could only look for a few seconds before I had to focus on something else in the room.

Triple A's eyes bored into mine, the two bullet holes in his forehead also staring at me.

The squeak of Sasha leaning forward in her old chair broke where my mind was heading.

"I've never seen anything like this, or heard of anything like this. A gun for hire wouldn't deliver a message in person like Triple A did, yelling at us from the sidewalk. Hired guns do the job quietly, and hope the crime delivers the intended message, or their employers follow up with another one. He boldly attacked us, and that is not his MO. He's hired for his discretion. He was a pawn, but in who's chess game?" She stood up and walked right to the image on the wall, pointing at the two perfect bullet holes in Triple A's forehead. "This is professional. Why would a gun for hire be of any interest to a professional? It seems like a waste of time. None of this makes sense. Are we looking at a drug cartel? Or not?" Sasha stared at the crime scene photo, trying to find anything. A clue, an answer.

"The big drug cartels of the eighties would do this all the time." A booming voice rang into the room, making all three of us spin around and face its owner.

A barrel chested older man came around the corner. His thick salt and pepper hair, edges sharp from a fresh buzz cut, and the pale blue button down with a tweed jacket, screamed law enforcement or car salesman, but in that moment, he was a stranger in a restricted office. I reached for my gun, cursing again that I had never bothered to grab mine from the house. I was getting sloppy.

The large man met my eyes, smiling at us. "I apologize for scaring you ladies." His deep Boston accent held onto every inch of every syllable he spoke as he dug into the pocket of his black slacks, quickly flashing a worn gold badge. "I didn't mean to interrupt the debriefing, but I got a call from my guy at your station, Captain Tiernan, about the situation at your home. Ten minutes later I'm getting emails from the FBI fingerprint unit that good ole Triple A finally met his match." He walked over to the photograph on the wall, lightly smiling at a still startled Sasha. The man rubbed at his chin, squinting at Triple A. "Yep, two shots in the forehead. Looks exactly as if two pennies were set side by side. Professional."

Turning to Morgan and I, he motioned to the mugshot. "This stinks to high hell of drug cartel. It's probably one of the old Colombian ones who've tried to rebuild their empire since DIY meth cooks began to kill the market. Triple A is the typical side casualty of a cartel bent on seeking out revenge. The big boys hire the little guy, pay him a hefty sum to entice them to do exactly as they ask and be bold about it. When the job is done, they eliminate the poor schmuck as fast as possible. They take the money back, leaving no witness who could be coerced into spilling the beans." The man paused as he put his hands on his hips. "Coffee? Anyone?"

Morgan spoke first, her hand firmly wrapped around her sidearm, ready to put two holes in this man. "Hi, I'm Agent Adams, that's Agent Clarke and apparently you already know Captain Tiernan. Pardon my manners, but who the hell are you? And how the hell did you get in here? This office is restricted."

The man threw a toothy grin at Morgan, walking over to her with an outstretched hand. "I apologize, my mother did raise me with manners. Agent Angus Duncan, DEA, but for the love of Mary, call me Gus."

He walked over to me, shaking my hand. "I know who each of you remarkable women are, especially you, Captain." Gus tightly squeezed my hand, then moved to stand next to Sasha. "As for how I got in here? My security clearance exceeds even your beloved SAC Reagan's." Gus grinned. "Now, about that coffee? Where can a man get a cup?"

Sasha pointed to the corner. "There's a coffee machine over there, but I don't think it's been turned on since the nineties." I noticed her hand clenched around the concealed holster under her shirt.

Gus clapped his hands. "Ah, perfect. I'll make us a fresh pot." He hustled to the machine, and as he busied himself digging in drawers for filters, Morgan shot me a look. I slid off the desk, sighing. "He's a friend of my father's." I waked over to Gus fiddling with dusty coffee filters as he filled the pot with a bottle of water.

"Excuse me, can I take a look at your badge again? I've been a little paranoid lately." A paranoia set in motion by another one of my father's old friends.

Gus laughed, handing me his badge. "Sure thing. Trust me, I'm legit." He hit the brew button on the coffee machine. "I headed over when I got the call from the FBI lab boys. You two ladies walked right past me as I chatted with the DEA liaison for this office. He was the one who escorted me down here."

I stared at the badge and the picture ID, handing it off to an extremely suspicious Morgan. Gus pulled a chair out and sat down. "I can understand why you gals would be a little wary, especially after meeting Triple A like you did." Gus leaned back in the squeaky chair, looking at the crime scene photos still lighting up the wall. "Triple A has a knack for first impressions." I watched as his eyes settled on Sasha's bandaged arm and took a breath, throwing an arm over the back of the chair. "Looks like what you have on your hands is a drug cartel doing their damnedest to get you to throw in the towel and abandon your case."

Morgan piped in, giving Gus a hard look. "If you want

to call almost burning Emma's house down a first impression. Why would a drug cartel want them to throw in the towel? They're working a thirty seven year old homicide cold case."

Gus pointed to Sasha. "Agent Clarke, in my briefcase over there, you'll find the files on Bellico and the evidence we processed from his murder scene. It looks like your homicide has drug ties."

Sasha walked to the soft leather case Gus dropped as he stared at Triple A's mugshot. "What do you mean Agent Duncan?"

"Gus, call me Gus. I'm far too old to give a shit about formalities." He pointed at the files in her hands. "Yeah, the file on the top."

Sasha pulled out a thick file from his case, handing me a chunk. Gus swiveled in the chair, the coffee machine bubbling to let him know it was done. He slapped his thighs in excitement. "Cups?"

Morgan huffed, shaking her head. "I'll go steal some from the cafeteria, leave you three to talk. I have to call Aaron and see where he's at. I also need to yell at a few receptionists for not announcing our guest here." Morgan gave Gus a hard look before muttering in Russian as she stomped towards the elevator.

Gus laughed harder as he dug around in the old desk drawers. "Ah! Here we go." He pulled out an old FBI ceramic mug, making both Sasha and cringe as he blew out, what I could only assume, was twenty years of dust. I shook my head as Sasha frowned at him. "Morgan will be back with clean cups."

Gus held up a hand, chuckling. "Little dust won't kill me." He filled the cup and took a huge sip of black coffee. "Perfect." He slumped back down in the chair, waving for us to continue reading. "When the fibbies and local deps finished processing most of the Bellico scene, they stumbled upon his basement lab. We got the call to process the lab, as is standard policy with drug labs. When we ran the chemical batch numbers, it traced back to a trail of meth we've been riding for the last five years. It's a weird new brand of methamphetamine. Synthetic, real low quality, but high powered stuff. It's popped up here and there around the country. It's starting to hit the south pretty hard over the last few months." Gus leaned forward in his chair. "Bellico was cooking meth, or it was set up to look like he was a cook. A full beginner's meth making lab sat in his basement, the chemicals were all there, it looked like he was making some extra retirement money producing tiny batches, tiny potent batches. My lab boys are dissecting the chemical structures, comparing it with what we found in the basement to the samples we've pulled off junkies."

    I read over the files. All of what Gus was saying was right there in my hands. Full color photographs of a lab in a basement. Bellico's basement. Sasha handed me her file, trading hers for mine. Her brow was furrowed in concentration. "Gus, these lab reports also hint at him trying to make synthetic cocaine." She glanced up at him.

    "Yep, synthetic cocaine is becoming popular lately. A lot of the bigger cooks out there, love using it as a component in anything they can. It's highly addictive, and cheap to make, generating repeat customers."

    I set the file down on the desk. "It looks like this case is pretty cut and dry. Agent Clarke and I can hand it off to you and return to our cold case. A homicide cold case." I was relieved and agitated. This case needed to be handed over. I wanted to go back to digging through dusty old files and police reports, not be the target of firebombs and packages filled with body parts.

Gus drained the rest of his coffee, spinning the empty cup in his hands. "As simple as that may seem, the powers that be, want you to stay on this case. At least for a little longer." He looked up at me. "I know it's the last thing you want to do, but it goes well above me and SAC Reagan." He stood, dropping the empty mug into his blazer pocket. "Monday morning be at the DEA office by nine. My boss wants to meet you and discuss what you saw at the Bellico scene, then collect statements from you. He may cut you loose after that." Gus shrugged, walking past Sasha and I, collecting his files. "In the meantime, watch your asses. Triple A might not be the last shitbag for hire you come across." He snapped his leather briefcase closed, saluting us. "Monday morning, nine a.m." Gus walked out of the room in the same silent way he came in.

Sasha looked over at me. "I know I've said this a million times, but what the hell is going on?" The exhaustion on her face had tripled in the few minutes Gus had arrived and bombarded us with information.

I moved to her, pulling her into a hug. Feeling her sigh as she wrapped her arms around my waist, holding me tight as if a hug was exactly what she needed.

"Sasha, I can't tell you that. I'm just as confused as you are. All I know is, I hope come Monday morning we can pass this off to the DEA and wash our hands, go back to deal with greasy retired cops and solve the Heaten case." I held onto her, resting my chin on the top of her head. "I have no idea why any of our bosses want to keep us on the case, it's a little odd. Unless there's a jurisdiction struggle." I let out a slow breath. More than anything I wanted to stop all case work and try to build a life with the woman in my arms. Take my father's advice as I saw the light at the end of the tunnel in her eyes.

Leaning back in Sasha's arms, I smiled, pressing my

palm against her cheek. "Can I finally take you home?"

"Yes, please." She leaned into my hand, closing her eyes. "Please take me home, Emma."

I held onto Sasha's hand as we grabbed a few things and walked to the elevator. The doors opened to reveal Morgan standing there with three coffee mugs in her hands.

She frowned when she saw us. "Don't tell me, you no longer need the coffee cups, and I missed the best parts of the story."

Sasha laughed as she threw an arm around Morgan. "I can use them at the apartment. I never bothered to buy coffee mugs." She then slid an arm around my waist. "Emma will fill you in on everything, including the best bits, as you drive us to my apartment. I think I'm going to lie down in the backseat and let you two talk. This has been a strange day." She sighed, leaning into Morgan's side.

Morgan groaned as she walked with us into the elevator. "I almost shot that old shamrock when he busted in through the door. I thought I had an accent. It's like the Wahlberg brothers live in his mouth." She shook her head as Sasha, and I, burst into laughter.

*****

Sasha passed out in the back seat of the car as we drove to her apartment. I filled in Morgan as best I could, giving her a quick rundown of everything she missed. I was overwhelmed with information and the exhaustion was setting in. I was losing the finer details of everything Gus dumped into our laps with every yawn that slipped out.

When we pulled up in front of Sasha's building, Aaron was sitting on the front steps. He hopped up as I opened the car door, hands on his hip, looking me over with a parental eye. "How are you? The agent?"

I gave him a tired smile. "I'm fine. Sasha is good, knocked out and asleep in the backseat."

Aaron bent down, peering into the back window. "Her arm?" He smiled at Morgan as she came around the back to open the back door as quietly as she could.

"It's good. She's good." I felt my voice shake a little, the emotions weaving their way back in. I jammed trembling hands in my pockets. "I feel bad about waking her up. She needs the sleep."

Aaron winked at me. "Not a problem." He motioned to Morgan to open the door slowly. He silently leaned into the backseat and pulled Sasha out, picking her up in his arms with a smile. "Get the door, I'll carry her upstairs." He moved so smoothly Sasha barely made a move other than to rest her head on his shoulder, still completely passed out.

I ran after him as I heard Morgan quietly swoon over Aaron's chivalry. I had to admit, it was a dashing sight to see Aaron carry Sasha, and for a moment, I was jealous I wasn't able to carry her.

Morgan and I swept the apartment while Aaron laid Sasha on the bed in her bedroom. I covered her up in a blanket and closed the door behind me. I found Aaron and Morgan standing at the front door, whispering, stopping the second they saw me. Aaron handed me the apartment keys. "Your house is secured. I have an undercover unit sitting on it until I say they can leave. The crime scene boys are done collecting evidence and I'll release the scene in a few hours. I have my cousin's recovery company coming out to clean up and replace the window. You'll be able to come home in a day." He looked at the bedroom door. "Both of you."

I grabbed him in a hug, sighing as I whispered. "Aaron, what would I do without you?"

He blushed when I let him go. "All that matters is you're safe." He cleared his throat. "If I hear anything or we get any leads on Triple A, you're my first call." He nodded and glanced at Morgan. "This little lady has offered to let me sleep on her couch until the house is back in order." Morgan's eyes widen, shrugging as she turned to busy herself with rearranging her purse.

Aaron chuckled, slugging my shoulder. "If you need us, we're two floors above you. This entire building is government apartments filled with agents." He waggled his eyebrows in the goofy way that was typical Aaron.

I slugged him back, grinning. "You two get some rest. It's been a late night for all of us."

Aaron nodded in agreement, motioning to Morgan as he opened the door. Morgan hugged me again, telling me to keep an eye on Sasha and take care of her. Aaron smiled, and as Morgan walked out the front door, he paused. "I don't know what I would do without you either, Emma." He dug under his coat, setting my gun on the small kitchen island. "Stop leaving this where you can't get it." He smiled tightly and holding my gaze a moment longer.

I swallowed hard, whispering. "Thank you."

Aaron nodded and left the apartment, clicking the door shut.

I double checked the locks, and windows, then took slow steps around the apartment, stopping in the middle of the living room. Sasha's apartment was stale, bland, with very little decoration. She had furniture, nice furniture but there was no life to any of it.

I'd never been to her apartment since she came back to Chicago. She'd shown up at my house and never left, and I never wanted her to. Now I wanted her there even more, she needed to live somewhere she could thrive in. Not a stale concrete boxed provided by the FBI.

I grabbed a water bottle from the fridge and went to the bedroom to check on her. She was curled up in a ball in the middle of the bed. I watched her sleep for a few minutes, thinking and digesting the last few hours.

Sasha was my world. She was truly my everything, and what I said to her in the hospital was not born out of adrenaline and frayed emotions, it was the hard truths I had to face. We were truly partners in every definition of the word.

Sasha rolled over, groaning slightly as she bumped her arm. She was flushed and beginning to sweat as the day caught up with her.

I sat down on the edge of the bed, running the back of my hand across the warm skin of her forehead. "Sasha, wake up. We have to get you out these clothes, and you need to drink some water." Her body was beginning to react to the antibiotics and overheat.

She sat up with a soft smile, blinking a few times. "How come you never ask me that when I'm healthy and ready to fool around?" She took the water, taking slow sips.

"Because the only time you wanted to fool around was at my parent's house, and if I remember, the desk in my office has seen the best parts of you a few times." I pressed a hand against her forehead, no fever. "Let's get you into some pajamas." I stood up, taking her hand.

She set the water down, looking around

her room, confused. "Wait, how did I get into bed? Last thing I remember, I laid to down in the backseat to keep myself from throwing up. Morgan still drives like she's running from the cops."

"A very handsome, dashing man carried you to bed." I helped her to her feet, holding her arms to steady her.

"I'll have to thank Aaron in the morning." Sasha moved past me and started opening drawers. "The closet over there has extra clothes, take what you want." She smiled as she faced me. "I want to take a quick shower then sleep until Monday."

"As you wish, my love." I said it softly, bringing a bigger grin to her face.

Sasha kept her smile as she disappeared into the bathroom. I changed into one of her Chicago Blackhawks t-shirts, and a pair of linen shorts that hung off me. I was falling asleep as soon as I crawled into the bed, barely hearing Sasha come out of the bathroom, rubbing a towel through her hair.

The room filled with a strange quiet I wasn't used to. I laid in the bed, facing Sasha as she dropped the towel on a chair, pulling back the blankets on her side of the bed. When she was under the covers, she slid in as close as she could next to me, her arms taking their usual place around my waist. Neither of us said anything as we both quit the fight with exhaustion, letting sleep take over.

*****

I woke up startled, unsure if it was a dream or a nightmare that pulled me from the depths of sleep. I was sweating, my heart racing, as I rolled over to find Sasha. My hands slid across the mattress only to find the space next to me empty and cold. I sat up, the room was empty.

My heart crawled up my throat as I hopped out of bed, bending over to my jeans to pull my gun out of the back pocket. I held it tightly while I stood in the darkness, listening for anything that would push my instincts in one way or another.

Opening the bedroom door slowly, I saw a small light coming from the far corner of the living room, right where the bookshelf was pushed against a wall next to a large window. I crept into the room, my gun at the ready.

Sasha was sitting in the high back chair near the window, curled up in a ball with her legs tucked under her chin. She was staring out the window, the curtain pulled back just enough to let the late morning light fall across the floor in slivers. I set the gun down on the bookshelf that was closest to the kitchen as I walked over to her. "Sasha, come back to bed."

She never took her eyes off the window. "I couldn't sleep."

I sat on the edge of the coffee table in front of the chair, Sasha turned to me. She smiled as she saw what I was wearing. "Blackhawks shirt? Isn't that blasphemy for a Red Wings fan?"

I smirked. "It is, yes, don't tell anyone." I leaned forward finding her hand with mine. "Are you okay?"

Her smiled faded. "I want to lie and say, yes, I'm okay, but I'm too tired, Emma." She turned her gaze back out the window, her hand covering mine as it sat on the armrest. She slowly ran her thumb over my knuckles. "I remember the first night I sat with you after Evan shot you. I sat like this in a chair, holding your hand and staring out the window. Watching the world carry on with their day as usual, while I sat praying you would be okay. Hoping my world would wake up, look at me, and smile." Sasha leaned her head against the back of the chair. "I was so angry after you called about my transfer out of your unit, I actually gave up on you. I gave up on an idea of ever there being an us. The anger overwhelmed the love I felt for you."

Her eyes moved from the window to look in mine, glassy with unshed tears. "Then I saw you in that hospital bed, barely fighting for life. Your body was so tired from what he did to you. I was tired, worn down but spent every night by your side, afraid of what morning could bring and if I'd ever get to tell you how much I love you." She paused, blinking the tears free, allowing them to find a path down her cheeks.

Her own bad memories clouded over her eyes. "You are the reason this still beats." Sasha held a shaky hand against her heart. "I hold everything in for you. I suffer through the bad nights and the fears I have, for you. Because you need me, and I need you. I made a promise that night I would be strong for you, be the one to break down the walls and hold you up, no matter what."

She let out a soft sob, so soft I had to clench my jaw to hold mine at bay. I had to let Sasha talk, say what she needed to in this moment. She'd kept it bottled up for so long, I was surprised it was trickling out, rather than exploding out with heavy sobs.

Sasha sniffled, wiping her cheeks. "I hate waking up alone. Even though I know you're distracting yourself with work to chase away the nightmares. When I wake up from a bad dream or a bad memory I haven't dealt with yet, I wake up alone and I panic. I panic because just the simple sight of your side of the bed empty... it scares me."

Sasha squeezed her eyes shut. "I can't lose you, Emma. To the past or to your fears." She let out a choked breath, opening her eyes to find me. "I need you here, with me. Because I'm scared, I'm tired, and all I want is to wake up and have you next to me." Sasha smiled weakly, sobs slipping out. "I'm so tired."

I held onto her hand as I sprang up, pulling Sasha up out of the chair and into my arms. Letting her completely fall apart, letting her be the tired one. "Let it out, I've got you." I felt the tears track down my own face, but held her tight as she sobbed harder as her hands clutched at my back, desperate to pull me closer.

After a few minutes, her breathing evened out, but her grip on me, remained strong. I dropped my arms, and lifted her up, just like Aaron had earlier. She said nothing, just buried her head into my shoulder, her hand clutching to my neck, as I carried her back to the bedroom. My heart broke at how light she was, realizing how much she was sacrificing to be the strong one in this partnership, this relationship.

I set Sasha down on the bed and crawled in after her, pulling her close. Her arms resumed their strong hold and I held her like I should have every night she was in my bed. I ran a hand through her hair whispering. "You'll never be alone again, I promise you."

I held her until she fell asleep in my arms. Never once letting go.

CHAPTER 15

The muffled sounds of the Miami Vice theme woke me up. I didn't move, not wanting to wake Sasha up as she pressed against my side, sharing my pillow. I stretched my arm out over the edge of the bed, moving only a few inches so my fingertips could snag the belt loop of my jeans. I pulled the jeans closer and dipped my hand into the front pocket for my phone. Hitting ignore, I silenced the catchy eighties theme before it grew louder. I squinted at the screen, my fingers moving fast as I typed out a text.

Aaron, I told you to stop changing my ring tones.

Hey at least you always know it's me.

I laid my hand on Sasha's back, checking to see if she was still warm from the meds. She stirred slightly under my touch, sighing hard, smushing herself deeper into the pillow. I kept my hand on her, glad I didn't answer the phone. She needed to sleep after the last couple days of high emotions and adrenaline.

You woke me up. You almost woke up Sasha.

I was tired and very much enjoying lying in bed with Sasha. We had the day off before we were due at the DEA office the next morning. I had plans of staying in bed with her and not moving until life came to pull us back into reality. My phone buzzed with Aaron's reply.

I feel bad, you never sleep past five, I'll make this quick. My cousin will have the house back in shape by tonight. You'll have to pick out a new couch and a new coffee table, the old ones are toast. But the keys will be in my hand by bedtime.

I smiled. Finally, something good was happening, however small it was, I'd take it.

Perfect, it will be good to go home.

I looked over at Sasha, still sleeping. She looked at peace, it was a rare sight to these days, and I wanted to memorize it. I set my phone to silent, placing it on the side table. I rolled over to pull the covers over us, when Sasha felt me shift and opened her eyes, smiling as she adjusted her pillow. "Hi." Her voice was the soft raspy one she had from the nights she slept the hardest.

"Hey, how are you feeling?" My fingers moved on their own, brushing away the stray hairs that escaped her loose ponytail.

Sasha moved her arm out from underneath the pillow, yawning a smile out as she moved a little closer to my side. "Ok? I feel really groggy. I think it's from the painkillers the nurse begged me to take." She gingerly moved her arm, reaching for me when her eyes fell to the bandage. "Shit, I'm leaking." She sat up quickly, holding her arm up trying not to touch me or anything else as she frantically looked to see if she stained the bed. I saw her arm had seeped blood through the thin gauze.

Sasha threw back the covers, padding to the bathroom. I was two steps behind her. "Let me."

She waved me off and kept pulling at the gauze, trying to find an edge to unravel it. I had to cover her hand with mine to get her to stop, pulling her chin up to look at me. "Sasha. Let me." She nodded slowly, still tired, still hazy. I patted the stone grey marble sink counter. "Hop up here, it'll give me better light."

I dug around in the cabinets, pushing past toilet paper and a basket full of sample sized hotel soaps. The basket was crammed full of tiny, perfectly packaged soaps in all sorts of shapes. I held one in my hand shaped like a turtle, about to make a joke about how much she loved soap when she whispered.

"Kitchen. Cabinet next to the stove. I have a full med bag I borrowed from Metro. I kind of forgot to give it back to them."

I stood up from the cabinet. "You forgot?" I blinked at her a few times, curious about this sudden confession of theft.

Sasha smiled, resting her head against the mirror. "You freed an entire biology class worth of frogs. I stole a med bag. Guess we're both criminals."

I laughed. "Guess so." I pointed at her. "Don't move and stop picking at it."

Sasha held up both of her hands in mock surrender as I went to the kitchen. I found the massive dark blue med bag tucked next to cleaning supplies. It was heavy, and when I opened it up next to Sasha in the bathroom, I found it to be completely stocked.

I shot her another look as I dug out rolls of gauze and a pair of gloves. I waved for her to give me her arm, moving to stand closer to her. I unwrapped the dirty gauze, noticing her flinch when I press too close to the stitches. "I'm sure we can call and get you some more painkillers."

"No, I'm fine. I hate feeling like I could slip into a coma for days. I want to try and enjoy the day." I saw her look at me out of the corner of my eye. "With you."

I tossed the dirty gauze to the side, taking a closer look at the stitches. Everything was on its way to healing as it should, no signs of infection or pulled stitches. I had to look away from her arm after a few seconds, my stomach twisting with that forever underlying fear.

I wondered where the sudden inability to look at

blood and injuries like I once did, came from, but I just couldn't look at the gore and remain detached and scientific. It was something that worried me, knowing there was more behind it than just losing my taste for this kind of work. I dabbed at the edges, wiping away the little bit of blood leaking out. "How do you feel about Sunday brunch?" I glanced up. "Aaron told me about a bar by the pier that has a fantastic bloody Mary bar."

Sasha smirked. "That sounds amazing, Emma." She knew I was following through on a promise I made in Virginia while interviewing Exeter.

I spoke while wrapping her arm. "You can shower first, I'll make the coffee. Hopefully, you've used your coffee machine in this decade and there isn't thirty years of dust in it." I secured the gauze edges with tape, stripped off the gloves and dropped them into the trash can. I then moved to stand in front of Sasha, sliding my hands to her waist as she instinctively held onto my shoulders, squeezing them as I lifted her off the counter.

When she was back on solid ground, Sasha slid her hands to my back, pulling us together. I felt her heartbeat against my chest, grounding me. "Thank you, Emma." It was soft but held more weight than a thousand words.

"You're welcome."

Sasha stepped out of my arms, examining her new bandage. "Nice work doctor, but how do I keep it dry?"

I winked at her as I handed over the plastic wrap I also pulled from the cabinet. "With this. Cover your arm in it and you will be waterproof."

Sasha chuckled, taking the box. "You really are a Boy Scout."

"I was a Girl Scout. They wouldn't let me join the Boy Scouts." I smirked, kissing her on the cheek. "Hit the showers, kid, I'll have hot coffee waiting for you."

Sasha kissed me back. "Aye, Aye, Captain." She turned her back to me, starting the shower while I packed up the med bag. I hesitated when I saw Sasha pull off her shirt, revealing smooth skin and the toned muscles. My heart begged me to reach out and run my fingers over every inch. I took a steadying breath, leaving Sasha to her hot shower.

It wasn't right to hop in the shower with her. It didn't feel right when I saw how tired she was, how emotionally drained she was, and how sore her body was from me throwing her to the ground. I silently hoped tomorrow morning the DEA would graciously take this case off our hands and I could convince Sasha to slow down on the cold case.

Tucking the med bag back into the cabinet, I set on the task of finding coffee and figuring out how to use the extremely fancy coffee maker she had. Mine at home was simple. Insert filter, insert coffee, hit brew.

I found a single serve package of coffee in a drawer with a filter, but now stared at the coffee maker as if it was an advanced biochemistry equation. But unlike an equation, I had no idea where to start.

When I opened the top and determined that was where I should start with a filter, I heard a soft whisper of paper gliding across the wood floor by the front door. I glanced and saw a white piece of paper settle its glide a few feet away from me. On the front in black ink was the word *Captain.*

I stopped everything, listening past the muted sounds of Sasha in the shower. I couldn't pick up the sounds of footsteps walking in any direction past the front door. I saw no shadows break the stream of light drifting under the door.

Bending down, I picked up the thin white sheet,

checking again to see if someone was waiting on the other side through the peephole as I stood up.

Suspicion flooded through my body as I flipped the page open.

Emma. Meet me outside in the park across the street. Sit on the third bench facing the small pond. Don't bring Sasha. We need to talk about the drugs.
Reagan.

I held the sheet of paper in my fingers. I'd recognized Reagan's handwriting from the case files I read with her notes and signature. I chewed my bottom lip, thinking. Nothing about Reagan tipped me off to be suspicious. She was more of a blatant deception type of gal, not one to throw me a line and trap me in the shadows. All the times she deceived me, it wasn't from setting up a hole for me to fall in. She simply left out the information I hadn't asked for. My gut also told me it had to be important if Reagan was going the note slipped under the door route.

I headed back to the bedroom, pulling on jeans and double checking my gun was loaded. I knocked on the bathroom door. "Sasha, you're out of coffee. I'm going to run down to the shop at the corner. You want anything else?"

Sasha mumbled through the running water she wanted a couple of those silly pumpkin muffins. I told her I would be back in a few, walked past the kitchen and grabbed the single serve packet of coffee. Jamming it deep into the trash as I ran out the door.

*****

I was on edge walking into the park. Even though the park was filled with families walking together, building snowmen and embracing the minimal amount of fun winter offered, I was wary of why I was summoned here. I pulled the hood up on my sweatshirt, finding the third bench facing the frozen pond dotted with hockey players giving it their best. I sat down on the empty bench, clutching onto the grip of my gun hidden in the front pocket of my Red Wings hoody. I kept alert, watching the hockey players, envying the ease they had on the ice. The hard snap of a slap shot being fired off, took my attention for a split second, and I barely noticed when the bench shifted with the weight of someone taking a seat next to me.

Before I could look to my right, they spoke.

"You can relax. I can see you gripping onto your gun. Never mind the fact you're so tense, you're not paying attention to your surroundings. I've been standing next to the bench for the last three minutes." Reagan's voice was just loud enough that only I could hear it. I turned to look at her, a permanent scowl on my face. I really hated this woman.

Reagan was bundled up, looking nothing like the stoic and pretentious federal agent I'd always dealt with. Her hair was tucked up underneath a Chicago Cubs hat with a large scarf draped around her neck, covering most of her face. The sunglasses she wore covered the sides not allowing anyone to see which way she was looking. She looked completely different, and if I hadn't met her numerous times before, I wouldn't have recognized her.

"I didn't notice you, because I was looking for a harpy in an over starched pantsuit." I smirked at the cocked eyebrow Reagan gave me. "Secret notes slipped under my girlfriend's door breeds cautionary steps, hence the gun." I leaned back into the wooden slats of the bench. "Why not a phone call, email, or just barge into the apartment like you do my office?" My voice was hard, tinged with the ever present irritation this woman caused.

Reagan smiled in amusement. "That's why I like you, Emma, ballsy and bold." She tilted her head in my direction. "Did you tell Sasha where you were going?"

I shook my head, cringing at her use of Sasha's first name, it felt far too personal for my taste. "Not yet. I'm doing my best to protect her as this cold case becomes fresh homicides and digging in the bowels of drug cartels."

I turned back to the hockey players. "Aren't you going to be at the meeting tomorrow, SAC Reagan?" I was getting more irritated as the cold air bit deeper, soaking into the thin material of the old sweatshirt.

Reagan set a white bakery bag down in the space between us. "In that bag is an interesting autopsy report from Fairfax County Medical Examiner's office. You won't have to bother finding Captain John Walker. He's currently lying in a steel cooler after a mysterious accident at his house. An accident that left him bleeding out in his garage with his ears missing." Reagan sipped at the coffee in her hand. "The collected statements will be of key interest to you and Agent Clarke."

I went to dig in the bag when Reagan shook her head. "Not now, Emma. Wait until you get back inside. I'm not here in an official capacity. I'm here because this case has a thick slime on it and tomorrow the DEA will try to pull it from our hands. The FBI will allow it, since the drug evidence trumps our murder investigations."

Reagan crossed her legs, casually looking around the park and the bustling activity. "I don't like where it's headed and the jackass you will meet tomorrow, I like even less. Patrick Ellis and I go way back, back to my days in the NSA and I was trying to get him to work with us to assist in the investigation of a Columbian terrorist threatening our ports. Ellis thought his DEA investigation took precedence over the safety of thousands of Americans. Ellis was always of the mind frame law enforcement was basically his way of playing big boy cowboys and terrorists. No tact and selfish." Reagan paused when a family of four walked by us, giggling and smiling. "He irritated the fuck out of me. Still does."

"NSA?" I knew my mouth was open in shock. Reagan had more layers than an onion.

Reagan nodded with a smirk, holding the coffee cup in both her hands. "There's a lot you don't know about me, and it will stay that way." Reagan pulled her sunglasses off, looking at me. "There's also an old blood analysis report from Angela Heaten's murder. It's ancient, may not have much to offer, but it's more than you had, and more than Latham was able to hide under old comic books." She paused again when a man smiled at my Red Wings sweatshirt, jokingly hollering. "*Go Blackhawks!*"

Reagan smiled back at the man, picking up where she left off. "My contact who got me the copy of the autopsy report, which was completely altered, found the analysis report in Walker's basement." Reagan folded her sunglasses up and tucked them into her pocket, standing up. "I can't touch this case. I can't be involved with it as the FBI is being redirected to assisting in hand off of the information you and Agent Clarke gathered at the Bellico scene."

Reagan paused. "But you can, Emma. This is a cover up. I can spot it from miles away because that's all I did in the NSA. Cover up the things better left in the dark corners of life, all in the name of protecting guilty in the name of protecting the innocent." She raised an eyebrow. "The credo of all government black operation efforts."

Reagan took a step away, when I huffed at her. "Why are you doing this? We don't exactly have the best working relationship."

Reagan paused, her infamous pretentious smile appeared, the one that irritated the fuck out of me. She shrugged, watching the hockey players. "Because, you fight for the truth where others ignore it. You're still uncorrupted and want to do the right thing. My gut tells me the truth was covered up over thirty years ago and it's clear more lies will be brushed under the rug to protect whatever shitstorm you and Agent Clarke have started." Reagan tilted her head towards the sun, taking a deep breath. "I'll see you in the morning, Captain. Oh, and when we see each other, don't acknowledge me in any polite manner. Let's try to stick to our usual course of heavy distaste for one another." Reagan tipped her coffee cup at the bag. "Enjoy the doughnuts." She turned and walked away, meshing into the small crowd of people milling through the park.

I relaxed the death grip on my gun, pulling my sweaty hand out of the pocket. I took a deep breath, letting out slowly before I grabbed the white bag and calmly walked out of the park.

I left the park without looking back and walked to the corner coffee shop. Standing in line I noticed nothing out the ordinary, no one following me. I began to relax a little as I gave the simple coffee order to the exasperated barista behind the counter, almost forgetting Sasha's muffins, I was so lost in thought.

It took me a minute to get through my head that if Reagan was once NSA, she knew the spy game. She knew how to get in and get out without drawing attention to what she was doing. I smiled to myself, picking up the coffees and the brown paper bag of muffins.

Reagan was a spy.

What an intriguing thought, one that made perfect sense why she was such a stone cold bitch with a dead heart.

*****

Sasha was dressed, sitting at the kitchen table when I returned to the apartment. I handed her the brown bag of muffins with her cup of coffee. "You know those muffins are nothing but sugar?"

Sasha nodded, unwrapping the muffin. "I know, but they're my favorite and only available during the holidays. I like to eat them until I want to throw up, then wait a year to repeat the cycle." She smiled, taking a huge bite.

I bent over, kissing the corner of her very full mouth. "You're a little goofy sometimes, you know that?"

Sasha shrugged. "Will it stop you from loving me? My muffin binging?"

"Never." I set my coffee down. "I'll be right back, I want to take a hot shower. It's freezing out there." I took two steps before turning to her. "Aaron called this morning, we can go home tonight. The house is ready."

"I'm ready to go back to our house." She grinned at the words, our house. "I told him to stop breaking into your phone, and you should probably change your password. He knows you better than you think." She paused and giggled. "SASHA1? I'm flattered."

My face turned a bright red making Sasha laugh harder. I grumbled under my breath Aaron would be kicked out of the house by morning.

When I was back in the bedroom, I pulled the white bag and my gun out of the sweatshirt pocket. I opened the bag and saw the thick stack of neatly folded paper wrapped in the tissue the bakery uses as a barrier between dirty hands and your doughnuts. I caught glimpses of the seal from the medical examiner's office and in the middle was yellowed, ancient sheets of paper.

I furrowed my brow and closed the bag, rolling it up in a dirty t-shirt. I wanted to read the files and the report, right then and there. But at the same time, I wanted to keep Sasha in the dark until after the meeting tomorrow. That way if Reagan was trying to be tricky, I could at least protect Sasha. I stuffed the rolled up shirt into my bag and headed to the shower.

I also wanted the day to be untainted by case work, just bloody Mary's and fancy omelets were in my near future.

*****

After a day of consuming bloody Mary's, eggs every which way we could imagine while sitting staring at the lake, Sasha and I went home. We talked about random things, enjoying the quiet company of each other. No badges, no guns, no Aaron. Just her and I starting a new tradition as promised.

At the house, our house, Sasha ran upstairs to drop off our things while I walked the living room, surveying the repairs. Aaron's cousin had done a remarkable job in a short time frame. He had installed bulletproof glass at the request of Aaron and repaired everything back to its original state. The living room was empty aside from my favorite leather chair and the bookshelves lining the far wall. The giant couch I loved and the old wooden table I hated where the only casualties of the firebombing. I was secretly glad the table had taken the fall. I'd hated it from day one even though it was Elle's favorite.

I folded my arms and stared at the empty spot it

once occupied, maybe it was a sign. A rebirth of many to come. Sasha and I could find a table we both liked. Together.

I sighed and shook my head. Why was I thinking such domestic thoughts in that moment? What had become of me? Was I finally loosening up to the idea of having the life I wanted, lost and never wanted again, until her?

"What are you thinking?" Sasha's arms came around my waist, her chin settling on my shoulder.

I laid my hands over hers against my stomach. "I'm thinking its time you move out of that concrete box you call an apartment and move back in." I turned in her arms. "I mean, I do need a new couch and a new table, you have both of those and they're really nice. Really, really nice."

She cocked her head to the side. "You're asking me to move in with you just for my furniture?"

I shrugged. "Maybe. What are your detective instincts telling you?"

Sasha squinted. "Hmm, they're telling me a private interrogation may be in order, upstairs."

"Oh really." I pulled Sasha closer, my lips hovering over hers, our breaths mingling. I could feel her suck in a slight breath, waiting for me to close the gap.

We both turned to the front door as Aaron pushed it open, bellowing. "Hey Emma! Look! I even got the deadbolt fixed!" He hustled over, holding a hand up in the air like a game show host. "You guys like what Kenny did?" Aaron walked around the living room, hands on hips, admiring his cousins work. It amazed me that one minute he could be a dashing hero, then an intense brilliant detective, and then slip so easily into the most annoying little brother anyone could have.

Leaning my forehead against Sasha's, I sighed.
"Forever interrupted."

"It's our curse." Sasha laid a soft kiss on the corner of my mouth, peeling out my arms as Aaron barraged her with twenty questions about her arm.

I took the opportunity and ran upstairs, grabbing the white bag from my dirty laundry and locking it up in the bottom drawer of my office desk. I stared at the desk, my eyes falling to the badges sitting next to my computer. One day we would have our unbroken moments.

"Emma! I talked Sasha into watching the game down at O'Malley's. You're coming with us and you're the DD."

I groaned, turning to go back downstairs, hearing the two people I loved more than anything in this world, giggle like two little kids.

CHAPTER 16

Sitting in the cold, grey reception area of the DEA field office, anxiety was the one feeling that kept surging past my attempts at remaining calm and cool. I couldn't stop smoothing out the dress shirt I wore. So much so, Sasha had to squeeze my thigh to get me to relax. It was Monday morning and she was back in agent mode, but she as anxious as I was. We'd arrived fifteen minutes early and was escorted to sit in the cold, lumpy plastic chairs the government favored.

I went to stand up to walk off the building irritation when Gus came around the corner, big smile on his face. "Ladies! Welcome, follow me and we'll get this started."

I turned to pick up my briefcase, looking at Sasha. She smiled tightly and nodded at me, standing up and smoothing out her grey and blue pinstriped business suit. I wanted to take her hand as we followed Gus, but then remembered where we were and that I was hiding something from her, and it wasn't doughnuts.

Gus escorted us to a side conference room, similar to the one I sat in as Operation Eclipse was unraveled to me. The table was huge and unnecessary for the five people already occupying the room. Reagan sat off to the far end near the window, making notes on the notepad in front of her. A few seats down from her sat an older man, I guessed to be around Gus's age, maybe a few years younger. He sat perfectly still and oozed politics and law enforcement.

He wore a perfectly tailored navy blue suit, his hair was cut with precision, highlighting the best parts of his salt and pepper hair, and when he turned to look at Sasha and I, his perfect brown eyes smiled when he stood up to greet us. He was politician handsome. The worst kind of handsome in my book.

I had an instant distaste for him.

Gus stood off to the side making introductions. "Captain Emma Tiernan, Agent Natasha Clarke, allow me to introduce Deputy Administrator Patrick Ellis."

The man held out his hand and when I took it, he grinned. "Ah, the infamous Emma Tiernan. It *is* a pleasure and an honor to meet such a remarkable fellow law enforcement officer." I kept my smile tight. His handshake was a little too firm. It felt like he was trying far too hard to impress me. Ellis then introduced himself to Sasha, motioning towards the empty seats. "Please take a seat and we'll get to the debriefing. You both obviously know SAC Dana Reagan from the FBI."

Reagan looked up from her notes, giving Sasha a genuine smile. "Agent Clarke, always good to see you." Reagan glanced my way, her smile fading to the usual tolerant one she reserved just for me. "Captain Tiernan."

I pulled Sasha's chair out for her before I took my seat, clenching my jaw when Ellis started to speak before sitting in a plush leather conference chair. "From what Gus has told me, you ladies have done an outstanding bit of investigation work. I know I personally appreciate the headway you've made with the Bellico case. It's opened up so many doors for us."

Sasha spoke first. "Thank you, sir. I'll admit, it was something we definitely stumbled across, but we're happy to provide any leads we have, and will continue to come across."

Ellis grinned a full set of pearly white, baby kissing, teeth. "I appreciate the tone of teamwork in your voice. It's rare to find agents who are willing to share information with another agency." Ellis shot a look at Reagan, and I watched her tense up. "But, Agent Clarke, jurisdictions do get in the way. I called this meeting with the two of you and your direct supervisor, to inform you the DEA will be taking full control of the Bellico case. From now on, all we will need from you, is your assistance in tying up the informational loose ends of the case when you *stumbled* across the Bellico scene." Ellis' tone was beginning to get patronizing, I immediately understood why Reagan hated the man.

Ellis tugged at his sleeves, his fingers rubbing his cuff links in a manner that brought attention to the fact he was wearing very expensive designer cuff links. He was flashy, and I was drawn to the flash. I focused on it, my instincts kicking in.

No cop, agent, or lawman in general who was worth his weight, was this flashy. Ellis was trying to make up for something, or wanted to silently broadcast his success. It was unusual, and the profiler in me kicked in gear. I watched Ellis in a way he'd never notice I was watching him. I remained alert, but silent as he pulled the case from us.

Sasha, on the other hand, was pissed. She looked at me before turning back to Ellis, her eyes wide with shock. "Excuse me, sir? This is technically the FBI's case. I was the first agent on scene and the evidence both I, and Captain Tiernan, have received over the last few weeks, ties into the original cold case we were assigned. The one we've been diligently investigating." Sasha straightened up in her seat, her temper idling through her voice. "I politely request Captain Tiernan and I stay on the Bellico case. We have more leads to investigate and interviews to conduct."

Ellis held his smarmy smile. "And you've also become targets of whichever cartel you've upset." He pointed at Gus. "Agent Duncan has filled me in on the Triple A murder. I can tell the both of you, it's clearly a drug cartel hunting you down, searching out your permanent silence. That alone, begs you to be removed from the case. For your safety, of course."

　　Ellis stood up from his chair, walking closer to Reagan. "I have already spoken with SAC Reagan and she's in agreement. More so her bosses are in agreement, that due to the overwhelming nature, the drug related evidence, the Bellico case should be turned over to DEA, effective immediately. We are now the lead investigating agency on this case."

　　Reagan's jaw clenched so tight, I thought it would snap right in front of us. I watched Ellis as Reagan cleared her throat. There was something about him that bothered me more than just his shiny hair and perfect suit.

　　He gave me a crooked vibe, the same vibe I got from Exeter but worse. He had that same greasy look in his eyes, but it felt more determined, more directed, even as Ellis glanced my way with a kind smile.

　　Reagan leaned back in her chair. "Unfortunately, Deputy Administrator Ellis is correct. The Section Chief over the BSU has decided chasing drug manufacturers is better left to the DEA and the vast resources they have. You, and Captain Tiernan, will assist for however long it takes to transfer all drug related information and statements taken in this case, to the liaison, Director Ellis assigns to you. Then you will return to the cold cases you have on your desk."

　　Reagan paused for a moment, tapping her pen on the tabletop. "I also have to request, Captain Tiernan, that whatever information Detective Liang collects on the firebombing incident at your house and the Triple A murder, is turned over to the DEA." Reagan met my eyes. "However long that may take. I understand arson incidents can be tricky to tie up." She held my gaze for a moment.

　　I understood exactly what she was telling me with that stone cold stare.

　　Sasha huffed, shaking her head as she glared at

Reagan. "I'm sorry, but I don't understand, ma'am. This is our case. I want to see it through to the end. For God's sake, body parts were sent to us and you expect me to hand it off to the DEA like nothing happened? Drop a case like nothing into the hands of an agency who will give two shits about the murder and only focus on chasing chemicals?"

I knew Sasha was pissed off, pissed off enough to let her professional face slip away and into the former Chicago street cop who never played politics. Normally I'd also be in Elli's face, calling him a piece of shit, but I already knew how this was going to play out, thanks to Reagan. I wanted to maintain the upper hand and let us walk out of this meeting like wet dogs, beaten down and looking for cover.

Sasha threw me another hard look. Her anger cascading my way for not standing up next to her, and fighting for a case that already cost us more than we both wanted to admit.

Sasha looked back at Ellis. "I thought the DEA prided itself on professionalism, and as I recall from an email that just fell in my inbox from you, Deputy Administrator Ellis, the DEA's mission is to be an open door asset to all its brother and sister agencies. Hmm, seems someone is upset the FBI has the good toys to play with and now wants to take them away." Sasha was on a roll, her flush face showing she was a few breaths away from a complete blow out.

Reagan looked down at her notepad, trying to hide the gentle smirk as Ellis spoke as firmly and politely as he could, even thought it was evident Sasha talking back got under his skin. I watched as his eyes focused on the wall past Sasha. A calming technique my therapist taught me months ago.

"SAC Reagan has been given her orders, and now,

Agent Clarke, you've received yours." He walked closer to Sasha. "I suggest you follow them."

Something in his tone hit me funny and I looked at the man. The politicians sparkle in Ellis's eyes shifted to something dark, something I'd seen in the numerous criminals I'd interviewed, and chased, in my life as a cop. Something I'd also seen in Evan's eyes every time we stood face to face. Darkness, evil. Or maybe it was because he was more a politician than a cop. In my experience, politicians were far eviler than any killer I'd met.

Ellis recovered his composure quickly, pulling at the shiny cufflinks, his fake salesman smile returning. "I must be off. I have a meeting with the Secretary of State about his trip to Argentina next month."

He turned to Gus. "Agent Duncan if you could please fill these lovely agents in on what we will need and when we will need it." Gus nodded and dug out his notepad, walking out of the room to talk to the receptionist outside.

Ellis walked over to Sasha and I, holding out his hand. "Again, it's been a pleasure. I do hope you make headway on that cold case of yours. I always say the cold cases are the hardest to crack, but the most rewarding." Sasha said nothing. Her face told me she was three seconds away from losing her temper on the man, but held it in for the sake of her career.

I smiled as I took his hand. "They are the most rewarding. I do enjoy sifting through the mistakes made by overexcited and incompetent men."

I watched as Ellis flinched. He cleared his throat. "Good day, ladies." Ellis exited the room leaving a cloud of arrogance mixing with his terrible cologne.

Sasha exploded the second Ellis left the room. "Reagan?! What the hell? We're being pulled off the Bellico case? It's mine, you know that, I know that! It's a homicide as well as a drug crime, why can't we share jurisdiction?"

Reagan stood, tugging on the edge of her blazer. "Because that slimy asshole you just met, is in line to be the next Drug Czar to the President. Ellis is trying to fluff himself up to the point no one can see past him. He was the one who pulled you from the case and had our bosses agree with the move. He has stronger ties than I thought." Reagan let out a sigh. "Do what is asked of you, Agent Clarke. That's all I can enforce in this matter."

Reagan said nothing while Sasha stammered to say something to try and convince her boss. Reagan ignored her, making an exit and disappearing, Gus reappearing in her place. He gave us a sheepish smile. "Emma, I'm sorry about this. I had to report what I found to him. I didn't mean for Ellis to take over the whole case. But this is big, it's a big lead. One us old guys have been looking for the last thirty years."

Sasha stood up and walked out of the conference room. She was on fire and irritated, just like the first day I'd sent her to dig through physical files with Eddie in the basement. Quiet curse words followed her out the door. I looked at Gus, fully understanding why Reagan secretly met me in the park, and why the files were shoved in a bakery bag. There was something more to this case and the bodies piling up next to me.

I smiled at Gus. "No worries, you and I both know politics supersedes justice." I stood up, grabbing my briefcase and Sasha's bag. "Meet Agent Clarke and I tomorrow at her office. We'll have what your boss wants."

I nodded at Sasha standing outside, arms folded as she stared out the massive windows. "Plus, it will give her the time to cool down. Trust me, I've dealt with that woman's fierce temper a time or two. Let her be for a day."

Gus chuckled. "She must have a little Irish in her." He

stood, laying a hand on my shoulder. "I really am sorry. I know you're one hell of a detective. I've seen it in your work, and it's an honest damn shame you're being pulled off this one. I think out of all of us in the DEA, or FBI, you would be the one who could've solved it."

I smiled. "Maybe, Gus." I patted him on the arm. "See you tomorrow." I walked out of the conference room towards Sasha. Gus was right. I could solve the case and would solve it. It was apparent someone out there wanted me the furthest away from this case, which only drove me harder as my suspicions tripled during the meeting.

I said nothing to Sasha as I gently grabbed her elbow, guiding her out of the building. She was still angry, and I let her vent in the car back to the house. She called Reagan names, Ellis names, and swore up and down that it was the biggest pile of horseshit she'd ever seen in her police career. Pulling people off a case and handing over it over to another agency on minor details.

Back at the house Sasha threw her dress jacket on my leather chair and turned to me, hands on her hips. "Why did you have so little to say in there? It's like you were mute and wanted this case to go away." She was now directing her temper at me. "I felt like I was alone in there."

I held out my hand. "Come." I motioned to the stairs. "Let's go to my room."

Sasha frowned. "That is the furthest thing from my mind, Emma. I'm a little pissed off at you right now."

I grabbed her hand. "Just come upstairs." I pulled her after me, feeling her resistance as she finally followed.

"Emma, I just want to drink until I'm so drunk, I forget how badly I want to go to my office right now, and shred every damn piece of paper we've been ordered to give to those DEA dickheads."

I smiled as I walked into my office, letting go of her hand before bending to unlock my drawer. "That would be destruction of evidence." I opened the drawer and pulled out the white bag as Sasha flopped onto the bed. I turned to find her laying on her back, her hands covering her face.

She groaned in frustration. "Maybe I should look at early retirement and become a secretary or a cab driver."

I sat down next to her, setting the white bag on her lap. She peered through her hands, shooting me a look. "Cupcakes? You brought me up here for cupcakes? Is there whiskey in them?"

"No, but it is something I've been saving for you since yesterday. I haven't even looked at it."

Sasha grabbed my arm, pulling herself upright. She opened it, looking at me as she shoved a hand in, pulling out the thick stack of papers. "What is this?"

I leaned against her as she unfolded the stack. "It's a gift."

Sasha's eyes locked onto the autopsy report. "John Allen Walker? Wasn't he the Captain next up on our interview list?"

I nodded. "Yup."

She sifted through the pages faster. "He died two days ago? There's witness statements and this autopsy report is the original uncorrected one. The coroners first draft." She set the autopsy report down on the bed in between us, pulling open the last ancient sheet of paper. "Holy shit! This is blood analysis from Angela Heaten. It's the original report." Sasha set the last sheet on her lap and stared at me. "How?"

I smirked, shrugging. "Reagan. She was the reason you ran out of coffee the other morning."

Sasha glared at me. "SAC Dana Reagan? The stone cold bitch who just pulled us from a fresh homicide? One that was rightfully ours?"

"The one and only." I picked up the autopsy report and started glossing over it as Sasha stood up.

She huffed, her arms folded as she held onto the thirty year old piece of paper. "What the hell is going on, Emma?" Her face flushed red with anger. I was two seconds away from being on the receiving end of her infamous temper if I didn't start talking and start talking fast. "You let us get pulled off the case. You knew we were getting pulled off the case. Why didn't you tell me?"

I chuckled. "You know I love it when you get all red and blustery." My comment earned a grumble from Sasha about unnecessarily pushing her buttons will get me nowhere. "Anyway, yes, I knew. Reagan set up a meeting in the park yesterday. Call it an impromptu recreation of a James Bond movie, but she handed me those files and asked I keep you out of the loop. She knew we were being kicked off the case, and knew those files in your hand would disappear as soon as possible. Reagan asked to keep you in the dark so your reaction would be genuine when Ellis made his power play."

Sasha huffed, her face fading to a normal soft pink color. "Reagan, my boss who hates you as much as you hate her?"

"Yes, but we share a common interest. This case isn't simple. Its more than a girl murdered in a park and an old retired cop being murdered and his parts mailed to us. I haven't quite figured it out, Reagan is only facilitating things out of her undying hate for Ellis over the last decade." I pointed to the stack in Sasha's hand. "Those are our quiet approval from your boss to keep digging as much as we can. And whoever her ghost in the wind is that handed them over to her."

Sasha let out a sigh as she dropped onto the bed

next to me. "That's why you were quiet during the meeting and eyeballing Ellis. I just figured you were happy the case was being taken from away us." She nudged me with her shoulder. "I should have paid more attention to the last fifty rules in your *how to be a detective* handbook."

I smiled, sliding my arm around her waist. "I wanted to protect you until I knew for sure the DEA was taking lead. I now know I can trust Reagan to have our back, even if it is from the shadows." I took a slow breath. "It's up to you, Sasha, if you want to keep digging deeper into this. I have a bad feeling it's only going to get worse from now on, the further we go."

Sasha laid her head on my shoulder. "So, Reagan is former NSA." She turned slightly, her chin resting on my shoulder. I watched the gears turning in her head as everything sank in. "I want to see this through, Emma. I've never given up on a case and won't start now." She smirked. "Plus, Ellis pissed me off so much, I want to show him up. Prove him wrong."

I squeezed Sasha as she kissed the edge of my jaw. "Then I suggest we start with Walker's autopsy report."

Chapter 17

The autopsy report was spread out along the top of my desk. I sat on the floor against the bed, watching Sasha pace with sections of it in her hand. Her face was furrowed in deep thought. I'd only glossed over the report until I was met with black and white copies of the crime scene and morgue photos. I had to give in and move to where I was now seated, letting my mind try and find any reason why I continued to fail at stomaching the biggest part of my job. Death.

"Emma, did you read the scene techs notes?" Sasha held up a sheet.

I shook my head. "I only read through the medical examiners preliminary notes."

Sasha handed me the sheet, tapping at the corner with her finger as soon as I took it from her. "Read there. Even the tech noted something was suspicious and the scene looked like it was a setup. A murder setup to look like an accident."

I ran over the notes. Quick, concise and to the point, but full of doubt. "We need to get our hands on the final copy of the report. Something to compare what the first reports said was suspicious, versus what the final said was an accident." I set the lone sheet in my lap, glancing at my watch. "I can go to the station and pull it. I'm certain by now its public access." I looked at Sasha. "You think you can do your magic and find Walker's personnel file?"

Sasha smiled at me. "I can do better." She walked over to the closet, pulling out a black soft side laptop case. She set it on the desk, moving some of the reports to the side. Unzipping the case, she spoke. "I grabbed a few things from my apartment before we went to the DEA." She winked. "You can help me move the rest of my things in later. But this," She pulled out a sleek, shiny black laptop.

"Needs to stay with me at all times." She set the laptop up and turned it on, sliding my desk chair over and sat down. I stood up from the floor and walked over to her, taking in the small details of the laptop that told me it was very expensive, and very state of the art.

"I never took you for a tech geek." I leaned over Sasha, watching as she quickly navigated through setting up firewalls and masking my IP address.

"I don't tell many, wouldn't want to ruin my street cred." She clicked around the desktop. "But actually, it's Morgan who's the tech geek in my life. She taught me everything she knew about computers and hacking. It was something she fell upon one day and excelled at." Sasha tapped at the top edge of the screen. "This little machine here was a gift from her. Custom built for me on the FBI's dime. After Operation Eclipse, Morgan was bored in her surveillance assignment and started building laptops for field agents. Custom to the agent, what they were doing and needed. She threw this one my way as an early birthday gift." Sasha leaned forward, squinting as the Fairfax County seal popped up on the screen. "Best part, no one knows I have it."

I turned away from the screen. "What's the deal with the little hotel soaps stashed in your bathroom?"
I was starting to wonder if Sasha had a criminal past like Morgan did. It always seemed to be the best cops were former criminals in one way or another.

Sasha kept her eyes on the screen. "They're souvenirs." With two clicks she pushed the laptop my way. "Here is the final Walker autopsy report."

I stared at her a second longer, eyebrow cocked. "Souvenirs?"

Sasha nodded slowly. "Yes, souvenirs. I never traveled much as a kid when I lived with my mom. I was always stuck with the bare, dirty apartment walls. When I went to my grandparents, they took me places. National parks, amusement parks, and nice hotels. They showed me there was more to the world than moldy walls and screaming neighbors." Sasha smiled tightly. "I was always mesmerized by the clean smells of the hotel soaps and how they were made to look like seashells, stars, and fish. I would take one or two with me when we checked out of a hotel. It helped chase away the memories of the dirty tub in my mom's apartment, and how I had to take baths with liquid dish soap."

She leaned back in the chair. "It's dumb, I know. But it reminds of good things and comes in handy when I have guests."

I bent closer, kissing her cheek. "It's not dumb, it makes perfect sense. I thought maybe you were a soap hoarder or a…"

Sasha interrupted me. "Or a petty soap thief?" She winked before stealing a kiss. "I've always kept to the straight and narrow. As a street cop, a homicide detective, and as a federal agent" She motioned to the laptop. "That has become a convenience now. especially after the last few weeks and our surprise house guests." She took a deep breath. "I want to keep us safe, Emma, even more as we continue with this case." The look in her eyes was serious, she was shifting into the same protective mode I had from the moment I knew who Evan was and what he was after. I nodded in silent agreement and focused on the lengthy autopsy report set before me in digital format.

John David Walker, age forty five, was laid out before me in cold color autopsy photographs. I quickly clicked past those and onto the final report the Medical Examiner submitted.

I sought out the cause of death first. Exsanguination

due to a torn axillary artery in Walker's left shoulder. He bled to death within a matter of minutes. I kept reading. Toxicology came back clean. Blood tests came back cleaner. Walker was not a smoker. He didn't drink and took relatively good care of himself. Yet, it appeared he had a minor slip and fall accident in his garage, causing him to fall on something that punctured his shoulder, tearing the artery.

    To anyone who read of the autopsy report, it was an open and shut case of accidental death. Tinkering in the garage gone bad and Walker met his maker while his blood mixed with the oil stains on his garage floor.

    I pushed the laptop towards Sasha. "This is clearly a cover up report. It's meant to cast away any suspicion that Walker's death wasn't an accident." I reached for the reports still spread around my bed and picked up the scene techs notes and the original handwritten ME report from Reagan. I scanned both and found one major consistency between the two.

    Both of the reports found it suspicious the puncture wound that was Walkers fate, wasn't a through and through injury. The wound was only deep enough to reach the artery and cause the bleed out.

    I read over the scribbly pen of the medical examiner. *"Fatal wound appears to be intentional. The way the artery is torn suggests it was targeted and not an act of fate. The tool markings also fail to match up. Take castings of both."* I looked at Sasha. "Are there pictures of the item Walker fell on?"

    Sasha peered over the screen of the laptop. "Yes, I think in the autopsy photos there are scene photos." She pushed a few glossy pictures around until she grabbed one. "Here."

    I took the glossy color photograph of Walkers garage

after his body was removed. It was easier to look at, but still made my jaw clench when I saw the large pools of coagulating blood.

Sasha pointed to the left bottom corner of the photograph. "The tech took a wide shot with the item as it was found."

I spotted a large posthole auger on the floor next to a larger pool of blood. The edges of the tip of the auger were covered in blood. I instantly grew suspicious, flipping through the other photographs until I found a closeup shot of the tool. The second I looked at that photograph, I was right. There was no feasible way Walker fell onto the auger and produce the grievous injury he received. The auger tips were sharp enough to penetrate his skin, but the hole would've been bigger, and with Walker's height and weight, the gravity of his body falling, would've pushed the auger all the way through. The entire auger, tip to shaft, would've been covered in blood and remained in his body until the medical examiner removed it.

I took a breath, tossing the photographs to the side. Closing my eyes, I leaned back in the chair. "Walkers death was a setup. He was murdered."

Sasha's fingers stopped moving over her keyboard, cutting short the soft clicks that had set a strange rhythm while I looked over the photographs. "Are you sure, Emma?"

I nodded, my eyes still closed. "The evidence is there. Of course, only in the unedited reports. The physics and dynamics of what supposedly caused his death are inconceivable with the evidence presence. There isn't enough blood at the scene. He was murdered with a strange precision. And by the looks of the scene, whoever it was, was in a hurry to shut Walker up for good. Fudging the science and leaving us with silent evidence." I opened my eyes and looked at her. "The question is, who would want to kill Walker two days before we were about to interview him?" I stood up from the desk, walking to the bed so I could lie down. The day had been long and weird with all the smoke and mirror spy games.

I called after Sasha, who started typing again. "Use your fancy computer and dig up everything on Walker and Bellico. Anything that puts their names together, tag it and save it. I want to know why these two died in close proximity of each other." I covered my face with a pillow. I was exhausted and all I could think about was how delightful sleeping through the next week would be.

Sasha appeared in the archway that connected my room to the small office. "Did you want to look at Heaten's blood analysis report or do you want to go to bed?" Her voice was soft in the way it always was right before we both went to bed together. I knew the moment she crawled into bed with me, I would be wrapped up into her arms like a mummy. Something I would eagerly welcome tonight especially after holding out on her about Reagan during the DEA meeting. I truly really hated it when I pissed her off, and her rookie temper showed itself. I lifted a corner of the pillow up and looked at her with one eye. "Read it to me?"

Sasha smirked, pushing off the wall and walking back into the office. She came back a second later, crawling into the bed to sit next to me as I continued to lay there. "Did you want me to read the whole report or just the highlights?"

I mumbled under my pillow. "Highlights."

Sasha began reading the blood analysis notes.

"*Traces of Levomethamphetamine is present in the blood. Could be discounted by the sample origin use of over the counter allergy medicine. There are minute traces of a* substance that could be recognized as cocaine, but not enough to positively identify." Sasha flipped a page. "Blood also contains small traces of codeine and benzodiazepine. Not enough to qualify as an illegal dosage."

Sasha paused, tapping the file. "There's a weird little handwritten note underneath the analysis's signature."

I threw the pillow away and sat up, looking over her shoulder as she read.

"For Coroner, can you run for hydrophilic/lipophilic balance and see if you can possibly check the blood-brain barrier permeability. Something is not adding up. Either this patient had a severe cold, or it was a drug cocktail overdose." Sasha pointed to the date scribbled next to the note. "It's dated a day after the report was submitted."

I gently pulled the report from her hands and reread the report. I started mentally cataloging the chemicals in Angela's blood. It took a minute, but it finally dawned on me. "I think she was given a crystal meth cocktail." I looked up at a confused Sasha. "It didn't hit me right away because meth wasn't super popular in the early eighties. Back then it was cocaine and heroin hitting the streets hard. Meth was always in the background, but the kids of the eighties really had no idea what it was unless you were well and gone into drug use."

I pointed to the chemicals. "Levomethamphetamine. It's an over the counter drug, but it's a component used by basement meth cooks. It's used all over the place these days in home labs because it's so easy to get. Back in the eighties it wasn't that easy to get without an extensive prescription from your doctor. It's one of the more expensive ingredients, but a very potent one in any given meth recipe. Codeine and the benzos would add that extra little push." I took a deep breath. "This possibly is a home brew of some very expensive crystal meth, but then the cocaine traces point to it being a designer drug."

Sasha turned back to the report, scanning it. "But everything is in minute trace levels. I can understand why the analyst would brush it off as too many cold and allergy meds mixed together."

I nodded. "Exactly until he slowly put it together and came to the same conclusion. Mix all them together and you'll have one hell of a drug that packs a punch but is very hard to trace." I rolled out of the bed, excited as a few more pieces fell into place "All the drugs listed are still heavy hitters in small doses, in barely traceable doses. But when you think about it for a minute and you're trying to run a blood test for a suspicious death, it would lead one to look deeper." I ran a hand over my hair, settling it on my chin. "It could be meth, but it could also be a hybrid cocktail Angela stumbled upon." I breathed out a sigh. "Does the report have the exact levels in her blood?"

Sasha flipped pages. "Yes, the analyst listed the exact levels he found."

I nodded excited. "Perfect. Is there someone you trust in the FBI labs? Like really trust?"

Sasha looked up at the ceiling, "There's Chris at the Chicago office. He has a small crush on me and was good about keeping things to himself when I was undercover."

I clenched my jaw when I heard undercover.

It would forever bother me when I heard anything related to the days where I was living a lie.

I gave her a curt nod. "Send him the chemicals and the trace levels listed. Make up something about a new case and ask if the chemicals could be manufactured into a narcotic, and what viable form. Pill, crystal, liquid or powder. I have a hunch if we find a lead there, and it works, it'll take us back to Bellico."

Sasha nodded and got up from the bed, heading back to the office.

I remained in the bedroom. Standing in the middle of it as my mind raced over chemical structures and lies. I would have to look over Angela's original autopsy report to pull more things together. I knew she was strangled, and her body dumped.

A crime that in my days in homicide would've been a pretty cut and dry case. But now there was the added blood analysis report, throwing an extra little cog in the overall mystery.

I now understood why Reagan wanted to keep me on this case like a dog on a fresh bone, there was more to the story and it was revealing itself one strange page at a time.

It was not only Reagan, but Latham, the blood analyst, and the other good people on the right side of the law, who questioned why they were being blacked out like their reports had been when things didn't make sense. I had puzzle pieces that made sense, I just had to figure out how they all fit together.

I left the room and went downstairs, grabbing a beer on the way to the living room. I stood in front of the huge window, taking in the view of the lake at night through brand new bulletproof glass. Sipping the beer, I tried connecting the dots in my head.

Bellico had links to drugs through the home lab, and he was linked to Angela by being at her crime scene. Exeter was connected to Bellico, but it was a thin string of a connection. Exeter was also connected to Angela when he was the first officer on scene. But nothing led me to believe he was any dirtier than the stains on his shirt.

Walker was connected to Bellico in ways we still had to connect. It would've been helpful if Walker had stayed for a few more days, and I could've asked him these questions face to face.

Those were the Heaten murder connections. The other dots I needed to connect were the drugs and why I had a hired cartel thug trying to burn my house down with Sasha and I in it.

As I stared at the light from the skyscrapers bouncing off the tips of the lake water, I circled back to the drugs. The murder connections were slowly merging with the strange new development of drug cartel involvement.

The drugs would be the main bridge between everything and everyone. It would make sense because of the DEA railroading Sasha and I off the case. They knew more than they wanted to share. The weirdness from Reagan, her wanting me to push harder on this case and providing me with the original reports. If that wasn't a sign, I didn't know what was. I had to find the next lead to take.

I drank the rest of the beer, twirling the empty bottle around between my fingers. This case was going to get complicated and take us deep into the depths of a dark unforgiving world.

My father worked Narcotics for a short period of time and when I was promoted to detective, he advised me to never transfer to narcotics. He told me the world of drugs was a vicious world of human depravity, one that would suck the most honest person in and change them.

I kept staring out the window, drifting off to thoughts of when the time would come, would I find peace in my life and find the complete happiness I was starting to crave? I hadn't been wholly happy in years and even with Sasha by my side, I still felt like something was missing. It was possible I was forever living in a world of darkness and had only one beacon of hope. A beacon I was hesitant to rely on once again. Fearing it would be snuffed out like so many other beacons in my life.

Her hand found my elbow, and Sasha pulled me closer as she slowly broke me from my trance. "Chris has my email. He's already working on compiling it all. He said he should have something for us in the morning." Sasha kissed my shoulder. "Come to bed. Work is done for the night."

I smiled and looked down at her. Her hair was up, and she still wore her pantsuit. Her hazel eyes told me she wanted nothing more than to let her hair down, crawl into my old sweatpants and stop being flipping the pages of old cases and convoluted lab reports.

I slid my elbow from her grasp, finding her hand with mine, linking our fingers together. Enjoying the way she always seemed to squeeze my fingers whenever we held hands, it was as if she was afraid to lose any hold she had on me. I turned to look at her with a smile. "Well, what would you like to do for the rest of the evening?"

Sasha smirked. "Is Aaron coming home anytime soon?" Her eyes glinted with the slightest hint of mischief and desire.

"He won't be home for a while, maybe not until tomorrow. He called me while we were at the DEA. He picked up a new case over on the southside. He's going to be tied up taking witness statements."

Sasha nodded, turning to walk away, pulling me with her.

Upstairs in my bedroom, heart began to race. Sasha always had a way of making that happen right before we consummated the tension hovering around us. Begging for us to kiss, touch and indulge in the way our bodies reacted to one another.

Sasha closed the door and walked to the desk, stopping mid unbuttoning of her shirt, and looked at the desk and the bed. She immediately started picking up the paperwork we'd spread out, tucking it back into files and envelopes. I walked over to help. Sasha was like me. We wouldn't be able to focus on anything else if a case file was within view.

Sasha spoke as she collected the original Heaten blood report. "Can we have a late start tomorrow? At least until Chris gets back to us. I'd really like to sleep in tomorrow." She looked up. "With you next to me."

I smiled and nodded, handing Sasha a thin stack of papers. "Of course. I was thinking, after breakfast I might call my dad. I want to ask if he has any old buddies in narcotics who could help us. I need some expert advice on drugs, drug cartels, manufacturing and dealing. I have a hunch, but I need more information and I can't think of anyone who has expansive knowledge of the inner workings of the drug world."

Sasha paused, her eyes settling on the now clean desk. She slowly set the stack of papers in her hand down. "I might know someone who can help us and not cause ripples in the pool we're trying to hide in."

I leaned on the edge of the desk facing her, running my hand down her arm to find her hand, holding it as I pulled it up to my lips, trying to reignite the small fire she started with that smirk. "Who would that be? Another lab tech or fellow agent who has a crush on you?"

Sasha half smiled and shook her head, looking up at me, she removed her hand from mine, placing it on the side of my neck and met my eyes. The look in her eyes was serious even as she stroked my pulse with her thumb. "No fellow agent or lab tech who has a crush, but I'm sure she might have loved me at some point in my life."

The sharp pang of jealousy raced through my body. I had to hold back from reacting even as Sasha's fingers settled on my pulse, feeling my heart shift from desire to controlled jealousy.

Sasha moved closer to me, her hand moving to the edge of my jaw. "Emma, I mean my mother."

I could feel my eyes widen on their own. "Your mother?"

"Yes, my mother. My mother who is serving two consecutive life sentences for an endless list of drug charges. She would be the only person I know who knows the business from the inside and not have to worry about retaliation. I can probably also work on getting her a plea deal, reduce her sentence if she helps us. She was tied to a major drug cartel when I was a kid, her insight could prove to be useful." Sasha turned away, looking at the wall.

I could tell this was a struggle of an option for her. I pulled Sasha closer, wrapping my arms around her so she could lean back but still be in my grasp. "Are you sure? I can find other people. Agents, cops, or former junkies to help us. I don't want you to feel like you have to do this. It's just a case and I know it's a difficult relationship between you and your mother."

Sasha smiled. "That will never change. The difficult part." Sasha closed the space between us, laying her head on my chest, sighing deeply. "But I don't want our relationship to change, Emma. If talking to my mother means we can close this case faster and move on with our lives, and away from the death threats and constant need to look over our shoulder, I can suffer through a couple of hours talking to the woman who gave me birth."

I held Sasha tightly. "Just promise me."

She cut me off before I went further. "I know. You don't have to say it." She leaned back in my arms. "As long as you're with me, that's all I need." She leaned forward, her lips pressing against mine in a quick gentle kiss. "I love you, Emma. I promise you that will never change."

I smiled, bending forward to return the kiss. This one not as gentle or quick as hers. I grinned against her mouth when I heard her moan like she always did when I kissed her hard. I moved my hands to the front of her shirt, unbuttoning the last few buttons. I looked at her after parting from her lips, pushing the shirt off her shoulders. Her face was flushed, her eyes hazy and full of desire. I grinned, removing her shirt and tossing it to the floor. I glanced at the bed, then back to Sasha. "You never told me exactly what you wanted to do for the rest of the night." I traced a finger over her collarbone and down between her breasts. "I don't want to make an assumption."

Sasha's breath caught when my finger pulled goose bumps when it dragged along the waistband of her pants. Before I could get any further or say another word, I was shoved to the bed by an eager woman, who told me to stop talking right as she straddled my hips.

The second I felt Sasha bite my shoulder, I prayed to God Aaron was utterly swamped with witnesses for the rest of his life.

I would literally kill him if he interrupted us.

Chapter 18

I leaned forward, looking at the stone gate welcoming us into Alderson Federal Penitentiary. "You said your mother was convicted and sentenced to multiple life sentences? How did she wind up in a minimum security prison camp?"

"She's an informant and proud of it. She was at Coleman down in Florida for a long time. Then realized talking would get her a better bed. They moved her to Alderson three years ago." Sasha kept her eyes forward as she drove up to the guard gate. She was tense. Had been since the flight down to West Virginia. She barely looked at me as I handed over my identification for the guard to scrutinize.

"We don't have to do this." I spoke softly as I took my wallet back from Sasha. She clenched her jaw and gripped the steering wheel with white knuckles.

"She's expecting us." Her jaw twitched as we drove along a winding road lined with trees. The debate was over for now. I knew when Sasha had that steely look in her eyes, I'd come up against impenetrable walls. The only thing I could do now was be there for her.

*****

"The visit will be monitored via video. Please make sure you maintain a safe distance from the inmate." The guard spoke in a bored monotone voice as she led us down a cold hallway. "We understand this is an official interview and will not interrupt you for routine inmate movements. When you're done, please hit the button on the wall and we'll come down to collect the inmate." She stopped in front of a cold grey steel door. "Any questions, Agent Clarke? Captain Tiernan?" Her face was void of emotion.

Sasha clutched her briefcase. "Not at this time, Thank you."

The guard nodded once and opened the door to reveal an even colder room with a small metal table and chairs. She waved at the two seats closest to the door.

"You can sit here. I'll go collect inmate Porter." The guard left us in cold silence.

I shivered, running my hands over the sleeves of my suit jacket as I sat down. Sasha sat next to me, her head down as she began pulling files out of her briefcase. I caught the slightest tremor in her hands and went to reach for her, when the sounds of chains rattling down the hallway broke me from it. The door creaked open and I turned to the sight of two more guards escorting a smaller woman between them. The woman was tall, thin and looked exactly like Sasha, just twenty some years older. She also looked elegant, clean and nowhere near the picture I had in my mind. A ragged woman lost to the life of drugs and crime. If I'd seen her on the streets, I would have pegged her for a trophy wife, not the vile woman in the files Sasha hid from me.

Alison Porter glared at me for a moment before she caught sight of Sasha sitting next to me. A small smirk crossed her face as she was shoved into the chair on the other side of the table. The guards linked her handcuffs through the large metal ring in the center of the table. I watched Sasha swallow before clearing her throat. "Ms. Porter, I'm Agent Natasha Clarke of the FBI and this is my partner, Captain Emma Tiernan. We'd like to ask you a few questions regarding a homicide cold case." She kept her head down as she turned a few pages.

Alison laughed, leaning back in the chair as the guards left us alone. "So, we're going to be all formal and shit?" She shook her head, looking around the blank room.

"I should've known this was business. You were always a tight ass, Nat."

Sasha's jaw twitched. "You were once linked to the Alvarez Cartel from the early eighties into the early nineties as a drug mule and manufacturer of synthetic narcotics." She turned over a page from the chemical analysis report Reagan gave me.

I felt the skin on the back of my neck bristle hearing the name of the Alvarez Cartel. They were big dogs in the eighties. My father once ran surveillance on them, told me they were nasty and vicious. "Can you tell us what kind of synthetic narcotics were being produced at that time, and where you might have distributed them?"

"Hi, how are you? Good to see you too, Nat. It's only been eight years since I last saw you. Maybe open the conversation with your manners. I know your grandmother raised you better than this. I *am* your mother, or did you forget that?" Alison hissed at her daughter, making me shift in my seat and go into protective mode. "You brat."

"Mrs. Porter, please. Stick to the questions." I held up a hand, smiling to ease the tension in the room. I guess I was playing the role of good cop.

"And who the fuck do you think you are?" Alison waved a hand my direction. "You reek of city cop. City cop wearing a cheap pantsuit, so piss off. I want to talk to my daughter, not you." She cocked an eyebrow, staring me down. My temper flickered and she caught it, grinning as she laughed. "I hit a nerve. Perfect." She waved me off as she twisted in her seat, facing Sasha. "Who is this bitch? Some trainee you're trying to impress?"

"Mrs. Porter. If you're not willing to answer the questions, we will leave." Sasha finally looked at her mother. The hard, unforgiving tone set Alison off.

"I'm your *God damned* mother, Nat! Or did you throw

that away with everything else?" Alison screamed as she leaned forward, her face a bright red. Her handcuffs scraped against the metal ring, balking at the tension.

"You threw me away! Or did you forget that?!" Sasha screamed back, startling me. "You stopped being my mother a long time ago, Alison. You chose drugs over me. You chose the random men, the late nights, and alcohol over me." Sasha's hands curled into tight fists. "I will walk out that door and end all communication with you. I don't need you."

Alison huffed, staring at her daughter until she rolled her eyes with a chuckle. "You got me there, kid." She held her hands up in defeat, sitting back down, throwing on a mask of false sorrow. I only saw a woman was a master of manipulation, constantly playing her next card, especially when it came to her daughter. "Drugs and booze were a lot easier than raising a kid, but you did bring in a nice paycheck from the state." She winked at me, leaning back into the chair. "Let's make a deal. I'll answer your questions if you answer mine. One for one."

I spoke before Sasha. "There are no deals here. There will be no deals. You'll answer her questions, or you won't." I glanced at Sasha, trying to silently communicate I had her back.

"You're fucking my daughter, aren't you?" Alison laughed, shaking her head as I tried so hard not to blush, or react. I suddenly wished I'd read the full file in Sasha's briefcase to prepare. I also understood where Sasha got her intelligence from. This woman was sharp, brilliant, and would use it to her advantage. "You don't need to answer my question, *Captain.* It's written all over your face, in the way you look at her." She scoffed looking at her daughter, watching Sasha's cheeks pink up with embarrassment.

Alison scoffed, looking right at her daughter. "Classy,

Nat. Real classy. Screwing a street cop. I'm glad your college education is paying off."

Sasha shifted in her seat. "I'll take your deal." She half whispered the words, and I saw the flicker of a young girl scared of her mother. "As much as it disgusts me, we need your help." She sighed. "The Alvarez Cartel." She glanced at her mother, silently asking her to pick up the conversation.

Alison rolled her eyes. "Were a bunch of fucking idiots who thought they were the next Escobar, but they lacked the balls." She held up her hand, examining very clean nails. "I started as a mule for them. It was easy money and diaper were expensive." He gaze flickered towards Sasha. "And because of their lack of organization, I was able to move up and become a distributor. More money, more travel." She sighed, laying her hand flat on the table. "Where do you live, Nat?"

Sasha shuffled a few papers, pulling out an old report with the DEA logo on it. "Chicago." She slid a sheet across the table. "When you testified two years ago, you mentioned in your deposition about the cartel wanting to expand into methamphetamines and other man made narcotics. Explain?"

Alison smirked and grabbed the sheet of paper. "I saw you standing in the back of that courtroom. You hid behind a massive corrections officer, but I'd know my daughters' eyes anywhere. Big hazel eyes, filled with eager hope, desperate to save the world. You kind of inspired me to be a little more honest when the prosecution questioned me." She scanned over the sheet. "The youngest brother, Carlos, wanted to branch out. Import and export fees were killing them on cocaine, cutting into their profit margin and heroin was too risky since they had to go through the Middle East to get the highest quality, the purest shit.

Carlos was interested in a synthetic cocaine with an extra kick. He wanted a cocaine that took you on a trip, not just make you the flash. He also wanted to cut out the Middle East and keep things local."

She set the sheet down, folding her hands over it. "I'd ask you about your love life, but." Alison looked my way. "It appears things have changed fom the days when you thought you were going to marry Tom Cruise." She looked me up and down in a slow judging manner. "Are you living together?"

Sasha sighed deeply. "No. I spend most of my time in D.C. It's closer to grandma and grandpa." She glanced at me, communicating me with a look to go along with the bullshit she fed her mother. She clearly didn't want her mother to know anything about her family, and that her grandparents moved to California three years ago. "Tell us more about the cocaine Carlos wanted to make."

I wanted to grab Sasha and beg her to stop answering her mother's questions, stop feeding the woman scraps, but I saw the long game. Alison would talk more for every scrap Sasha threw her way.

Alison stared at me, making me very nervous. I was literally caught in the middle of a chess game between mother and daughter. I was half tempted to stand up and leave the room, let the two women battle it out. She kept her eyes on me as she spoke. "He held a meeting in Detroit. A strange place for a meet, but it was far enough off the main pipeline to prevent suspicion from the other cartels. He had some guy he claimed was a chemistry genius. They divvied out samples in tiny dime bags with the strict instructions to stay in the Metro Detroit area. Sell off our loads in twenty fours, then report back the results." She squinted at me. "You look real familiar to me. You're a cop, right? Chicago?"

I opened my mouth to tell Alison this wasn't about me, when Sasha's hand fell to my thigh. She squeezed gently, answering for me. "She is. She's a Captain with the Chicago Police department."

"I do recognize you from the TV and the newspapers when my baby here cracked that serial killer case. I was a bit of a celebrity here for a hot second. Not like you think, though. Having an FBI agent for a kid sets one up for a few sleepless nights and beatings in the shower." Alison leaned forward. "Leave it to my kid to start fucking a cop because someone told her to. I was proud of her for being so good at that undercover job. Slipping in between the sheets and doing her job to the nth degree. I knew a part of me was in there. I thought, maybe I did teach my baby girl a few useful life lessons." She winked as my cheeks turned red with anger. Alison laughed as I suddenly stood up from the chair, almost knocking it to the ground. "What? That one got under your skin? You're too easy." She then turned back to Sasha. "You're in love with this hot shot? I see the way you look at each other. I can smell her on you." She grimaced with disgust.

"Mother." Sasha spoke the word with icy distaste. As if the word alone burned her tongue.

"Oh shit. You do love her." Alison tilted her head up towards the drop ceiling and fluorescent lights. "My kid. The constant fuck up."

The sight of Sasha flinching lit the final match. I stormed across the room to the edge of the table, yelling. "Fuck you, Alison! You have no clue who your daughter is, and what she's become. All you see is the weak parts you choose to exploit her with. I see the game you're playing. This isn't a fucking game. So, knock it off and answer the questions before…"

Your mother and father were my best customers in

Detroit. Garth and Jackie Atkinson. Hardcore junkies with tunnel vision for one thing. Heroin. And I was happy to supply them." Alison squinted, leaning closer. "The second you sat down, I thought I was having a flashback from my own junkie days. But then it clicked. You look just like Jackie. A mirror image of your mother." Alison grinned. "I met you once. I think you were about three. I was leaving the city and Jackie hit me up for one last buy. I gave her all I had and held you while she shot up. You were a cute baby."

The rage boiled over at the sound of my biological parent's names. Names I left in a file buried at the bottom of my desk drawer I reached across the table, wrapping my hands in the collar of Alison's orange jumpsuit, pulling her up as her handcuffed wrists pulled her down. "Shut the fuck up, you piece of shit." My voice cracked as I screamed in her face. I blinked tears away and caught the look in Alison's as Sasha scrambled to push me off her mother. She chuckled and whispered with a wink.

"Got you."

I growled, throwing her back into the chair as guards burst into the room. I shoved past them and out into the hall. I walked down the hall, kicking the double doors at the end of the hall open, and walked outside. The day was unusually warm and sunny for winter in the south. The bright sun bore down on me, adding to the heat of rage sloughing off my body. I tore my jacket off, curling the collar in my fist. I was angry, beyond angry for letting that woman find a hole in my wall and bury the knife deep. I let her use me as a pawn.

"Fuck."

"Ma'am. Is everything okay?" The first guard we met stood behind me. Her blank face held a hint of concern. "Did inmate Porter attack you?"

I shook her my head, waving her off. "Everything is

fine, but I won't be continuing the interview. Please ensure Agent Clarke has someone in the room with her." I ran a hand through my hair, looking up at the blue skies as my body still trembled with anger.

"I understand." There was a pause. "Porter is manipulative as hell. Don't let anything she said get to you. She's a former junkie, but smart as hell. I think manipulating people is her replacement for drugs."

I sighed, looking over my shoulder at the guard. I wanted to tell her to screw off and point me in the direction of the closest bar, when an idea popped in my head. "Has Porter had many visitors during her stay here?"

"A few. But it's been sporadic over the last few years. I can show you the visitor logs if you'd like. We also kept track of her visitors when she was down at Coleman and the other facilities she was housed at." The guard finally broke a smile. "I also have a bottle of whiskey I confiscated from a visitor last week."

I blew out a breath. "Show me the way."

*****

The main office was cool and comfortable. The guard, Sally, set me up at a desk and gave me access to the visitor log database, along with Alison's phone records. She set up a laptop next to me with a
streaming video of Sasha continuing with the interview of her mother.

"I figured it would be easier this way. You can watch without Porter watching you." Sally patted my shoulder and sat at another desk across from me, pointing at the cup of black coffee next to my hand.

"Enjoy the coffee. You look like you could use it."

I half listened to the interview while searching visitor logs. I could hear Sasha and her mother go back and forth.

It was a verbal chess game and I wasn't sure who was winning. For every step Sasha took, her mother matched her. But at least it sounded like Alison was giving up pieces of information.

Skimming through the visitor logs starting from the date she was transferred to Alderson, Alison hadn't had many visitors over the last few years at this facility. Sasha only visited once as an adult, and the visit was short. No more than a half hour. I flipped a few pages, looking for a pattern when eventually the log grew empty as time passed. I glanced at Sally. "Porter isn't a very popular woman?"

Sally shrugged, scooting over to the laptop. "She's an acquired taste. She had more visitors at Coleman, but we were certain those were her drug buddies. It's one of the reasons why she was moved up here. That, and she gave up information in trade for a transfer to a safer facility." Sally reached over, clicking a few times, pulling up Alison's file. "Porter had eight different incidents at Coleman. Nothing she incited, just random attacks. When they were investigated, it was determined Porter was being targets." She pointed at a report. "Coleman's investigating team could never find a link before she was moved."

I skimmed over the files. Alison was a horrible woman, but not violent. She chose to use her words over fists. I clicked on the visitor logs, trying to find a pattern when Sally spoke up.

"Wait. Porter had a visitor two weeks ago. A man." She leaned forward, clicking through the logs. "Damnit. Carlson didn't log it."

She stood, grabbing another laptop. "I'll find the footage of the visitor. He came in from D.C. and wanted to talk to Porter. Claimed he was an old cop friend of hers who wanted to see if rehabilitation was working. He was a big guy. Dressed too nice to be a cop, retired or not." She clicked the video. "That's him. I think his name was J. Higgins. I escorted him to the visitors' room, but left when Carlson took over."

I leaned forward. The man was large and wore a baseball cap covering most of his face. A large bushy mustache covered the rest of his face and the angle made it almost impossible to clearly see his face. "What did they talk about?"

"I'm not sure. The visit lasted a half hour and ended when Porter suddenly asked to be taken back to her cell. She looked pretty shaken when he showed her whatever it was on that phone." Sally pointed to the man taking out his phone and holding it up to Alison. I watched Alison's face turn pale, and look away from the phone as she motioned for the guard. When she was escorted out of the room, the man stood and turned towards the camera, his head still tilted down and avoiding the only good angle in the room.

I groaned until I saw the old English D on the cap, he Detroit Tigers logo, and something in my gut clicked. "Fuck." I dug in my pocket and pulled out my phone and sent the pictures of Bellico and Walker to Sasha. "Sally, do me a favor. Go and tell my partner to show the pictures I just sent her to Porter."

Sally nodded and left the room. A second later she appeared in the room, leaning over to Sasha. Sasha glanced at her as she took out her phone. I turned the volume on the laptop up. Sasha's face carried a confused look as she opened my message and read the instructions I'd written. She took a deep breath and set the phone in the middle of the table, asking her mother. "Do you recognize these two men?"

Alison smirked. "Are these former boyfriends? You want my motherly opinion? I like the lady cop you brought with you. She's got a fire in her belly." She leaned to look at the phone. The second she did, all the color drained out of her face and she turned away. "No."

Sasha sat up straighter. "No what?"

Alison shook her head. "No. I'm not saying shit. You can't make me."

Sasha looked over her shoulder right at the camera as if she was looking right at me, before turning back to her mother. "Mom. These two men are dead and can't hurt you. Tell me what you know about them."

Alison shook her head. "I want a deal." She glanced at her daughter and the tough, intelligent fire was gone. Replaced by fear. "I'll tell you everything, if you move me."

Sasha paused. "I can only do so much, Mom."

I grabbed my phone, typing out a message.

Reagan. Reagan is former NSA. She can move her into the shadows. Give her the deal. I have a theory.

I watched the screen, my leg bouncing as my gut feeling was twisting into thick knots.

Sasha read the message, tilted her head and let out a sigh. "Fine. I'll move you."

Alison's eyes lit up. "Somewhere no one can find me? That means any of the people you work with, and for." She bit her bottom lip. "Drop this one in the sea, Nat. Drop whatever you're working on into the great beyond and walk away."

I watched Sasha's shoulders fall. "And in the sea is where you'll find me." She sighed. "I always hated that poem. I'll have Emma make the call now. Tell me what you know."

Alison nodded, pointing at the phone. "Those two are cops. Shady, dirty cops I worked with all along the East Coast. They showed up at the meeting I told you about. I thought they were new muscle, but they were dealer handlers. Always on our ass and watching us. The fat one, Bellico, even arrested me three times. Roughed me up and told me to watch my ass if I wanted to stay alive. The other asshole, Walker, he snorted most of the inventory and blamed me when I came back short." Her face twisted. "They found out about you, Nat. They knew I had a daughter and went to use you as leverage to keep me on the line. That's when I disappeared for good. Told them I sold you off to the courts and you weren't a problem."

Alison laughed, shaking her head. I swore I saw a hint of regret in her face as she looked at her abandoned daughter. "These aren't people you can negotiate with, Nat."

Sasha swallowed hard, wringing her hands. She was struggling with what her mother just said, and saw the interview was about to come to end. I rushed out of the small office and headed back to the room. I asked the question the second I walked in. "Who was the man who visited you two weeks ago?"

Alison's eyes landed on mine. I could almost feel the fear in them. "Higgins. I thought the fucker was dead, until his ghost walked in here."

"Higgins. And who is Higgins?"

"He's the man who wiped out Carlos and took over the cartel. He's the man who got Walker to find the chemist who could make all the synthetic drugs imaginable. Especially those listed in that toxicology report my daughter has been hiding from me." She waggled her fingers at me, indicating she wanted to read the file. I handed it over.

She held it with trembling hands. "I didn't smoke away all of my brain, just most of my motor functions."

I sighed, hating how quick this woman was. She saw everything and was smarter than I gave her credit for.

Alison read over the report, squinting a few times. "This concoction is Higgins and his chemist, one hundred percent. The chemist was hard for levomethamphetamine since it was new to the market and you could buy it in bulk at a drug store with no question. The first batch was death in a baggie. The science wasn't right."

I sucked in a slow breath, trying hard to keep my composure. We'd just hit gold with a huge lead, and I didn't want to lose it. "Who was the chemist? And why was Higgins coming to see you?"

Alison slid the toxicology report across the table. "I never knew the chemist's real name. I have no idea where he came from, all I know is he was kicked out after a rash of overdoses hit the D.C. area. Killing the random junkies we gave samples to. I think one of them was a kid. Last I heard of the chemist was fifteen years ago. Meth lab explosion turned him into ash. Word was Higgins died in the fire too, I was wrong about that." She looked at me, then Sasha. "Higgins is dangerous. He's connected to powerful people, and I don't mean that in a cliché way. He's tied into the government somehow. Whether he's a cop, or he's in bed with senators, he's untouchable. He came here to warn me." She paused, squinting at me. "You're getting too close to something big and bad. That's why those two fucks are dead and I'm getting my first visitor in years." She leaned forward, covering her face with her hands. "He's going to kill the both of you. It's not an if, more of a when."

Sasha glanced at me. "Mom."

"No, don't, Nat. I fucked up again. This was all a trap. Higgins has the jump on you. Knew you'd come to me for information. You need to get me out of here tonight and then get the fuck out of dodge." Alison looked at her daughter with glassy eyes. "Get me out of here, and I can help you. I will help you."

I stared at the woman, trying to read if this was another chess move. Sasha went to open her mouth when I grabbed her shoulder. "Let us make a few calls. We'll be back." I squeezed Sasha's shoulder, silently asking her to leave the room with me.

She nodded, collected the files and left the room with me. The second we were out in the hall, she let out a huge breath. "Shit."

I moved closer to her, pulling out my phone. "I'm calling Reagan. She can move your mother, and I think she has a few questions of her own to ask.

This Heaten case extends past a girl's murder. It's a cover up, and I think Alison and Reagan have the final pieces we need to put this together."

Sasha's hand fell to my wrist. "You don't have to help her. The things she said to you, about your parents. I'm not sure they're true. I'm not sure anything she said is fully based in honesty. She's manipulative."

I nodded, clenching my jaw. "She stopped manipulating us the second you showed her the pictures of Bellico and Walker. She's afraid. So afraid she's willing to sacrifice her ego to save her life." I sighed, hitting Reagan's number. "As for my parents. I'll never know the truth, and I'd like to keep it that way."

I stepped back as Reagan answered the phone. "Agent Reagan."

"I'm calling in a favor, Dana. Do you still have a few shadows in your pocket from your NSA days?" I glanced at Sasha and saw the weight of emotional exhaustion settling on her shoulders.

Chapter 19

"We vetted her mother, but since her grandparents were the sole guardians, we didn't dig any further." Reagan stood next to me in the underground garage of Alderson. "Her mother had become a state's witness and we looked past her past. She was a valued informant for the DEA and ATF. Who knew? Who knew this woman had these ties?"

I chuckled. "You did, Dana." I folded my arms across my chest. "That's why you gave me the toxicology report in a doughnut bag. You had a hunch and you needed Sasha to play the daughter card. How long did you suspect Alison had information?"

Reagan smirked as Alison walked out of a side entrance with Sasha a step behind her. "Forever?" She glanced my way. "Honestly, I had no clue. I just gave you the information, it was your brilliant girlfriend who decided to tap into the mind of a convicted drug mule." She winked. "We should get moving. The quicker I can move Porter into protection, the better." She went to take a step, when she paused. "Oh, one more thing. Director Ellis called my office, asking where the files were. You might want to start packing things up and head to the Chicago office by the end of the week. The DEA wants to start their own investigation. It's a shame we've just taken their best chance at solving this one away." She chuckled, walking towards the van Alison was being loaded into.

I stood off to the side, watching. Alison was wearing normal clothes that hid the handcuffs and chains wrapped around her waist.

Sasha helped her mother into the van, and I saw a moment pass between them. Sasha shook her head and stepped away, keeping her head down as the van door slammed shut. I made my way over to her as the van drove out of the garage with three all black cars following.

I laid a hand on the small of her back. "Are you okay?"

"I grew up thinking she never cared about me. That I was just an inconvenience in her life, an easy paycheck." Sasha swallowed hard. "I'm confused. Torn about what I feel for my mother now." She looked up at me, her eyes glassy. "You know she just told me she likes you? Thinks you're good for me."

I chuckled, moving closer to her. "I think it's the other way around." I bent down, kissing the top of her head. "At least we've gotten the meet the parents part out of the way."

She sighed. "Yeah, but mine is a convicted felon." She stepped away from me. "Can we go home? Reagan will call us in a day or two when my mother is settled in her new living arrangements."

"It's nice down here. No snow and sun, maybe we can stay an extra day or two." I smiled when Sasha poked me in the side. "We can leave now. Reagan arranged a flight home for us." I stepped away, letting my hand slide down her arm. "I want to get back to the office and secure copies of the files we have. Ellis is breathing down our necks. He wants us to hand over the case immediately."

Sasha and I walked to the car parked outside the facility. She scrunched her face up, shaking her head. "That man is annoying. I don't understand his sudden interest in a cold case long abandoned by his agency."

I sighed, sliding into the driver's seat. "From what I understand, it's a power struggle. He wants credit if it's solved. Reagan has a heavy distaste for him, and I see why." I turned the car on as Sasha got in. "I think our best bet is to find the link that brought Bellico and Walker into the drug dealing side business." I glanced at her. "We need to find the files on the Alvarez cartel, and do it quietly."

"My mother is scared. I've never seen her scared." Sasha sighed. "I'll have Morgan sift through the video footage and see if she can get a clear image of this Higgins."

I sighed, nodding. "She's safe. Oddly enough, I trust Reagan. She'll make sure your mother has protection." I started the car, glancing at Sasha. She was staring out the window, her brow furrowed, lost in thought. I reached over, covering the hand sitting on her lap. "Our flight doesn't leave for another four hours. Sally pointed me in the direction of her favorite hole in the wall diner. She claims they serve up the best cornbread in five counties. What do you say to having lunch and talking about my weeklong stint as a high school cheerleader?"

Sasha smirked, tipping her head down to look at our hands. "Your mother already told me that story. Even showed me the pictures." She looked up, meeting my eyes. "I love you, Emma. Thank you." She squeezed my hand.

I leaned over, kissing the side of her head, murmuring. "I love you, too. Let's go get some cornbread and maybe a shot of moonshine."

Sasha only smiled, pulling my hand closer into her body.

*****

"I found the Alvarez files. It took me most of the night of backtracking and doing loops around the mainframe security." Morgan sat on the countertop of my kitchen island, a bowl of popcorn sitting in her lap. "Not everything I did was illegal." She winked at Aaron standing next to me with a beer. "He can testify I used my federal credentials until I ran into the access denied screens of the DEA."

She pointed at me with a handful of popcorn.

"Which, by the way, gives me all sorts of hinky feelings. Why would the DEA have cartel files buried in red tape? Alvarez was a mid-level cartel. Nothing like Escobar or El Chapo. It doesn't make sense when the thousands of other mid-level drug dealers, gun smugglers and tobacco smugglers are wide open to all agencies." Morgan nodded to Sasha. "Even my CIA contact couldn't access the files with his super stellar clearance."

Sasha sighed, pulling at the label on her bottle of beer. "No, it doesn't make sense." She sat next to Morgan, hunched over and still lost in thought.

Meeting with her mother and unraveling another layer of Alison had Sasha quiet, distracted ever since we stopped for lunch. She'd grown almost silent during the flight back to Chicago, and hadn't spoken more than ten words since Morgan arrived.

Morgan managed to navigate the elaborate databases with the help of Aaron. She was currently downloading the files using a dead drop ISP address based out of Siberia. We wanted the files, but didn't necessarily want anyone to know we were the ones borrowing them. Morgan made it look like a bored kid in the winter wasteland was testing his computer skills. It would be another hour before we could peel back the layers of the Alvarez cartel along with Bellico and Walker's involvement.

Morgan reached over, snagging Sasha's beer and taking a huge drink. "You good, Sasha? You've been playing it quiet since I got here. You haven't even touched the doughnuts Aaron brought from that overrated bakery you love." She leaned back, patting Sasha on the cheek. "You okay?"

Sasha smiled tightly, shrugging as she stood. "I'm just tired. It was a long day and the weather shift is getting to me." She buried her hands in the sleeves of her sweater.

"I think I'm going to take a hot shower and then lie down. Get me when the files have downloaded." She glanced my way, catching my eyes before leaving the kitchen.

Aaron sensed the tension in the room. "What happened in West Virginia?" He moved closer to Morgan.

I smiled, picking up her half empty beer and took a sip. "We went to talk to her mother."

Morgan dropped the handful of popcorn. "Her mother? The great ghost Alison?"

I nodded, taking another sip. "Yes, Alison. Mother of the decade. It was a long shot, but she turned out to be a very valuable long shot. She's where we got the info for the Alvarez cartel." I sighed, rubbing my forehead as a tension headache was threatening to take over. "It wasn't fun for either of us. I think Sasha is struggling with seeing another side of her mother. The careless drug dealer who wants to have a heart of gold and repent." I chuckled. "Alison is a banshee in an orange jumpsuit."

Morgan squinted. "That's rude to speak of your future mother in law like that."

"It's rude of her to tell me she once held me as a baby, watching my mother overdose on the heroin Alison sold her." I clutched the beer bottle. "It's rude for her to crawl into my mind like a morbid therapist and use her daughter against me." I sighed. "Alison Porter might be a dirty drug dealer, but she's incredibly brilliant. Brilliant and dangerous." I glanced at the stairs leading to the bedroom. "Sasha kind of shut down the moment Reagan showed up to take Alison into protective custody."

"She never really talked about her mother. I only knew about the phone calls from the penitentiary on holidays. It's probably why Sasha hates Christmas so much." Morgan sighed. "Are you okay?"

I shrugged. "I've been through worse." I smiled a

little as Morgan and Aaron chuckled. "I can't be upset over a family I never knew. But I can be upset when someone messes with the family I have."

"Where is her mother?"

"In a safe house in an undisclosed location in the city. We all agreed it was best to keep her close, but hidden. If her intel on the Alvarez Cartel is good, it might draw out the creepy crawlies." I frowned. "I just need one good lead. Not more dead bodies and random body parts showing up in the mail." Morgan's laptop dinged, signaling the files were downloaded. Morgan slid off the counter, grabbing her computer.

"Let's see if Momma P came through." She clicked on a few files, filling the screen with old DEA and FBI case files. There were a few old video clips from the last three prisons Alison was housed at. Courtesy of a link sent over by Sally giving Morgan a back door to access all visitor logs in the federal system. I sat next to Morgan, leaning over to look at the screen.

"Can you run a facial recognition program and see if it picks up anything from Alison's visitors over the years? Go back as far as the files go. She mentioned she'd been on the bubble with the cartel since she was arrested. Looked for someone named Higgins. Alison was petrified Higgins is still alive." I looked up at Aaron. "And can you go back to the station and talk to Vice? Ask if any of them had dealings with the Álvarez Cartel over the years? I know in the late nineties the cartels were using Chicago as a main trafficking hub. Heroin and cocaine."

Aaron chugged the rest of his beer. "You got it. I'll call Kirkman. He's been vice since the dawn of time. He's a walking encyclopedia of drugs and drug dealers."

He rushed out the door, promising to call me as soon as he got anything.

I moved to the fridge, pulling out two more beers for Morgan and I. "How long will this take, Morgan?"

"Depends on how many visitors Alison had during her incarceration." Morgan eagerly took the beer, glancing at the staircase. "You should go check on her. Sasha doesn't do well stewing in her own thoughts. No matter what she says." She winked at me, motioning to the cupcakes sitting on the counter behind her. "She can't resist devil's food cake cupcakes."

I smiled, grabbing a cupcake. "Duly noted." I moved towards the stairs, calling over my shoulder. "Come get us if you find anything."

I found Sasha sitting on the floor in my office, her back against the desk. She had her head down in her hands. She had changed out of her pantsuit and into a pair of flannel striped pajamas and her FBI academy shirt. Sasha looked defeated, tired and the sight hurt my heart.

I sat down next to her, leaning into her shoulder. I heard a soft sigh fall from her lips as she leaned her head back against the desk. I held up the cupcake. "Word is these cupcakes make you weak in the knees?"

She half smiled, looking at me. "They used to. But something else came along and made me weaker in the knees."

I rolled my eyes, nudging her with my shoulder. "I really hope you don't say it was me who ruined your love of cupcakes." I began peeling the paper away from the cupcake. "Are you okay?"

Sasha shrugged, pulling her knees up to her chin. "How did you deal with everything when the world fell apart?" She tilted her head in my direction. "Not saying mine is in utter shambles, but my mother is a hard pill to swallow. No matter how small the dose."

"I relied on Aaron a lot. He came through for me when I didn't think I needed him. I sat in silence quite a bit in between my ridiculous outbursts."

I pulled the cupcake apart, handing half to Sasha. "But mainly I talked. I talked to whoever would listen. Aaron, my Mom, my Dad. People I trusted." I glanced at her. "You. You were a huge part in healing the cracks in my foundation." I smiled, swiping a finger through the icing. "I've been on shaky ground for weeks, but every day with you, the shakes are fading. Meeting your mother helped. She pisses me off so much, I forget how scared I've been. Maybe I should fire my therapist and visit your mom every Monday." I laughed, licking the icing.

"I know I caused a few cracks in your foundation, and I'm doing everything I can to be there for you." Sasha sighed, staring at the cupcake in her hand. "I'm having a hard time with my mother suddenly having the desire to be in my life again. I always felt like I was an inconvenience she only kept around for the checks. But after you left the room, she told me she'd had plenty of time to sit and rot in her life choices. She has serious regrets about being such a shit mother. I believe in her need to fix the rift between us, it's just hard to digest after all these years. The distance, the hate, the anger. They're not small things I can overlook with a smile and a hug."

"Alison is a master manipulator. It's a shame she chose the drug life, she would've been an incredible interrogator. She has a knack for getting under your skin and pushing out your secrets."

Sasha shook her head. "Not with me. My Grandmother taught me to look in my mom's eyes when I was talking to her. When she tells the truth, she won't ever make direct eye contact. The truth scares her. She can't bullshit the truth." She leaned back against the desk, shoving the cupcake in her mouth. "But I guess when you live your life in lies, the truth can be scary."

"Interesting fun fact. I'll have to keep that in mind the next time I'm in a room with her." I shifted, facing Sasha, taking her hand in mine. "I don't want you to ever think you owe her anything. I don't want you to think she's right about any of the terrible things she tells you. And I don't want you to ever think you're alone in this." I ran my thumb over her knuckles as she squeezed my hand. "You're incredible, Sasha. If anything, your mother should be envious of who you've become."

Sasha smiled. "Thank you. Thank you for always being my champion even when it seemed hopeless. I know I'm swimming in a sea of self-pity right now, but the day has been overwhelming. No one ever wants to think their parent is a key player in a massive drug cartel, let alone a possible witness to a cold case murder that's turning into multiple murders."

I shrugged. "I'd take your mother over my murderous brother any day." I stood up, tugging her hand. "Let's forget about our crazy families and eat the rest of the cupcakes. Morgan is downstairs pulling footage from all the prisons your mother was housed at. I think she can be persuaded to call it a night."

"That girl is a bigger workaholic than I am. She'll be reviewing footage all night on your kitchen counter while eating all our food." Sasha stood up, grabbing my other hand.

I chuckled, taking my cell phone out of my pocket. "True. But she has a weakness for a handsome Chicago detective who owes me a million favors." I tapped out a quick message to Aaron. Asking if he would take Morgan to dinner, giving Sasha and I the night to decompress. "I can't believe I'm saying this. The evidence can wait. Your mother is safe with Reagan, the footage is going nowhere. Let's take the day and come back tomorrow refocused."

Sasha opened her mouth in mock shock. "I do believe I will have to write this down in my memory book. The great Emma Tiernan, Detective extraordinaire is taking a night off in the middle of a case. I'm shocked and awed!"

"Shush." I leaned over, kissing the shock off her face. "In case I didn't say it today, I love you." I could feel the tension leaving the woman as small smile covered her face.

Sasha blushed, grinning. "I don't mind hearing you repeat yourself." She looked up. "I love you so much. So much more than any favorite cupcake." She laughed, moving past me to leave the office. "I'm making dinner tonight."

I squinted at her back. "You mean you're heating up the leftovers Aaron brought over from his mom's house."

Sasha held her hands up. "A chef never tells her secrets."

CHAPTER 20

I sat in the kitchen, looking out the window into the garden as the morning sun worked on melting the newest layer of snow the night had given us. My laptop was sitting on the far edge of the table, a half full cup of coffee next to it. Morgan had compiled footage of Alison's visitors and sent it over in the wee hours of the morning, waking me from a deep sleep. I had the half notion to review it while Sasha slept, but now that I was sitting down, I wasn't too eager to get started. I wanted to spend a few minutes watching the snow melt, sip my coffee, and think about what I wanted for breakfast.

Tomorrow was the deadline for us to hand over everything we had to the DEA field office. They would get everything we had, minus the original files stashed away in my safe. I sighed, I needed to call Reagan later and figure out what her game plan was. How would we cover up the fact we were still working the Heaten case under the radar? People were getting killed over this case and I had the sinking suspicion the DEA knew the who and why behind all these deaths. Maybe they could help explain why we were being sent random body parts of the victims. Another question I had no answers to.

The FBI had matched all the body parts to each victim who was also on our list of witnesses. It was Walker's ears in the box, Bellico's hands, and his eyes sitting in that jar next to his body. I was pretty sure if we hadn't kicked down that door and found him, his eyes would be on a first class trip to our desks. Another warning note attached to the jar.

The FBI hadn't found any trace evidence to give us a possible suspect. All the DNA collected at the scene belong to the victims. There were no signs anyone else had been in either man's house. Each crime scene was unusually spotless, giving me another gut feeling I had to untangle.

A gut feeling that told me our guy was possibly law enforcement with the knowledge how to clean up after himself and leave no clues behind. But the violence of the dismemberments and murders had drug cartel stink all over it.

Maybe our suspect was a pissed off cop who was caught up in the drug business by Walker and Bellico. They shorted him on a deal and kicked him to the curb, leaving him holding the proverbial bag for the last thirty years. And now, as we dug up a cold case, he was cleaning house, just like Triple A was sent to mine to do. Exacting his revenge and shutting mouths before names slipped out of one. I scribbled on my notepad. Most of my witnesses were dead and the others gave me everything they had, and that everything led me nowhere. I groaned and reached for the laptop, clicking the file open. I'd watch it once, then have Sasha watch it with me, see if anything stood out to her.

The file went all the way back to late 1983. The footage was grainy and skipped every three seconds.

I was thankful Morgan edited and isolated Alison's visitors. I half watched on fast forward. Very few people went to visit Alison that year. There was a lawyer and a news reporter looking for a cold case story to research for. In early 1984 the same lawyer stopped by twice. I knew he was there to go over the last of her appeals, and by the exasperation on his face, the lawyer had failed to get any traction. I kept watching through the winter and spring, the poor lawyer was diligent that's for sure. Then summer hit and Alison began having a few more visitors. I clicked off fast forward and scooted closer as two men came to visit her. One looked a lot like Bellico. I frowned when I couldn't zoom in on the frame, the eighties still being a little behind in technology. I groaned when audio wasn't an option.

I watched in silence. The guy who looked like Bellico, came with his buddy twice a week all summer long. A few times a guy who wore a blue baseball cap and a thick mustache, joined Bellico. But again, zooming in wasn't an option. The camera was fixed overhead to watch if things were being passed between the inmate and visitor. I marveled that for a federal prison, Alison was left in a small room with nothing but a cheap folding table between her and Bellico. She was a high risk prisoner, but got the fancy delights of face to face visits. No hard wired glass and nasty black telephone handsets.

I watched all of 1984. Bellico's buddy dropped off in the fall and was replaced full time by baseball hat. I scribbled down notes on times and dates. If there was at least a pattern, I could sit with Alison and use it as a talking point. She would know who these people were, including the baseball hat who always kept his head tilted away from the camera. It was like he knew he was being watched and knew how to play the cameras.

I clicked onto 1985 with vigor. In winter of 1985 Alison's parents came to visit, a tiny Sasha with them. I didn't need to audio to understand the conversation. I could tell by the hand gestures and blurred frown on her grandparent's face, it wasn't a happy time for anyone. I shut the video off when little Sasha went to hug her mother and Alison politely stepped away from her own daughter. I swallowed a lump and hit pause. I should've known at some point I'd come across footage of Sasha and her mother.

"I actually remember that day. I just turned five and mom was serving a short sentence for a misdemeanor drug possession charge." Sasha's sleepy voice half startled me. "I think she was in upstate New York then. I'd spent the year with my grandparents, thinking nothing of my mother being gone, or in jail. I was having too much fun running in a big backyard and sleeping in a warm bed. I was too young to understand my mother was a criminal and we were at a jail. I do remember the guards to be very nice. One bought me a candy bar out of the vending machine." She yawned, squinting at the clock. "We have today off, why are you up so early?"

    I smiled, standing up to go make more coffee. "I woke up to pee and decided to sort out the files we're giving back. I'm making sure we have copies of everything we needed to keep going." I grabbed the bag of coffee, handing Sasha my half empty cup. "Then Morgan sent us the video files of your mothers' visitors over the years. I couldn't resist." I bent over, kissing her cheek. "I should've waited for you. I didn't think you'd be in the videos."

    Sasha smiled. "That's because I've always fudged the truth about mom and prison. Kept things close to the chest. My grandparents were my babysitters until I reached the legal age to go with them permanently. Mom signed me away without a second thought." She leaned against the counter next to me. "They took me here and there to see her. Hoping I'd be the one thing that could change her ways. It never worked. The drug life was more her style than being a parent." Sasha's gaze drifted to the coffee maker. "She never cared until I became an agent and could help her."

    "You don't have to watch them. I can recruit Aaron to sit and look for patterns with me." I tapped the button on the coffee maker. The air quickly filled with the smell of fresh coffee.

    "It's fine. She's always going to be the one part of my life I can't predict." She met my eyes. "We have a case to solve, no matter the personal ties."

    I let out a slow breath. "Boy, don't I know that." I leaned over, kissing Sasha's temple before resting my chin

In the space between her neck and shoulder. "We'll spend the morning reviewing footage, before packing up the files."

"I hate that we have to bow to the DEA." She grabbed my hand. "It's a homicide cold case, not an active drug case. My mother already gave the DEA everything she knew over the last thirty years. As far as I can tell, it's only street cops involved with the cartel." She paused. "It doesn't make sense. Why is the DEA so adamant in taking this one away from us?"

I squinted at her, I'd been asking that same question over the last few days. "We should put the DEA on our suspect list. I'll ask Reagan to get us a list of agents involved in the Alvarez Cartel investigations. Check if any of them were linked to our dead street cops." I stepped away, filling a mug with the Cubs logo with fresh coffee. "Shall we?" I waved to the laptop sitting on the table.

Sasha smiled. "No other way I'd rather spend a snowy morning."

Four hours into the footage, Sasha tapped the space bar, pausing the video. It was from Alison's short stint up in a New York Federal prison. A quick stop over before she was released and arrested four months later for the crimes, she was now serving life sentences for. "This guy."

She tapped the screen. "He's shown up four times. The last two were within a six month period. He's always in a baseball hat, sunglasses and keeps his face away from the cameras. Mom doesn't like him. She's sitting sideways. She always did that when she hated the person she was speaking with. It allowed her to make a quick escape from the conversation and the room."

I leaned over. "I noticed him in '84, but he disappeared from '86 to '92." I squinted at the screen. "The video quality is better, but the facial features are still too pixelated." I sat back in my chair, picking up my half eaten doughnut. "We still have at least thirteen more hours of footage to go through."

Sasha grabbed her phone, shooting me a wink. "Morgan? Hi, I need you to do something." She rolled her eyes. "Yes, lunch for a week, on me. Can you run that test program the IT boys created? The one where it finds patterns and landmarks in video footage? I'm sending you a screen cap of a guy from mom's visitor tapes. I need you to collect all the times he visited my mom. I'm hoping in the later years the quality improves and we can identify him." Another pause. "As soon as possible."

When she hung up, she glanced at me. "After lunch we'll have baseball guys greatest hits. Can you hit up Reagan?"

I grinned, shoving the last bit of doughnut in my mouth. "Aaron has the list. Reagan hand delivered it to him at the park. He should be here in an hour with a white bakery bag full of Danishes and an unedited list of DEA agents assigned to the Alvarez cartel."

Sasha stood up, stretching her arms over her head. "Perfect." She cocked an eyebrow my way. "Would you like to join me in the shower?"

Through a full mouth, I grabbed her hand, half dragging her behind me. "Only if you wash my back, and front." The sound of Sasha's giggle, and the way she squeezed my heart, made a little bit of the weight of this case disappear.

CHAPTER 21

"Reagan is strange. I felt like I was picking up the country's nuclear codes." Aaron flopped down on the couch.

"She's former NSA and holds a wicked grudge against Ellis. She's trying to stay out of the mix, while staying firmly in the mix." I sat next to him, digging in the white bakery bag. I handed Aaron a Danish as I unfolded the thin sheet of paper and read off the names. "Agent David Coranado. Agent Roger Whitaker. Agent Lawrence Vale. Agent Patrick Ellis. And lastly, Agent Pierce Salt."

Aaron sat up. "Wait, Agent Patrick Ellis? Isn't that the dickhead Deputy Administrator who's taking the Heaton case from you?"

I closed my eyes, tossing the paper on the coffee table. "Fuck." I stood up, rushing to Sasha's laptop. Messaging her to hurry home with lunch. I whispered another fuck as I ran Ellis's name through the secured database. His entire file popped up and it was filled with nothing but heroic commendations for a job well done. The man was squeaky clean and on the road to the top. Which in my eyes, immediately made him suspicious. "Ellis has to be connected. I don't know how yet, but there's a reason why he's pulling the case from us."

Aaron appeared next to me. "Didn't you get a weird vibe off of him at that meeting?"

"Nothing other than he's a pompous dick bag." I sucked in a breath. "Reagan hates him. She has for years. But she has nothing on him other than he's a greasy player who's used her as a door mat a few times." I tapped the counter. "I need his case work. I need to know what he worked, who he worked with at the street level. The Alvarez case was huge and involved everyone, not just federal agencies."

"What if you pickle him?"

I looked at Aaron. "You mean run at him like a usual suspect?"

Pickle him was a code Aaron and I used on cases where we were interviewing a suspect who wouldn't budge an inch. We'd pepper them with random questions, feed them like we were feeding a drunk shots of whiskey, trying to pickle them into confusion. Eventually they'd slip and give us a sliver of something to go on. It was our version of good cop, bad cop, but not as cliché. "He's smart. But too political for his own good. I think if I chip at him like that Alderman from the eighth district, he'll slip. If anything, he'll kick me out of the room and ask the FBI to censure me and strip me of my bars."

Aaron chuckled. "But you technically don't work for the FBI."

I grinned. "Exactly."

Sasha walked in the front door, hands full of greasy brown paper bags. "I ran as fast as I could. Tony's was busy and they ran out of meatballs." She handed Aaron the bags. "What did you get? Morgan is sending over the greatest hits of baseball hat."

I pointed at the sheet of paper on the table. "Ellis worked the Álvarez Cartel case. I can't get into his case files to link any of other suspects to. I'm going to take a soft run at him in the meeting tomorrow. I want to see his reaction."

"Deputy Administrator Ellis?" Sasha sat on the edge of the coffee table, picking up the paper. "He's so clean, his asshole squeaks when he walks."

Aaron choked out a laugh. "Yeah, squeaky clean usually means dirty as hell." He bit into his massive Reuben sandwich. "Emma and I can tell you stories of how the clean ones are usually the worst society has to offer."

I tapped Sasha's knee. "I want to talk to your mom later. Show her the footage of baseball hat, maybe she knows who he is. I want to go into tomorrow's meeting prepared to hammer Ellis if I need to."

Sasha nodded, reaching for a club sandwich. "I figured. I have the safehouse address. Mom is on Lakeshore, tucked up in a secured luxury condo. I asked them to keep her close in case we needed her for information." She gave me a look. "We can head over whenever you're ready."

I squeezed her knee, a silent thank you. My heart began pounding like it always did when I felt like I was about to break a case. That strange adrenaline surge mixed with fear.

*****

"This place makes me want to become an informant." I stood in the marbled lobby of the condo building Alison was housed in. It was one of the most expensive building on Lakeshore and a perfect place to house a federal prisoner. Not many would suspect the NSA to truly have a safehouse like this. That only happened in the movies.

Sasha nudged me. "Stop gawking before the security guard get suspicious." She walked to a random mailbox, opened it with the small key and pulled out another set of keys before dropping the first one in the box, closing the door. "Let's go up. We only have a few hours."

I followed her into the elevator. "It's all I need." Leaning against the wall, I jammed my hands into my pockets. "Here's hoping the high life has softened Alison's edges. The last thing I want, is to go a few more rounds in the mental boxing ring. She's a firecracker. But at least now I know who you inherited your intelligence from."

"She's scared." Sasha nervously smoothed out the edges of her jacket. "Meaning she'll be a thousand times worse about picking through your brain. She gets meaner, smarter, when she's scared." Sasha cocked an eyebrow my way.

I let out a slow breath as the elevator dinged, the doors opening. "Great."

Following Sasha out, I offered a professional smile to the man in khakis and a sweater standing at the door. He screamed federal agent/ex-military. I held out my badge and ID card, meeting the man's intense stare.

"Thank you, Agent Clarke and Officer Tiernan. You have three hours with the prisoner. Not a minute more." He held out our wallets. I snatched mine back, opening my mouth to correct him.

"Captain Tiernan." Sasha's tone was hard as she corrected him. Equally as hard as the glare she threw at the guy. "Her title is Captain." She pushed past the agent, pushing the large maple door open with palm. The agent seemed unfazed, giving me another hard, uncaring glare of his own. In a way, I didn't blame him. Babysitting witnesses and prisoners was the shittiest of shit details. NSA or not.

The interior of the condo was as opulent as the lobby. Dark woods adorned the walls, plush rugs covered the floor while leather soaked furniture dotted the living room. There were floor to ceiling windows lining the walls, the hazy glint of bulletproof glass took the shine off them. A female agent walked out a hallway, a soft smile on her face. "Agent Clarke, Captain Tiernan, I'm Agent Madeline Coolidge. Alison's handler for the duration of her time in our custody."

I half smiled at her, waving at the windows. "Bulletproof glass with one way mirror effect. Which mafia did you confiscate this place from? Italian, Russian, etc.?"

Coolidge chuckled, stopping to stand next to me. "SEC fraud busted by the FBI and eventually confiscated by us. Stockbroker was inside trading and grew paranoid when his clients turned against him. He cut a deal with the CIA and by proxy us. We took this place off the FBI's hands for the duration of investigation, and we kind of kept it." She looked at me, smiling as she answered my unasked question. "Russian and Italian mafia clients. Let's just say Mr. Stockbroker went willingly to the super max in Colorado. We seized this condo and four other properties. And before you ask, Reagan called in a few favors to provide Alison with this level of protection. All we ask is the NSA is allowed first dibs on any information we find useful."

She turned to Sasha. "Your mother is just finishing up in the bathroom. You'll have three hours at most to speak with her."

Sasha nodded. "Will we have privacy? The nature of our conversation is sensitive."

Coolidge cocked her eyebrow. "Reagan mentioned it was a private family matter." She paused, making direct eye contact with us. Her silent way of communicating she'd been fully briefed on the true nature of our visit. "I've set up the office for you. It's soundproof and free of wiretaps." She motioned to the room to her left just as Alison walked into the room.

"Nat." Her tone was soft, almost motherly. She stepped forward, her eyes landing on me. "And the street cop lover. What a lovely surprise!"

"Mom, this isn't a social visit. We need to show you a few things, ask a few more questions." Sasha glanced at Coolidge. "I'd like to get started."

Coolidge gave a curt nod and escorted us to the office. "You have three hours." She didn't wait for us to get comfortable before exiting the room, closing the massive oak door behind her.

    I took a seat in the plush leather couch, Sasha next to me and Alison sitting in the leather wingback facing us. Alison kept staring at me like I was a museum exhibit, studying my face, ignoring her daughter setting up the laptop on the table in front of her. "You look so much like your mother. It's like looking in a photograph."

    I knew she was baiting me. "We reviewed all your visitor logs and the footage from those visits over last twenty five years." I motioned to the laptop. "There was one man who visited you far more than anyone else." I paused, hesitating before it spilled out of my mouth. "More than your family." Alison flinched as Sasha huffed out my name in a harsh whisper. I was playing dirty and didn't care. This woman had pressed plenty of my buttons. Alison looked down at her hands, her cheeks turning a soft red.

    "A friend compiled all of his visits over the years for your daughter and I." I reached over, pushing the laptop closer to Alison, hitting play on the video. "Who is the man in the baseball cap?"

    Alison's eyes flicked to the screen. She clenched her jaw and turned away. "He's someone better left unknown." She was scared and slowly pulling back from us. Long gone was the cocky convict.

    Leaning on my knees, I squinted at the woman. "I need to know who he is. He's the only solid suspect we have in a cold case homicide gone tits up. He's also the only suspect I have in the death of three other people. People who were suddenly murdered right when your daughter and I began digging in the death of a sixteen year old girl." I scooted to the edge of the couch. "I need to know who he is outside of the baseball hat and a cheesy mustache. I need to know who Higgins really is."

    Alison's eyes grew to the size of small moons, giving

me the tiniest bit of hope. "You told us he visited you a few weeks ago, and there he was. Baseball hat and avoiding the cameras. Scaring the living shit out of you. We did you a huge favor, Alison, put you in protective custody where no one can touch you. Give us a little something back. You know who he is. If you didn't, you'd still be sitting in your West Virginia cell, watching soap opera reruns, counting down the days until you can call your daughter and make her feel guilty for living a motherless life."

I was done playing games with this woman. I didn't care if she was the mother of the love of my life. Our lives were in danger and she was too chicken shit to help us.

Alison closed her eyes, shoving the laptop away. "Leave it alone. He'll only hurt you, kill you to keep the silence." Alison opened her eyes, looking right at Sasha. "Trust me, Nat. He's pure evil, nothing you want to handle. Pure evil with more power than you can imagine."

I chuckled, shaking my head. "I've had my fair share of pure evil. This guy is nothing compared to the monsters in my closet." I glanced at Sasha, feeling the surge of pain of almost losing her at the hands of the Carpenter family.

Sasha swallowed hard. "Mom, please. Tell us what you know. We need any lead we can get. This simple cold case has taken a turn. A big enough turn that has you scared and spilling your guts to the DEA." She pointed at the laptop screen. "Who is Higgins? Is he tied to any of the agencies? Is he a cop? Is he a politician?"

Alison looked up. Her jaw twitching. "Am I really safe? These people are powerful, and have the keys to every door."

Sasha nodded. "You're in NSA protection. You're off the grid and off the radar for the usual departments you've dealt with in the past. The FBI are under the impression you're in the process of being bounced around until a spot in the California penitentiary opens up. The DEA will have your interview notes nailing the remaining members of the Alvarez cartel. That's enough for them to forget your existence. Only Emma and I know you're here. My boss pulled the strings to slip you into the shadows. At the first hint of trouble, they'll protect you." Sasha let out a slow breath. "You're as safe as I can ever make you, mom."

She chuckled. "A shame I never did the same for you. But penance for my sins can wait." Alison's gaze fell to the laptop. "The last time he saw me, he threatened to kill you, Nat. Kill you and send me your body parts one by one." She looked at me. "He also threatened to kill you, Emma. Kill you in front of Nat, record it and make me watch. Told me I could sit and watch as the only person my daughter ever loved, be torn away from her. A reminder of how I always failed my daughter." Her eyes turned glassy, as she licked her lips. "I promised him I'd never tell you his name. But he never said anything about giving you clues." She looked directly at me. "I'm still not sure about you, cop, but you love my daughter like she's the air you need to breathe. Word has it you're a bit of a genius?" She grabbed the notepad and pen next to the laptop and started scribbling.

I furrowed my brow. "I'm not sure what any of this has to do with the case. If anything, you're wasting our time." I stood up, pissed off at being played by this woman. "If you're not going to answer our questions, fine. Live in fear and regret." I turned to Sasha. "I'll be outside. Use the last two and a half hours however you choose. I can't be in here anymore."

"I like your fire, copper. But your temper needs a lot of work. Ever try therapy?" Alison swallowed the smirk, tipping her head down as she softened her tone. "I can see you getting pissed off, it's so easy and I can't resist pushing your buttons." She glanced up, tossing the notepad on the table. "One of the upsides of living in prison most of my life, it gave me time to pick up hobbies. Reading, writing, drawing. Art therapy has done wonders. My art teacher thinks I have a natural talent." Alison tapped the edge of the notepad before showing it to us. A perfect abstract rendering of Higgins without his baseball cap and mustache stared back up at us. "He never took off his hat and I knew that mustache was fake. Luckily for me, he took off his sunglasses during the last visit. Just a split second, but it was enough of a last puzzle piece to put everything in perspective. This is the best I can do." She looked at me. "Now, genius, do your magic. I read up on you. Expert in facial recognition, the best in the Chicago Police Department."

    Picking up the notepad, I stared at the face staring back up at me. The sketch wasn't bad, but it wasn't good enough for me to recognize who Higgins was in the flesh. His eyes were crooked, throwing the entire image off and his jaw was longer than humanly possible. I'd have to have Morgan clean it up in one of her programs and run it through the databases. "You could give us his name, not draw me an abstract sketch."

    Alison shrugged. "I could, but I've never ever given up a name and snitched. I'd like to keep that reputation intact." She stood, stepping closer to me. "Keep Nat safe. Once you get his name, it's going to be the end. He won't stop until everyone of us is dead and his name disappears in the wind." She turned to Sasha, sitting in silence. "Now, if you don't mind. I'd like to talk to my daughter for a moment. Alone."

    I rolled my eyes, tore the page off the notepad and left the room, folding the sketch up and jamming it into my pocket.

    Coolidge met me outside near the windows. "Did

you get what you need?"

"Yes? No? Who knows? The woman is a pain in the ass who loves to manipulate. We might have a lead, or we might have another dead end." I huffed, rubbing my eyes.

"I'd trust her. I basically live with that pain in the ass, and all she talks about is how brilliant her daughter is." Coolidge smirked, looking my way. "And how even more brilliant her cop girlfriend is."

I shook my head, looking over my shoulder as Sasha walked out. Confusion painted all over her face. "Emma, we can go now."

"Are you okay?

"Yeah. Just confused like always when I visit my mother." Sasha shifted her briefcase. "She suddenly wants to be a part of my life. Asking if she can call more, email and add me to the visitors list at the next prison she's housed at. And not one mention of pulling strings for appeals, or more money for the canteen."

She met my eyes. "She also wanted me to tell you, she really likes you." She scrunched her face up in utter confusion. "You two bicker like an old divorced couple."

I smiled, shaking my head. "That's the second time she's said that. She knows my buttons and likes smashing them." I motioned towards the door. "Let's get back to the office. We need to pack up the rest of the files for the meeting tomorrow. I also want to double check we kept copies of everything."

Sasha sighed. "Why do I have a really bad feeling about tomorrow?"

I said nothing, my silence confirming I shared the same bad feeling.

Chapter 22

"Would either of you like any coffee? Director Ellis is running a few minutes late."

I shook my head at the pleasant secretary as Sasha accepted the offer. I was already on edge, I didn't need caffeine to amp me up. I also saw through the bullshit Ellis was pulling. The waiting game was an old trick. The longer he made us wait, the less time he would have for us. He'd swoop in, collect our hard work and shoo us out the door. I sat at the conference table, picking at the edges of the stack of banker's boxes Sasha and I hauled across town. It was everything we'd compiled during our investigation, minus the hard copies of the original files Latham and Reagan gave us. Those were locked in my basement safe hidden under Aaron's Supergirl comic books.

Morgan was back at her apartment working on Alison's sketch. Running it through the million identification programs she had access to, Aaron was by her side running them through the databases he had access to. The moment Sasha and I walked into the conference room, they weren't anywhere close to finding a match to Alison's abstract drawing. I had half the mind to storm down to the safe house and strangle a name out of the infuriating woman.

Sasha was pacing the length of the room, arms crossed with a look of complete frustration on her face.

"Are you sure you need coffee? You're going to wear a path into that fancy carpet. With our luck, Ellis would bill us to replace it." I leaned forward, smiling at the look Sasha gave me.

"I'm frustrated. Our first case in this new unit and it's yanked out of our hands right as we get close to any leads." She ran a hand over her hair. "The DEA is going to bury this, and that girl will never get justice. No one will get justice."

"We'll get it for her." I caught her hazel eyes. Sasha was tired, exhausted. The last few weeks had run her through the ringer, then topped it off with the cherry of her absent mother wanting to repent for her sins. "I promise."

The large doors swung open and Ellis and Gus waltzed in, the secretary hot on their heels with a tray of coffee. She went to set it down when she was waved away by Ellis. "No thank you, Nora. This meeting will be quick."

I rolled my eyes, standing up and shoving the boxes to the middle of the table. "Here's everything you've requested." I glanced at Gus giving me an apologetic look. He knew the raw deal we were being handed, but his hands were tied.

Ellis grinned, plucking at the silver cuffs highlighting his expensive blue suit. The man was impeccably dressed and looked nothing like a DEA agent. He looked more like a politician who sold you piece of shit cars on the side. "Ah, perfect! My team will get started immediately." He motioned for Gus to grab the boxes before he turned to Sasha. "Agent Clarke, your cooperation will not go unnoticed. I'll ensure your supervisor receives a letter of commendation to add to your file."

Sasha's jaw twitched. "Of course. Interagency cooperation is critical. If you need anything, or have any questions, Captain Tiernan and I are available."

Ellis cocked an eyebrow. "*If* I have questions, I'll surely search you out." He turned to face me. "But sadly, Captain Tiernan, you're no longer required and your access to this case has been removed." He gave me a sympathetic smile. "Federal jurisdictions. The shiny gold badge Reagan gave you is now null in void."

I shrugged, looking dead in the man's eyes. "I could give two shits about a shiny gold badge. Sir."

Something shifted in his gaze. The politician glimmer

slipped away, replaced by something else. Something else that had my stomach dropping. I swallowed hard, clenching my fists as my gut screamed at me. Ellis chuckled, turning away from me. "Street cops have such class."

When he looked up, the politician glimmer was back. It was only a split second, but it was enough of an angle for my brain to click. He checked his watch. "I have an oversight meeting in five minutes." He nodded towards Gus. "Thank you again, ladies." He waved to the coffee on the table. "I'm sure Nora can fix you a coffee to go." He took one more glance at me, then left the room.

"Fuck." I let out a slow breath, yanking my phone out of my pocket. I pounded out a quick text to Aaron. "We need to go home immediately."

Sasha dropped her arms, her eyes wide. "What is it?"

I waved at the camera above her head in the far corner. "I think I left the oven on. I wouldn't want the house to burn down."

Sasha nodded. "We better go, then." She quickly collected her things, grabbing both of our coats before following me out of the conference room.

She waited until we hit the solid streets of Chicago. "It's a good thing I paid attention to you and Aaron's dumb code talk. What is it?"

I bit the inside of my cheek, my adrenaline pouring into my veins. "I know who Higgins is."

******

Morgan sat at the kitchen table running Alison's drawing against Ellis's head shot from the DEA website. "It's a ninety three percent match. The extra seven percent is hard because the drawing is so free form." She turned the laptop around. Ellis and Alison's drawing staring back at us. "Most courts accept anywhere between eighty five to ninety nine percent as long as the key facial mapping points match." She pointed at his eyes, nose and mouth. "These all match."

Sasha let out a slow breath, looking at me. "How?"

I shrugged even as more adrenaline raced through my body. "When I was a kid, I was pissed Lois Lane was oblivious to the fact Clark Kent was Superman. How could one pair of black framed glasses throw off a person's entire face? It became a strange obsession and it led me onto the path studying facial forensics." I reached for the beer Aaron set down in front of me. "I'm a huge nerd, I know, but I never wanted to be Lois Lane, swindled by a pair of glasses."

I took a large drink from the bottle, hoping the beer would take the edge off my nerves. "There was a split second in the conference room, right when I told Ellis I didn't give a shit about his jurisdictions. His eyes shifted and he turned the right way. It was as if Alison's drawing came to life in front of me. The rest all fell together once my gut pointed at him. Everything makes sense it would be Ellis. DEA insider, worked on the Alvarez task force, worked with the three dead detectives. Then pulling the case from us out of the blue?"

"I know the FBI loves it when other agencies pick up a cold case of theirs. They don't have to spend money or manpower, and if the case is solved, they can step in and take credit. I've never heard of a cold case being pulled at the stage the Heaten case is at. No strong suspects and a bunch of dead bodies." Sasha stood up from the table. "It never made sense why Ellis wanted our case so bad. Until now."

"So, your lead suspect is a Deputy Administrator for the DEA. How in the hell are we going to prove he's behind anything in this case? We can't barrel in with accusations, they'll just think you and Sasha are starting a pissing match in retaliation of losing the case." Aaron held his hands up. "How are you going to play this one, Emma?"

I looked at Sasha. "Alison. Alison is the first step. And now that we know Higgins could be Ellis, I need her confirmation. Once we get that, we start the push. Alison is a solid witness for the state, everything she's ever given them has been good intel." I moved closer to Sasha. "Are you okay?"

She nodded. "I'll call Reagan. See if she can meet us and set up another meeting with mom." She left the kitchen, phone in hand as she dialed Reagan.

I looked at my two friends. "This is going to get real messy in the next few days. We're about to accuse a huge federal player of a handful of felonies. I won't be upset if you both decided to fade into the shadows and play ignorant. Ellis is dangerous."

"And a psychotic serial killer obsessed with you isn't?" Aaron smirked. "We've faced some pretty dark monsters together, Emma. No point in cutting bait now." He looked at Morgan. "What about you?"

Morgan stole his beer, chugging it. "I didn't join the FBI to shuffle papers."

I grinned. "Alright then."

Sasha walked back in. "Coolidge gave me thirty minutes and that was a hard sell. It's rare for anyone to have this much access to a witness. Mom is starting to feel like a snitch. If I let her sit, she'll go quiet and we'll never get anything out of her." She tossed her phone on the countertop. "Reagan is on her way over here. She wants to be briefed in person, her own paranoia is starting to shine through." Sasha smirked. "The woman actually sounded giddy when I mentioned we found a suspect."

I sucked in a deep breath. "Did you want me to go with you?"

"She's in a safe house run by the NSA. It'll be a thirty second meeting. I just need her to confirm Higgins is Ellis, as soon as she does, I'm leaving."

I hesitated. I wanted to go with her, but again she was right. Alison was safe and I certainly didn't need to get into another back and forth with the woman. I figured I had a lifetime of that ahead of me. "Okay."

Sasha walked towards the front door, slipping her coat on. "I'm going over there now. The sooner I can get the positive ID, the sooner we can take him down." She smiled, reaching for my hand. "Save me some pizza?"

I grinned. "Of course." I bent down, kissing her firmly. "I love you."

Sasha blushed. "I love you." She glanced out the window, the snow blowing as the wind whipped around the house. Winter had settled its claws in the city with no intention of letting go. The night was going to be cold, fiercely cold. I grabbed a scarf from the coat rack by the front door, and wrapped it around her, smiling as she sighed like an irritated child. "Stay warm." I kissed her once more, making her promise to be careful.

The second the front door closed, I headed back to the kitchen where Aaron and Morgan were strategizing our next move.

*****

"I knew that son of a bitch was a greasy piece of shit." Reagan leaned over the table, staring right at the two faces of Ellis. "I got you, you bastard."

"Whoa there, don't wear your heart too close to your sleeve." Morgan gave the Special Agent in Charge a shocked look. "Plus, it's weird to hear my boss swear as much as I do."

I hopped up on the edge of the kitchen island. "Sasha is with her mother, hopefully getting the confirmation we need to prove Ellis is Higgins. After that, we'll bring him in for questioning." I huffed, reaching for a doughnut. "Looking over everything, we literally have squat on him. Just the word of a junkie drug dealer and her personal dealings with him. We still haven't connected Walker's and Bellico's deaths to the great Ellis." I glanced at Morgan to pick up the debriefing.

"The FBI labs are sifting through the evidence from the Walker and Bellico scenes again, along with the boxes of body parts sent to you and Sasha. So far, nothing. No trace evidence, DNA or anything we could go off of. I've even gone through the cameras at the shipping place the boxes of joy came from, and nothing. The kid dropping the boxes off was interrogated and cleared. He was paid to pick them up at a random warehouse with instructions emailed from a dead email account. I couldn't even trace an IP, it bounced around to Russia, South America, then a hub in Alaska." Morgan leaned back in her chair, staring at the second laptop she'd brought. "All we have is word of mouth and that's real thin ice. Real thin ice that could drop us into pool of shit if this goes south."

Reagan chuckled. "Ellis is a slippery fuck. He's covered his bases well."

I looked at the woman with irritation. "You put us on this trail, tell us how to nail this guy."

Reagan cocked an eyebrow. "If we get confirmation, I'll pull him in. We have enough probable cause with Porter naming him to at least pull him in for questioning. Then we'll go from there. Ellis never did well under pressure in interviews. He always stumbled when pressed. Between the three of us, we can talk him into a circle, and he will slip. He gets pissed when he gets flustered and forgets his lies."

"Fine. But we do this quickly before more people disappear or end up pieced out in UPS boxes." I sighed, rubbing at my forehead. I had a sinking feeling Ellis could be a bear trap. He'd sink his powerful teeth in us if we fucked up, and I'd be left limping my way into a second retirement.

The nod Reagan gave me told me she understood my fear. Alison was the next target and I wasn't sure even the NSA could keep her safe.

I left Reagan with Aaron and Morgan, opting to take a short walk to the corner deli for more food. Morgan required an incredible amount of food to keep her moving, and Reagan wasn't showing any signs of leaving in the next hour or two. The request for food was oddly welcomed, I wanted to walk and clear my head. We had a thousand different clues, but not one damn thing to connect them all together. I took a deep breath of the cold afternoon air, the crisp air igniting all of my senses. I glanced at the snow covering the streets, the sun reflecting warm shards of yellow off the ice on the sidewalk. Even with the sun, the temperature hovered around the low twenties, the windchill taking that even further. I made a mental note to pull out the extra blankets. Sasha always complained about how drafty the house was.

I smiled, burying my chin deeper into the collar of my coat. These little domestic thoughts had been floating in my head more and more over the last few days. Maybe it was because I'd met her mother, or maybe it was because Sasha was my rock in this world and was slowly pulling me out of the rubble I'd been standing in since Evan.

My father had been right. She was the light at the end of the tunnel, and when I focused on her, the darkness faded away. I was still broken, fractured and scarred, but I had a reason to stop sulking.

    Sasha was the reason.

Sasha was worth it. She was worth everything.

My phone vibrated against my hand, pulling me out of the dreamy blissful haze I'd slipped into. I pulled it out, keeping my face buried in the thick wool coat.

> *-They've opted to move mom. It's gotten too dangerous now. Can you meet me at the safe house? -*

My gut twisted as I told Sasha I'd be there in fifteen minutes. "Dammit." I rasped the word out, knowing this was going to happen. Alison would soon disappear into the NSA shadows after identifying Ellis. I spun around on my heel, heading back to the house and my car, fumbling with cold fingers to call Aaron and let him know.

I barely took one step before lighting struck the back of my head. The phone tumbled out of my hand as the world went black with a pulsating pain radiating through my skull. My eyes closed a second before my cheek struck the frozen concrete below.

Chapter 23

I gasped. Sucking in a massive breath of frozen air, coughing it all back up the second it hit my lungs. I gasped a few more times, coughing and wincing at the incredible pain flooding my head. The first rational thought outside of the pain was, I was fucking freezing.

My eyes hurt from the raging headache and wouldn't open more than a squint. I swallowed hard, moving to reach up and feel the damage done to my skull. I must've slipped on some ice, taken a nasty fall and cracked my head open.

But my right hand wouldn't move, neither would my left. I blinked, forcing my eyes to work. My hands were bound together at an odd angle, thick rope holding them tightly to the side posts of a metal chair. My ankles were also bound to the legs. Thick heavy rope wrapped around my legs, thighs, waist and upper chest. I tried to look around, but the rope around my neck was too tight, I couldn't move without choking myself.

I was completely immobilized, wearing nothing but my underwear and thin tank top. My thick, warm coat, jeans and sweatshirt were gone. No wonder I was fucking freezing. I was half naked in the middle of a Chicago winter.

I squirmed, feeling the patches of my bare skin balk at the movement. I was stuck to the metal chair where my skin made contact with the frozen metal. I began shivering, scanning the area ahead of me, trying to figure out where I was. My panic was fighting me as memories of another time, another time waking up tied to a chair, pushed through. I clenched my fists, twisting my wrists trying to fight my way out of them and the ropes. I soon felt the warm trickle of blood slide into my palms.

"The greatest part of Chicago winters? The beaches become no man's lands. No one will bother us this far north."

The voice came from behind me. It was a man's voice, but I couldn't pinpoint who it was. I tried to turn and look, but couldn't. The ropes were tied too tight for me to move and cut into frozen skin like tiny shards of glass.

"Don't worry. I'll make proper introductions in a moment, Emma."

"Kidnapping a cop is an amateur move." I forced the words out around chattering teeth. The cold was starting to bite deep, sinking its icy talons into my skin.

The chair suddenly tipped back, I had to squint as the sun bore down into my eyes. "Perhaps." The voice was closer, almost above me as it yanked the chair, dragging me backwards. "You forced my hand, Emma. Forced me to take drastic action." The voice let out a slow sigh. "I had to rush this. The weather report predicts the lake will be completely frozen by morning." The sound of water sloshing against rocks filled my ears, I was near the lake. I swallowed down the rising panic. I couldn't lose my shit just yet.

The voice dropped the chair hard, my teeth slammed against each other. A shock of cold lighting filled my body as my feet were submerged into ice cold lake water. I gasped as my entire body seized and slipped into panic.

A gloved hand fell to my shoulder, patting it "Won't you excuse me for a moment?" He stepped past me, stopping a foot in front of where I sat in the water. He reached down to pull a thick blanket off a lump on the beach, half covered in sand, and tossed it to the side.

Sasha squinted at the sun, covering her face with her hands. The shiny silver of the handcuffs around her wrists caught the light, making me flinch as the sliver jabs of light blinded me.

I shook my head. "No." The word shivered out from

my clenched jaw.

    The man turned to face me, pulling down the thick collar of his heavy black coat. He tugged at his sleeves, fingers rubbing those stupid fucking cuff links.

    "Ellis."

    He nodded with a smile, removing the scarf wrapped around his neck. "The pleasure is all mine." He moved next to Sasha, moving another chair from the tall grass, setting it right next to her. He sat in the chair, reaching down to yank Sasha into a sitting position by her arm. She whimpered, trying to pull away from his grasp. Ellis yanked harder, shaking his head. "Relax. The sedative I gave you is still too strong. You won't be able to run, Agent Clarke. You'll just stumble like a newborn calf and fall on your face." Ellis grinned, looking my way. "When you fell onto my radar, I dipped into your personnel files. Then your therapy files, and wow, what a fascinating read. The horrors you endured at the hands of the Carpenters? I was impressed. Impressed at how you survived and bypassed death a few times." He waved at the chair I sat in. "I found inspiration in the way Evan tortured you, the chair. I knew it would paralyze you, the memories. The mind can be a beautiful trap if you know how to utilize it." He let out a slow breath, turning to look out at the water. "You're a strong woman, Emma. Incredibly strong. It's a shame I have to do this."

    "How about you let me go, and we can work this out. I can show you how strong I am." I wanted to beat the living hell out of Ellis. Choke that stupid grin off his face.

    He chuckled, leaning over to wrap his scarf around Sasha as she began to shiver. "You've fucked with the wrong man."

    He stood up, walking over to kneel close enough to me, I could feel his body heat prickling my frozen skin, but he was still far enough way the water didn't touch his nice shoes. "I was hoping you wouldn't trust a junkie piece of shit prisoner. But you did." He sighed dramatically, shaking his head. "For a cop who's escaped a monster once before, you'd think you'd learn to look over your shoulder." Ellis removed a leather glove and pressed warm fingers against my knee. He smiled, blowing on the tips, warming them before slipping his hand back in the glove. "You're well on your way to hypothermia." He stood back up. "It should only take a few more minutes."

"Why don't you just shoot me?" My teeth chattered. My whole body shivered violently. I glanced at Sasha sitting in the sand, tears streaming down her face. "Don't make her watch this. Just kill me and let her go."

"Ah, bargaining. Nice move, Emma. At least you're not negotiating with me, I hate when people negotiate. It's a foul tactic." Ellis turned to look at Sasha, drugged and helpless as she watched from afar. I swallowed hard as another memory forced its way in. A memory of the last time she saw me bound to a chair, fighting for my life. "You're a coward. A real man would've shot me."

"I'd love to shoot you both, right between the eyes as you look at me, but where's the fun in that? It's too quick of a death considering all the aggravation you've caused me lately." He clasped his hands in front of him. "I have a plan. A well thought plan that took me days to perfect, I'd hate to ruin it." He took a dramatic breath in.

"The way you're about to die, are dying right now, is a trademark kill of the Volokhov Bratva. They'll find your frozen body welded to this chair and my intel will provide them with plenty of suspects to chase. Maybe even they'll trail off onto a possible copycat version of Evan, I'll have to make a note of that when I'm back in my warm car. I could sprinkle a little evidence from the Latin Murders to make it

Authentic." He motioned to Sasha when he caught me staring at her. "She won't watch you die, that's too cliché even for me. And she won't die in the same fashion as you, if you're worried about that. I'm keeping her for a few more days to get her mother to come out of hiding. Then I'll kill them both. Alison was a great employee, but then the she sobered up and found a heart. I can't have employees with a heart."

Ellis smirked. "Everything was fine until Reagan got a bug up her ass about my presence and gave you an ancient cold case. Then add a little bit of a mother's guilt and love for her daughter, and we've really screwed the proverbial pooch." He pointed at the rising water now covering my calves. "Should we see if the water or the cold kills you first? Drowning or hypothermia?"

"Why did Angela Heaten have to die?" The words chattered out. My lips felt heavy like blocks of ice, frozen solid.

Ellis rubbed his chin, squinting at the sun. "She wasn't supposed to die." He huffed as if he was irritated by the question. "She was only supposed to get high and then tell all her friends the fun she had. She was supposed to be a marketing tool as we targeted a younger audience. She was also the test subject for my chemists' synthetic cocktail of cocaine and meth. A random teenager in a crowd of random teenagers. Instead, it killed her. Ruining my new marketing plan to expand my side business."

He tipped his head towards me. "Any good businessman will tell you dead bodies are a sign of very bad business. The Alvarez Brothers already lost millions on dumb business moves, giving them a shitty reputation. After I killed them and took over, I didn't want that terrible reputation to follow me as I took us into the future." He paused, flicking a piece of lint off his collar. "Honestly, that girl was an inconsequential road bump in this whole adventure. That is until you, and your Agent started digging too deep. Her death began to open too many doors I thought were left locked tight."

I blew out a harsh laugh. "Taking over the Alvarez cartel worked twofold for you, didn't it? You got an empire and a promotion." My tongue fumbled over frozen lips. "You killed Walker and Bellico. They were getting scared, scaring you in the process. They had nothing to lose if they talked. They were walking dead men." I shivered uncontrollably, my words felt like lead balloons around my frozen tongue.

He nodded, winking at me. "You're correct, Captain Tiernan. However, Bellico did lose his hands, ears and eyes while he was still alive. His tongue was next, but I ran out of time. He was a day away from calling you and confessing everything, I had to stop him before he did that. He was another good employee who grew a conscience." Ellis walked back to his chair, nudging Sasha awake. "I was very successful at both jobs for a very long time. Who would ever dare to suspect a Deputy Director of the DEA to be the kingpin of one of the largest drug cartels in the United States?"

Ellis sat down, crossing his legs. "And as soon as you freeze to death, I can continue on my path to success and complete power." He ran a hand over Sasha's hair. "I'll tell her you loved her very much. It'll make her death a little easier to swallow, knowing you're already on the other side waiting for her."

My entire body was numb, the water now up to my waist. I could barely keep my eyes open. "They'll know it was you." My raging anger at Ellis couldn't break through the freezing cold numbing my senses. I was literally frozen to the chair.

"Perhaps." Ellis sighed, looking at the lake. "You should close your eyes, Emma, and rest. It's only going to get colder and I'd hate for you to waste more energy."

"Fuck you."

Ellis chuckled as he stood from the chair. "And fuck you too, Emma." He bent down, lifting Sasha up into a firemen's carry, tossing her over his shoulder like a rag doll. "Shouldn't be much longer before your colleagues receive a 911 call. A kind dog walker found your frozen body half submerged in the frozen lake." He shrugged, flashing his politician smile. "Maybe I'll even attend your funeral. A sign of interagency support. Do you like lilies or tulips?"

I went to call Ellis a piece of shit but found my mouth couldn't move. Hypothermia had its grips in me and wasn't letting go. I let out a slow breath as my head fell forward, my eyes hazily focusing on the water now at the bottom of my breasts. My eyes slipped shut as I gasped for air, my chest locking up as my lungs froze.

In the distance, I heard two loud snaps cut through the air. Snaps that sounded a lot like gunshots, but my mind was too far frozen to recognize it. My eyes grew heavy as they begged to close and allow my body to search out warmth.

The world went dark and quiet, yet I swore I heard Sasha's raspy voice screaming my name.

*****

I woke up encased in warm white blankets in a white room. I sat up, wincing at the ache filling my entire body. It was a dull, throbbing ache. It took a minute to realize I wasn't in a hospital room, and I was grateful for that. I hated hospitals. But then the sudden thought hit, was I in heaven?

I pushed the warm blankets back and looked down at myself. I was dressed in warm blue plaid flannel pajamas with thick woolen socks on my feet. I took another minute to look around the room, searching out signs I was on the other side. There were a few large photographs on the walls, a bookshelf in the corner with a few books on the shelves, with more stacked on the floor.

I went to stand, wobbling on rubbery legs so much, I had to grab the side table next to the bed to stop from faceplanting. My sleeve slid up, revealing the raw red marks of rope burns staring back at me. I closed my eyes as the memories sifted in, sending a shiver down my spine.

"You're awake."

I opened my eyes to Sasha leaning against the doorframe of the bedroom. She looked tired, beyond tired. I nodded, opting to sit back on the bed. "This isn't heaven."

"No, it's not. It's Morgan's apartment." She pushed away from the doorframe and walked right towards me. Her hands slid across my face, holding me still as she kissed me hard. I leaned into the kiss, covering her warm hands with mine. She broke away, pressing her forehead against mine. "Emma."

I nodded, softly kissing the corner of her mouth. "I know that tone. Let's not talk about it right now."

She leaned back, her hazel eyes glassy with unshed tears. Her eyes roamed over every inch of my face, memorizing it.

I pulled her to sit next to me on the bed. "Ellis?"

"Patrick Ellis is currently sitting in a maximum security federal prison. He's being charged at the end of the week when the prison doctors clear him for arraignment." Sasha grabbed my hand, winding her fingers in mine. "He needed another surgery for the gunshot wound in his leg."

"I thought I heard two gunshots."

Sasha frowned. "I woke up when he dropped me in the trunk of his car. I landed right on top of your coat. The hard lump of your gun smashed my hip. Thank God you always carry a backup." She paused. "When he went to close the trunk, I had just enough strength to point and fire. I shot him in the kneecap and upper thigh. He fell instantly, disabled and in excruciating pain. I climbed out, handcuffed him and stole his cell phone. I called 911 and then Aaron."

Sasha sniffled. "Luckily, Aaron already tracked your cellphone when you failed to answer his calls. The state troopers arrived just as I ran out into the lake to drag you back."

She turned to look at me. "You were blue." Her words faded away as she looked down at my hand.

I covered Sasha's hands with both of mine. "How did he get the drop on us?"

"The agent outside of mom's safe house was a mole for Ellis. He contacted Ellis when we left with the sketch. The call from mom was bait to draw me out to the safe house. The text to you, was from him. I was already heavily sedated by the time he sent it, there was no way I could intercept him. He stuck me with some weird cocktail that knocked me out into a strange waking dream state. I could hear everything happening around me, even if my eyes weren't open."

I tipped my head down. "Alison?"

"Was moved after that first visit in the middle of the night. Agent Coolidge had a gut feeling there was a mole. As of right now, I don't know where mom is. I just know she's safe." Sasha leaned against my side.

I kissed the top of her head. "Where's everyone? And why am I at Morgan's apartment?"

"The team is at my office, putting together the rest of the evidence the prosecutor asked for. I'm going with Reagan in the morning to interview Ellis. We're at Morgan's apartment because it was the closest to the hospital and free from press. They've swarmed around you, us, again. A cop being tortured by a DEA director turned cartel leader has caught a few headlines. They've been following me for the last few days." Sasha looked up at me. "Plus, her room isn't as drafty as yours. The doctor said you need warmth on top of warmth while you recovered from severe hypothermia."

I plucked at the pajama shirt. "Tell her I owe her one."

"She already has a list of demands when you're ready." Sasha's eyes welled up. "I love you, Emma. Please don't ever forget that." She swallowed hard. "I love you."

"You know, even as I sat in that chair, I never thought I'd never see you again." I reached over, tipping her chin up with my fingers. "I wasn't sure I'd survive, but I knew I'd see you again. I think after everything we've survived, nothing can tear us apart. I'm done being scared, Sasha. I'm not going to let the monsters win." I ran my thumb under her bottom lip. "I love you so much."

Sasha blinked, a few tears running down her cheek. "I love you, too."

I grinned, scooting back into the bed, pulling back the heavy covers as I patted the empty space next to me. "Take a nap with me before we face reality again? I heard sharing body heat is the best way to warm up."

Sasha shook her head with a smile as she crawled into the bed. I laid back as she snuggled deep into my side, resting her head over my heart. I pulled her as close as I could, soaking up the warmth of having her in my arms once again.

We had so much to talk about, another monster to deal with, but right now, all of that could wait. I just wanted a few hours with the woman I loved and be grateful I survived to have this moment with her.

Chapter 24

~Three Days later ~

 I spun aimlessly around in the creaky old metal chair, Aaron sitting on the edge of the desk next to me, a file in his hand.

 "He's facing seventy two different charges. Ten RICO charges and a hefty charge of assaulting a police officer, kidnapping a federal agent, and resisting arrest." Aaron cocked an eyebrow at me. "And he confessed to full responsibility for Angela Heaten's death. That lady of yours is one hell of an interrogator."

 I chuckled, still spinning in the chair. We were back in the basement office of the FBI field office. "Reagan and my lady are a hell of a team. They went full bore on him, aided by testimony from Alison. He had no ground to stand on. Morgan was also able to tie fiber evidence from that fancy coat he wore trying to kill me, to the Walker scene. My testimony on his confession of dismembering Bellico was enough to close that case. And Ellis's mole confessed to killing the fire bug who blew up my living room." I stuck my foot out, catching the edge of the desk to stop the spin. "The Alvarez cartel has been dismantled. Gus is in California running busts on the last few pockets of dealers and labs." I let out a huge sigh. "The cases are closing up nicely. My frostbite, and rope burn is almost healed. Sasha's mom is back in federal custody at a low level facility upstate. They're repairing their relationship and moving through the past. Everything is calm right now." I glanced at Aaron. "I think it's time to retire." I leaned back in the chair, grinning.

Aaron laughed, shaking his head. "Bullshit. You know you have at least five years' worth of court appearances ahead of you. The Alvarez Cartel had a heavy run for over thirty years. Ellis will be pulled from his cage to limp in front of a judge to answer for everything the DEA and the FBI find on him. The court time overtime is going to be incredible for your paycheck." He grinned. "Sasha is one hell of a shot. I heard Ellis will have a permanent limp and reminder not to fuck with the dream team. Tiernan and Clarke."

I nodded, picking at a piece of lint on my sweatshirt. I'd given up wearing pantsuits until winter was over. No matter what I wore, I constantly felt cold and only felt warm if I was wearing the thick new Detroit Red Wings sweatshirt Sasha bought me. "I'm serious, Aaron. I think it's time to retire. Do something with my life other than chasing criminals and getting tortured." Deep down I was still dealing with being caught by Ellis and tortured in a way where I couldn't fight back. At least with Evan, I'd fought back. "I feel helpless." I whispered the words out in the large empty office.

Aaron let out a breath. "You weren't. You aren't helpless, Emma. You stayed alive long enough to keep him talking. He told you so much and it gave Sasha a chance to wake up from the sedative cocktail. The doctors told me your body shut down in the subzero temperatures, but you didn't die. You were frozen and all they had to do was pop you into the microwave to thaw you out. Kind of like one of my hot pockets you hate." He grinned at the dirty look I threw him.

"*You survived*, Emma. Never feel helpless for surviving." He reached over, grabbing my hand. "And do you really want to go back to medical school? Go be a doctor? Or would you rather ride a desk as a Captain for a few more years and get that full retirement? Get yourself a boat and sit out on the lake with the other retired cops?"

I shrugged. "I know. I'm just airing out idle thoughts. Honestly, I just want to marry Sasha and be a stay at home wife. Maybe I'll take up writing crime novels or professional video game playing." I smiled at Aaron as his eyes grew to the size of dinner plates.

"Marry Sasha? Did I hear that right?" He looked around the room. "We're in a federal building, you can't bullshit me in one of these. I'm pretty sure it's a federal crime if you do."

I laughed. "You heard me right. The idea hit me the other morning when I woke up in our house. She was curled into my side, her book smashed between us with her glasses crooked on her face. I want that every day of my life. I want to introduce her as my wife, not just my FBI partner. I want the life I've been avoiding for years." I sat up when I heard the elevator ding in the distance. I pointed at Aaron. "Don't you say a God damn thing until I figure out how to ask her. I don't want her to think I'm still thinking on a half frozen brain." I jabbed my finger in his chest. "Do not mention my ranting about retirement either. I'm not sure about anything. I could retire tomorrow or end up taking another promotion in the department."

"Did I hear you say retirement, Captain Tiernan?" Reagan's voice made me groan. I still hated this woman, even if she was my strongest ally.

I turned to her and Sasha walking towards us.

Both were dressed to the nines in official federal pantsuits, arms full of manila file folders stamped with the FBI and DEA logo. Sasha dumped her stack on the desk next to Aaron. "Hi." She smiled, a soft blush covering her cheeks.

I reached for her hand, smiling as I spoke to Reagan. "I'm still on medical leave, Agent Reagan. The great city of Chicago doesn't want me back for a few more weeks. And I was informing Detective Liang I felt like I was retired. Too much time on my hands with nothing to do."

Reagan's hands fell to her hips as she gave me a critical look. "I can tell a liar from a mile away." She motioned to the stack of files Sasha had set down. "We've just about tied up our involvement in the Ellis case. The final depositions are set for tomorrow, and Agent Clarke has gone through her internal affairs investigation and come out clean." A huge grin spread across her face. "I knew that piece of shit was dirty from the first day I met him. The joy I will have for ages, sending him up the river without a paddle, is too great to put into words." She met my eyes. "I owe it to you, Emma. Latham also sends his regards. He stopped by my office yesterday, handing over every original file he ever kept. He told me since all the shadows of the past are gone, he didn't need to hide the truth anymore."

I rolled my eyes. "You owe me a trip to somewhere warm and sunny." I squeezed Sasha's hand. "But you're welcome. I'm just happy we closed the Heaten case and her parents finally have the peace and justice they've been searching for."

Reagan nodded, bending over to her briefcase. "I've also spoken to my bosses. You remember when I made you a temporary agent at the start of all this?"

"Of course. I returned the gold badge and ID card when I walked in today." I tapped my chest, the visitor sticker half peeling off my sweatshirt. "I'm a visitor."

Reagan stood straight. "I'm following through on the offer. I want you to come on board with the FBI full time. You'll be partnered with Agent Clarke and continue to work cold or stalled cases for now." She held out a thicker black wallet, a shiny gold badge hidden under the smooth leather. "Full benefits, pay bump that puts your Captain pay to shame, and all of the technology and resources you dreamed about while sitting in that cramped office at CPD."

I shook my head, frowning. "We had a deal, Dana. One that precedes this one."

"I'm still honoring that one. Two years and you're out. You and Sasha. Full retirement and no one will ever bother you again." She looked at me with soft eyes. A look that told me she wasn't asking out of a power move, but because she truly valued me as a fellow investigator. "You're one of the best, Emma."

I bit my bottom lip, looking at Sasha who stared at me with a hopeful look. "You're on board with this?"

"The feeling of putting Ellis away for life and closing a handful of open cases, and giving families peace? It's an addictive feeling, it's given me a new drive." She gave me a sheepish smile. "You don't have to do this with me. I'll happily date a medical student again, Emma."

I glanced at Aaron who shrugged and nudged my shoulder. "You're way too good to quit, Emma. You're one hell of a cop and think of the overtime you can squeeze out of the FBI!" He winked at me. "If you leave the department, Agent Reagan promised I'd finally be promoted to Lieutenant and would join a task force between the FBI and the Chicago Police Department. We'd still be working together, Emma."

I was backed into a corner.

I looked at Reagan. "One more stipulation." I glanced at Sasha. "For the both of us."

"And what is your final demand, Tiernan?" Reagan crossed her arms over her chest.

"Sasha gets a three week vacation, effective immediately. When we're back, I'll swear in as an FBI Agent." I smiled, turning to Sasha, suddenly frozen on what I really wanted to ask her. My spontaneity turned into pure fear as I looked into the big hazel eyes of the woman who owned my entire soul. "Two years like you promised, and that's it. No more cops, no more agents."

She nodded. "I promise. Two years."

I turned to Reagan. "You have a deal."

"Perfect." She pulled out a thick file, beat up and torn at the corners. "Your first case. A series of unusual murders in the swamps of Louisiana that no one can figure out, six to be exact. We'd like to label it a serial killer on the loose, but haven't been able to connect any of the murders to officially deem it a serial murder." Reagan tapped the top flap. "Take it on vacation if you'd like, read it over. Your first day as an official agent, you'll be flown down to the Louisiana office to start from the ground up." Regan snapped her briefcase shut, looking at the clock on the far wall. "Agent Clarke, you're officially on vacation. If I need you, I'll give you a call." She then pointed at Aaron. "Detective Liang, I believe you and I have an afternoon meeting with the Superintendent. He's got your new Lieutenant bars ready. Agent Adams will meet us at the car." She threw me a look over her shoulder. "I'll also inform the Superintendent to begin filing your transfer papers immediately. You can hang up those stiff white uniforms for good, Agent Tiernan."

Aaron rushed over, scooping Sasha and me into a hug. "About damn time." He dropped us and ran after Reagan waiting for him at the elevator. The second we were left in the empty basement office, I leaned against the edge of the desk, sighing.

Sasha stood in front of me, resting a hand on my shoulder. "You don't have to do this if you don't want to. Reagan is a whirlwind and she sucks you in before you even know what hit you. You can retire, you can stay at the department or, you can work at a coffee shop. I don't care, Emma. I just want you to be happ…"

"Marry me." I blurted the words out like an excited teenager.

Sasha's mouth fell open. "What?"

I sucked in a breath, standing up. "Will you marry me, Natasha Clarke? I literally don't have a clue what I just agreed to, or what deal I made with that devil Reagan. I don't even want to think about the hell the swamps of Louisiana hold, all I know is I want to marry you. I want you by my side. I want a forever with you. I want the life I've ignored for so long, and I want it with you. You're my light at the end of every tunnel." I chewed on my bottom lip. "I don't have a ring. This was so last minute. I did look for one last week, but couldn't find one perfect enough to show you what you mean to me."

I went to ramble on when I was silenced by warm lips pressing against mine. Sasha's hands fell to my hips, gripping me tightly, pulling me closer into her. My hands fell to her back, pressing her deeper against my body as I kissed her back.

She broke the kiss, breathless. "Yes."

I grinned. "Yes?"

She nodded. "Yes, I'll marry you." She grinned, running her hand across my cheek. "Forever, yes."

I laughed, tears filling my eyes. "Well, I guess we'd better go ask Reagan what the policy is on Agent to Agent relationships."

Sasha kissed me deeply once more. "After our vacation. I want to spend time with you, just you, before we get tangled up in policies and rules."

I nodded in agreement, taking her hand. "Let's go home, Sasha." I bent down and picked up the heavy file Reagan left. I knew there was another monster we'd have to chase, more shadows to peel apart and more evil to face. But that could wait.

First, I was going to enjoy my vacation and take a moment to live.

Thank you for purchasing this book and supporting an independent author!!! If you're interested in keeping tabs on me and the future works that will certainly follow in this series and other original works, head on over to Facebook and find me at Sydney Gibson at Facebook.com/sydney.fivesixthree

And then to enjoy some of the nonsensical tweets and updates with future novels and the ongoing fanfiction I still occasionally putter with, find me on Twitter at Syndey563a.

Lastly, keep an eye on my Amazon author page. There, you can keep updated on blogs, sales, and what I'll be writing next!

If you love the cover art and want to reach out to the artist, KM West Creative, you can find her on Twitter @km_west_

Thanks to each and every one of you readers! I wouldn't be here if it wasn't for you!

Sydney!

[Type here]

Printed in Great Britain
by Amazon